When Oceans Rage

By Rolynn Anderson

To Josh

Happy Reading!

Rolynn Anderson

This is a work of fiction. Names, characters, places, and incidents are either the product of the author's imagination or are used fictitiously, and any resemblance to actual persons living or dead, business establishments, events, or locales, is entirely coincidental.

WHEN OCEANS RAGE

Contact Information:
https://www.rolynnanderson.com

Publishing History
Print ISBN: 978-1-951453-02-2

Digital ISBN: 978-1-951453-03-9

Published in the United States of America
Rawhide Press

Cover Art by Nick Castle
Formatting by Enterprise Book Services, LLC

When Oceans Rage
By Rolynn Anderson

Talent is nurtured in solitude; character is formed in the stormy billows of the world.
Johann Wolfgang von Goethe

Grant me the stormy seas over a life of ease, the toil and madness of a life of effort, and adventure, and meaning. The safe harbor is not for me, not for long. Let the fearful stand at the shore and point as we head into the unknown, toward that vast horizon where the bold become legend.
Brendon Burchard

Rolynn Anderson

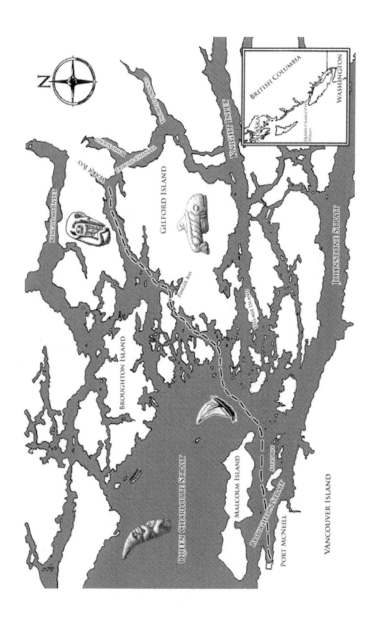

iv

1

Jill Morrell entered the cavernous conference room and read disaster in her bosses' body language. They sat in the far corner, stiff-backed, chins jutting. CEO Mary Watkin, black-suited, thin, and hollow-cheeked, looked as if administration had sucked every lipid molecule out of her. And VP Calvin Crystal's grim expression did not match his casual company uniform of blue polo shirt and tan pants. On the table, no cups of coffee, bottled water, or plate of cookies deformalized the moment.

Seattle, we have a problem. A big one.

Jill's five-year work history as Drone Division Supervisor for Baldur Industries flashed before her eyes.

She walked past seven high-backed chairs lined up like grave markers against a shiny mahogany table. Lemon furniture polish scented the heavy air.

Pushing her hands into the pockets of her khakis, she asked, "Mary? Calvin? Why does this feel like a wake?"

"Have a seat, Jill. We've got a glitch to work out." Mary mustered a wan smile. "A troubling issue came to our attention yesterday, so let's deal with it today."

Pain pulsated over Jill's right eyebrow. "Define 'troubling'."

Calvin said, "It's about your security clearance."

From Calvin, Jill expected serial posturing, so she focused on her boss. Less bullshit. "Mary. Cut to it. I'll quit before you fire me. Know that."

Mary's eyes opened wide in surprise. "No quitting or firing. A misunderstanding, I'm sure. Please pull up a chair."

Jill remained standing, her stomach roiling from the tension.

Calvin said, "Our yearly updating of security clearances is underway, hastened by the new government contract in your charge."

"Reluctantly."

He waved his hand. "You're perfect for it. Point is, the FBI discovered your father was recently incarcerated for killing a man. He pled guilty to manslaughter, a five-year sentence." Calvin paused, all but preening with the drama.

Jill blinked, images of her stepfather racing through her mind. He was a milquetoast. Sweet. Brainy. Not a murderer. "Mike?"

"Your *biological* father. Al Morrell," Mary clarified. "He apparently shot and killed a man in Port McNeill, British Columbia. A fishing partner." She cleared her throat. "Why didn't you tell us?"

A vision of Al punched into her mind. A quiet man. Half-Samoan with hazelnut brown skin and curly red-brown hair. He'd left the family because of bouts of depression, making a new life catching shrimp off Vancouver Island. Jill was four when he ditched them. The handful of times he'd visited since had been awkward events.

Al killed someone?

When Oceans Rage

Sliding into a leather chair, Jill said, "News to me. I haven't communicated with my father since I graduated from college." She did the math. "Seven years ago."

Calvin said, "His lawyer mailed you a notice."

Jill rolled her eyes, the movement transferring pain from right to left brow. "I'm always a month behind getting my mail. It piles up in my P.O. box." She thought for a moment. "Why assume I've kept the information from you?"

"The FBI blindsided us, Jill. Their inquiry puts your new classified project in jeopardy."

"I don't keep up with my father. His actions do not affect me or my career."

Calvin raised a holier-than-thou eyebrow. "Not true, Jill. Absolutely not true."

Leaning Jill's direction, Mary said, "When your father went to prison, his last act was to deed his fishing boat to you. Coupled with its fishing license, the vessel is worth a million dollars."

Jill drew in a breath, too stunned to speak. *I own a million dollar boat?* Her headache spiked.

"Your father bought the trawler at a government auction years ago, confiscated from drug smugglers," Calvin said, almost smirking.

What happened to having her back? Five years she'd invested in this company and now they believed she colluded with criminals? Baldur Industries, named after the Norse god of light and radiance, of peace and forgiveness. *What a joke.*

She stood. "The FBI must know I'm estranged from my father, but you two leapt to the conclusion I'm tainted by him. Luckily, you won't have to endure more embarrassment. I quit."

Their expressions morphed from self-righteous to shocked.

"No! We can fix this," Mary said, pushing out of her chair. "Obviously you weren't aware of your father's crime and you had no idea he gave the boat to you. We'll explain the information lag to the FBI."

Jill laughed. "A boat with a history of running drugs, captained by a killer, who gives a million bucks of dirty assets to his daughter." She narrowed her eyes at Mary. "Obviously you didn't stand up for me, or we wouldn't be having this tête-à-tête." She shook her head in disbelief, her emotions careening from fear to fury. "So the FBI gets to *run* with this mythology. From now on I'll be harassed, bugged, and dogged by them."

Calvin remained seated, his hands clasped, head wagging. "The news was unsettling to them and to us."

"I can't believe you assumed the worst. After I've given Baldur my best thinking and energy, you let them tag me as a crook? This gets out— and it will—my reputation is on the line. My leadership questioned."

Mary stepped closer to Jill. "You're project manager because of your expertise, Jill. Now that we know Al Morrell means nothing to you, we'll smooth your way with the FBI."

Means nothing to me?

"Smooth my way?"

Calvin's hand waved again, as if in absolution. "You'll tell the Feds what you told us and refuse to take possession of this...this..." He looked down at his notes. "*Jig's Up*. A fishing boat." He said the word 'fishing' with his nose crinkled like he smelled rotten cod. "You explain your estrangement with your biological father to the FBI, promising to cut ties with him. Pass the clearance tests with ease. Slide through the interviews. The polygraph. The lifestyle poly..."

When Oceans Rage

Jill gripped the back of her chair. *Jig's Up*? Her father had nicknamed her Jigs when she was four. He'd named his boat after *her*?

Calvin's last words rang in her ears, and she repeated them aloud. "A lifestyle polygraph. Interviews, plural." Shaking her head, Jill said, "You've set me up for a lifetime of scrutiny by the FBI and you want me to deny my father before I know anything about his so-called crime. This boat I'm supposed to own you want me to dump, sight unseen." She walked halfway to the door before she turned to her bosses and glanced at her watch. "My letter of resignation will hit your e-mail in minutes. I'll call security to escort me out in an hour."

***

"Going somewhere, boss?"

Jill raised her eyes from sorting through her top drawer to Lynda Flynn, a drone sensory device specialist. "Seems so."

"We can see you packing through the office windows. The steam blowing out your ears isn't hard to miss, either." Lynda leaned against Jill's desk, her brunette pageboy and bangs set against concerned brown eyes. "They sent me to find out if this is for real or a negotiating tactic. You vying for a promotion here at Baldur or did a head-hunter grab you for another company?"

Squinting out to the lab where dozens of engineers were busy at work on drone tech, Jill noted not one person looked her way. "Forget advancement, Lynda. I'm done. Precipitous, actually. I wasn't keen on the new project."

"Who's going to lead if you leave? Shit, Mary could lose *her* job by letting you go."

"My quitting may be a victory...one way to kibosh an immoral contract in our race against China's drone industry."

5

For a minute, Jill considered Lynda Flynn's chances at taking the lead. Nope. She was a one-note engineer. Any of her crew capable? Probably not. The position required proficiency with robotics generally, drones specifically. Navigation and mapping sensor knowledge; communication component savvy, too. A *ton* of pressure.

Lynda didn't fit the profile.

The woman peered into the box Jill had half-filled. "Not much to take home. It's your brain Baldur wishes you'd leave behind. And the crew doesn't want *any* part of you to go."

How to respond? The woman had always been friendly to Jill, but she wasn't a pal even if she acted like one. *As if I know what a pal is.*

Did Lynda truly speak for the other employees?

Jill anchored her fingers on the box's handholds as a mother of a headache hit her. She was aware her colleagues regarded her as a tight-ass scientist with little interest in them, a workaholic focused on how things worked. Not human relationships. They called her 'RoboJill' behind her back but how could she take umbrage? Her best friend, waiting for her at home, was a DJI Matrice 210 RTK-V2 Drone.

"Tell us how we can keep you here," Lynda said. "A petition? Work-stoppage?"

Jill test-lifted her take-home box. Light. Inconsequential. All her files and her computer stayed at Baldur. Security guards would riffle through her pictures and trinkets looking for secret papers and tiny thumb drives. They'd use X-ray on her purse and might bring in a dog to sniff out hidden computer chips. Technology was a piranha industry, within the U.S. and amongst countries. Baldur had to be number one or die. If they could erase her memory now that she was leaving the company, they'd do it.

Lowering her voice, Lynda said, "Baldur is crazy to let you go. China will snap you up at three times your salary, and Mary knows it."

The idea of jumping out of the crazy industry suddenly had appeal. "I'm done, Lynda. And I don't want to draw more attention to my departure. Please say goodbye to the staff for me."

Lynda raised a brow. "Baldur doesn't want you working for their competition. I'd watch my back if I were you. Still, none of us would blame you for working with China. I've got contacts there if you're interested."

A uniformed security guard knocked on the door and Jill heaved a sigh. "My escort. Good thoughts to you and the staff. My last words to the crew are: intimidation's making me leave; I surely won't be intimidated to stay."

***

The earworm buzzed through her brain as she drove from Seattle to Vancouver and up the east side of Vancouver Island. *I know nothing about boats, but I want to see* Jig's Up. *I don't know my father, but I refuse to give him up. When tested, I take his side. Why is that?*

A week ago she'd quit a career, partly because her bosses wanted her to be squeaky clean, even if their prize project wasn't. Did she care about Al Morrell, much less his damn boat? The questions bugged her the entire day as her car gobbled up the miles to the end of nowhere.

Her father's attorney had said the vessel was docked in Port McNeill, on the northern reach of Vancouver Island. GPS initially directed her to the big city of Vancouver, where she bought a ferry ride to Nanaimo for herself and her Mazda 3. A long drive up the coast of Vancouver Island brought her to Port McNeill, where she parked her car in the marina lot and headed to the office. 'Get a daily parking slip,' said the sign at the entrance to the car park. A day? A week? How long would she stay?

Jill pulled on the collar of her sweatshirt, starting to sweat on an unusually warm March afternoon. In the brisk wind on the ferry, she'd been comfortable in long pants, a warm top, and slip-on tennis shoes. But with blue skies and temperatures in the 80's, her wardrobe choices were all wrong. She'd expected cool breezes from the ocean; what she got was still, heavy air, rank with fishiness.

At the marina office desk sat a wiry guy, black-rimmed glasses set against almost white, neatly combed hair. Fifties, maybe. Greg Hanley was his name. After she introduced herself, his eyebrows winged up and he smiled. "Al's daughter?"

"I am."

"Same russet hair color. Curly. Brown eyes. Defined cheekbones."

"Guilty." She smiled before remembering Al was in jail. She pinched her forehead in confusion. *How does the daughter of a convicted felon act?* What did these people expect of her?

"I have your keys to *Jig's Up*."

Hearing the boat's name again was unsettling. Her father had nicknamed her 'Jigs' twenty-six years ago. Was *Jig's Up* his daily reminder of her existence?

Why didn't he tell me?

Why didn't I ask?

She fingered the keys Al Morrell had touched. Used. On a boat with her name. "Thanks, Mr. Hanley."

When Oceans Rage

"Call me Greg."

She nodded. "Greg. I'm worried about the condition of the boat. How long since anyone tended to her?"

He stroked his chin. "At least four months. Owners pay me for moorage, but I don't maintain the boats docked here. *Jig's Up* could do with some attention, that's for sure." He pointed to the end of a finger, a narrow wood pathway jutting off the main dock. "There she is, ma'am. Cheery-looking from here with her burgundy hull. One of the biggest prawning boats in the fleet. But up close, you'll see she's not so pretty." He paused. "Pollution, salt, and dirt are murder on boats. After weeks of bouncing at the dock, your rig's got hull-scars and a fair amount of seaweed growing on her bottom. Definitely in need of TLC."

Jill thought of her father, now moored in prison. Untended, as well.

Greg cleared his throat. "There's one more problem with the boat."

"The inside's a mess, too?"

He shook his head. "We've had some break-ins. Happened during a three-day downpour, when everyone stayed away from the marina. After the deluge, I checked each boat. Two of them, including *Jig's Up,* showed evidence someone tried to jimmy their doors." Another throat-clear. "I hired a security guard, and he's sleeping on your boat."

"Why?"

"The burglar broke the lock. I tried to reach Al to have someone install a new one on *Jig's Up*, but I couldn't find him in the prison system. I wrote to his attorney, but no response yet."

The marina door squealed open, followed by a man's whistle. "Who's your new girlfriend, Greg?"

The marina manager stepped from behind his desk and stood next to Jill. "Daryl Wisson, meet Al's daughter, Jill Morrell."

Wisson took her hand in both of his instead of shaking it. Rough workman's hands, a square, muscular body. Blond hair, mostly hidden by a baseball cap, and hazel eyes, boldly assessing her head to toe.

Greg took her elbow and escorted her to the door. "See you later, Daryl. Miss Morrell gets a tour of the marina before I show her *Jig's Up.* You're going out for a training session, I hear."

"I am. We are. Don't let anyone in my moorage." He squinted at Jill. "You up for a little adventure, sweetheart? We're taking my prawner out for a couple hours to train a new crew member. You might enjoy the experience. See how your dad made a living. Understand how a prawn boat works since you now own Al's."

Jill blinked, the invitation and Wisson's knowledge of her new possession unexpected. Was the whole marina aware she'd been deeded *Jig's Up*? When Greg didn't say anything, Jill focused on her boat gently rocking in the wake of a passing boat. *I own a prawn boat and I have no idea what that means.* Clearly the fisherman was a full-of-himself guy, but his offer was worth considering, especially since his whole crew was involved. "A generous invitation. I'd like to observe the process."

Wisson's eyes sparked with interest. "Excellent. One hour. My boat sits one finger down from *Jig's Up.*" He pointed as he moved ahead of them to the gangway. "*Lady Luck's* her name."

"Fine. See you in an hour."

She accompanied the manager as he explained the scope of Port McNeill's marina, tucked behind an enormous sea wall separating public and commercial moorage from the B.C. Ferry dock. But her focus kept tracking back to her new possession. When they reached *Jig's Up*, she was surprised at how the boat loomed above her, a giant among the other fishing vessels. Her burgundy hull, unique among the gray and cream-colored hulls in the marina, made Jill smile.

Like to make an impression, do you, girl?

Greg released a section of railing and gestured for Jill to hop aboard before he joined her on the deck. He showed her the chipped wood near the keyhole. "Thieves almost got in," he said, and handed over the keys. "The lock doesn't work anymore. Better get it replaced right away." He stepped away so she could open the starboard pilothouse door. "The guy staying here is Ray Stewart. Hails from Campbell River. I'll let him know to stay at his sister's while you're here."

She panicked for a moment, thinking about being alone in a strange town, on a boat with no working lock. But sharing close quarters with a stranger was as discomforting a proposition. Jill pinched her forehead again, overwhelmed by the sheer amount of incoming information and decisions to make.

"Thank you. I have a lot to learn." She hesitated. "About fishing for shrimp."

A moment of quiet, then Greg said, "You want to watch out for Daryl. But he does know prawning, so you'd learn from him."

Jill pulled open the right, no, *starboard* pilothouse door, and looked at the helm, barely registering Greg's assessment of Daryl Wisson.

"I'll be going now. If there's anything you need, you know where to find me." He turned and jumped from the boat to the dock while Jill marveled at the electronics, dials, and meters filling the area behind the wheel and overhead, each device inviting her to tinker with it. A compass as big as her palm held center position among the instrument displays. *All this is mine?*

Circling its base was a thin rawhide necklace, a bone carving of a whale at the end of it. Native art, by the looks of it. She reached out to touch the whale charm. Did the necklace belong to Al?

Had he left it for *her*? Or was it here to protect the boat?

A tall captain's chair, permanently mounted, was positioned behind the wheel. In a cubby-hole to the right of the wheel, Jill saw a roll of duct tape and a colorful assortment of bungee cords of all lengths. It seemed Al had the practical and the spiritual covered if the whale charm was indeed a totem of some sort.

She knew about bungee cords and duct tape, but struggled to name other things she saw on the boat, a vocabulary unto itself. She'd fried her brain with hours online memorizing boating terms and vessel types. Now, here she was, aboard a trawler, teak wood and diesel fuel fusing into a strangely pleasant tang.

A fishing boat. A prawner. Hers.

Jill noted a twin door on the left, no, *port* side of the pilothouse, located behind the second mate's chair. A u-shaped, cushioned seating area with a permanent workspace/dining table, took up the area aft (rear) of the portside door. Opposite the table was a single-counter galley/kitchen. Cooktop, small oven and refrigerator, sink. Under a wall of half-size windows exposing the huge stern section of *Jig's Up,* sat a pot-bellied stove with two ratty chairs on each side of it.

When Oceans Rage

She maneuvered the narrow steps leading deep into the bow of the boat, revealing three hooked-open doors. On the left was a bathroom, in boatspeak, the head. Toilet, sink, shower with a plastic curtain. Simple. Complete. The right door led to two stacked beds, a rumpled sleeping bag in the bottom bunk. The compact second cabin, apparently Ray Stewart's crash site. His stuff must be in the hanging locker, a small closet to the right of the bunks. The third door gave entry to the master quarters at the prow of the boat, with a queen island bed and a hanging locker on the port side. *My bedroom. My cabin.*

Teakwood strips lined every inch of her cabin's walls except for the overhead areas, done in some puffy cream-colored fabric. Sound absorbing. Softening the effect of so much wood. The overall feel was rich, warm, and soothing. The spicy, pungent aroma of teak pleased her. A cocoon. Perfect place to sleep.

Mine.

For how long?

From somewhere outside came Wisson's insistent voice: "Jill? We're ready to head out. You comin'?"

She hurried up the stairs to the pilothouse and opened the starboard door. "On my way. What do I need to bring along?"

"Nothing. It's a scorcher today, so you won't need a jacket. You'll observe. Help if you want to." Wisson glanced in the direction of *Jig's Up's* helm. "I've only got half the tech you do." His longing look quickly changed to stubborn. "My rig's rough but it's cheaper to run than this baby. Plus, it has a great crew. You'll see."

She grabbed a ball cap from a nearby hook and hopped off *Jig's Up,* taking a moment to steady herself on the undulating dock. She drew in a deep breath, the scent of adventure in the air.

"Lead the way."

As Jill followed the prawner to the adjacent finger, her history flashed across her mind once again. She'd made a series of jarring moves that were well out of her comfort zone these past several days.

Would learning how to prawn be a dive too far into the unknown?

2

In a coastal town as small as Port McNeill, news took less time than ocean mist to spread through the community. By nightfall any event would be chewed to bits at The Tides Tavern.

Tonight, Ray Stewart wanted to hear the fishermen's version of prawning with the Morrell woman, so he ordered a round of beer for a table of regulars. Since Ray was fairly new to town, as was a veteran prawner named Jim Livingston from Washington State, they pulled up their chairs to the table, listening and learning.

Ken Bailey leaned in, his beer belly divided by the table's edge, whiffs of garlic and stale lager delivered with his story. "Daryl let her come along when we were training this new guy from Vancouver. We told him we couldn't bait the shrimp traps, 'cause it's off-season, but we practiced layin' 'em down and bringin' 'em up, using the pulleys."

"How'd she do?" Ray asked.

"Made it the best damn day of prawning I ever had, even though it was boilin' hot out there," Ken said, grinning. With a toothpick, he pulled a chunk of food from between his teeth, stared at the dab of leftovers at the end of the stick, and sucked the food back into his mouth. "The new guy, Morrie, was slow and clumsy. She came over to bail him out, 'cause he almost fell overboard each time he tried to work the gear. We got a good laugh out of that." Ken tested the pointy end of the toothpick with his finger. "Have to say, she was a quick study on the pulleys." He pointed the little stick at Ray. "That's when she made my day."

Ray took a swig of beer to hide his impatience. "How so?"

Ken grinned. "Morrie and the lady wore the wrong clothes for prawning. Loose sweatshirts. Too easy to get snagged in the pulley system. When Morrie got caught once, we told him to take off his shirt. To make him feel better we took ours off, too. For safety. Blisterin' hot day. One a them climate change effects. Before we knew it, she whipped off her sweatshirt. Stood there in one a them thin tank tops. We stopped workin' at the sight of her rack. God, she's built." Ken shook his head. "Then she raises an eyebrow and cool as you please, says, 'Modesty can kill'. Made us laugh our asses off. Yessir, best day of prawning ever." He shut his eyes and rolled his toothpick to the side of his mouth. "She's one a them pretty but tough gals. Quick learner. Comfortable around equipment. I'd fish with her any day."

"Would Wisson hire her?"

Ken scowled as he twisted his empty beer glass on the table. "We're stuck with Morrie and all the boats are full. 'Cept hers. She owns a prawn boat, but she's not saying she'll take it out to fish. Don't know if she'll hire a crew, either. You're green so I doubt she'd hire you." A glance at Jim Livingston. "If she takes you, you'll end up in charge." He chortled. "Want to join the pool we got on her? I'd say you two young'uns have the best chance to win."

"Pool?" Ray asked.

Ken nodded. "Daryl's feelin' sorry for her and asked me to start a 'centive pool."

"Incentive?" Ray swallowed the last of his beer and planted his feet, ready to get up from his chair. He'd learned what he needed to know.

"Uh-huh." Ken pulled the list out of his pocket and counted the names. "Twenty bucks a pop and I'm the one collecting. Money goes to the first dumbass who signs up to work on her boat." He leaned in, conspiratorially, his belly crowding the table. "Daryl found out she's a Seattle white-collar who's never handled a boat before. He's pushing guys to work with her, one a them charity cases." He frowned at Ray. "You or any poor schmuck who signs up to fish with a greener like her deserves a bonus."

Jim shook his head and wandered off, but Ray stood, reached for his wallet, took out a twenty and handed it over. Ken pinched a pencil from his pocket, asked Ray to spell his last name and added it to a long line of entries. *Thirty names?*

Ken looked up with a phony smile, the pencil poised over Ray's name and said, "Almost forgot. One more condition. To win the pool, you gotta get hired by her *and* get in her pants." He folded up the list with the twenty-dollar bill, elbowing his buddy. "Daryl ain't too happy about our 'rider.' " He cackled when he raised his eyebrow at Ray. "You still in?"

Ray nodded slowly, the beer bitter in his mouth.

Ken stuffed the list and money into his jeans with a triumphant grin. "She put in her own twenty, sayin' she might need our help finding a crew. Joke's on her about the rider. She's gotta screw *herself*." He barked a laugh.

Ray suddenly wished he hadn't thrown his money in the pot, but Ken was a grade-A gossip in Port McNeill and Ray wanted to keep the man yakking. "I thought she went back to her job in Seattle. Greg said she left the end of the week and he hadn't seen her since."

Ken threw up his hands. "Maybe we shoulda been friendlier, eh?" He glanced at his pals and gave a crooked leer. "Not MeToo enough?"

Ray twitched an eyebrow. "Money back if she bails, right?"

Ken nodded.

In a few steps, Ray left the tavern and stood on the porch, breathing in fresh salted sea air. He glanced at the marina, tension mounting. He didn't like the way Ken and his buddies had piled on the poor woman, but he couldn't let empathy get in the way. *Jig's Up* was his and the sooner Jill Morrell put his boat in her rearview mirror, the sooner he could take possession.

***

"No new locks. Perfect," Jill grumbled as she pulled open *Jig's Up* starboard pilothouse door without using her key. "Must mean Greg still has his security guy staying in my boat." She dumped her luggage on the floor and glanced at the galley where she saw a man's well-worn leather jacket, a paperback, and an empty beer bottle. "How hard is it to install deadbolts?"

She wondered what to do next. Greg Hanley hadn't been in his office when she'd blown by on her way to *Jig's Up.* Guess she was about to meet Ray Stewart, security guard.

When she heard a toilet pump in the head, Jill announced her presence: "Hello. Owner on premises."

No response from below. Maybe she had a squatter on board.

She propped open the starboard door in case she needed a fast exit and checked the dock for boaters. Not a soul in sight. Naturally. She waited for whoever it was to emerge from the head.

Shuffling and the sound of a zipper had her dialing 911, her thumb over the 'send' button. *Does 911 work in Canada?* The doorway darkened and the narrow hallway filled up with a man. *Big.* Her heart skittered as he all but leaped up the three steps from the cabin area into the galley to confront her. *Intimidating.* She straightened her shoulders, cleared her throat and backed toward the pilothouse door.

"Are you Greg's security guy?"

It unnerved her when his height, way over six feet of stolid, spoke volumes, but he didn't say a word. *Mid thirties? Damn fine looking.* He pushed his hands through dark brown hair, leaving it more tousled than before. "Jillian Morrell?" Deep, mellow voice.

"I am." She took her finger off the 'send' button.

"Ray Stewart." He offered a hand and she scrambled to put the phone in her back pocket before offering her own hand. "Pleased to meet you," he said as they shook. "Greg knows. I'm staying on your boat until you get proper locks...or you return...or both of the above."

Jill glanced out the window in the direction of the marina office. "I arranged for the installation weeks ago."

He shrugged. "Some kind of mix-up. And there's also a problem with unpaid moorage fees, eh?"

"Damn it. I set up the bills to be paid electronically." She swallowed a curse and made an attempt to sound more friendly. "Sounds like technology has failed us once again."

He said nothing.

Thinking he didn't buy her story about the lock or the payments, she said, "Why don't we talk to Greg? He probably figured I wouldn't return." She leaned over to cup the glass-domed compass with her hand and put her index finger on the whale charm. *Good. Still there.* "But I'm back. For good."

He stared at her. "You are?"

"Sorry to roust you out of my boat," she said, feeling anything but.

He leaned against the galley counter. "Greg's paying me to watch over the whole marina as well as secure *Jig's Up*," he said slowly. "We've had a string of burglaries..."

And hers was one of the most well-equipped boats in the marina. She got the picture, drew in another fortifying breath, and surveyed the interior of her boat. *I don't even know my boat well enough to figure out what might be missing.* She glanced at the helm electronics, relieved when she found all the spaces filled with equipment. A peek out the port window to check the back-deck depth finder. Still there, too. "Are they stealing stuff from outside or inside the boats?"

"Both."

Jill waited for more detail but got none. "Well, it appears I should thank you for watching over *Jig's Up*. Again, I'm sorry you've lost your crash-space." She tried to look apologetic when she handed over his jacket and book, but she was eager for him to leave. Settling in was her sole focus.

A curt nod. "Did you let Greg know how long you're staying?"

When Oceans Rage

His gaze moved to her suitcases, then traveled slowly up her body to her torso, and then her breasts. She waited until he raised his eyes to hers and cocked an eyebrow at him. Clearly he'd heard about her first prawning experience from highly unreliable resources. "Actually you can tell Greg I'm back permanently. I'll make some calls about new deadbolts and the automatic transfer snafu and see him shortly."

The flash of a frown. "Fine. I'll make my rounds. Okay with you if I come back later to pack up?"

She was about to protest the coming-back-later idea, but before she could say a word, he'd hopped off the boat and headed to the marina office.

The array of technology at the helm caught her attention, as enticing as a display of sweet rolls. *Later, Jill.* Suitcases to haul in. Unpack. Mae C languished in the trunk of her car, waiting for a place in her new home. Where the hell would she put her drone? She'd figure out something because Mae C was going with her, no matter what.

Descending the stairs to the sleeping quarters, she discovered Ray's sleeping bag and pillow on her bed instead of on the lower bunk in the second cabin. The drawers under the queen were filled with his stuff.

Interesting. He'd moved from the second cabin to the first and frowned when she told him she was back for good. Who else in the marina, besides Ray Stewart, was counting on her not to return?

***

Ray found Greg Hanley three fingers down from *Jig's Up,* fiddling with an electrical box, his black CAT cap bobbing up and down with his efforts. He must have felt the movement of the dock as Ray approached, because he sat back to wipe sweat off his forehead, pushed up his glasses, and calmly took in Ray holding his book and jacket.

"She's back, eh?"

"Oh, yeah. Says she staying and brought luggage to prove it."

"Ka-ching! The pool's still on."

Ray squatted to get a closer look at the plug Greg was dismantling. "She'll be up later to prove her moorage payments are on track."

Greg said, "I figured." He pointed his screwdriver at Ray. "You'll go back to your sister's?"

"Reluctantly. She's hard to live with these days."

A nod from Greg. "You tell Jill who you are?"

"No. She surprised me. I'll wait a bit while I scope out the situation."

"In a town this small, she'll hear about you from someone else if you don't explain yourself."

"She's nothing like what I expected."

Greg clicked his tongue. "Has the feel of a primary female, like a rare breed of shrimp. Look it up since prawning might be your new career. I think she's one of those snappy-eyed women who sets her mind on something and won't let go." Greg surveyed the mess of wires in the power box. "She's not hard to look at. Not as stacked as the stories say, but..."

Ray remembered Jillian's cocked eyebrow, acknowledging his interest in checking her out. "But still impressive." *With warm caramel skin and enough curly red-brown hair for two women.* He shrugged off the image. "I'm thinking she'll dabble at fishing and go screaming back to her cushy world in Seattle. Why would I start a wrestling match when she might not be interested in a fight?"

Greg squeezed his chin. "Life goes on whether she stays or not. I pay you to take security walks through the marina, random, from eleven to two a.m., eh?"

Ray nodded. "I bartend at The Tides from five to ten and protect the marina eleven to two. But hear this: if Jillian Morrell goes out prawning, I'll be cruising with her, however short *her* season is."

3

She stood below sea level.

Jill had stashed her last piece of clothing in a drawer under the bed. Now, in the bow of the boat, with her feet on the floor at the foot of the bed, she was unnerved by the fact her knees and her feet were below saltwater. But dry. *Jig's Up* was a trawler with a deep keel and a rounded bottom. Like a sailboat's construction, much of the living space was below decks, including the massive freezer buried in the stern, geared to chill 900 pounds of shrimp at -55 degrees. Under her stateroom's floorboards, 1600 gallons of diesel sloshed in four aluminum tanks. Two more containers, made of stainless steel, stored 530 gallons of municipal water, but an onboard saltwater conversion system created even fresher water on demand.

Thousands of pounds of liquid floating under the surface of an ocean. Mind-boggling.

She'd sleep underwater.

With two strangers.

Her crew would occupy the bunk beds in the second cabin, sleeping so close she would hear them snoring. Sharing one bathroom. Vying for space in the tiny galley. The food and beverages she'd bought since cleaning out Ray's food filled the little fridge and two cupboards. Where would her crew store their stuff?

She mounted the narrow stairs to the pilothouse, careful not to trip. Again. She'd banged both elbows and hit her head on a low-hanging cupboard already. Her left hip had smacked into the jamb of the narrow pilothouse door more times than she could count. Was the boat making a point about the folly of moving from a two-bedroom, two-bath, Seattle condo to live with a couple of strangers in less than 300 square feet?

With a sigh, she shifted to the pragmatic. Mae C hung from a hook next to her bed, looking like a giant insect crawling up the cabin wall. Later she'd secure the drone so it didn't bounce during heavy seas. Clean sheets on the queen, clothes and bathroom stuff stowed. Time for a cup of tea.

She headed for the starboard side of the pilothouse to the galley and pulled cream from her under-the-counter refrigerator. While she waited for water to boil, she eyed the captain's chair and all the equipment on the helm console as well as the readout screens lining the space above the window. She couldn't wait to pore over manuals and test out instruments: radar, hydraulic pumps, GPS, plotters, autopilot, compass, inverter, compressor, stabilizer, bow thrusters. With a warm mug in her hand, she slid into the big helm chair, relishing the smooth tan-colored leather, seating her so high she could see beyond the prow of her boat.

A far cry from outfitting drones for Baldur.

Banging on the pilothouse door startled her out of her reverie. She looked at her watch and peered into the dark. A disembodied face filled the pilothouse window. Stewart.

"Sorry," he yelled from outside. "I know it's late, but I saw your light on. Making a security check." He raised an eyebrow at his duffle and a bag of groceries sitting on the deck. "And picking up my gear. And food."

With the door partly open, she said, "Sorry about that. I wanted to unpack. Organize." Her tone of voice let him know she wasn't sorry at all. This was her boat and what she said went.

He hoisted his gear and food. "I was running errands all day. Meant to get back sooner."

Sounded like an apology. She opened the door wider. "Join me for a cup of tea? Sorry I can't offer coffee. Not a favorite."

"Sure." He dropped his bags, entered, and stood next to the galley, running his hand through his short dark hair, messing it up instead of taming it. A couple cowlicks and a shadow of a dark beard gave him a casual look. Even though she was five foot eight, he loomed over her.

Stewart cleared his throat and avoided eye contact when he took the cup from her. He didn't sit down when she waved him to the table, either. "So, Ms. Morrell…"

"Jill."

With his eyes on her, he said, "Jill. You surprised us by coming back."

She frowned. "What do you mean, 'coming back'? And who is 'us'?"

"Greg figured after a grueling six-hour training session on Daryl's boat and without hope of hiring a crew, you'd give up on shrimping."

Jill crossed her arms. "Nobody checked with me."

"You plan to stay?"

She nodded. "What took two weeks was the paperwork around quitting my job and clearing out of my apartment in Seattle. *Jig's Up* is my boat, deeded to me by my father. Since yesterday, it's my only home. Today, April 1, marks the beginning of my new profession." She paused. "Hope the fact it's Fool's Day doesn't refer to me or you."

"No shit? You're going to fish?"

"No shit."

Stewart sucked in a breath, squared his shoulders and announced, "Need a partner?"

She blinked. "Partner? Do you have any experience shrimping?"

"Uh, no." He fell silent.

"That's your pitch?"

"I guess it is. My situation is pretty straightforward. The lumber company in Campbell River where I worked closed down six months ago. My sister moved from Campbell River to her father's home outside of Port McNeill, so I came to spend time with her. I work at The Tides plus three hours security duty here, but both are temporary." His eyes homed in on hers. "I'd sign on with you for the season."

"No experience with prawning, yet you're asking for an equal share of the profits?"

The man raised his eyebrows. "I'd be learning with you. Like all coast kids, I worked grunt detail on fishing boats through my high school summers. Still, I admit I've never worked on a prawner."

Jill squinted at him. "So why push for a partnership?"

"You can't fish alone, and word on the dock is all the boats are crewed-up."

"So I've heard."

"I'm willing to do it for forty percent share and room and board."

"Room and board?"

"We'll be spending every waking hour prepping for the season." He paused. "I need a place to stay because my sister and I aren't the best roommates." A few swallows of tea and he set his mug aside.

Jill shook her head. "I don't like making snap decisions about something so important. Let me talk to Greg and whoever else has an opinion about you."

"Few people know me here and I've only been working for Greg a short time. I'll get you the phone number of my boss at the mill soon as I find out where he transferred." He washed out his cup and placed it in the sink. "It's a good offer."

She plucked a small plastic bag off the couch and handed it to him. Ray flushed at the sight of a half dozen condoms mixed in with some toiletries from the bathroom.

"I think that's the last of your possessions. You get your former boss's reference. I'll ask around about you."

He squared his shoulders, appearing ready to say something else, but Jill opened the door to usher him out. "Catch up with me in a couple of days and I'll let you know if you're in the running. If so, we'll begin negotiating."

***

By the time Ray returned to the marina office, he'd worked himself into a serious lather.

Why didn't she stay the hell in Seattle and make his life a whole lot easier? And why hadn't he told her the real reason for his interest in *Jig's Up?*

He stared out the window at the dimly lit docks, realizing he should have reminded the woman to rig some kind of a lock for the starboard door. She was the only female in the marina, a sitting duck for guys like Ken Bailey. Ray thought about the fishermen in the bar telling the tank top story to anyone who would listen. By now she had breasts the size of cantaloupes and was every guy's wet dream.

Foolish? Yes, she was.

He didn't feel right about the pool money he'd given to Ken, but was even more unsettled by his inability to tell Jill how their lives were horribly entangled and antagonistic. He should be upset she had returned to Port McNeill intent on prawning, but instead he was impressed by the look of wonder and excitement in her eyes when she beheld the boat's electronics. She'd won some respect from Daryl's crew because she'd jumped in to help and showed she had skills. Was that why he couldn't tell her straight out what *Jig's Up* meant to him and his sister?

Like Greg said, in Port McNeill no one got to keep secrets. If Ray didn't tell Jill Morrell the truth, someone else would.

***

"You're in danger, Jill. I can't believe you've already spent a week on Al's boat when every minute is a bomb ticking."

Adjusting the cellphone to her ear, Jill said, "Drama, Mom. I arrived April Fool's day and waited for something bad to happen, but apart from a fishy smell and the big winds we're having today, I like it here so far." Jill took a seat behind the helm and touched the whale carving with her index finger. "I'm not fond of rocking-at-the-dock, but I put out a couple more fenders to guard the hull, and I've stopped the banging, at least. Inside, the boat is cozy and clean. New deadbolts went in today. Once I replace two crappy chairs, my interior decorating's done."

"Al's in prison for killing someone, Jillian. Won't they confiscate the boat? For restitution?"

"I don't know what kind of reparations the Canadian government will demand. Because I have dual citizenship, I think I'm allowed to own the boat free and clear, but I'll look into the legalities now that I have some time."

"Accepting a gift from a man in prison? How does that feel?"

Jill scoffed. "We banked $250 a month from Al until I started college. He fronted me $20,000 for tuition and came to my high school and MIT graduations. Maybe he's simply hoping I'll care for his property in his absence."

Her mother was quiet.

"*Jig's Up* is the boat's name."

Her mother remained silent. Typical. The only way Jill and her mother had dealt with Al leaving was not to talk about him.

Rose Morrell clicked her tongue. "I'm worried you might be depressed like Al was, sweetheart. He had a thriving business as a mechanic in Seattle and he walked away from it. From us. Haven't you done something similar?"

Jill palmed the rounded glass of the ship's compass. "No, Mom. I enjoyed my first years at Baldur, because I got to build drones. The big money I made and my condo were bonuses. But Baldur named me to lead a new drone project where my job was administrative, not hands on. Worse were the questionable ethics of the contract. Ridiculous security standards, untrustable bosses. I would have gotten depressed if I stayed."

"And the headaches? When did you eat last?"

Jill didn't answer.

"You forget meals and you isolate yourself like your dad did."

She couldn't deny either.

"You're sure the thing with Dave isn't part of your running away from Seattle?"

Breath expelled. Easier topic. "Over. Done. He wanted to own me. I'm relieved he moved on and married someone else."

Her mother said nothing.

"I am not Al, Mom. And remember he got control over his depression with medication. For all we know, prawning helped him heal. Admit it. The Al we saw at my MIT graduation was a healthy man."

"Even so, he wouldn't expect you to dump your job at Baldur to be a fisherwoman. Al assumed you'd be an astronaut and go to the moon and back, not haul shrimp in Canada."

Jill pulled on her ear lobe, doubt creeping into her mind. "Put that way, I look a little crazy, don't I?" She sighed. "The moon has appeal. Still, I lost the buzz at Baldur."

"And you're feeling it on *Jig's Up?*"

"I am. Could be temporary, I admit. But I had my last headache when I got fired at Baldur. I should be stressed, but I've been fine since I got here."

In a quiet voice, her mother said, "Maybe Al knew you needed the boat. He loved us enough to leave us. Could this be another way to show he cares?"

"He was always nice to me, to us, Mom. He isn't a man who would kill."

"How can we know for sure? You're in Port McNeill with no support system. People think your father shot someone, and they'll treat you badly. Worse? If Al didn't shoot the guy, maybe the murderer is still in town and his next target is *you*."

A knock on the door startled Jill enough to end the conversation, promising her mother a call back. She peered out into the darkness, unable to make out who her visitor was. Stewart? Wisson? Setting the phone on the table, she stepped to the door.

"Lynda? What in the world are you doing here?" Jill opened the starboard door and let her colleague in.

Round-eyed and open-mouthed, Lynda Flynn entered the pilothouse. "Is this the twilight zone? What the hell?"

Jill laughed. "Hard to believe GPS brought you here, isn't it? We're close to the end of civilization, for real. Everything north of Port McNeill takes a ferry or personal craft to get there."

"This is yours? Seriously?"

Unease hit Jill when she considered Lynda's presence on *Jig's Up.* Lynda had traveled a whole day to get to Port McNeill. Why?

"Don't freak out." Palm up, Lynda said, "I took a vacation day from Baldur because I wanted to check on you. When we heard you'd taken over a fishing boat we worried you'd cracked up. Mary gave me your marina address, where they'll send your last check. I said I'd try to get you to return to Baldur, but that was an excuse to get your address. Period."

"I've sold my condo and signed the exit papers. Not going back. Tell them prawning is my next career."

Lynda shook her head and thumped a bottle of wine on the galley counter. "They'll never believe it so I better take pictures of you and the boat. Hard evidence you've lost your marbles."

When Oceans Rage

Jill struggled to make sense of the surprise visit. Lynda wasn't even a friend, yet she was teasing Jill as if they were the best of pals.

"Glasses? I heard you like chenin blanc," Lynda said. "After that bitch trip from Seattle, I'm ready to drink." She unscrewed the bottle and held it up, waiting.

Removing a couple of plastic tumblers from the cupboard, Jill said, "You didn't come all this way just to feed the company grapevine."

"Sit. Sit. You must be exhausted after clearing out of your apartment and downsizing like this. Total whiplash." Lynda growled out her words. "I'm pissed Baldur didn't value the years you dedicated to them."

When Jill seated herself next to the pot belly, Lynda turned her back on Jill, poured the wine and pivoted to present Jill with a glass. She took a sip, enjoying the taste until a question slithered into her mind. The woman couldn't be counting on a *Jig's Up* overnighter, could she?

"It's late Lynda. You have a place to stay?

"Drink up. Yes. Done. The Tides. Yelp told me. Wine good?"

Lynda clinked her plastic glass with Jill's and they both took swallows.

"Very. Thanks for bringing it." Jill squinted at her. "Did Baldur pay your way here?"

Lynda leaned next to the galley stovetop. "I'm on my own dime, but they hope I'll entice you to return. I...I was curious. Wanted to put my mind at ease about your abrupt flight from the company." Lynda surveyed the tight quarters as if she were viewing an alien world. "Or not."

Jill drank the wine, thinking *Jig's Up* was feeling more comfortable by the moment. While Lynda rattled off gossip about the Baldur drone crew, Jill relished the idea she had little interest in the company anymore. As for the people she'd worked with, it wasn't that she didn't care. She'd simply never connected with any of them on a personal level.

Including Lynda. So why was the woman here?

"I loved your condo with its view of the Cascades," Lynda gushed, taking Jill's glass and refilling it. "Why did you sell it?"

"Boat maintenance and moorage is expensive. I couldn't afford two homes on a prawner's salary."

Lynda stood at the top of the stairs leading to the sleeping quarters. "Is Mae C down there?"

"She is."

"Hard to believe Baldur let you keep her."

"I bought her with my own money and never took her to work."

"But the modifications. The upgrades you told me about."

"My own parts. My private tinkerings." While Jill drank more wine, she narrowed her eyes. "Why did you bring up my drone? What's Mary saying?"

Lynda tipped her glass and took several swallows. "It's just that we've got a huge hole to fill since you left. Mary wants me to take lead on the new project, but the learning curve is so steep I'm feeling desperate. One wild idea I had was you'd give me a tutorial using Mae C. That's the only reason I brought her up. Desperation. Pressure. Feelings of inadequacy. You could teach me, Jill. Bail me out."

Jill considered the request for two seconds. "Can't, Lynda. Won't. Mary and Calvin are responsible for preparing you for the job. Not me. Not Mae C. I can't believe they aren't giving you the support you need."

"But, I—"

In the next moment, Jill felt her body rise above the chair, giving her a helicopter view of the top of Lynda's head. Damn if the woman didn't have a bald spot. The boat expanded to twice its size and jerked crazily from side to side. A mother of a headache coming on? Had she forgotten to eat today?

She shook her head to clear it. "No, Lynda. And you...er...I...I'm not comfortable with you here. To make a go of prawning, I have less than a month to learn the trade, hire a crew, and get my boat in working order. I don't have time for Baldur. Or tutorials. Now, it's late, and I've got silly...uh...so...some charts to study. You have a nice night at The Tides and...and a pleasant trip back to Baldur tomorrow morning. Give...give my best to the team." She put her hand to her forehead, feeling strangely buoyant again. Had the wind come up? Was the boat rocking, the movement giving her vertigo?

She gulped, failing in her attempt to rise and escort Lynda out the door. "Goodbye," she said, forgetting what the word meant. "Hello?" Another shake of the head. "Tell them I'm fine but let them know I've cut ties with Bad...Baldur. Co...completely."

A flash of annoyance in her expression, Lynda drank down the last of her wine. "No call for bitterness, Jill. I came as your friend and I'd hoped to spend time with Mae C."

When Lynda's smile stretched a yard long, as insincere as The Joker's, Jill clutched at her chest. *What's wrong with me?* "Help me, Lynda. I'm rising into the air. Hang on to my hand so I don't float."

Lynda bent down and pressed Jill's hands on the chair arm so hard Jill groaned.

35

"I've got better things to do than handholding, you self-absorbed bitch. Your drone and I are about to have a little conversation." She grabbed Jill's purse off the bench seat. "Knowing you, Mae C is locked up tight. You'd never let her out of your sight, would you?" The woman stalked to the top of the stairs leading belowdecks, digging in Jill's purse for her keys.

Inside her head, Jill produced a scream that should have wakened the dead.

4

Ray couldn't understand what he was seeing.

From his vantage point on the deck of *Jig's Up*, he spotted Jill sitting on a chair, jaw and neck muscles taut, as a woman dug in what appeared to be Jill's purse, the woman's irritated expression and angry words seeming to stymie Jill's efforts to rise.

He'd come to the boat expecting Jill to be alone, prepared to explain his complicated relationship with her and the boat. Finally. No matter how late it was, he was determined to follow Greg's advice and get the whole story off his chest.

But Jill had company. Unwelcome? Should he wait until morning to unload his news? Maybe the woman was a lover, a partner. He shouldn't interfere in their private argument.

A pang of discomfort hit him. Jill was a stranger in Port McNeill, a green, crewless captain. Out of her depth and realm. The enraged woman wasn't helping, that was for sure. And shit. He was security. He was here.

Ray banged on the door.

The woman gave him the finger.

He pounded again. Yelled, "Security. We've had complaints."

With a sour expression, the woman hollered, "This is between Jill and me." She appeared to take a steadying breath. "We'll quiet down. Leave us alone."

"Open this door. I want to talk to Jill."

"She's had too much to drink. I'll handle her."

"Ma'am. I will not leave until you let me talk to her. She is an owner on the dock. I work for *her*."

The woman rolled her eyes. "I'm her friend. When she gets like this, she's impossible. She'll cool down. I know how to help her."

Jill's mouth opened in an 'O' and her eyes twitched. Was she asking for help?

"Ma'am. I'm coming in."

With a shrug, the woman pushed open the door, almost sending him backward over the railing. What the hell? He glanced at the half-empty bottle of wine on the galley counter, an empty glass in Jill's hand. As soon as he knelt next to her, she grabbed his hand, eyes riveted to his. "What's going on, Jill? A little too much giggle juice, eh?"

"Storm. Helicopters. Bald spots."

"Are we free associating? Why don't you tell me how you're feeling and how I can help?"

"Bad. Fly. Wine."

Lynda stepped in front of Jill. "I think she mixed pot with booze again. She was like this when I got here. Don't worry, because I'll watch over her and make sure she gets some sleep."

"Who are you, ma'am?"

"Her friend. From work. She's lending me Mae C so I can learn how the drone works."

"Mae C?"

"Right. Jill's best friend is a drone. Mae C is down there somewhere. Probably locked. I'll find her keys in here." The woman held up Jill's purse.

"You're Jill's second-best friend, then? Known her for years?"

"Five and counting. I get frustrated when she's like this. Sorry I was pissy when you were at the door. Booze makes her stupid."

"So how do you sober her up?"

"Coffee. Tons of it. I was just about to brew some."

"Why don't you do that? I'll hold her hand and you get the coffee going. She seems to need someone to hang on to."

With a huff, the woman began searching through the cupboards while Ray watched.

He squeezed Jill's hand and rose. "Funny you can't find any coffee even though you say it's her go-to beverage."

Jill's guest stared at a cupboard brimming with various types of teas.

"Your purse, ma'am?" he asked, picking up a Coach bag from the floor. When she reached for it, he pulled it away, and rummaged around until he found her wallet.

"Hey! You can't—!"

"Lynda Flynn," he read from her license, and memorized her address.

She snatched the wallet and the purse from him. "How dare you! I ought to—!"

"Get out of here Lynda Flynn. If I were you, I'd leave Port McNeill and never come back. You are *not* Jill Morrell's friend."

The woman straightened, grabbed the empty wine glasses, squirted soap in each and washed them in the sink. "You have no right to make me leave."

Ray crowded her at the counter. "I've got your name, ma'am, and I know where to find you. I'll figure out your game real soon. Count on it."

When a flicker of fear showed in her eyes, he smiled. "Go."

She screwed the top on the wine, pushed the bottle into her purse and left, slamming the door behind her.

***

Jill had been drugged. Ray was sure of it. After years living with an alcoholic stepfather, he knew about drunkenness. Jill Morrell was not hammered with booze.

GHB, ketamine, LSD, mushrooms. One. Not pot mixed with alcohol like Lynda Flynn said. Ray had been a wrestler at UBC, so recreational drugs were not for him, but he'd seen friends messed up by all four.

Had Jill chosen this particular trip? Didn't seem so. She was flying and so far, not liking any part of the journey. In fact, she was gripping his hand so hard it was numb.

"Flynn is gone. I kicked her out." He studied Jill's face. "Was that the right thing to do?"

She didn't respond to his question. Instead, she writhed on the chair, muttering about Mae C. The drone. The machine Lynda Flynn had wanted to take with her.

Ray had a hundred questions to ask Jill about her job, the drone, her co-workers, and Lynda Flynn in particular, but now was not the time to ask. Instead, he'd help her through her agony, hoping for answers later.

For a second, he considered telling her his sorry secret. A trial balloon. For practice. She wouldn't judge, much less listen. But he dismissed the idea when she hooted, "I'm flying.

I'm a kite!" She giggled and pushed her curly hair away from her face.

"What's so funny?"

"Lynda's mouth was two yards wide. And she's bald on the top of her head." She put her fingers to her mouth and looked into the dark night. "Did you know this boat is sinking?"

"I hope not," Ray said, helping Jill rise out of the chair.

"All boats are in the process of sinking, mister. They yearn to founder, don't you know?"

"Alas, you are correct." When he steadied her on her feet, her curls brushed his cheek. The fresh almond smell of her shampoo and the thinness of her arm made her seem vulnerable. But not for long. When Jill recovered and Ray told her why he was hanging around *Jig's Up,* she'd be pissed as could be.

She smiled. "I like you. Show me the top of your head."

Ray did so. "What do you think?"

"Not bald."

"Glad to hear it. Want to walk a bit? Stretch your legs. Have some tea?"

"Tea me."

"I'll boil water."

She held on to his hand. "My boat is determined to sink and I can't let it." After a survey of her cozy spaces, she shook her head. "If I'm in charge of this vessel, the poor thing is underhelmed."

"Clever turn of phrase, Ms. Jill. But you're smart and you'll learn." He helped her slide into the bench seat.

"You are my friend. Lynda isn't."

"I thank you for the compliment," he said, checking his watch. She'd come down from the drug in about eight hours and he'd have to confess his sins against her.

And then she'd pitch him into the sea.

***

Mae C smiled at Jill from her perch on the cabin wall, and Jill grinned back, relief bringing tears to her eyes.

She turned her head the opposite direction to see Ray Stewart sleeping next to her, her hand in his. He wore a tee shirt and jeans. Barefooted.

She looked down at herself. Tank top. Yoga pants. *Thank God.*

"What the hell happened?"

At her words, Ray stirred in his sleep, so Jill pulled her hand out of his and rolled off the bed. When her feet hit the floor, the fact it was dry produced another wave of relief. *Why?*

She stumbled to the head, peed, and looked into the mirror, touching the top of the head of someone she barely recognized. Dizziness had her slamming down the toilet cover and sitting, her head between her legs.

Ray's muzzy voice: "Jill? How ya doin'?"

"I'm gonna make some tea. Then I'll tell you."

A chuckle. "Perfect."

She'd gulped down half a mug of Earl Grey before he joined her in the galley, looking nervous, guarded. Palm up, she said, "Relax. The tea helped. I remember enough. I owe you, Ray Stewart. When Greg hired you to secure the dock, he got a gem."

Ray's grin brightened the pilothouse. He practically swaggered over to the stove to pour his own mug of tea. "You're amazingly calm for what happened to you last night."

"I know. Right? Do you think I'm still on it?"

Checking his watch, Ray said, "Shouldn't be. Maybe residual. I googled it last night to get the deets."

"You think LSD?"

"Maybe. But ketamine, Special K, could have given you hallucinations, too. Or mushrooms."

"She wanted to distract me, not kill me. She spiked my wine lightly, don't you think?"

"I'd say so. Easiest to buy up here in Canada is psilocybin—magic mushrooms. Powdered form. Illegal to possess in the U.S. but a wide-open market here."

"I don't remember everything."

"Supported by Google. The blood draw will tell us more."

Jill fingered the bandage in the crook of her arm, trying to recall her hospital visit. "I need a play by play. Sit. Please." She pointed to the two ratty chairs. "Now."

As Ray described his part in the encounter with Lynda, Jill took in the matter-of-fact way he delivered the information. Exacting detail, almost emotionless. Like he was trained to observe objectively. He said, "I took you to emergency and they drew blood. Constable Burns met us at the hospital but took a statement from me since you weren't coherent. He's expecting you to stop in this morning."

"They released me into your custody? Do they know you?"

"Greg vouched for me. Burns knows I'm marina security."

"You brought me back to the boat? Then what?"

"You wouldn't let go of my hand, so I had to sleep with you." That's when his eyes dropped and uncertainty tainted his words.

"Did we...uh...sleep?"

Rolynn Anderson

He blinked. "Solidly. I haven't slept so hard in months."

Jill rubbed her chin. "I've never taken a drug like LSD. Have you?"

"I was in sports at University of British Columbia. Didn't partake."

"I'm surprised there's no hangover. I feel darn good. Too good."

"Which is why people take LSD or 'shrooms, or K, as they are called on the street. For the most part your trip seemed to make you happy. And sleepy."

"Weird that I have lots of energy and I'm looking forward to breakfast, a meal I usually skip." She rose and opened the refrigerator, taking out butter, peanut butter, and bread. "So this morning the constable and I need to talk about two crimes: Lynda Flynn's and my father's."

Ray's expression shuttered. "Oh?"

"I've confined myself to this boat long enough. I don't want to be the only person in town who's ignorant about what happened."

"Listen, Jill, I —"

With a head-shake, Jill said, "Nope. Today, I get the facts."

"But I came over last night to—"

She put up a hand to stop him. "No need to apologize. I'm lucky you showed up." Dropping a slice of bread into the toaster, she said. "Let's focus on today. You're a witness to Lynda's burglary attempt, so you should make sure you've told Burns everything you know. I'll slap a restraining order on her, accusing her of drugging me. Lynda wants my drone and she can't have it." Jill glanced at her new deadbolts. Then she took in the yards of glass encasing the pilothouse, rendering door locks useless if a

44

burglar broke the windows. "She can't set foot in this marina, ever again."

Ray nodded. "I'd like to know more about your drone and why Lynda Flynn wants it so badly, but I also have some things to explain about my sister and me. You sure we can't talk now?"

"Positive. We focus on the crime while it's fresh in our minds." Jill put her hands on her hips. "Lynda and Baldur are determined to steal Mae C and we can't let that happen."

***

Al Morrell admitted to taking a man's life.

Jill sat in the Port Hardy police station, re-reading the police report on Bill Parrish's death by gunshot. Her father had pled guilty to manslaughter, admitting he killed Bill Parrish when he attacked Al's girlfriend.

In a crisp brown RCMP uniform, Constable Burns sat behind his metal desk, ramrod straight, his red hair buzzed short. His eyes were on her, waiting until she finished the report. "Any questions?"

"A million. But let me try a summary first. Parrish was a terror when he was drunk and obviously had a snoot full when he followed Adrienne Riley home that night, presumably jealous about my dad's relationship with Adrienne. My father arrived at the scene in his own car and says he shot Parrish as the man raised a brass vase to hit Adrienne a second time. Al can't or won't talk about the missing pistol."

Burns folded his hands. "That's a good overview. Since we didn't recover a weapon and we found no gun residue on your father, his story doesn't make sense."

"Why didn't Al take the case to court? At the very least he could have pled self-defense instead of waving off the trial and accepting a manslaughter conviction. What, he's serving five years when he could have gotten off with no prison time? I don't get it."

"I feel the same way, Ms. Morrell. Your father had a clean record, whereas Mr. Parrish was known to be a mean, violent drunk with two DUI's on his record. I tried to get Mr. Morrell to take the case to a jury, but he refused. Vociferously, mind you. Mr. Morrell's lawyer was thoroughly frustrated with your father's stubbornness. Still we can't force people to go to trial. He must have had his reasons."

"And you have no idea what they were?"

"I can guess. Jury trials bring out traumatic, painful information. He may have been protecting you, someone else, or himself. He's the only one who can provide those details."

Jill rubbed her forehead in frustration. "But he made sure no one could find him to ask, right? His note says I'm not to contact him, to respect his privacy."

"That was his plan, miss. Here in Canada it's not a matter of public record where a criminal is incarcerated. Still, he can't keep that secret for long. Eileen Parrish and her stepbrother, Ray Stewart, are suing your father for the boat. They'll be sending a subpoena to your father's prison and Al will probably have to show up in court to defend his right to keep the vessel."

Jill stared at him. "Ray Stewart? He's suing me for *Jig's Up*?"

The constable hesitated, apparently realizing he'd stepped into something unpleasant. "I hate to be the one to deliver bad news, ma'am, but an attorney for Ms. Parrish and Mr. Stewart contacted us about the matter. He wants to locate Al in the prison system so they can serve him with a summons."

"I ask again. Ray Stewart?"

"Bill Parrish is Eileen Parrish's father and Ray Stewart's stepfather."

"Ray, the guy who works security at the Port McNeill marina? He brought me to the hospital last night."

Burns nodded, eyes averted.

Jill pressed fingers to her forehead. "Logging, right? Company shut-down in Campbell River." She paused. "Unless he made that up."

"I'm sorry. I assumed you knew his relationship to Bill Parrish."

She dropped her head into her hands. "That must be what he was trying to tell me this morning." A moment later she raised her eyes to Burns. "Why are they suing me for the boat?"

After he'd picked through a pile of papers, the constable pulled a folder out and opened it. "Fishing license, ma'am. Category 'W,' the symbol for prawning. Worth $777,000. Eileen Parrish says your father owes her $500,000 for the license."

Jill pushed her fingers through her hair. "What the hell? Why didn't Ray tell me? Or Greg? Even Wisson?"

Silence from the constable.

"Do you know Ray?" Jill asked.

"I do." He cleared his throat. "He moved to Port McNeill four months ago, after his stepfather was killed. Evidently the death of Mr. Parrish led to some mental health issues for his younger half-sister, Eileen. They've been living in Parrish's house out on Mine Road." He paused. "I like your father, ma'am. And the fishnet of gossip here on the north coast of Vancouver Island calls Al a good man."

"A good man, but how about smart? He gives me the keys to a boat, and says I'm not to contact him, even to show gratitude." She glanced at the constable and shook her head. "Then I find out someone's fighting Al for ownership of *Jig's Up*?"

Burns leaned over, his eyes targeting hers. "Your father may not know about the suit yet. Listen, I'll do anything I can to help you get Mr. Morrell out of prison. He's the only man I've had to lock up I don't think deserved it." He stood, straight-backed, seeming to reinstate his proper role and ending the meeting. "Now, this thing about who gets the boat? That's for the courts to decide."

"I'm still processing the fact my trawler is worth a quarter of a million tied to a license worth more than three times the value of *Jig's Up.* I can't believe it."

"The Fishery Department will have a record of how much Al Morrell paid for the license, but they might not know what Mr. Parrish contributed to the cost of it."

Jill suppressed a growl. "And you can't tell me where my father is?"

"As I said, in Canada, prisoners aren't required to disclose their locations. Eileen and Ray will get a court order to find him, then they'll petition to claim the prawn boat." He cleared his throat. "It's between you and them now, ma'am."

She shook her head as she stood. "How would I know licenses were attached to boats?"

"They aren't. Always."

"What?"

Burns leaned against his desk. "In your case, the boat and license are separate entities."

Jill shook her head, finally understanding the rub. "Without the license, I can't use my boat for prawning."

"If you could find the paperwork regarding who made payments on the license, you'd have a leg up. Check with Maggie Muldoney, your father's attorney, who's here in town. Visit the Fisheries Office in Port Hardy. They'll show you records of payment on the license."

Numbly, Jill stared at Burns. "I found nothing aboard except for trap inspection tags and my father's checkbook. All the license payments are in order, signed by Al Morrell."

Burns looked sympathetic. "Then you've got more research to do, haven't you? Port Hardy will help. Ray Stewart hasn't been in town long, but word on the street is he's smart and loyal to his sister."

She made a sound in the back of her throat, troubled by a vision of clutching Ray's hand all night long. A rival, not a friend.

The constable reached for some documents. "This morning, Mr. Stewart reported on your burglary suspect. We have a call into the Seattle police about Lynda Flynn and we'll let you know when they've tracked her down and questioned her. The tox report on your blood draw could take weeks. We have the tumblers which held the wine, but we understand Flynn washed them out, and she took the wine bottle with her. A cunning woman. You'll fill out a restraining order before you leave today, eh?"

Half an hour later, Jill stumbled out of the RCMP building and into the sun, holding a copy of the police report and a restraining order. She looked at her watch automatically but was too distracted to register what it said. Campbell Way was straight downhill to Broughton Boulevard.

The least troublesome problem she'd faced all day was walking to the marina. So she did.

"Jill?"

Ray Stewart sat on a park bench next to the Wells Fargo bank.

Why is he *here?*

Already dizzy from the flood of information about her father and Ray's fight for Al's boat, his presence was confusing, dislocating. The man had stuck with her after she'd been drugged. She'd slept with him all night hand in hand, drunk tea and eaten breakfast with him, too. When he'd tried to confess something this morning, she'd cut him off. Which meant she caused her own blindside. Brilliant.

Seagulls screeched overhead, the ferry horn blew, and the smell of decomposing sea life filled the air. *How did I end up in Port McNeill?* She made it to the bench and grabbed the back of it to steady herself. Ray frowned and asked her a question, but the buzz in her brain blocked out his words. Turning away from him, she shut her eyes and tilted her head to get rid of the noise.

Ray took her elbow and helped her sit down with him.

Foot traffic at the bait and tackle store was robust, and a string of people laden with bulging laundry bags trudged from the marina to the laundromat. Two men hauled a fifty-pound shiny white halibut up the stairs of the Seahorse Restaurant.

She'd quit her job at Baldur, burning her bridges behind her. Lynda Flynn had wanted Mae C badly enough to drug her in order to steal her drone. And now Jill sat on a bench in a fishing town she hadn't known existed, with a guy who could take a boat she never knew she wanted.

"Could I get you some water?"

The buzzing stopped. "No, thanks." She stared at him. "Why are *you* here?"

He shrugged. "After I filed my report, I decided to wait for you." He tipped his head toward RCMP headquarters. "You talked to the constable."

"I did."

Ray's gaze followed the flight of an eagle.

"I now understand why you were sleeping on my boat. Why you took the marina security position. Why you kept showing up. Why you slept in my bed last night." When he didn't respond, she waved her hand. "No need to play dumb, Ray. I know who you are."

"Burns told you about my stepfather."

"And my father's case."

"We are not our fathers."

"But our lives are intertwined because of them."

Ray leaned back on the bench, still focused on the sky. "I came to your boat last night to confess and you know how that worked out. This morning, I tried again. Probably not hard enough." He took a breath. "My goal is to help my sister, not rip away your livelihood."

"You pretended to crash on my boat because of a bad lock and an unpaid bill."

He raked his fingers through his hair. "I was waiting you out. Thinking you'd go back to Seattle. Making it easier on you...and me."

Jill slapped her palms on her knees. "Watching me stumble around, with all the fishermen as witnesses? How humane is that?"

"My stepfather is dead, my sister has gone bull-goose loony, and I can't pay for the therapy she needs."

"I heard she was your half-sister. An adult. Why do you feel responsible for her?"

"She's ten years younger, newly divorced from an abuser, alone in this world except for me, and in a very fragile state."

Jill shook her head. "All I have is my father's checkbook, showing Fishery Department payments made on schedule."

"Bill gave him cash for his portion. Or so he told my sister."

"Any receipts, IOU's, or bank transactions to prove your stepfather paid Al?"

"Nope. Bill didn't even have a bank account. But everyone knows Bill crewed with Al."

"They worked together. Doesn't mean your stepfather paid into their business."

"My sister swears Bill contributed money to the license. Fishermen on the dock regarded them as good partners. Everyone was surprised when Bill's jealousy over Adrienne got ugly and Al kicked him off the boat."

Jill waved a hand. "He said, she said. Until I can find my father and ask him directly about Bill's stake of the fishing license, we're at an impasse."

"We both need answers."

She nodded, the energy eking out of her. Holding her head in her hands, elbows fixed to the top of her thighs, she said, "My father refuses to see me. Even if I knew where he's incarcerated, Al made it clear he won't talk to me."

Ray was quiet.

Jill pulled her hat off and shook her head. "Damn it, I'm wired to be pragmatic. I'm gonna fish. I need a crew. Did you get a reference?"

"Not yet. The mill's locked up tight and no one's answering any of the numbers I call."

"So, no references? No prawning experience. And you want my boat." Jill remained with her head down, thinking how trivial references were, given the circumstances. The man had stuck with her when she was at her most vulnerable. He'd saved Mae C. Didn't that count for something?

If she held Ray Stewart responsible for Bill Parrish's actions, then Ray could hold Al Morrell's alleged crime against her. She felt her heart constrict and laid her hand on her chest in a futile attempt to arrest the pounding. Was she supposed to give up the prawner *and* her father?

The smell of burnt bridges filled the air.

Beside her, Ray said quietly, "I'll get the references even if I have to travel to Campbell River."

She pressed fingertips to her forehead and relaxed, letting her subconscious do the work as she would if a machine problem stumped her. When she closed her eyes and breathed deeply, Ray's bright yellow condom packages popped into her mind. She smiled and turned to him. "I've got a fishing boat with no crew, and I won't hire you without references. You have a girlfriend in town. Take me to her. Now."

5

Ray looked stunned.

"You want to meet my girlfriend?"

"I saw your condoms."

Warmth slid up his neck to his face. The woman was sharp.

"I want to see if she'll vouch for you."

She also had good instincts. He nodded resignedly. "If that's what it takes. But she's an ex-girlfriend. Donna Rueff. She owns the store over there—Donna's Specialties. Next to the bait and tackle store."

Her display window showed off kitchen and garden sundries along with gifts and books.

"You really want to interview Donna about me?" Ray said, turning on the bench to face her.

"Who in town knows you better, other than your sister?" Jill shot back as she stood.

"This is crazy. You must still have drugs in your system."

"Nonsense. I feel good. Actually better than I have for a long time. Optimistic. Charged up. This is the best idea I've had all day."

Ray caught her elbow as they waited for a couple of cars to pass. "Careful. No one stops for pedestrians on this road." He was still guiding her gently by the arm when they reached the entrance to the store, but wasn't aware of it until he saw Donna watching from inside the open door. He quickly pulled his hand away from Jill's arm and shoved it into his pocket, thinking about what to do next. How could he make this conversation short, focused only on his Campbell River work experience?

Donna leaned against the door jamb, arms folded. "This is a surprise, Ray. I heard you were in town."

"Hey, Donna. Sorry I haven't been by to say hello."

"You've had four months."

The two women stared at him expectantly.

"Uh...Donna Rueff, meet Jill Morrell. I'd like Jill to hire me as a partner for the May prawning season. My boss from the mill is nowhere to be found, so Jill needs a reference. From you. About me. A little bit about my mill security gig and we're out of your hair."

The women eyed each other with interest, Donna's pretty face framed by shoulder-length straight blond hair. He'd called her his calm, blue-eyed beauty. Steady and conventional. And Jill? Six inches taller than Donna. Light caramel complexion, a riot of bronze and russet curls framing prominent cheekbones. She could pass for one of those edgy, intriguing models in a high-end fashion magazine.

Jill ended the silence by cocking her head in his direction. "Ray, here, wants to be my sidekick in exchange for free room, board, and a forty-per-cent share of the season's take. I have no experience at prawning; nor does he. Do you understand my hesitation?"

Donna raised her eyebrows and nodded.

"Wait. I—"

"Let us work this out, Ray." Jill turned her body to close him out physically as she focused on Donna. "You know something about his work history at the mill. Based on that, should I hire him?"

Folding her arms again, Donna straightened. "They liked him in Campbell River. Gave him a raise. He'd earn a good reference from the supervisor." A glance at him. "He's strong, not afraid of hard work." She paused for a moment and added, "His sister, who used to clerk for me, is his focus right now. I'm impressed how he's taken responsibility for Eileen."

Ray felt awkward, standing there as they discussed him like he wasn't there. "I'm also organized and pick up after myself. Not a bad cook, either," he added, half-jokingly.

Donna raised an eyebrow but said no more.

A woman walked toward them, aiming for entry into the store. Ray suppressed a sigh of relief and moved away from the door. "Good enough, eh? We should let Donna get back to her customers."

"Thanks for your comments, Donna." To Ray, Jill said, "I'll make up my mind tomorrow, after I've gathered more information. See you at the marina."

Donna and Ray stood side by side, watching Jill walk across the street. Ray turned to her. "Appreciate it."

She nodded. "I could have said commitment hasn't been your strong suit." She put up her hand to stop his response, looking irritated. "You want the job on the prawner because you're determined to safeguard the boat. For your sister. After years of distancing yourself from your family, I see a change, Ray. That's why I didn't bring up your past history of estrangement."

Ray was silent, knowing Donna's assessment was accurate. Because he couldn't get along with Bill Parrish, Ray's relationship with his sister had suffered.

"You sure about working with Jill and leaving Eileen alone?"

He shrugged. "Her therapist is trying to figure out what sets Eileen off when I visit her. We got along so well in Campbell River, partly because I put a stop to her ex-husband hounding her. But something flipped in her mind when Bill was killed. It could be she's angry I abandoned her when she was a kid, leaving her with a drunken father followed by an abusive husband. I never even went to her wedding. Only showed up when her marriage had fallen apart, and now this." He paused. "I'll admit I haven't been there for her and she probably thinks I'll ditch her again. The doctor says until he drills down to the reason for her resentment, I need to stay away. Since I've lost my bed on *Jig's Up,* I'm sleeping on a cot in the marina office. Or crashing at Greg's until I get a high sign from Eileen's shrink."

Donna nodded. "You hired Sasha Morgan full time to watch over Eileen when you're working."

"My sister likes Sasha. But the expenses for the psychiatrist, Sasha, and the attorney are draining me dry. Plus her household expenses. I've got to earn more money fast."

Donna surveyed her store. "The plan was for Eileen to manage this store so I had time for my art, but she's too sick. Last time she took a shift, she could barely follow a thread of conversation, much less close a sale."

He touched her arm. "It's okay. She can't be in charge of anything until she gets healthy. I'll keep Sasha on salary and earn money prawning. It's the best solution I can think of."

"Jill knows who you are, right?"

"Only that Eileen is my sister and Al Morrell is in jail for killing my stepfather."

Donna squinted at him. "She doesn't know about your years in Nova Scotia? Or your family history?"

"Look," he growled. "She's inexperienced. Never had a boat in her life. Doesn't know a prawn from a minnow. My job is to ensure she doesn't sink *Jig's Up* or sell it and abscond with the money. The details of my past have nothing to do with running a fishing boat."

She frowned. "Your lawyer can't approve of this."

He looked away. "It's Eileen's suit. I'm her power of attorney, so it's my job to protect her assets." Ray stuffed his hands deeper into his jeans pockets. "The court case could take a year, so I might as well earn money prawning, bunk free, and protect *Jig's Up.*"

Donna shook her head but said nothing.

A second customer walked in the door and Donna greeted her warmly. Over her shoulder, to Ray, she said, "See you later."

"We can talk more tonight, eh?" When Donna didn't answer, he pivoted and left the store, his eyes on Jill's retreating figure. He glanced back at Donna, who also had her back to him. Add in Eileen and he was 0 for 3. Three women who wanted nothing to do with him.

So far, his plan to make a new life for himself and his sister in Port McNeill was not going well.

***

Jill sat on one of her tangible successes of the day. She'd talked a furniture store into taking the two ugly chairs off her boat when they delivered twin brown leather ones, aluminum framed, comfortable as gloves.

Security first. She rose and screwed eyebolts into the back frames of her new furniture. Next she pushed each chair against the hull to align with the hooks already attached to the wall. She snapped the hooks into the eyebolts and smiled, impressed by Al's system and her purchase. "Under heavy seas, these puppies stay put." She nodded, satisfied she'd made her mark on the boat's interior.

She glanced belowdecks at her cabin, where she'd applied an extra lock to secure Mae C next to her bed. *Can't steal my drone, either, Lynda Flynn.*

The boat tipped starboard. Daryl Wisson stood at the door so she beckoned with her fingers, motioning him to come in.

"What's up, neighbor?"

"Just bein' neighborly. A couple of transporters want to meet with the prawners. These are freezer trucks that take our product to market. Thought you might like to hear their spiels."

"I saw the flyer on the bulletin board, but I thought you guys favored TriFoods."

Wisson smiled and moved his eyes from her breasts up to her face. "Been doing some homework?"

Jill nodded. "More than you know. Tea?"

"Don't mind. Yeah, well, we wanna keep TriFoods on their toes. And you never know, one of the other two might be worth considering, eh?"

"Makes sense. I'll go. Save me a seat." She handed him a mug and pointed to her BC Sport Fishing Guide and a computer printout. "What's with the interchangeable shrimp and prawn terms? I've read everything I can about our particular crustacean and I don't understand why we call it a prawn."

Wisson arched his eyebrows. "You might want to keep that little secret to yourself, eh?" He picked up the Sport Fishing Guide and appeared to skim the page discussing shrimp versus prawns. "Seems they're still helping with the cover-up."

Jill glanced at the computer printout of the research she'd done and took a swallow of tea. "The only real prawns are caught in the Gulf of Mexico and in Australia. We're catching *shrimp* up here in B.C."

He nodded. "Funny that the Aussies and Louisianans call prawns 'shrimp' and we do the opposite."

"Marketing ploy?"

Wisson smiled as he drank from his cup and set it down. "People up here think the big prawns are more difficult to catch. And better eating. So we call ourselves prawners."

She glanced at the shrimp drawings. "But we're catching Spots, Sidestripers, Pinks, and Humpback shrimp, right?"

"Spot shrimp are our favorite. Big as prawns, so we call 'em prawns." He grinned and held out his hands to show a measurement. "Ten inches. Every woman's dream."

Jill rolled her eyes. "Focus, please. I appreciate your knowledge, not your innuendos. Sit. What else can you tell me about prawns?"

"Fine, fine. Always on the business," he groused, sitting opposite her at the galley table. "But I have to finish with one more sexy tidbit about prawns," A sly grin. "You ready for a gender-bender story with a twist?"

"Long as it's true."

"It is. I swear. Ocean shrimp grow up male, becoming females in the final year or two of their lives. Some species bypass the male phase completely and function only as females. They're called primary females." He clicked his tongue.

She smiled. "Cool concept." A pause. "So, how much money is in the pool?"

Raising his eyebrows in mock surprise, he said, "Pool?"

"The pool giving a bonus to whomever signs up with me. Your idea."

Wisson grinned, his wind-burned face crinkling up. "Maybe six hundred bucks."

"You're in."

She watched him calculate the effect of his response. He shrugged. "Yup."

"I have no hope of hiring a local."

"Don't see a line-up of applicants standing outside."

She leaned forward and his eyes returned to her breasts. "Up here." She used two fingers to point to her eyes. When he dragged his eyes up to hers, he grinned.

Jill cocked an eyebrow. "Seriously. Anyone express interest while I was gone?"

He peered into his mug, scowling. "Dunderheads."

She looked out the window. "Damn." Then she had a thought. "Al had a third partner? Where is he?"

"Name's Jack Canter. He's on his own boat now, out of Campbell River."

No help there. "I hear an experienced prawner from Washington State is looking for a job. Jim Livingston. Has he approached you?"

"Nope. Know of him but nothing about him."

"Ray Stewart? Marina security?"

"Yeah?" His expression clouded. "You thinking of hiring him?"

"I may have to."

"He wants your boat, lady. He could damn well throw you overboard, say you slipped, hit your head, fell in the drink, and drowned."

Jill rubbed her eyebrow. "Don't need the drama. I need to talk to people who know him. References. Nothing about him on Google; Constable Burns says the man doesn't have a record. He worked security at Campbell River, too. It's not his fault the mill shut down."

"He's never prawned." Wisson's lip curled in disgust. "Wears boat shoes like he's going yachting." He paused. "The man's a stalker, watching your every move."

"And you and the rest of the fishermen don't? Come on. He's got a vested interest in the boat and he needs a salary. Why call those bad motivators?

"He's in the pool," he warned.

"So's every guy. Ray needs money. He's—"

Wisson rose, slammed his mug down, and headed for the door. He turned to her and growled, "Don't take him on, lady. If you do, we'll probably be fishing your body out of the water, shark-belly white, and bloated."

She stood, ready to protest.

He shook his head, walked out the door and threw back, "Good tea. Rotten decision. Later, eh?"

She resumed her seat at the bench, a hollow feeling growing in her belly. *Who can help me?* She thought about her fifteen minutes with Al's lawyer, Maggie Muldoney. The brash, red-headed attorney had chanted 'That's privileged information' so many times Jill wanted to hit her. Al had forbidden Muldoney to name his prison, much less reveal details about the crime. The attorney kept saying she was sorry. Like Constable Burns. Everyone was sympathetic when Al should be the most contrite of all for the mess he'd dropped on his little family.

A glance at her watch. Tonight she'd meet Adrienne Riley, a woman whose knowledge of Al might help Jill tweak her next steps to fill out a crew as well as stay out of danger.

Wisson's vivid picture of her drowned body swam in her head. If Ray Stewart was a threat to her, who could she hire instead?

***

Ray nursed his beer at The Tides, waiting for his shift to begin. He'd picked a corner stool, a good vantage point for watching who entered the restaurant as well as the bar. The dimly lit room, made cozy with an elongated gas fireplace opposite the bar, wasn't a bad place to end a fisherman's work day. Flames danced artfully, causing a muted lightshow on the rough-board interior of the bar. Fishnets, anchors, bright orange and yellow buoys, and blue plastic fenders decorated the walls. A distressed wood dinghy hung from the ceiling. After a few beers, this dreamy view of the fishing life could lull patrons into forgetting the downsides of their chosen career.

Ray's first visits to the bar since Bill Parrish's death hadn't been pleasant because they reminded him the man drank too much, hounded waitresses, belittled everyone, then expected Eileen to take his drunken ass home at midnight. The more he learned about his stepfather's dark last days, the less he liked the guy. But Ray had gotten used to The Tides, enough so he appreciated the money he earned here as a bartender. That the bar/restaurant was gossip center of the town, met his goals as well.

He glanced at Parrish's drinking pals, the same guys who'd laughed about Jill's virgin prawning experience and bought into the incentive pool. Men who hadn't bothered to attend his stepfather's funeral. Friends? Right.

Jill walked in the front door and boldly surveyed the room, the restaurant entrance on the right and the bar to the left. She wore fitted dark pants and a navy blazer over a yellow knit blouse. Conservative. Not like the woman who'd removed her sweatshirt in front of strangers quipping, 'Modesty can kill.'

He held his breath until she waved away the hostess and came toward the bar, the gentle corkscrews of her hair backlit by a droplight. "She's no angel," he reminded himself. Her irritated expression proved him right.

"Again? What's with you, Ray? Why are you here?"

"You said you were meeting someone at The Tides. A possible recruit, I figured. I want the job, eh? And I'm on the top of your list since I probably own part of the license."

She frowned. "God, you're persistent. I'm not recruiting. I told you I'm meeting with Adrienne." She surveyed the bar. "This is your nightly haunt? You and Donna?"

"Donna and I dated in Campbell River. We split before she moved to Port McNeill."

"Your stepfather hung out here, I understand. Now you do?"

He stared into his beer. "I start my shift bartending at five. Five to ten, five days a week, but only until the prawn season starts." Ray gestured to a stool. "Do you have time to join me for a drink? Take the opportunity to interview me more thoroughly?"

She looked hard at him and straightened her shoulders. "Are you sure you're ready for some tough questions?"

He met her gaze. "I need the job. Fire away."

She hopped up on the chair and motioned to the bartender. "Gin and tonic, thanks." She turned to Ray. "You're in Port McNeill because your sister's ill."

"What does that have to do with prawning?"

"It might interfere with your work."

"It won't," he said stonily. "She had a breakdown after Bill's death. She's under twenty-four-hour care."

"I'm sorry she's sick, Ray. She lives outside of town, you said."

"In my stepfather's house. West of town, on Mine Road."

"Are you sure you can leave her for hours every day? Even overnight?"

He pushed his hands through his hair. "The sight of me sets off my sister, so until her shrink figures out why, I manage her care and the suit from a distance. In the four months I've lived in Port McNeill, I've been crashing wherever I could, most recently on *Jig's Up*. Since you returned, I sleep on Greg's couch or the cot in the marina office." Ray gulped his beer. "It's a shitty way to live."

She nodded and shifted her attention to the man who brought her drink. "Excuse me a minute. Bartender?"

"Pete." Ray said.

The man seemed wary when he joined them, his neutral expression and dark, shadowed eyes warning her he wasn't interested in any sad stories. A graying beard and mustache hid his age and emphasized narrowed lips.

"I'm Al Morrell's daughter. I haven't seen him since I graduated from college, but, surprise...now I own his boat."

Pete nodded, seeming more interested in the glass he was polishing than anything she had to say.

"Did my father ever come in here, Pete?"

"Just the restaurant part, to have dinner with Adrienne. I know him by sight."

Jill said, "I can't imagine my father shooting anyone, so I'm doing a little research of my own. I read the police report and learned this is the pub Bill Parrish frequented. You and a woman named Milly are the regular bartenders, so I assume you know the clientele. The constable called Bill Parrish a 'mean' drunk. What do you think?"

The polishing cloth stilled. "Accurate description." Pete stared at the fireplace for a few moments. "He'd go bad at the end of his fourth drink, usually. Pick at anyone in the room. Found each person's hot button. Even mine." He resumed a vigorous cleaning of the wine glass in his hand. "The more people he pissed off, the better he liked it."

Ray shifted in his chair.

Eyes lowered, Pete said, "He made us dump right back on him to keep the game going. By midnight, you could cut the self-hatred in the room with a knife." He gave Jill and Ray a thin smile. "His daughter would pick him up before the punching began. Smart man. At least as far as that went."

Jill sat up. "Eileen came here every night to bring him home?"

Pete shrugged. "If she didn't show by midnight, I called her. Parrish always drank too much to drive his own car home."

"But something else happened the night he died."

Expression shifting, Pete held the glass to the light, moving back a step. "I had emergency surgery to remove my appendix that day. My sub didn't know to call Eileen. Bill left here under his own steam around one in the morning, I've been told."

Pete excused himself to help a customer, leaving Jill and Ray to sit quietly, sipping their drinks. Jill consulted her watch. "I'm heading into the restaurant for my meeting with Adrienne."

"I'll get your drink. You go ahead."

She chewed on her bottom lip. "I don't owe Al anything, but I still have a need to understand what happened between him and your stepfather. Tonight I'm meeting with the woman Al was supposedly protecting when he killed Bill Parrish." She raised her hands in a gesture of helplessness. "We'll get back to the job interview later. Thanks for the drink."

He watched her retreating figure, drawn once again to the way the light silhouetted her slim body and curly hair. He shook his head to clear out the vision and remind him of his mission, his sister's misery giving him purpose. He raised his glass in a toast to Eileen. *We'll get the best help for you, Sis. I promise.*

As Ray tipped his glass to drink the last of his beer, a dark thought grabbed him. His contentious relationship with Bill Parrish had pushed Ray to move across the country after he finished college, leaving his sister to fend for herself. And now, Parrish's death and his sister's breakdown kept him in Port McNeill. Would his life always be colored by his dark ties to his stepfather?

6

Adrienne Riley rushed to Jill's table fifteen minutes late, red-faced and apologetic. She shook Jill's hand, introduced herself, then blurted, "I had to run home and make sure Beth was set up with dinner at a friend's. It took longer than I thought. Sorry."

Jill had to smile. Adrienne's round, kind face and pleasantly plump body exuded warmth. She wore black slacks and a colorful Native-designed sweater. "I'm happy you could meet with me on such short notice. Please sit down. I'll bet you've been on your feet all day."

Adrienne grinned as she collapsed into the chair across from Jill's. "What a joy to relax and get served instead of serving. Ever since my thirteen-year-old granddaughter came to live with me, I've barely had time to breathe."

"You work full time and you're raising a teenager. Should be a medal for that."

Her brunette bob, salted with gray, bounced as she talked. "Mothering at this stage in my life is a shock to the system." Adrienne took a swallow of ice water. "I'm divorced. Al and I are...um...*were* a couple."

With a nod, Jill remained silent.

"I heard you're living on *Jig's Up.*"

When Jill hesitated, Adrienne pleaded, "Listen, nobody knows better than I do how much people talk about each other in this town. I've learned a lot about discretion since the shooting. So anything you tell me stops with me. I just know Al would be so proud you're running the prawner instead of selling it. He'd want to know everything about your decision to keep it, which translates to: So do I."

Jill closed her eyes for a moment, exhausted from the tumult of the last weeks. It might not be the smartest thing to do, but she did need someone to talk to. "I was four when my mother split with Al. His gift of a trawler came out of nowhere. Since I can't ask him why, I thought maybe you could tell me his reasons for giving me *Jig's Up.*"

"When did you first learn the boat was yours?"

"About a month ago. All hell broke loose at my job because corporate got wind I inherited a boat from a convicted felon."

Adrienne sobered. "I'm so sorry your world got turned upside down because of this."

Jill offered up a wry grin. "That it did."

"What a shock it must have been."

Jill nodded. "I learned where *Jig's Up* was moored, called my mother, then drove up see the boat."

"What was your mother's reaction?"

Jill raised an eyebrow. "You really want to know?"

Adrienne hesitated. "Well, not if you don't want to—"

"She flipped. Said if I took the boat, I'd get hurt somehow. She was upset I didn't reject the gift outright, which is what my bosses at Baldur suggested. Since my mother and I can't believe

70

Al killed anyone, the possibility I've chosen to move to a town with a killer on the loose doesn't sit well with her."

Adrienne sat back, fingering the menu. "She's worried and I can imagine why."

When the waitress hovered for the second time, Jill said, "Let's order something. What's special here?"

"Halibut fish and chips. Fresh and prepared perfectly."

"Done." Jill ordered and resumed her story. "Al didn't know I was facing some issues at Baldur Industries, when he deeded me the boat. His incarceration surprised me as well as the security clearance folks investigating my background. It was a quirk of timing. The FBI found out about Al's guilty plea and the boat before I did, and accused me of hiding the information. I'm lucky they haven't sent the IRS after me. Yet."

Wide-eyed, Adrienne sipped on water and waited for more.

"Al's boat added a welcome distraction, something I could deal with instead of wrangling over moral issues and investigations. Despite my mother's warnings, I ditched the big city and big business and came to Port McNeill."

Adrienne smiled. "You got to the dock, then what?"

"Greg Hanley gave me the keys, told me where slip 'D-10' was and presented me with a sealed envelope containing a letter from Al and a business card for his attorney. Would you like to see the letter?"

"Oh, yes. Anything from Al. I miss him so much."

Jill reached in her purse for the paper and handed it to Adrienne.

Dear Jillian,

Forgive this intrusion into your life. I'll be incarcerated for the next several years. I won't give you details or make excuses.

I had a lawyer draw up the papers transferring ownership of *Jig's Up* to you. Please contact her for the title and other important documents.

The boat is yours to do with as you please.

I do not want nor do I expect us to start communicating. I ask you to respect my privacy.

I wish you luck. All these years, I've carried you and your mother in my heart, but I realize my gift to you of *Jig's Up* is too little and too late. If only I had been worthy.

Al

Adrienne had tears in her eyes when she placed the letter on the table. "He's lousy at expressing emotions. I expect you were hurt when after all those years, this note was all you got."

"Well, it's awkward as our relationship has always been. Over the years he sent money without comment. This time he gave me a boat and forbade further communication. Not the most gracious gift offering, but not shabby either."

Their food arrived, stacks of tempura-battered halibut, French fries, and cole slaw. Jill folded Al's note, put it back in her purse, and decided to be kinder about Al's actions. "He meant to save me from embarrassment."

Adrienne raised an eyebrow. "He wanted you to focus on your career, not his problems." After a wistful glance at the purse holding Al's words, she focused on Jill. "But you decided to keep the boat in the family. That's wonderful news."

Is it? They ate in silence for a while, until Adrienne said, "So tell me what happened when you saw *Jig's Up*."

When Oceans Rage

Jill smiled at the memory. "Love at first sight, all fifty-one feet of her. She's bigger than other prawners because of her high profile, a good four feet taller than the rest of the boats. Has a regal look because her front cabin windows angle forward, so she looks streamlined instead of boxy like most trawlers." Glancing in the direction of the marina, Jill said, "And Al kept her clean. Gel coat's in good shape and every piece of equipment is in excellent condition. Even though it sat unattended for too many months and needs polishing and maintenance, it's the best rig on the dock."

"Al was so proud of that boat. Especially his high tech toys."

"That's when lust took over. The electronics on *Jig's Up*, all yelling 'Try me! Try me!' At night I dream about how stabilizers work. And bow thrusters. Principles of hydraulics. The engine room? Playland. Like an addict, I am obsessed with learning how to make every machine on *Jig's Up* function perfectly."

Adrienne made a motion with her hand to continue.

"I bought a sleeping bag and moved into *Jig's Up* that afternoon. After a few days, I locked up the boat and drove back to Seattle. Gave myself a couple days of soul-searching, and said no, again, to Baldur. They were less than pleased. Wanted to raise my salary, my pension, my benefits; they even apologized for questioning my integrity."

"Their loss is Port McNeill's gain."

"Engineers aren't easy to come by. My boss could lose her job because she ticked me off." Jill took a deep breath, recognizing she'd left a career where her skills were sought after, stepping into a world where she lacked capability.

"Sidenote—I have yet to start the engine and I've docked a boat the size of *Jig's Up* one time in my life, with a tutor at my side."

Adrienne said, "You love *Jig's Up* the way Al does. He'll be so pleased." She moved a cluster of fries to the side of her plate. "If only we could tell him." Raising her eyes to Jill's, she forced a smile. "We can't be whiners, can we? I know what you need from me, so let's get to it." She took a deep breath. "I love Al Morrell and I know he loves me. He went to prison because he was protecting me from Bill Parrish that night. And he's still shielding me by accepting man...manslaughter and going quietly to pri...prison without a trial." She dabbed at her eyes with her napkin. "I can't believe this hap...happened."

Jill reached out and touched Adrienne's free hand. "I know this is hard, but I've got to understand more about how Parrish died in order to fight for *Jig's Up.*"

Adrienne stilled, staring at Jill. "What do you mean, 'fight for *Jig's Up'*?"

"Bill Parrish's daughter is suing Al for the boat."

Adrienne's mouth opened in disbelief. "No friggin' way." Then she smiled exultantly, "Ha! They'll never find Al to sue him."

"Why did he do that, Adrienne? I need to meet with him. At first I was relieved I didn't have to face Al, but now with this puzzle of Bill Parrish's death along with the civil suit, I *must* talk to him. It's not only because I want to keep *Jig's Up* for Al. I have to understand what happened that night. The constable's encouraging me to fight for my father, but Al's lawyer won't help. Everything's 'privileged'."

When Oceans Rage

Adrienne smiled. "You remind me of Al, honey. You're gettin' on your high horse like he would."

Jill squirmed, feeling flattered. "He would?"

"Oh, yes. The squinty glare along with the speechifying. Must be genetic." Adrienne laughed. "I find it charming."

Jill shook her head and looked away. "It can get old. Ask my mother or any ex-boyfriend."

The waitress interrupted to take away plates, so Jill redirected the conversation. "What prompted Al to refuse a court trial?"

Adrienne drank some water, set down the glass and smoothed the front of her blouse. "Al and I made a point of having dinner together once a week and he'd drop over to the house a couple evenings a week as well. Say, one weekend a month he'd take Beth and me on an outing. 'Road trips' he called them." She gave Jill a sheepish look "He was taking it slow. Too slow for me. I love Al and so does Beth. Formalizing that bond was tricky. For Al."

Jill nodded.

"I worked a late shift at The Tides. A Thursday. After I waitress during the dinner hour, sometimes I help out in the bar. When I do, they rarely make me stay until closing at two. That night I left around one."

Adrienne gulped and put her hands to her face, squeezing her eyebrows. She peeked out between her fingers at Jill as if the memory were too difficult to manage. "You have to understand, Bill Parrish was a horrible man when he drank. He regularly harassed all the waitresses, but because Al and I became a couple, he targeted me. Bill had been interested in me for years, but I had no interest in return. So when I started seeing Al, Bill got jealous. Ugly jealous. To the point Al threw him off the boat."

"They'd split up, you mean?"

"About a year ago. Bill's behavior at The Tides, especially toward me, ended their partnership. Al was looking to hire a new team for this season."

"I see," said Jill. "What happened after you drove home that night?"

"Normally, Eileen, his daughter, picked up Bill at midnight and I didn't have to think about him being around at closing. All I can figure is, Bill drove to my house sometime before I left The Tides. When I got home, Bill's car was parked in front of it. I called Al right away but could only leave a message. I was about to punch 911." Tears brimmed in Adrienne's eyes. "I may have imagined it, but I thought I heard Beth shouting. I sneaked through the side door of the garage where I keep a gun in a lock box next to my fishing gear."

"You have a gun?"

"Yes. And I know how to use it...for shooting the big halibuts before we haul them aboard. Around here most of us carry handguns when we fish." She paused. "Anyway, I loaded the thing and walked to the living room where Bill was standing." She shivered at the thought.

Jill nodded. "Take your time, Adrienne. Try to give me every detail."

Adrienne knit her eyebrows. "It's hard to remember the rest, because everything happened so fast. I was mad Bill was in my house, barring my way to check on Beth in her bedroom. I know I yelled for him to get out. I pointed the gun at him but I never intended to shoot him. Good Lord, I've only ever shot fish!" She shook her head. "He must have realized I wouldn't...you know, how they say 'Don't pick up a weapon unless you plan to use it'. They're right. Bill wasn't scared at all."

When Oceans Rage

Rubbing her eyes, she continued. "Suddenly he lunged at me with one of my brass vases in his hand. I threw up my free hand to protect my head, and a good thing I did. Sprained my wrist, but he still hit my head hard enough to crack it open and that's the last I remember until I woke up bleeding in Al's arms. I saw Bill lying on the floor with blood all over his chest." She shuddered. "There was blood everywhere. His, mine, all over me and Al. Al told me Bill was dead and the police were coming."

"So you never knew when Al came in? You didn't see or hear Al shoot Bill?"

"No. For all I know, *I* could have shot him, which is why I doubt there is a killer on the loose here in Port McNeill, but Al says he did it. He wouldn't discuss the details. And I can't remember anything after Bill attacked me. When Al said he wanted to take the plea bargain and keep the whole event out of court, what could I do? He refused to explain himself." Adrienne teared up again. "I haven't talked to him for months, and likely won't see him for years." She dabbed her eyes with her napkin again and stared at the wet spot she'd produced. "He's so stubborn."

"No kidding."

Adrienne straightened, and gained control of her emotions. "I promised him I'd let the case drop. He'd say you should do the same thing."

"But his admission of guilt makes it possible for the Parrish family to sue for the boat. Would Al want them to take the boat away from me?"

Adrienne's eyes narrowed. "When he finds out about the suit, he'll be furious."

"And he'll be found. As soon as Ray and Eileen serve a subpoena, we'll know the name of his prison."

Adrienne closed her eyes. "I need to see him. Desperately." She looked at Jill, her sorrow making Jill's heart ache. "I can't bear waiting five years."

"You think he'd ever ask for a court trial?"

"Opening the chance for me to be implicated? To force me to testify? Never."

Jill bowed her head and willed herself to view the future Adrienne had accepted. She sighed. "Well, a civil suit like this one could take months. A year. In the meantime, I take good care of Al's boat and do some prawning to support myself."

Adrienne grinned. "Now that's a picture sure to please Al. He said you'd probably sell the boat."

"Wait. He talked about me?"

"On the last day I saw him, before he went to prison. I guess he assumed you and I might connect up one day."

"How could he know what I'd do?"

"He guessed you'd seek me out. The stubbornness gene." Adrienne reached over to touch her arm in sympathy. "He'll be proud to hear you've decided to prawn even while he questions the wisdom of it." She looked at her watch. "I better pick up Beth."

Jill grabbed her purse as Adrienne stood. "Dinner's on me, Adrienne. Let me pay for the babysitting, too."

"Nope. I took Beth to a neighbor's. Didn't cost a cent. Thank you for the dinner, though. I'm so happy to meet you. I pray Al gets a chance to see you soon."

Jill stood as well. "Let me think on what you've told me. I'll keep you up on anything new concerning Al."

Adrienne enfolded Jill's hand in both of hers. "Please. The minute you find out where Al is, let me know. Even if he won't let me visit, I'd like to write to him."

As she watched Adrienne scurry out of the restaurant, a familiar feeling overwhelmed Jill. Judging Al had been her lifelong pursuit, his image looming as heroic some days, villainous on others. Was Al a doting boyfriend and surrogate grandfather? Was the boat a gift from him or a curse? Or were they all being duped by a con artist?

***

"Stalk much?"

Jill stared at Ray as he rose from a bench in the restaurant's entrance. He smelled of soap and sage, hair tamed, and clad in jeans, cowboy boots, tee shirt, and leather bomber jacket. Ready for an event. Had she forgotten something?

"Thought I'd go to the company meeting with you. If you decide to hire me, I'll need the same information you get about our distributors." He cleared his throat. "Since we're both neophytes."

"It's a free country." She walked down the steps. "I'm going back to the boat first, so I'll meet you at the café."

"I'll walk with you and raise more arguments in my favor. Reasons why you should hire me. Wouldn't mind hearing about your talk with Adrienne Riley."

Jill ambled into the night, determined to keep the details of Adrienne's story to herself.

"This way," he said, touching her arm.

She considered the direction she was moving in and realized she had erred. "Things look different in the night." She turned and slipped on some loose gravel. He caught her elbow, helping her to rebalance.

"I'm fine," she said, pulling away. "The drugs are out of my system."

He said nothing as they walked on, Jill thinking if she made a list of pros and cons, the negatives mounted against hiring Ray Stewart. He hadn't been up front about the rivalry over *Jig's Up*, his experience on a fishing boat was limited, and if she had to stand by her father in court, she couldn't be sympathetic to his family. Sharing any information with Ray about Al's case? Folly. Could she live with the guy for more than a month and keep details about the crime to herself? Was the fact she liked the look and the persistence of the guy a pro or a con?

She consulted the stars for inspiration, disappointed when the big dipper blinked steadily, signaling nothing.

Halting at the top of the marina gangway she said, "Give me a reason I haven't thought of for hiring you. Something oddball. Crazy."

Ray stood in place, chewing on his lip. "Neither of us knows anything about prawning."

Jill laughed. "Which means we can't show each other up, can we?" She narrowed her eyes at him. "Another?"

"I smell good."

That, he did. "Next."

"Close quarters. You're probably not used to people crowding you." He shrugged. "I'm a two shower-a-day guy because I sweat a lot. I keep my clothes clean. Shave every day."

He stuffed his hands in his pockets and grinned while she shook her head. *This is nuts. I'm nuts.*

She descended the gangway briskly, but stopped halfway down and turned to face Ray, startling him. "I don't have time for this."

"Time for what?"

"Time to interview people about whether or not I can trust you as a partner.

"Okay?"

"Daryl warned me about you. Said you'd likely push me overboard and call it an accident."

He stared at her, open-mouthed.

"But I don't sense that Donna is afraid of you. Frustrated maybe, but not frightened." She pivoted and descended to the flat dock. "So I'm going to take a chance on you.

"You're not happy about it."

"Actually, I am. You need the money as much as I do. We're both motivated to care for *Jig's Up*." She paused, giving him a measuring look. "And they say we should keep our enemies close. However..." She cleared her throat.

"However?"

"You get thirty percent of the profit along with room and board."

"Okay."

"I'll write it up."

"Go ahead."

"This is all about the business. Making money."

He nodded, but not with the vigor she hoped for.

"Ray?"

Again, he nodded, but she swore she saw discomfort flick across his eyes. Shit. What was she *doing*? The man was determined to take *Jig's Up* from her, so she could never trust him. No matter how good he smelled.

***

By the time he sat through the transport meeting with Jill and debriefed the information with her afterward, it was going on midnight when Ray buzzed Donna's doorbell. She was a night owl like he was and probably steaming over the weird conversation with Jill. He'd promised to return and the need to settle things between them weighed on him.

Donna answered the door looking polished despite a long day at the store. Her blond hair was trussed up in a new way and it seemed to him that her makeup was fresh.

She gave him a thin smile. "Wait a minute, Ray. Let me get my coat. We'll talk out here on the porch."

"We will?"

"We will," Donna said, draping her coat over her shoulders and closing the door behind her.

Ray added up the evidence: she had company inside, male company. He stuffed his hands in his pockets, feeling stupid. Of course she'd move on with her life. She was an attractive, engaging woman. "Sorry. Didn't mean to interrupt. I said I'd come back tonight and finish our conversation. Apologize for…uh…Jill. It wasn't planned."

Donna clutched her coat against the coolness. "Planning isn't your strong suit, Ray. Nor is communication. Out of the blue you bring a stranger to my store and let her corner me. Then you show up here at midnight to explain why."

"I've been at wit's end since Bill's death. Taking care of Eileen and scrambling to earn money. It's been a rough time."

Looking sympathetic Donna said, "I'm sorry about Bill, of course." She dropped her head and sighed. When she looked up, she had tears in her eyes. Tears he didn't have the ability to explore because he felt unmoored, disturbed by his sister's mental state, and adrift without a decent-paying job.

He looked into the night for answers. "I was wrong to bring Jill to you for a recommendation. But I need to work on that boat. Eileen's boat."

Donna gave a wry smile as she put her hand on the doorknob. "Listen, your show of support for Eileen is admirable, but don't hold it against me if I don't trust it. You abandoned your sister years ago; don't you dare desert her now." She shivered. "It's cold out here, and I've said what I needed to. I'm going in. Good night."

She closed the door softly behind her. A disappointing sound. To experience her lack of faith in him was painful. He was doing his best in an untenable situation, but she wasn't going to fight for him, if she ever had. Still, he took heart she continued to care about Eileen's welfare. Donna had been, and remained, a good friend to his sister. That was enough for now.

He zipped up his jacket against the wind and walked down the steps carefully, feeling enough out of balance to flub up the simple task of putting one foot in front of another. Of the handful of women he'd dated over the years, had he given his loyalty to any of them? Was Donna right? Was he even capable of supporting his sister, especially if she got sicker?

I've alienated Donna and I'm about to partner with an adversary.

The urge to hop a plane back to Nova Scotia was so strong he snagged his phone out of his back pocket and unlocked the browser to check flights.

Ray growled at the screen, jammed the cell back into his jeans, pulled up his collar and headed to the marina office for another shitty night of too little sleep on a narrow, uncomfortable cot.

Tomorrow, he'd transfer his stuff to *Jig's Up*. A step up? Yes. A step forward? Doubtful.

7

Sounds like whale farts bounced along the bottom of *Jig's Up*, making Jill smile as she cleaned windows inside the boat. In fact, the bubbles vibrating along the hull were made by a scuba diver assessing the trawler under its waterline. With Ray stationed on the dock to assist the diver, Jill remained in the pilothouse until the diver was finished, music on to lighten her mood, jazz tunes syncing pleasantly with air pinging off the boat hull.

Every inspection she'd lined up, each long overdue, made her anxious. No one had fired up the boat's engine for months. Would she run?

"Hull looks decent overall," the diver told them as he sat on the edge of the dock, black rubber suit dripping with water, a mask perched on his head. "Bottom paint's still thick, but your zincs are way too thin, everywhere. The anodes will eat up your props if you don't get new metal on, pronto. Good we caught 'em in time."

"What's your next step?" Jill asked.

"Install new zincs around the big prop as well as the stern and bow thruster propellers.

Later, while the diver screwed in zinc plates, scraped junk off the props and cleaned the hull,

Jill ticked through their accomplishments. In the third week of April, after four days of cleaning *Jig's Up* inside and out, now a diver tended to the bottom. Next up for Ray: Polish the burgundy hull and the creamy-colored gel coat of the pilothouse, to brilliance.

She glanced at the helm, itching to start on the electronics and the engine. But first came an inventory of spare parts followed by a buying trip to Campbell River. She wouldn't fire up any motors on the boat until each had an oil change and a good greasing.

"We'll be up until midnight again," she grumbled, stretching the soreness out of her shoulders. A glance at Ray's location on deck helped her calculate how close he was to finishing his task. Inventory was a two-person job so she couldn't get started without him.

On this sunny day Ray was down to cutoffs, a sheen of sweat reflecting the light on his bare shoulders, arms and chest. Intense. Focused. Ray applied rubbing compound and polish to the beige gel coat on the boat's exterior, eradicating a haze of salt, dirt, and pollution. The man worked hard, with an astounding level of thoroughness. He'd clearly read the manual about gel coat oxidation: apply a dollop of rubbing compound to a three by three-foot area at a time, remove the excess with a second rag, administer a small amount of polish to the same area with a third cloth. The cleanest, and fourth soft cotton towel, brought a brilliant shine to the house.

On to the next three by three square. How many iterations? A hundred, just for the house; hundreds more to clean and buff the hull.

He polished as if the boat were his, or partly his. Was it? Would she discover records that her father and the man he'd supposedly killed were true partners in the past? Adrienne told Jill the two had split, but maybe they were in the middle of settling up finances before Parrish died.

Jill squirted window cleaner on the slanted windshield and leaned forward to wipe dirt off the glass. So far, the division of labor was working, but what about when they left the dock to go fishing? Ray admitted he didn't love electronics like she did, so she'd be the one to maintain diesel and electrical engines. Keeping the boat clean, handling lines, and hauling baskets was Ray's area; Jill would supervise the machinery. Missing was a third hand. An experienced prawner.

Ray had said, "You pilot, I'll pull shrimp."

She'd pretended nonchalance even though she could barely contain her excitement about taking the helm. "Deal. I do all the dirty work inside, including the bilges, and I get to pilot."

"Go for it, long as you know what you're doing. You fit in the cramped bilge lots better than I would. Why boaters call that tiny, greasy area 'the holy place' is beyond me."

Not the time to tell Ray how she'd occupied her down time in Seattle setting up the sale of her condo. How she paid Seattle's John Deere expert, Norm Dibble, for four hours of private instruction analyzing *Jig's Up's* engine, plus a half-day of tutoring at the helm of a boat like hers. How she'd taken Al's engine books home with her and after studying each one, focused on Nigel Calder's electrical and mechanical boat maintenance tome. She liked the man's candid style of writing. He berated boat owners for stupidity and laziness: "I *told* you to change filters more often!"

Jill walked to the bow, cleaning solution and rag in hand, ready to close a window and scrub it, when she spotted a girl leaning against the piling.

"I'm Beth," the girl said, as Jill did her best to place her.

"Adrienne Riley's Beth?"

The girl nodded, looking down.

"Nice to meet you, Beth. I'm Jill." She set her supplies aside, hopped off the boat, and reached out to shake the girl's limp hand. "I'll bet you know *Jig's Up* pretty well."

The girl shrugged, her bony shoulders hunched forward as if she were trying to hide her chest.

Jill pointed to one of the two lawn chairs on the dock.

"Want to sit for a bit? I could use a break."

Beth shrugged again but sat down right away. A noise from the flybridge caught her attention and she looked up, flinching at the sight of Ray. Her stony look made it clear the girl knew Ray was Bill Parrish's stepson.

Still, Jill introduced Ray formally. He waved hello with his rag and went back to work. *Thanks a lot.* What to do with Beth? Skinny, braces, and unruly hair. According to local scuttlebutt, no father in her life; an absent mother—something to do with drug addiction. Al, her father figure, in jail for murder. Way worse off than Jill was at only thirteen. Thank God for Adrienne.

"Your grandmother okay?"

"Yeah."

"School all right?"

She made a noncommittal sound.

Jill took a breath, inept at talking to a teenager whose body swam in a giant Guess tee shirt and saggy shorts, accentuating rather than hiding her reed-thin body. Bony knees, chicken legs, and scuffed sandals completed her waif look.

The girl shifted and blurted, "Can you get him out of jail?"

Jill struggled for a kind way to answer. "Al doesn't want our help, near as I can tell."

"Grandmum said you're like Al, smart and stubborn. So you're the one to spring him."

Jill opened her hands showing her helplessness.

Beth shook her head. "We gotta have him back. My grandmum's so sad." She eyed *Jig's Up*. "Grandmum said you don't know a thing about boats and you're short-handed. Put me to work on *Jig's Up* so you have the time to get him out of jail."

Giving a wry smile, Jill said, "We haven't been told where they're keeping him, Beth. Even if we came up with new information about what happened that night, your grandmother says he'd refuse to stand trial."

The girl's face scrunched. Jill couldn't tell if she was angry or scared. *What do I do with her?* "Is there anything *you* can tell me about the night Mr. Parrish died?"

"I was asleep in the back of the house," the girl answered, too quietly.

"With all the yelling going on between your grandmother and Mr. Parrish?"

"I sleep hard."

Interesting. Jill glanced at Ray who was buffing at a slower pace than usual. *He's listening.*

"You heard the gunshot?"

"I thought it was a firecracker. I went back to sleep." Beth pushed her hair behind her ears and

89

looked up at Ray, frowning. "His father hurt my grandmum and me. Al protected us."

Jill sat up straight. "Bill Parrish hurt you?"

Beth put her head down and muttered, "Al's gone and my grandmum's unhappy. It's hurt enough."

Jill glanced at Ray but he had his back to her. "Okay," she said, pulling herself out of the chair. "We could use the help, Beth. I'll do what I can about Al, but I'm not making any promises." She looked around for a boat task Beth could handle. "You can start by scrubbing the swim step. It's slippery with moss growth." Jill pointed to a brush and a bottle of biodegradable soap.

"Done it before." The girl popped up, grabbed the scrubber and cleaner and walked toward the stern section of the boat, her skinny body taking on a wiry strength. She stopped before she climbed aboard the swim step, eyes homing in on Jill's. She hesitated a moment, then said, "Take off your hat, will you, Jill?"

She did as requested, automatically shaking out her hair once she'd removed the ball cap.

Beth smiled for the first time, nodding. "Grandmum's right. You look like Al, 'cept you're pretty and he's handsome." Looking satisfied with her pronouncement, she climbed down to the swim step, poured soap on the scrub brush, and got to work.

Curious if Ray was still watching, Jill glanced his way. Big grin. *What's so damn funny?* Jill frowned, feeling as if she had been left out of the loop somehow. She turned her back on Ray and studied the girl. Find Al and get him out of prison? She'd told Beth, 'no promises,' but she'd given the kid hope by accepting Beth's help. Who was being more foolish?

When Oceans Rage

Jill could have used Al around when she was thirteen so maybe she'd help Beth get what Jill never got. Damn. Where had that bizarre idea come from? *I don't give a second thought to relationships.* What the hell did Lynda's drug do to her brain?

She climbed onto the boat and picked up the window cleaner, rattled about her rapidly rising list of responsibilities. Shaping up a boat was a no brainer, but running it and learning how to make money with it? The majority of boaters in the marina and her colleagues at Baldur expected…no, would be delighted, if she failed at prawning. Worse, Adrienne, Beth, and even Al would be on her conscience if Jill couldn't figure out why Al had left her to deal with this unholy mess.

***

Ray whistled while he polished, enjoying the sounds of Jill and Beth chatting as they worked on *Jig's Up* with him, returning the boat from neglected to sparkling. Jill's awkwardness with Beth interested him. When the girl had called Jill pretty and smart, Jill deflected the compliments. Not so clever was Jill letting a teenager talk her into stuff she couldn't deliver. Must be why Jill had stood at the bow in a near-catatonic state for several minutes after Beth tackled the swim step.

He'd laughed out loud. "You know, mushrooms can change the way you see the world."

She'd glared at him, throwing a meaningful glance at Beth. "No one has snatched my body or brain, Mr. Stewart. New topic, please."

Ray laughed harder, but he held up his hand in peace. "Quiz the Captain?"

Jill nodded but her raised eyebrow demanded caution.

"Why is this boat called *Jig's Up?*"

Jill closed her eyes.

"I thought that would be an easy question. Fun."

Beth poked her head over the swim step and grinned, a can of soda in hand. "It's Al's nickname for Jill."

He eyed Beth, then turned to Jill. "It is?"

She narrowed her eyes. "I was four. Dad took me fishing. I jigged for bait and I was good at it. For maybe five months before he left us, he called me Jigs. Didn't stick."

Beth said, "Did, too. He named the boat after you."

Speechless, Jill stared at Beth.

Ray leaned against the rail and tucked his rag under his arm. "Nicknames are important, aren't they Beth?"

The girl eyed him warily at first, then nodded. "Al was always bragging about you, your grades in school, your job. Everything. He used you as an example for me. Of persistence. Of using my brain."

Jill scoffed. "That must have fried you, Beth. I'm sorry."

With a thoughtful expression, Beth said, "I know, right? Dude, you are definitely up on a pedestal in my eyes and in my grandmum's, too." Beth shook her head. "Funny, I wasn't resentful." She was quiet for a moment, her fingers drawing the sweat off her can of soda. "But I had Al around and you didn't."

***

Ray dropped his rag and stretched, enjoying his bird's eye view of the whole marina from the bow of *Jig's Up*. On a bright day like this, all the boats sparkled in the sun, looking better than they were, full of promise for the coming season. Up close, however, every fishing vessel showed the ravages of years of rough treatment. These were workboats, not pleasure boats. Well-maintained, certainly, but with the fisherman's focus on efficiency, effectiveness, and heavy use, beauty lost out.

Through his job in Nova Scotia and his experiences as a kid growing up in Vancouver, he'd learned about a myriad of fishing boats. But prawn boats were special, wonders of complexity. Mazes of blue, orange and black cables snaked around the boat decks, delivering hydraulic fluid and electricity to pulleys, pumps, anchor winches, depth sounders and deck lights. A confusion of aluminum antennas, radar, VHF, single side band, GPS, and TV reached for the skies, while mast cables, radar reflectors, radar equipment, booms, winches, and pulleys angled to bow and stern. Most boats were loaded with net rollers, ice tanks, buckets, traps, anchors, and harpoons, leaving little room for people to maneuver. Yet, where Ray saw chaos, Jill found reason.

Ray's focus was a battle against salt and moisture. Every metal item on a boat yearned to rust, and in the saltwater environment, rust was the second color on any fishing boat. The primary color? Gray. To retard rust and bring some sense of nobility to a fishing boat, crews painted most surfaces a rust-retarding gray. Amazing how many shades of gray there were.

Forays against saltwater and salt air were no-win battles he was willing to wage, just as energizing as Jill's devotion to every machine on *Jig's Up.*

Ray smiled at the thought of Jill's effort to organize the boat's pilothouse. Inside the pack-rat houses of most fishing boats, disorder reigned. Anything to be kept dry had to be stored within, including clothing, electronics, food, and supplies. Wet and hardworking men filled the confined space with steaming bodies, their sweaty old-socks-and-oniony smell mixing with odors from toilets, engine oil, ripe bananas, mildew, hard-boiled eggs, body odor, and burnt coffee, overlaid by rotting fish. Ten square feet of stink. Men loved the life and most women hated it.

After a cushy life and high-power career in Seattle how could Jill adjust to the ripe, saltwater-infested life on a little boat?

He'd teased her about using sheets on her bunk. "Check every fishing boat in this marina. I guarantee you're the only one with sheets."

She started to protest but must have figured he was right. "Tough. I sleep better in sheets."

Movement on the dock caught his eye. Beth was leaving, making her way up the gangway the same time Jill began setting up a workbench in the sun, probably to catch the last of the evening light. He resisted the urge to call out to Jill when he saw how focused she was, so intent on her task. What was she doing?

He sat on a cooler in the aft section, mopped the sweat off his forehead and neck with a rag, and decided to take a break to watch her. He liked to watch her.

She wore a Mariner's baseball hat lately. He figured it got her hair out of the way so she could work without tendrils falling into her eyes. Too bad. Like Beth, he'd rather see Jill's curls. Since the hat hid her hair, he focused on her angular face and smooth, caramel complexion. Al was part Samoan, Jill had told him. The warmth of her skin came from her father.

At times in the last few days, she'd be talking to Ray and he'd drift off, imagining his finger tracing her fascinating jawline. It looked impossibly delicate, sharp, and smooth all at the same time. More than once, she'd shaken her head and stomped away, irritated when he'd lost the train of conversation.

She thinks I'm a daydreamer.

He tracked her fingers at work on the diesel stove pump. In moments she'd taken the machine apart and tested each section. He was amazed by the speed and confidence with which she'd attacked the thing, all the while humming some ballad he couldn't name.

She loves thing-a-ma-jigs. Another reason her nickname fit.

Ray was about to say something when Daryl Wisson appeared at the end of their dock, his eyes on Jill. Ray froze, not wanting to draw Wisson's attention to his presence. At the same time, he had the urge to yell for the jerk to go away and leave her alone.

"Hey," Wisson called out to Jill.

She looked up slowly, as if reluctant to be interrupted from her task. "Afternoon."

"Impulse pump, eh?"

Jill straightened. "Damn thing works fine for a couple minutes, then heats up and gurgles to a stop."

Wisson made some sound of commiseration.

"I was checking on whether it was a solenoid or diaphragm problem. It's the diaphragm. Gotta buy a new one."

He grunted.

She wiped her hands on a rag. "How're you doing?"

"Better now," Wisson grinned, his eyes on Jill's breasts. "Much. I've come to show you the new stuff I installed for hauling prawn traps."

"You talk to me, Daryl, your eyes are on mine. Got it?"

The man shuffled in place, looking annoyed. "Yup."

She said, "Excellent. I'll be over with a beer for you and me. When's a good time?"

"Whenever you've finished with the pump. An hour? While it's still light." Wisson wagged his eyebrows. "Wish I had an extra diaphragm for you—"

"Daryl, I warned you."

"No sense of humor, eh?"

"Understand?"

The jerk shrugged, turned and made his way down the dock. "See you in about an hour."

"Yup," Jill answered before she lowered her head to her work. Ray heard Jill clear her throat. She peered up at him with a half-grin.

Ray fumbled for his rag and stood up. "What?" he said looking down at her.

"That's the trouble with boats. Not much privacy."

"You knew I was listening, eh?"

"Of course. When you work, you emit all sorts of grunts and groans. And you whistle, like you did when Beth was here, refusing to bail me out. Then Daryl comes over and it gets real quiet up there."

His face grew warm. "Sorry. I was taking a rest. Couldn't help but listen in." He hesitated. "Jigs?"

She was flexing her arms and shoulders, preparing to sit down again. A raised eyebrow at the nickname, but she said, "Yeah?"

Ray looked around for help in what to say next. A passing seagull wasn't offering. "These guys aren't like your corporate boyfriends.

There's not a whole lot of rule-following out here."

"Point taken."

"You've heard we might have a thief on the dock."

A nod. "You fingering Daryl?"

"Everyone's a suspect."

"I've got Daryl's number, Ray. I'm using him, not the other way around."

"Someone's stealing prawn traps. Strings of them. All the guys are talking about it."

"Four incidents last season. Devastating because they steal the baskets along with the shrimp." Jill put her index finger on her chin. "I wonder if I could use Mae C to scare the poachers away from my traps."

"Your drone? Use it for surveillance?"

"I haven't worked out the nuances, but at the very least, you and I could talk up Mae C's powers so the bad guys leave us alone."

Ray scrambled off the deck and joined Jill on the dock, struggling to contain his excitement. "I think that's a great idea. And I wouldn't mind learning how Mae C works. So I can sound convincing about her abilities."

Ignoring Ray's offer, Jill said, "I've got some ideas how she can help us in other areas, as well."

"Listen, I'm teachable about technology. Especially when I'm interested. So, about Wisson's offer to demo the pulley. Mind if I come along to learn how it works?"

"I'll explain his method to you later."

He considered ways to shorten her visit with Wisson. "The inventory. When do we finish it and what time will we be ready to go to Campbell River tomorrow?"

She put her hands on her hips and squinted at him. "Let's work on the parts list tonight and tomorrow morning, hitting Campbell River early afternoon. I want to meet with Al's friend, Jack Canter, on the same trip. Okay with you if I set it up? You could do something else while I talk to him."

He folded his rag, feeling like the biggest liar on the coast. And he'd just warned her about Wisson being a user.

She frowned at his silence. "Ray?

"Uh, sure. I'll go with you to meet Canter. Inventory after your beer with Wisson?"

She smiled. "One beer with Daryl and I'm back."

He nodded. *Success.*

And then a wave of guilt hit him. He'd manipulated her into doing what *he* wanted. *Yep, buddy. You're as much of a user as Wisson.*

8

Jill popped out of bed early, unsettled by the tautness in her belly, usually signaling she was horny. *Really? Now?* It didn't help that a glance at her bedside table conjured Ray's package of condoms.

Absent the warmth of a man, she sought the heat of her tea mug, shivering in the morning chill. Her usual at-home outfits of yoga pants and short-sleeved tops, even augmented with a sweatshirt, weren't enough to fend off the cool coastal air.

She surveyed the marina from inside her boat, surrounded by men, like she had been at Baldur, all off limits. Gossip had run rampant about her tank-top episode on Daryl's boat, morphing at the speed of light into a topless event. Ray was off limits because he coveted *Jig's Up.* Meanwhile she worked with him side by side, head to head, warm body to warm body. Every day. Crazy-making.

Lust. What to do about it?

Her most recent ex-boyfriend, Dave, had demanded marriage way too early in their relationship. "How will marriage improve this?" she'd asked him after a torrid night of sex. But he'd insisted on taking the next step. Claiming her as his own. When Jill turned down his proposal, he'd found another woman to possess. A year later, married, he'd come back to beg for sex. Not on her life. Jill didn't poach her partners. They had to come to her free and clear.

"Smug this morning, Jigs?"

Jumping at Ray's voice, Jill sloshed tea on her sweatshirt and gave Ray the side-eye. "Too early for smug. Not enough caffeine in my system."

He stood at the bottom stair outside his two-bunk cabin, his eyes even with her chest. He reached in the head for a towel, clearly intent on wiping away the spilled tea. She intercepted, holding his wrist to stop him. "Not a good idea," she said, taking the cloth from him with her free hand.

He followed her upstairs and stood next to her. "What's not a good idea?"

Jill sighed, frustrated the sight of him attracted her, his hair mussed up from sleep in the most appealing way. And damn it, he *did* smell good. She groaned and shut her eyes. "Too close," she muttered, feeling an ache arrow through her loins.

And he'd called her Jigs.

When she opened her eyes, his blue eyes, dusted with gray, caught hers. She looked down to where his sweatpants could not hide his interest. "Double damn." She breathed in, forbidding her body to respond. Stepping away, she moved to the galley where she threw out her cold tea and poured boiling water into the mug, counting to five before she turned to face her partner-slash-adversary. "This is a professional relationship, Ray. What's more, we'll soon be battling in court over possession of *Jig's Up*."

He nodded with a wry grin. "You'll pardon the part of my body not down on the conflict."

"I'm serious, Ray. We're business partners."

Ray said nothing.

"I watched you with Donna at the store. One or both of you isn't satisfied with 'ex' status."

He came to where she stood at the galley and reached toward her, grabbing his cup from the galley sink. When she passed him the pot and a tin of tea bags, he poured, his eyes on his task.

Taking a careful sip of the hot tea, he said, "I wish we'd met under different circumstances, Jill. Shit, the baggage we're both carrying. We didn't choose these loads."

She stepped back and cleared her throat. "Or these close quarters."

"With a man who might push you overboard."

"I think you proved Daryl wrong by helping me through the drug episode. In the state I was in, I could have *fallen* overboard."

His eyes held hers for a moment. "Look," he said. "In the spirit of shoring up trust?" He frowned. "I gotta come clean about something."

She plowed her hands through her hair, feeling frustrated. *Beth, Ray, Al, Adrienne. What a bunch of complicated people!* "Spit it out." She sat on the bench and waited for Ray to sit, too. He remained standing.

"I'm in the pool with the rest of the prawners."

She put her elbows on the table and cradled her chin with her hands. "So? I'm in it, too."

"The pool's not what you think it's for." He shook his head. "It's for who you hire and screws you first. Package deal."

She covered her face with her hands. "Great. And you knew?"

"I'd already put in my twenty when I heard the rider. Forgive the pun."

Feigning calm, she laid her hands on the table. "You'll win."

"What?"

"You're living here. They already assume you're sleeping with me. As a matter of fact, you *did* sleep with me. Why not collect?"

"Not fair." He slipped into the seat opposite her. "I'd never do that."

"You need the money. Claim it. Plus if you say you won, the suspense is over. No more nasty speculation. God, I hate the way they treat me on the dock, like a dippy sex object. Maybe if you claim the prize, they'll put their attention on something else, someone else."

"Forget it." He smiled. "Though you tempt me."

"Tempt? Seriously? You want my boat, not me."

Ray knit his eyebrows. "You have no idea how attractive you are, do you? Your face is classic gorgeous and your shape? You're a knockout, Jigs."

Her stomach tightened and she scooted away from him.

Ray said, "Wait. I want to repeat what Beth said. You are a beautiful woman. The pool is about that, more than anything."

She pushed her fingers through her hair. "Nothing alluring here."

"What did you wear at Baldur? Suits and heels?"

"Logoed shirts and khaki pants. Regulation." Jill rubbed her forehead, thoroughly frustrated with the subject. "I don't care about any of this, Ray. I want us to be successful prawners."

Ray rose. "You already figured out loose tops won't work on this job. For sure, the clothes you're wearing aren't warm enough for the cool, wet weather on the ocean." He heaved a sigh. "I'm done with truth-telling. I came clean about the pool; I dub you beautiful but fashionably incorrect about how to dress for prawning. I will not collect on the bet."

She pushed out of the bench seat, flipped open Al's parts list, and drew a deep breath. "C'mon, Ray. Talking about clothes and weird relationships makes me nauseous. Please, let's work on the inventory."

***

Ray had changed into jeans and was pocketing the parts list when Jigs stepped up out of her cabin zipping a sleeveless fleece vest over her top. When she cast him a sharp look as if daring him to say something, he nodded and smiled, vowing to never wear sweatpants without underwear in her presence again. For the rest of the morning they worked together easily, both focused on their chores but willing to banter a bit and take breaks together when the need arose. She wasn't a grudge-holder. He admired her blunt and earthy approach to life which led to a vision of her as a sexual partner. A firecracker in bed.

Don't think about it. Get back to work.

Ray was using sandpaper to scour rust off a pulley disk when he heard a call from portside.

"Ahoy, the boat."

He looked below at a sun-faded red runabout bobbing next to *Jig's Up*, a hand reaching out to hang on to a fender.

Jill emerged from the pilothouse and leaned over the port railing. "Who goes there?"

"Dennis Hudson here," said a man who stepped out of the tiny cabin. Red-haired and freckled, with a weightlifter's body, Hudson looped his line around a cleat on *Jig's Up*, flipped

103

fenders out to protect both boats, and smiled up at Jill and Ray. "We run a marina in Waka Bay, up Tribune Channel. This is my wife, Camryn, and my son, Samuel."

A young woman climbed out on the little boat's starboard walkway and waved. Samuel, maybe six, hung his head out of the window and said, "Al is our friend, so you are, too."

After Jill and Ray introduced themselves, the father smiled at his son indulgently and said, "Al brought *Jig's Up* to visit us several times, so her new captain and crew are welcome, too. Since it's early in the season, we have lots of dock space."

"Thank you. We can't wait to explore the islands."

"Have you talked to your father?" Camryn asked. "We've tried to locate him with no success."

"He's made it clear he wants his privacy," said Jill.

Camryn pursed her lips. "Tough for you."

"Al loved this boat," Dennis surveyed *Jig's Up* and clicked his tongue. "Tricked it out with the latest in technology."

Samuel said, "Al was going to help us with our waterfall."

"Waterfall?" Jill directed her question to Camryn.

"Right. Al was talking us through a way to pull electric power out of the waterfall behind our marina." Camryn raised an eyebrow. "We're all dreamers."

Dennis shifted his weight, causing the skiff to lean to its portside. "We're sorry about Al's trouble and we hope you can tell us how to help him."

"Want to come aboard for a cup of tea?" Jill asked.

With a wince, Camryn said, "Wish we could. We've got frozen provisions from the grocery store and an hour's cruise home. We'll see you next at Waka Bay."

Dennis Hudson released the line around the trawler's cleat and ducked into the runabout. With his hand, he pushed off the hull and started his motor. Out the window he yelled, "Come visit soon!"

Jill's eyes followed the path of the runabout as it putted away from the dock. Once outside the slow-wake area, the engine revved and the boat flew across the water, disappearing from sight.

"Seemed like nice people. Waka's a good place to visit for our virgin voyage, wouldn't you say?" Ray took up his sandpaper, prepared to attack more rust. Then he remembered the spark of interest in Jill's expression when the Hudsons brought up the waterfall. "You're already designing a power system in your head, aren't you?"

She narrowed her eyes. "Let's go to Campbell River."

"Anxious to get this tub off the dock, huh?"

"More than ever. *Jig's Up* belongs out there, not caged in here."

They were on their way to Campbell River soon after, Ray at the wheel of his Jeep Cherokee with Jigs sitting next to him taking notes. In transit, they finished their list of spare parts and supplies to buy, then worked out a schedule of chores to complete before the prawning season opened May first. At the marine store, they divided up the 'what to buy' list, Jigs taking the electronic and machine-related stuff, Ray all the other.

Later, they pulled into the parking lot of the Discovery Shopping Centre with an hour to spare before the meeting with Jack Canter. Ray said, "Mind if I drop you off here? I've got a couple errands to run." He pointed out stores Jigs could browse in close to the restaurant. "Starbucks is over there."

"A beverage first, for sure," she said, smiling. "The hardware store next. See you in an hour."

Chai latte in hand, she passed by the hardware store and made her way to a clothing shop, with no idea why her brain directed her feet to do so.

She barely had a chance to look around the store when a saleswoman about the age of her mother came barreling her way. Jill sighed. She'd let the lady do the work, because Jill's presence in the store confused the hell out of her.

Unzipping her vest, Jill removed it, held out her hand for a shake, and read the woman's nametag. "Debbie, I need an expert. These clothes have been my casual style for some time. Now I'm a fisherwoman. I'm too cold in these duds for one thing, and I'm the only woman in a male-dominated marina. I need clothes that help me fit in rather than stand out. Are you up to the challenge?"

Debbie reached out her hand to Jill, smiling. "You've come to the right place, dear. Let me look at you here in the light."

The manager took Jill's vest away from her, set it on a chair, and said, "Hat off, please."

Jill removed the ball cap and shook out her curls.

"Gorgeous hair. Okay, turn around." Jill stood with her back to Debbie. "Now, face me."

Jill pivoted, her eyes on the surveillance camera over the door. Tiny. She wondered how it worked. Plug-in? Saltwater proof? Looked like top-of-the-line components. Could she use one like it in the boat?

Feeling a poke at her shoulder, Jill focused on Debbie. "Sorry, go ahead."

"You're five foot eight. Size eight. You have lovely curves, which we will not, I repeat, *not*, hide under a bushel." Debbie fingered clothes on a rack. "Your clothes are comfortable and well-made. Don't beat yourself up for choosing them. Warm, they are not. You need layers and safety."

"Safety."

Debbie nodded. "The outfits you wear on the boat need to be tucked in and close to your body. Anything loose will catch on equipment. Worst case? You'll be lowering a trap or an anchor, and flapping clothing will hook on chain or line." Debbie gave Jill an up and down look. "Actually the clothes you're wearing now fit the tightness criteria. We just have to get you warmer."

Jill nodded. "I already got burned by wearing a loose sweatshirt. I had to take the damn thing off when I was working traps last month. In front of four guys." Jill smiled ruefully. "And that dumped me into even bigger trouble."

Debbie winced. "I should say."

For the next half an hour, a delighted Debbie worked on Jill's new look. She picked out two pairs of tight-fitting but stretchy-comfortable pairs of jeans, some no-wrinkle wash pants and Jill's favorite, a set of overalls to protect her clothes when she worked down in the engine room. The shirts she bought were thick cotton, some short-sleeved and others long-sleeved, all with collars. Six of them in a variety of colors. She donned tan wash pants and tucked in a green shirt to wear to dinner.

Debbie and Jill peered into the mirror to evaluate their work. The clerk nodded. "See, the shirts fit fairly close to your body. They're warm like heavy rugby tops, but snug. Collar open and free."

Jill squinted, trying to see what Debbie saw. "Not scruffy like the fishermen's clothes." Jill clicked her tongue. "I'll fit in better when I get dirty."

Debbie laughed as she caught Jill in a side hug. "But you're warmer and more comfortable in these clothes, right?" Jill nodded. "And you feel pretty?"

Jill shrugged and refocused on the surveillance camera. Wireless? Bluetooth probably. No doubt came with a phone app. Debbie cleared her throat and Jill brought her attention to the woman. "I look okay. Tidy, except for my hair." She made a futile attempt to corral the curls behind her ears.

The clerk reached up to quiet her hand. "How many women do you think I see a day, Jill?"

She shrugged. "Twenty?"

"Try forty. I've helped hundreds of women. The majority of them would kill for your figure, your hair, and your face."

Jill grabbed her old clothes and bundled them. "You're a good saleswoman." After she paid her bill, picked up her packages, and thanked Debbie, she fast-walked to the restaurant to meet Canter. She slowed when she saw Ray pulling into the parking lot, pleased she could stash her purchases in the car.

She waved to Ray and opened the passenger door to stow her packages. He stared.

Jill said, "What?"

"New clothes?"

"Don't ask why. I hate shopping."

He stared some more.

"What?"

"Y...You should buy new clothes more often."

"I bought these for warmth and safety, Ray. Let's leave it at that and go to dinner. And stop staring at me, for God's sake."

***

Jill and Ray were already seated in the C-River Restaurant when Jack Canter showed up at their table, a beat-up golf hat in hand. He was a wiry-framed man in his late forties, both his hair and mustache dark brown.

After introductions, he zoned in on Jill. "Al told me he had a grown daughter, but I didn't pry."

Not interested in telling the estranged story once again, Jill nodded and moved on. "Tell me how long you worked with Al."

"I was naive when Al made me his partner, eh? Took him about five years to teach me what I needed to know." Jack ducked his head and smiled. "I was kinda slow and Al had a lot to teach."

"Do you still fish?"

The man nodded. "I bought a prawn boat out of Prince Rupert and fish from Comox and Campbell River." He paused. "Because of Al."

"What kind of a guy is he?" Jill asked.

"Pretty much a loner, living by himself on *Jig's Up* off-season. Devoted to that boat. Damned if I'm not the same with my rig. He taught me how to mind the details more carefully than the big things most people notice, eh? Regular oil changes and new filters. Protecting metal from salt."

"Did he do well as a prawner?"

"He was the best around. He could sniff out prawn locations like a pro. Even in light seasons, his traps came up heavy. He was never

109

foolhardy, but he'd go out in some pretty rough weather when the less skilled stayed in, eh?"

While the three ate an early dinner, Ray and Jill quizzed Jack about prawning and his forecasts for the upcoming season. Canter finished his sandwich and pushed away his plate. "Miss Al. He was a guy I could count on."

"So he made good money?" Ray asked.

Jack scratched his head. "Did when I was with him. He had a nice car he took on road trips, drivin' the side roads. Spent a lot of time on his computer. I think he invested because he liked to talk about the market. *Jig's Up* and prawning were his life. Didn't seem to need much more." Jack was starting on his dessert when he put down his fork and said, "Al and that boat saved my life, I want you to know."

How's that?" Jill asked.

"Well, he was at the helm, so I'd say *he* saved me, but Al swore it was the boat and the way it was constructed that insured my survival. Only two of us aboard and I was pulling in a basket on my own when my foot tangled in a line and I got yanked overboard. Now, I managed to get the line off my leg, but we were close to land so the waves and current carried me toward shore. I kept going under." He drank from his coffee cup. "I thought I was going to die that day.

"Al came right after me in *Jig's Up*, knowing there was no time to launch the dinghy. He crunched rocks on the way, he told me later, and hung up on some boulders in the process, but he got close enough so he could throw a line and help me climb aboard. Once he had me secure on the swim step, Al gunned the engine and we reversed our way back to deep water."

He wagged his head as if to question his own memory of the event. "We hunted for leaks, convinced we had three or four gaping holes in the bottom, but when we hauled *Jig's Up* out for a look-see, we found nothing but scratches and dents. The prop, protected by the keel, was in perfect shape."

Pride in the boat and his boss showed in his smile. "I broke my leg when it twisted in the fall with the line around it. If Al hadn't come after me in *Jig's Up*, sacrificing the boat to save me, I'd have drowned, eh?"

Jill nodded, silently saluting *Jig's Up* and her father. "You haven't seen Al for awhile?"

"Nope. But I heard he was in prison for manslaughter even before I got your call for this meet-up." He leaned toward Jill. "If Al killed someone, he had good reason to. From what you told me on the phone, he was helping a lady friend, so I'll bet he was protecting her."

Jill asked, "I don't suppose you knew Adrienne Riley or Bill Parrish?"

"Wish I could help there, but Al and I worked together out of Vancouver, mostly. Don't know anything about his life in Port McNeill." Jack placed his hands on the table. "I want to talk to him and thank him. And I'd sure like to help him the way he did me. If you find out anything I can do for him, will you tell me? Everybody needs family, especially in the tough times. You call when you find him, eh?"

Ray saw tears in Jill's eyes before she bowed her head.

While Ray settled the bill, they said their goodbyes. Jack left a phone number and asked Jill to keep in touch.

Taking Jill's arm, Ray led her to the car and tucked her into the passenger seat. She nodded her thanks but sat quietly well into their drive back to Port McNeill.

Ray used the silence to consider Jack's description of Jill's father. Hell, Al had steered his prized boat into the rocks to save a man. Maybe that same brazen rescue instinct, saving Adrienne, had taken over when Al killed his stepfather.

He touched Jill's hand and when she shifted position in response, he asked, "Did it help to talk to Jack?"

"I'm thinking about what a lonely life Al led in Port McNeill until he met Adrienne and Beth." She turned her face to Ray. "Then he goes to jail refusing to allow anyone to contact him for the next five years. Me? I haven't filled in my mom and stepdad on my new life, especially because my mother calls this venture crazy. And I cut every tie from school and my job at Baldur." She looked out her window and said softly, "My mom nailed it—Al and I have similar dispositions."

Ray waited, eyes on an always busy highway 19. He hadn't known Jill for long, but clearly she was the kind of person who kept her thoughts to herself. The only time he'd seen her happy was after she'd gone over every inch of the freezer generator and started the motor. Pure joy in her expression. Could he bring a similar reaction from her? He'd like to try.

"I should have gone looking for Al years ago, at the very least to thank him properly for funding my first year in college." She was quiet for a while. In a pained voice, "If I'd found him and gotten to know him, maybe he wouldn't be in jail today."

Ray slowed through the tiny town of Sayward.

"I'm going to hunt down Lynda Flynn and strangle her."

"What?"

When Oceans Rage

"My brain has changed since she drugged me. I *never* wallow in 'what ifs.' Angst over relationships? Not me." She shifted in her seat, palms pushing over her new pants. "I went shopping and actually enjoyed some aspects of the experience. Seriously, LSD, or whatever Lynda Flynn gave me, has made me a stranger to myself."

"Interesting you should say that. I told you, during your tripping hours, I googled one-handed because you had a vice grip on my left hand all night. I still say your reactions point to psilocybin, derived from mushrooms, easy for Lynda to buy in Canada. The drug's being tested by scientists to reduce depression and anxiety. The chemicals generate pathways to new parts of the brain, including pleasure centers."

"Fabulous. My personality altered without my say-so."

Ray didn't respond.

Deep sigh, then, "Al. I feel remorse about not contacting Al. Of not communicating with my mother." She sucked in her breath. "Something I've never felt so strongly before." The light glinted off her tears before she bowed her head.

He said, "Human."

She twitched, seeming surprised at the word. "What?"

"Human. Your reaction to Al walking out on you at age four is normal. If your mother's view of Al was negative, or even neutral, what would prompt you to connect with him?"

She was quiet for a while, sitting up straighter in the seat. A throat-clear, then, "No, Ray. I'm worse than Al. At least he had Adrienne, Beth, the Hudsons in Waka Bay, and a partner as loyal as Jack Canter. Me? I've got no one." She looked up to the roof of the car and sighed.

Ray went for levity. With a John Wayne voice he said, "Ya got *me*, pardner. Bona fide hand-holder, 'trip' advisor, and prawn partner."

Her silence made him feel foolish, especially since his offer was empty. A joke. A lie.

Once he maneuvered through the town of Woss, he drove the final leg to Port McNeill in guilty silence.

***

"Someone broke into *Jig's Up?*" Jill stared at her boat from the top of the gangway as if she could see evidence of violation from two hundred feet away. "Meaning they knew Ray and I had gone to Campbell River."

"An attempt. A couple of hours ago." Greg Hanley took off his glasses and rubbed his eyes as he leaned against the marina door jamb. "Broad daylight."

"Attempt?" Ray asked.

Greg said, "You gotta thank Billy on *Sea Star* in the moorage behind your boat. He saw a diver working with you twice the other day, so a third visit raised a red flag. Billy says a guy in a wetsuit climbed aboard *Jig's Up's* swim step, took off his fins and walked to the pilothouse door portside. The man tried the door, and when he kept yanking on it, Billy yelled at him and said you were gone. Billy saw something in the guy's hand, like a screwdriver, so he got suspicious. Anyway, Billy jumped off his boat and started walking toward *Jig's Up.* Since Billy's built like a Sherman tank, he's nobody to rile. In a heartbeat, the fella dived over the railing and disappeared, leaving his flippers behind. Billy alerted me and I climbed onto *Jig's Up* to examine the fins. Nondescript. Billy said the burglar had the shape of a man, and judging from the size eleven of these flippers, more evidence it was probably a guy."

"We owe Billy a six-pack," Ray said. "That wasn't our diver. He finished our work and had no reason to board *Jig's Up.*"

"Did Billy recognize him?" Jill asked, her voice tight with worry.

Greg said, "Full hood and goggles. Billy couldn't even tell what color hair he had. Smart guy choosing such a disguise. Must have known a diver had worked on your boat so a revisit might be missed by the other prawners." Greg grunted. "Here's one time the snoopy nature of fishermen is an advantage."

"What's being stolen?" Jill asked. "You hired Ray because of burglaries. Do you have any idea what thieves would steal from *Jig's Up?*"

"Electronics," Greg said.

"Computers and marked-up charts of fishing sites," Ray added.

"They snag anything made out of stainless steel, because it's expensive and won't rust." Greg rubbed his eyes. "The thievery's been going on for a year. I connect it with how long we've had trouble with unlicensed prawners stealing traps."

"A diver." Ray peered into the water.

"Yeah, a whole new concept. Rip-offs from the sea." Greg shook his head. "Used to be honor among fishermen."

Jill started down the gangway with Greg and Ray behind her. "Let's go see if he did any damage to the outside of the boat. Or if he got in, somehow."

"I already looked around, Jill. I called the constable; filed a report. Gave him the flippers to DNA test, though Burns said the saltwater probably destroyed evidence. You might discover something missing outside, but I doubt it. And because of Billy, he failed to get into the boat."

Her heart pounded with each step as she climbed to the port entrance. "Broad daylight," she muttered. "This guy was serious. Motivated." She scrambled down to her cabin, pulling in a breath at the sight of Mae C still hanging on the hull wall.

Behind her, Ray growled a curse. "Meaning, he'll be back and he'll get in unless we can figure out who he is and arrest him."

Jill glanced in the direction of Queen Charlotte Sound. "Time to get away from the dock, Ray. The marina doesn't feel safe, so let's take our chances on the seas." Jill breathed in. "I'll take a raging ocean over chaos on the dock any day."

9

Jill piloted while Ray studied charts on *Jig's Up's* maiden voyage. As soon as they hit the open waters of Queen Charlotte Straits, Jill sighed loudly enough to get a questioning glance from Ray. She wiggled tension out of her shoulders. "I'm so glad to get away from the marina."

Ray nodded, staring at the charts. "Yeah, I'm tired of cleaning, too. And docking drills. And sea trials in the confines of Alert Bay."

"Hell, I *like* cleaning and test runs compared to living in a fishbowl, looking over my shoulder for burglars."

Ray leaned against the chart table and gave Jill his full attention. "You think they're after us specifically?"

"Someone tried to break into *Jig's Up* yesterday. Witnessed by Billy. This boat. The other personal part comes from prawners gambling on us to make mistakes, betting on our failure. Except Billy and Greg. *They* seem to be on our side."

Ray stared out at the empty stretch of ocean and asked, "How about Wisson?"

"Daryl?"

Ray shrugged and turned back to his charts. "You had dinner with him last night. He plied you with wine, no? If you quit he can buy our license. More shrimp for him."

Smiling, Jill glanced at his profile, his serious expression contrasted by unruly hair. *Man-boy.*

He glowered at her. "It's not funny, Jigs. He's the kind of guy who gets what he wants—and not by using his charm."

"Are you saying he's dangerous?"

"He could be."

"And he warned me *you're* the one who will toss me overboard."

Ray's glower intensified.

"Listen, I can take care of myself. Not that I owe you any explanation, but Baldur offered self-defense courses for its employees. Since I led classified projects and often worked late into the night, the training seemed prudent at the time. Muscle memory type classes. Always a good workout."

"Jill, that's not—"

"I don't monitor your activities for safety, Ray. Keep out of mine."

His jaw clenched.

"Daryl's an expert and happy to give advice. Or should I say, eager. Compelled? No. *Obsessed* about giving me tips. He's the only fisherman on the dock willing to teach me, with marine electronics down cold. As I said, I'm using *him*."

"How do you know what he's sharing is truth and not misdirection to get us into trouble? We've read up on prawning and talked to Greg, Billy, and Jack about the ins and outs, but we lack experience. We won't know if Wisson is legit until the season starts and we try out his so-called skills."

118

She sighed. "Look, we've had a good week, accomplishing more than we thought possible, mostly without rancor. You think I don't know Daryl's a player? Give me some credit."

He didn't respond.

"I've been dying to get out here, away from the marina. Let's enjoy the fruits of our labors. *Jig's Up* is afloat, her engine humming. The bow thruster pushed us off the dock properly so I didn't look too inept at the helm. I've practiced that maneuver. What? A hundred times?"

Ray stretched his arms over his head, all the while keeping his eyes on the sea. "Sorry I'm cranky. We're both in tough spots."

"Apology accepted. Can we move on to your lawyer's sleuthing?"

He put up a hand. "He's good, I'll give him that. Took him less than a week to find your father."

Jill glanced at her GPS and veered left of Village Island. *Jig's Up* had autopilot, but Jill wanted to steer by hand until she had a good feel for cruising without electronics. "All I got from my dad's lawyer were refusals to find Al. Yours apparently used the Victim's Assistance Act, an option not open to me. Once your lawyer convinced the courts to reveal Al's location, his attorney notified me, too."

"Unless we question your father about the fishing license, we're stuck." He glanced at the radar readings. "Now that you know where he is, will you visit him?"

She chewed her lip. An image of Beth jumped into her mind. "I think so. Beth's at the age when she needs a father, a man, to tell her she's smart and beautiful when she doubts herself."

Silence from Ray.

"And Jack trusts Al. I'd like to as well."

Still no reaction.

"*Jig's Up* isn't mine, nor is it yours." At Ray's frown, she said, "It's selfish of me *not* to look into the killing. *Jig's Up* remains my boat if Al stays in jail. If he's found innocent, he'll reclaim the prawner and resume his career."

Ray combed his hands through his hair, leaving several clumps standing on end. "So to help Beth, you have to get Al out of jail, which means he gets the boat back. Didn't you say you'd burnt bridges with your company in Seattle? What would you do for a job?"

"Same goes for you, Ray. We're able-bodied adults. We'll figure it out." Jill glanced at the tachometer and goosed the speed a notch. "I talked to the constable again. Ran into him at the grocery store. He's still feeling guilty about Al being in jail. Encouraged me to keep asking questions." She studied the horizon. "Jack, Greg, the Hudsons, and the constable believe Al. Why shouldn't I?" She paused. "Victoria's a long drive from Port McNeill."

"My attorney's arranging his own visit as we speak."

"Never been in a prison before."

"Think he'll see you?"

Jill looked out at the quiet seas and took a breath. "Since I have to notify him a day before I visit, he could refuse me, but if he knows your lawyer has access, he'll assume I'm not far behind. He'll talk to me."

"But you and I can't share what our lawyers say to us. What a clusterfuck."

Jill tapped on the wheel, giving Ray his moment of angst. *I can't believe my brain knows what angst is!* "Enough of this. We have a beautiful day on the water and *Jig's Up* seems happy cruising the Broughtons. Since we got a personal invitation from Al's friends in Waka Bay, let's drop in on them first and explore further down Tribune Channel afterward." She zoomed into the chart, noting the names of Hudson Island and Mars Island on her portside. "A pretty route, don't you think?"

When he didn't answer, she glanced at him over her shoulder.

He'd closed his eyes and looked as if he were in pain.

"Are you all right?"

"Yeah. Sure. What's a safe topic we can talk about?"

Jill cleared her throat, pleased to move the conversation away from the suit. "I've heard about prawn holes in Tribune. Maybe the Hudson family at Waka Bay will tell us more about them." She shook her head. "We sure aren't getting tips on where to find shrimp from our buddies on the dock."

"Can't blame prawners for keeping those secrets." Ray paused. "The Hudsons. Nice couple. They like Al."

She smiled. "Yeah. Maybe they'll like us, too."

"You sure it's a friendship you're after, Jigs? What about that waterfall power plant they want to build?"

Jill winced. "I jumped on that train pretty fast, didn't I?"

Ray went back to studying the charts and Jill resumed piloting the ship in quietude. She thought about getting some time alone with Camryn.

"Ray?"

He raised an eyebrow.

"I'm going to grab Camryn for a conversation. She might be able to advise me about how to approach Al since my people skills are so poor."

He seemed to want to say something but instead, he nodded slowly.

"Did I just say that? Is my brain rebooted to the point I'm seeking relationship advice?" She gave a wobbly smile. "How about this? I barter for Camryn's help with Al, Debbie, and Beth in exchange for helping them with their water power plant."

"I don't think friendship requires bartering or keeping score, but I'm no expert. Hell, my *sister* won't even talk to me."

Nodding, she turned away from Ray, spotted a log in the water, and changed course to miss it. Once the seas opened up, she took off her hat, shook out her hair and pushed her fingers through it. "Ah. Much better. Sometimes hats make my brain feel tight."

They quietly watched the waters for a time.

"Ray, why did you start calling me 'Jigs'?"

"Suits you better than Jillian or Jill. Too formal."

"And I'm not?"

Ray grinned and held up his hands. "Not complaining, here. Your dad named you Jigs for your skill at catching bait fish." He smiled. "I found another reason."

"Which is?" She reached for her ball cap and re-anchored it on her head. "What if I don't like Al's reason or yours?"

"I was watching you repair the impulse pump that day when Wisson invited you to his boat." His smile grew and something in her lower abdomen fluttered. "You're so intent and intense when you work on any kind of thing-a-ma-jig."

She didn't know what to say about that.

He cleared his throat. "The thing about a nickname, Jigs? If it's a good one, it'll make fun of you a bit."

"I see."

"I'm guessing you have a love/hate feeling about your nickname."

She glanced at the rpms and pulled back the throttle a bit. "Maybe." Keeping her eyes on the GPS computer screen, she said, "I suppose I have the choice whether or not to answer to it. Or to make up a proper moniker for you." Her face tingled with warmth, so a little rattled, she pointed out the obvious. "The bay is just around the next bend,"

Jill prepared to pull into the large outer bay of Waka inlet, a baby fjord jutting off Tribune Channel. Steep mountains rose out of the sea, framing the entrance. Mid-bay was a small island with a lone tree welcoming them in. They chugged into Waka Bay, taking a left turn and heading for the floating marina Dennis and Camryn had been running for seven years, or so *Waggoner's Cruising Guide* said. As she entered the inlet, she took a deep breath, calmed by the rugged beauty of Waka Bay. Isolated. A water oasis. New-found friends. Another link to Al.

Ray said, "Not to be crass, but since you'll be seeing your dad in prison, be sure to take our chart along, so he can tell us where the good prawning holes are, eh?"

"Seems I'm not the only opportunist on this boat."

Ray shrugged. "Can't make money on sentiment, Jigs."

"That I know," she said, "That I know."

***

Dennis, Camryn, and Samuel grabbed lines from Ray, greeting Jill and Ray warmly. After he secured the spring line, Ray waited for Jigs to turn off the engine. She emerged from the cabin, the whale charm around her neck, her ballcap in hand. She shook out her hair, a 'getting ready for company' gesture. No new lipstick or a quick look in the mirror for this woman. Only a loosening of her curly mane.

She has no idea what that does to me.

He reached out his hand to help her climb onto the dock and was surprised she took it, but her focus was on Camryn, not him. Ray shook hands with Dennis and Samuel and gave Camryn a quick smile.

Jill surveyed the empty dock and said, "Nice to be here. Looks like we get you to ourselves."

Motioning for the group to sit on folding chairs, Camryn sank into hers with a sigh of relief, her son standing at her side. "We think we're ready. Boats begin showing up in May, about the time your prawn season opens. We might get a couple boats next weekend, the first wave of cruisers heading to Alaska."

Ray focused on the walkway from the floating dock to shore. "I read about your new bridge in *Waggoners*."

"Most important improvement we've undertaken," Dennis said. "For years, we had to row from the floating dock to the land and back again. Got old, fast. With the bridge finished we can begin our shoreline building projects."

"A hydro power plant and a house on dry land. Ambitious," Jill said.

"Amazing," Ray said, shaking his head. "I'd like to hear the story of how you got here."

"In this God forsaken place you mean?" Camryn said, shaking her shiny brown shoulder-length hair. "Every day I wake up in our doll-sized floating house, feeling like an alien drop-in."

Dennis leaned over and kissed Camryn's cheek. "I'm responsible for all this, and she's been a good sport through it all. We married out of college and I taught high school history, while Camryn made good money in marketing. We explored the Broughton area enough to know where we might set up a marina. Once we leased this shore, we brought in rafts and connected them." He pointed to the tiny house, painted light blue with white window shutters. "Bought that from a fish camp. Built the machine shed, the bathroom shed, and a gift shop slash office, all floating on rafts."

Samuel held up his hand. "Then they built me."

"Our best project, ever," Camryn said, grabbing her son for a hug.

Dennis shifted in his seat, his burly body a tight fit in the lawn chair. "We're an out-of-the-mainstream marina, with boats paying for space on our raft May through September. Five months of business, if the weather is decent."

"What about the rest of the year?" asked Jill.

Camryn sat back, her model-thin frame barely occupying her chair. "I was an accountant at the logging camp before Samuel was born, but now I am a stay-at-marina mom and dock manager while Dennis enforces Canadian regulations on local logging companies. We have a little rental in Port McNeill for the off-season months."

The change of cadence in the waterfall drew their attention ashore, where water gushed from a mountaintop three hundred feet high.

Camryn sighed. "All that power available to use and we still depend on a noisy generator. Makes me so mad."

Leaning toward Camryn, Jill said, "So, Al talked you through some ideas for extracting electricity from the falls. I guess I'm wired similarly, because ever since you mentioned the project, it's been agitating my brain. But first things first. We brought steaks, potatoes, and bagged salad for the whole crew. Up for an early Saturday barbecue?"

Samuel threw his hands in the air. "I love steak!"

"This calls for beers and a soda for Samuel," Dennis said.

Samuel raised his fishing pole in the air, his six-year-old body taut with excitement. He pushed his mop of thick brown hair off his brow. "I'm gonna fish off the dock until the steaks are ready."

Dennis tightened the strap on Samuel's life preserver and squeezed his son's shoulder. "Good idea, Samuel. I'll get Ray a beer." Dennis beckoned as he strode to the shed while Camryn and Jill veered off to talk on their own.

I'd like hear what they have to say.

Dennis gave Ray a speculative look before he bent over the cooler for beer. He arranged two chairs in front of the shed and said, "Camryn's going to tell me everything tonight anyway. Why don't we talk prawning and watch over Samuel from here?"

After a long pull on his beer, Ray said, "We've got one more week to prepare. The boat's in great shape, we've read up and talked to experts, and heard about some local prawn motherlodes. Wish we had Al's charts, because the talk on the dock is he was spooky-good at finding shrimp."

"We've also heard about the battle royale over possession of the boat."

"Moratorium. We make money catching shrimp and take good care of *Jig's Up.* Jill and I are in total agreement on those two aims."

When Oceans Rage

Dennis wagged his head. "Don't know if I could handle a relationship where you can't talk to each other because of the legal ramifications. But I get the problem: if the case goes to court, you could use information against each other."

"It's more complicated than that. Someone tried to break into *Jig's Up* even before Jill took possession of the boat. She was drugged by a Seattle colleague who tried to steal her drone, and someone, dressed up like a diver, tried to break into the prawner." Ray explained the drugging incident as well as the vandalizing in detail. "I can't help but be sympathetic about what Jill is suffering."

"I'd say the way you look at her isn't merely about feeling sorry for her."

Ray swallowed more beer to cool off the warmth blooming up his neck. "Don't know what you're talking about, man."

"You look at her as if she's edible."

Elbows anchored to his knees, Ray stared at the raft boards. "Damn."

"Does she know how you feel about her?"

"It's a physical attraction. Proximity."

Dennis shook his head. "The way she looks at *Jig's Up* is the same expression on your face when you look at her. This has all the markings of a train wreck."

Ray glanced at Jill and Camryn in the distance, then back at Dennis. "Thanks for the jolly assessment, eh?" He finished his beer.

Dennis drank his own down and belched companionably. "All I can say is, if you don't touch her, at least the train wreck won't have fatalities."

Ray nodded, feeling morose.

Dennis mugged at Camryn who put two fingers to her lips, blowing a kiss.

Ray groaned. "I'm not being fair with Jill."

"It'd be a good move to hire a third person for your crew. Someone with prawning experience. That would allow you to focus on the boat and prawning. Not her."

A feeling of loss made Ray's heart heavy.

Dennis wagged his finger. "If she does turn to you, it's a bad turn, not a win, man. You two are at cross-purposes."

"I know."

Dennis stood and patted him on the shoulder. "Let's get the barbecue going, eh? Enjoy the moment."

Ray nodded, but his heart wasn't in it. His sister's future depended on Jig's failure as a prawner and her turning the boat over to Eileen.

Dennis was right, no good could come of getting involved with Jillian Morrell.

***

"Time for you all to meet Mae C," Jill announced once they'd devoured Camryn's chocolate chip cookies. She was energized by her private conversation with Camryn, who'd urged Jill to trust her gut and dig into Bill Parrish's death, as well as to use every means possible to keep *Jig's Up* and Mae C safe.

"Who's Mae C?" Samuel asked, skipping over to Jills' chair and leaning into her shoulder.

Jill registered the warmth of the boy's presence and smiled at Samuel, quickly planning how to explain her drone in words a six-year-old would understand. "My best bud, actually. I named her after Mae C. Jemison, the first African American astronaut. She was an engineer and a physician who worked for NASA in 1992. Today she runs her own technology group."

Samuel looked perplexed. "Your best friend is on the boat and she's a girl?"

When Oceans Rage

With a hand on the boy's shoulder, Jill said, "She's a drone, a machine, but she's kind of like a person to me because she can do all kinds of cool things I can't do. She's clever, quick, and helpful, too." Jill rose and headed to the boat, noticing Ray and Samuel's expressions were identical in their excitement. Ray? Interested in something mechanical? What was that about?

Camryn said, "Samuel, you and I saw a drone in Port McNeill. Remember when we drove by the football field where a man controlled the little whirly machine with a remote?"

Eyes widening, Samuel caught up to Jigs and said, "Cool. You've got a drone on your boat and we get to meet her."

Ray and Samuel stood next to *Jig's Up* when Jill emerged from the pilothouse with Mae C. Carrying the machine two-handed she transferred the drone to Ray. "You can set her on the dock in front of the chairs."

With a giggle, Samuel said, "She doesn't look like a girl to me. More like a tarantula with his legs in the air."

Lynda Flynn's request for a tutorial about Mae C jumped into Jig's brain. Strange how explaining the drone to this group made sense; teaching Lynda Flynn had felt wrong. *I'm glad to be done with Baldur.*

"Great comparison, Samuel. Mae C looks like a big bug. Or maybe a donut with baby helicopter blades." Jill glanced at Camryn. "You might be wondering why I want you to meet Mae C. Beyond the fact she's a friend."

"Your friend is ours," Camryn said.

On his knees next to Mae C, Samuel scrutinized the drone, not touching it, though his fingers moved, clearly itching to handle the machine. "Did you make her?

"Good question." Jill sat cross-legged with Mae C between her and her audience. "I constructed my first drone in college, but when I was hired to work on these machines, I got the chance to buy Mae C. Since she'd been used for testing, I got her on sale. We're talking two years ago, mind you. I've added stuff to her, so she's definitely got more bells and whistles than when I bought her."

Samuel took a seat beside Jill. "She whistles?"

Smiling, Jill said, "I haven't taught her to whistle, yet, but she talks to me through her computer." She turned to the adults. "A geek at Baldur found a recording of Jemison's voice and rigged the computer to replicate her tone and accent." Pivoting to Samuel, Jill said, "What I meant was, I've made improvements on my drone since I bought her."

"What can Mae C do?"

"Why don't you make some guesses?"

With his fingers on his chin, Samuel said, "It has six little helicopter thingies, so I know she flies."

"Excellent. I've rigged this little girl to whirl so high you can't see her. Why do you think I did that?"

"She's a spy?" Samuel's eyes widened at the thought.

"She could be used that way. But Mae C likes to help people. By doing what?"

Samuel glanced at the mountain range climbing to dizzying heights behind the marina. "She takes pictures! Mae C could show me what it's like on top of the mountain. Where the waterfall starts." He stood, brimming with excitement. "Let's get her up there. Can we? Now?"

"Next trip, when it's not so cloudy. Any other guesses about what she can do?"

Samuel stood and turned to his mother. "Mom. Help me."

With a smile, Camryn said, "I'd like her to make a map of the land around here."

Dennis said, "Mae C could work with the police to find bad guys."

"To locate a forest fire," Ray said.

From Camryn, "Check the condition of a crop for a farmer. Where it needs water or fertilizer."

"Help a boat navigate through a tight spot or bad seas." Ray moved forward in his chair, clearly eager to contribute.

Samuel jumped up and down. "Find a bad grizzly bear."

"Good answers. Creative, which is the kind of work Mae C loves."

The group was silent, a distant boat motor the only sound.

Jill pointed to clamps around Mae C's legs. "What do you think these are for, kiddo?" She squeezed them open and shut to demonstrate.

Clapping his hands, Samuel said, "She carries stuff. Delivers stuff! A pizza!"

The adults laughed while Samuel smiled broadly.

Jill said, "Amazon is developing plans to deliver packages by drone as we speak. I know for a fact blood products and medicines are being delivered by Mae C's relatives in poor countries where roads are impassable for cars or it's too expensive or dangerous to fly into the area."

Rising from the dock, Jill brushed off the back of her pants and sat in a chair. "Now you know why Mae C is my first mate."

"Hey, I thought I was." Ray gave a fake pout.

With a headshake, Jill said, "Sorry Ray. That spot is taken. Mae C will keep an eye on our fishing buoys. We're passing the word around the docks we have a surveillance drone watching over our baskets. You've heard about trap-poaching, right? Last season over two hundred baskets were stolen. We think Mae C could protect our catch from thieves."

"What we say around the marina may stretch the truth." Ray sat back in his chair. "But the threat of being caught might send robbers to bother some other boat's traps."

Dennis asked, "Mae C has GPS?"

"Yes."

"Cameras?"

"Two. Gyrating." She turned to Samuel. "That means the cameras rotate and can take pictures all around her."

Samuel edged to his father's side. "I could make one, Dad. A baby drone that finds fish."

With a laugh, Jill said, "Unless the fish are swimming on the top of the ocean, Mae C can't see them. She could find evidence of a herring ball or a frolicking pod of dolphins, but she can't see what's down deep in the water. I sure wish she could tell me where the prawns are three hundred feet down." She stood. "Ray, we'd better head out to finish our exploring before it gets dark. The next visit, when it's not so foggy, I'll put Mae C up in the air."

Ray reverently picked up Mae C and waited for Jill to climb aboard before handing the machine to her.

Once she'd stowed the drone, Jill returned to the boat deck. "A six-year-old stole my thunder about why I introduced you to Mae C, but I don't mind. Samuel suggested flying Mae C up the mountain to map the waterfall. Brilliant idea. Mae

C will locate the best places to lay pipe." She took a breath. "Too bad Al isn't here, huh?"

Camryn nodded. "He was as excited about the project as you are." She paused. "You know it's rare for commercial fishermen to visit our marina, to tie up on the dock and pay for moorage. Mainly our marina serves pleasure boaters. But Al would bring Adrienne and Beth on occasion; a couple of times he came alone."

"Pretending to be social but focused on the waterfall, right?" Jill smiled. "I can identify."

"We don't know Al well, but we liked him," Dennis said. "Call on us if you need any kind of help." He paused. "Can you tell us about the necklace you're wearing."

She grasped the whale pendant. "Al left it draped around the compass on *Jig's Up*. For some reason, I put it on today." She gave a little sigh. "Some of my recent behavior is difficult to explain. I'm not usually sentimental, so...I apologize if I can't come up with an answer."

"Oh, there's a reason all right, if you believe in serendipity. That's a whale charm, probably carved from deer antler by an indigenous tribe. As early as the late 1800's. By the Kwakwaka'wakw."

Samuel giggled. "Dad likes to say the word 'cause it sounds like a crow."

Smiling at his son, Dennis said, "White people call this native band Kwakiut'l. Fewer than four thousand Kwakwaka'wakw are alive today, but their population used to number in the tens of thousands. This bay was the home of three thousand natives once upon a time." Dennis moved his arm to encompass the thick woods surrounding Waka Bay.

"Where did they go?"

"Many died of diseases brought by white explorers and settlers. Others moved to the lower forty-eight when fishing harvests thinned out in the Broughton Archipelago. Today, only three percent of the population speak the four dialects of Kwak'wala."

"So my father bought or found the carving?"

Dennis stared at the charm. "Or someone gave it to him out of respect."

"What do you mean?" Ray asked.

"The Kwakwaka'wakw believe whales symbolize wisdom and spiritualism, and since the mammals offered themselves up as food and oil for the native bands, whales came to represent a clan's wealth. Promise comes with this charm, too. If the owner is taking a journey, the charm will bring him, or her, safely home."

Jill lifted the bone carving, questions flooding her brain. Why did Al leave the necklace on *Jig's Up?*

And why did I put in on today?

After goodbyes and double-locking Mae C in the master cabin, Jill felt the flush of discomfort, a moment of concern for her drone. Had she and Ray shared too much information about the machine in Port McNeill? Was boasting about Mae C's powers endangering her girl?

Lynda Flynn's angry expression came to her mind. Maybe Al had kept the charm for protection against the Lynda's of the world.

In the isolated reaches of Waka Bay with the Hudson family, Jill felt safe, but Port McNeill came with dangerous people. Maybe she'd be wearing the necklace from now on.

10

"A prison that looks like a resort," Jill said aloud when she guided her car to the visitor parking lot at William Head Institution. If she ignored the high fence topped with barbed wire, the compound's low-slung buildings, dotting a pretty peninsula south of Victoria, B.C., had the look of a lovely getaway.

Al Morrell was assigned to a minimum-security facility, which the Canadian press dubbed 'Club Fed.' As a first-time offender and a sixty-some year-old man who pled self-defense, Al must have been deemed low-risk. He shared a small apartment with another inmate in a two-story motel-like building. Or so Google told her.

She switched off the ignition and took deep breaths, hanging on to the steering wheel. To take a whole day off prepping for the prawn season was crazy in itself, but to visit her father in prison was the bigger stress. Her stomach felt hollow and her sweaty palms slipped on the leather. Where would she find the energy to get out of the car and walk through the gates of her father's prison when she knew she wasn't welcome?

He could have refused to see her, but he hadn't. She tucked the whale charm under her shirt, again sifting through her reasons for wearing the necklace. *Move it, Jill. He's waiting.*

After being properly vetted by the prison guards, her clothing and purse checked for drugs or weapons, she walked into the visitors' section, rigged to look like a comfortable living room. He stood at a window, light shining off the bald top of his head, a wide fringe of curly red-brown hair from ear to ear. Turning, he moved toward her, his hand extended. She meant to meet him halfway, but her legs failed her, feeling wooden and unhinged. Because she couldn't remember the last time she'd hugged her dad, she drew herself up to her full height to offset her inability to move, and gave him her hand.

"Hello, Al."

"Jillian." His voice faltered. He cleared his throat. "I'm happy to see you." He motioned to two overstuffed chairs on the other side of the room. "Shall we sit?"

She stared at his face as she lowered into the chair. His was shaped like hers, but his skin glowed a warmer brown from his part-Samoan heritage. The eyes looking back at her were the same ones she saw every day in her mirror. Brown. Liquid in their richness. Such a contrast to his faded blue jumpsuit and scuffed tennis shoes.

"I've looked better," he said, glancing down at himself and touching his belly as if surprised to see it straining the front of his jumpsuit. "Lots of starchy food. My cheekbones, which used to jut like yours, are missing in action."

Good, he was eating. *And so am I.*

She waved her hand to dismiss his weight gain, but she didn't know what to say next, even

136

more uncomfortable in this fake sitting area than she was in the Campbell River clothing store.

The challenges she'd faced for five years at Baldur were nothing compared to the foreign worlds of a marina, a fishing boat, and now, a prison. For a moment she sat quietly, unable to put into words why she'd come.

He didn't want her to visit in the first place. Hell, he didn't want to see her ever again.

"Should I ask how you're doing? I have no idea—"

"I'm okay, Jillian. I work eight hours a day on a computer for the Province. All inputting. Lots of time to read, exercise, and converse." He shrugged. "I'll survive this. How's your mother? How is Rose?"

"She's confused. Worried about me. Isn't sure your intentions are good."

He smiled. "Astute. Always was."

"I'm committed to checking in regularly, assuring her I'm safe and haven't lost my mind."

"She deserves that."

"I've met Adrienne, Beth, and Jack Canter. The Hudsons, too."

Al nodded, shifting in his chair.

"None of them know I've found you. They'd like to visit. At least to write."

Al shook his head. "Let's talk about *Jig's Up*."

"You know about the Parrish civil suit."

"My lawyer called me about it. I've set it up so she'll help me fight the suit."

"You're aware the family is calling this 'fraudulent conveyance'?

Al nodded. "They say I gave you the boat to hide my assets from Parrish."

Jill hesitated. "Did you?"

Al's forehead lined with worry. "Absolutely not. I want you to have the money."

"I chose the boat."

He looked startled. "You want to keep *Jig's Up*?"

"That's my plan right now."

"Why would you quit your job in Seattle?"

Jill shrugged. "My position at Baldur got complicated. They found out about your incarceration and your million-dollar gift before I did, just when I was trying to get a higher security rating. The fact *Jig's Up* was originally used for drug-smuggling fired their neurons. Way too much intrigue for the FBI to handle."

His complexion whitened. "Oh, no. I never—"

"I was supposed to lead a drone team for a government contract. Needed an upgraded clearance. Not your fault, Al. I empty my mailbox once a month when I do bills. I got the letter from your attorney but didn't read it before the Feds sniffed out my windfall. I would have gotten everything sórted out eventually, yet when they questioned my integrity, I got angry. Seems like was ready to move on, anyway."

Al relaxed a little.

"The more I looked at the project and the reason why I needed a sky-high rating, the more I re-examined my role." She sighed. "Because the work is classified, I can't go into specifics. Let's just say I questioned the company's ethics, then got offended when they questioned mine."

He nodded slowly, taut lines across his forehead smoothing.

"So I went to visit *Jig's Up,* curious as hell. Fell in love with the boat. Quit Baldur, sold my condo, and moved onto *Jig's Up*."

"You didn't."

"I did. Hired a partner. Looking for a third. Getting ready for the season. I even brought along my chart for you to put 'X's' marking your favorite fishing holes." She gestured to the folded chart visible in her purse.

For a minute, Al sat shaking his head. He studied her as if seeing her for the first time as an adult. "Jillian, you're an engineer, not a prawner. When I gave you *Jig's Up,* the money from her sale was to give you an advantage, a chance to make job changes freely."

"What's wrong with prawning? *You* made a life out of it."

He brushed his hand over his bald pate. "Sure, I liked the life, but I didn't have your options. With the education and talent you have?" Al stood, stuffed his hands in his pockets and paced. "And it's not safe for a woman. I know the game, Jillian. You have no idea."

Jill straightened in her chair, ready for a fight. "So *Jig's Up* wasn't an outright gift? Strings were attached?"

He winced as he resumed his seat. "You're right. I didn't put any conditions in my letter, but I had no idea you'd keep the boat."

She rested her head on the back of the chair and took a deep breath. "I don't know how long I'll stay interested in prawning, Al. Right now, it intrigues me. The electronics, the engine. Took a course from Norm Dibble and read your Calder books for pleasure. Dismantled and repaired the diesel stove pump and rigged a new hydraulic system for the basket pulley. Found out I'm wired for charting and piloting." She shrugged. "It's fun right now, but I might get tired of it, eventually."

Al didn't say a word.

"I'm so much happier on the boat than I was at Baldur. Every morning I'm charged up. At Baldur for the last year, I lacked energy and interest. I got headaches. Forgot to eat."

He stared at her.

"The headaches stopped when I started sleeping on *Jig's Up.* I've gained ten pounds."

"But you only have days to prepare. And you're missing a partner."

"True. I'm working on filling the spot. An experienced guy out of Seattle named Jim Livingston is a possibility. You know him?"

"No. How about Jack?"

"Jack's busy in Campbell River."

"Who's your second?"

"He's green like me, but he's a hard worker. Motivated."

"Who is it? I know all the prawners in Port McNeill."

"He's not a fisherman, but he's learning fast, like me."

"Jillian, I asked for his name."

Jill hesitated, and in that second, decided not to tell Al that Bill Parrish was Ray's stepfather. "Ray Stewart. He's relatively new to town. We're doing a thirty/sixty percent split unless we get a third hire. Ray seems smart and quick to learn." To avoid talking about Ray, Jill asked, "Why didn't you take a self-defense plea to a jury and get off with a lighter sentence? I mean, I know you're probably serving time for something you think Adrienne did, but even so, you could have taken the case to trial."

"A court trial would force Adrienne and Beth on the stand. I won't have it."

"But—"

"Jillian. Please." He narrowed his eyes. "I serve out my time here. In five years, I get out and help Adrienne and Beth as best I can."

"So *Jig's Up* goes to Eileen Parrish?"

Al shook his head. "No, it doesn't. I'm going to beat the suit with a court fight denying fraudulent conveyance, not over why or how I killed Bill Parrish." His voice tensed. "If the courts accuse me of hiding my assets, I'll prove I gave you *Jig's Up* as a gift, yours to sell or keep. The fact you kept the prawner presents more of a challenge, but I'm determined to fight for your right to own *Jig's Up.* If I have to sign something to say I'll never accept the money or the boat back, I'll do it." He seemed to gather strength to deliver his next pronouncement. "Jillian, it's too dangerous for you to play investigator. I want you to stop."

Jill was surprised to feel her eyes fill with tears. *He won't let me help him. I've found him too late.*

She felt his hand on her shoulder and focused on it, still trying to control her emotions. A tear ran down her cheek and she hurried to brush it away.

Al smiled at her, his eyes warm with what might even be...affection?

"You would honor me most as a daughter by letting me decide how to live these next years." Before she could respond, he reached out to help her up. "You need to be going now."

Her emotions where so jumbled all she could think of to say was a quick, "Thanks for *Jig's Up,* Al. I'll take good care of her. You focus on yourself."

"Count on it." He pulled a piece of paper from his pocket. "Take this to my attorney. She'll give you a combination to my file box of privileged information, including my bank statements. Nowhere will you find a record of money deposited by Bill Parrish. I paid his salary in cash, Jillian. That's how he wanted it."

"He never contributed to the prawn license?"

"Never."

Jill stared at him.

"Among other things, you'll find a map of my most lucrative prawn holes. This note says you have my permission to visit the box any time you want to."

Jill nodded dizzily, feeling overwhelmed.

He tightened his hold on her shoulder. Softly he said, "You'll be fine. I'm proud of you, Jillian."

"I hope...I..." She put her palm on her forehead. "The thing is, machines are my friends. But the ocean. Current, tide, wind, waves. I've studied how to read the ocean, but I'm inexperienced. Unskilled. Wary. Will I find wisdom about the seas in your file box?"

Al smiled, his eyes holding hers. "The ocean's rage is never personal, Jillian. Vitriol from humans is what you should fear." He squeezed her shoulder. "You're my beautiful, brilliant daughter. Prawning or engineering...whatever you do, I support you." A pause. Al touched the rawhide string around her neck. "I'm glad you're wearing the charm. It will bring you and *Jig's Up* safely home, every time."

She straightened, still full of questions, but instead she gave him the kind of smile that showed him she was satisfied with the visit, and particularly grateful for the coordinates to Al's lucrative prawning sites. Taking his hand, she squeezed it, then walked out the door, flinching as the guard locked it behind her.

***

Stop looking out the window.

Ray was on his second drink in as many hours, reading a book on prawning as he waited for Jill's return. The tide was up, so he could easily watch cars come and go in the marina parking lot. Expecting hers. Growling at the stupidity of his surveillance, he turned his back on the scene.

Even then he found himself angling to peek at the parking lot as soon as his mind wandered.

Don't watch for her.

She walked into view and made her way down the gangway. Ray felt the tension flow out of his body. On this windy day, her jacket hugged tight to her slim torso and her hair blew crazily around her face. Jill's eyes homed in on *Jig's Up. Or on me?* She wore a quizzical expression while he puzzled over his own actions.

He'd lit up the cabin so Jigs would know he was aboard, but he wondered if his thoughtfulness made a difference. Pretending a partnership with Jigs, when his goal was to grab her assets was a monumental folly. *I should not be sitting here, waiting. This is sick.*

He swallowed the last of his drink, hopeful the booze would round off the sharp edges of his thinking.

"Hey, Ray," Jigs said, smiling when she opened the pilothouse door.

"Hey, yourself."

She put down her bag, took off her jacket, and stretched, eyeing his glass. "You pouring?"

He got up. "Sure. What's your poison?"

"Absolut, rocks."

While he got ice for her glass, she moved to the helm and brushed her fingers over the instrument panel. Lovingly. That she cared deeply for the boat made him feel all the more rotten.

She squeezed by Ray to get crackers out of the cupboard. The warmth of her body reminded him of the coldness to come between them because of the court case. Once she was seated opposite him on the table, Ray raised his glass. "Here's to better days."

She assented, accepted the glass he handed her, and took a sip of her drink. "First things first. You talked to Jim Livingston again?"

"You asked me to. I did."

"I wish we had an option, Ray. You've observed the guy during the last month and you don't like him much. Will we be sorry we hire him as a third crew member?"

Ray clunked his glass on the table, shaking his head. "He's been hovering at The Tides and around the prawners for weeks. Feels off to me. I mean, he's playing hard to get when there are no openings except on our boat. Is he dumb or wily?"

"Maybe he's watching how we prep *Jig's Up* for the season before he signs on, or he's waiting for one of the hired crewmembers on another boat to leave. He'd take a big risk by signing with us."

"Duly noted," Ray said. "Still, I wonder about the guy, and I definitely don't want to give him a room and board option. We're off the hook because he's renting the room in back of Donna's store."

"You gave him a deadline?"

"I did." Ray drank deeply. "On to your prison visit."

"After that place, the marina feels like nirvana."

"I can't imagine anything more depressing than visiting a father in prison."

She stared into her glass. "Hardest thing I've done in my life. I spoke with my father a mere fifteen minutes and I feel worse now than I did before."

The misery in her expression brought an ache to his heart. "Some good must have come from meeting him, eh? You got a chance to see your dad. He's an important part of your past. Of who you are, today."

She looked up, as if surprised by the notion. "We look alike. Our eyes and tanned complexions." A pause. "He's darker than I am. More stubborn, too."

"Hm."

She raised an eyebrow and Ray relaxed a little. *That's my girl.*

Her smile disappeared. "He won't let me help him. Forbade me to investigate the murder. Wouldn't come clean about that night." She sighed. "The visit was useless."

"A retrial?"

"It won't happen."

"What do you mean, it won't happen?"

"He refuses to go to court. Still protecting Adrienne, is my guess."

Ray was incredulous. "He'd rather see you lose the boat?"

She smiled ruefully. "He said he'd fight the fraudulent conveyance suit."

"From jail? He can't be serious."

She frowned at him and sat up straight. "My father owes me nothing, Ray, and he surely doesn't need to protect me. He's convinced he's doing the right thing by not going to trial. He begged me to stop sleuthing. Said it was a fruitless, dangerous path."

"You believe him?"

"I should abide by his wishes."

Ray's hold tightened around his glass. "He's set himself up to lose, Jigs."

"He asked me to move ahead. Like you said, the litigation could take a year or more. We have a boat to prep, prawns to catch and a partnership to nurture in order to be successful. In less than one week. To make money. And we both need coin." Jill looked miserable. "I can't talk to you anymore about the suit. Anything I say could be used against Al."

Ray blurted, "Your dad might have forbidden you to look further into the crime, but I want details about the night my stepfather died."

She met his eyes. "To help you get *Jig's Up* for Eileen."

"I want the truth."

Jill cocked her head. "You want the boat."

"I'm taking responsibility for my family. Finally."

"While you ruin mine." She drank the last of her vodka and thumped the glass down on the table. "Done here. Another shot of vodka, I might tell you stuff I shouldn't." She stood. "The pact stands: we talk of fishing and boat things only."

At her words, Ray felt such a loss, he couldn't speak. Her hunched shoulders, closing out the topic, felt like the beginning of his own prison sentence.

Arms folded in front, Jill said, "We *can* talk about one thing I brought back from my visit with Al."

"Besides a stubborn streak?"

Eyebrow up, again. She took a piece of paper out of her pocket and dangled it in Ray's face. "See this? Al's attorney gave it to me. Combination numbers insuring our success."

"To open a safe with money in it?"

She shook her head.

"Nothing about the crime?"

Another 'no' gesture. "It's prawning holes. Al's secret prawning holes."

***

"*Jig's Up* is the best-looking prawn boat in B.C.," Jim Livingston said as he stood on the dock, studying Jill and Ray, a backpack over his shoulder. Though he was average in height, Livingston had a gym rat's build, his tee shirt tight on muscly arms and chest. His shaved head and bushy black mustache completed the look of a tough guy. He offered a sarcastic laugh. "But this might be the least desirable crew-spot in all of Canada, especially without a room and board option."

Jill touched her necklace, her fingers seeking the smooth contours of the whale charm.

"You need work," Ray said, taking command. "And we went to the trouble of officially announcing the job opening so any qualified American could apply for the work permit. You're *lucky* to be working with us."

"Says you." When Jim threw his pack over the gunnel, Ray caught it easily, and they entered the pilothouse.

"If you need a nap during the day, the upper bunk's for you," Ray said, returning the backpack to Jim.

"Shit," Jim said, glancing belowdecks. "But if I climb all over you getting to the top, I'll smile before I sleep."

Ray harrumphed. "Use the ladder or die."

Jill ignored the banter and shook hands with Jim. "Ray tells me you've prawned in Seattle for years, so we're happy to have an expert aboard." She led the way to the galley. "The terms Ray explained to you are laid out in this contract," she said, sliding a document on the dinette his way. "Boilerplate for a share of the catch. No room or board included. Please sign, then Ray will show you around."

After he read and signed the paper, the man's eyes moved to her chest. *The story still had legs.* "No mythology here, Jim. The three of us want to make money catching prawns, and we're not too proud to let you teach us a thing or two. Despite the rumors, a rivalry over ownership of this vessel is not our focus. Attorneys and the court will have the last word in that matter. Until then, we work our asses off to make daily quotas."

Livingston glanced belowdecks. "I hear you've got a drone to protect our catch. It's the talk of the dock."

"Bottom line, we use tried and true methods to find shrimp. This boat is outfitted better than most in the marina. I know how every machine on *Jig's Up* works, and if any one of them stops functioning, I can take it apart and fix it. Including a water purifying system Al designed and built himself. You have those skills, Jim Livingston?"

He blinked.

"Didn't think so. I've ordered pizza to celebrate. Beer's in the fridge; grab your own. We're a team from now on."

Jim nodded. His next words came with less rancor. "But the drone is here, right? Keeping track of our pots."

A side look from Jill, again feeling uneasy she'd planted Mae C in the dock gossip chain. "My drone is aboard, but she can't catch shrimp. We can."

11

Jill's role as a primary female ended the next day.

With Jim Livingston on the crew, Ray watched Jill suffer from losing her position as the smartest person in the room. Or boat. Or at sea. All because she'd chosen to fish for the elusive Spot.

They stood on the dock next to *Jig's Up,* ready to load traps. "Get rid of these two oversize ones," Jim said, kicking the rim of one offending trap. "You've got 280 of the 124-inch perimeters. Not allowed to have any other sizes."

Jill blinked. "Why not?"

"It's a rule. Same as not fishing for more than one species per vessel per season. We're prawners relegated to one size of trap. I read up. The B.C. government requires consistency." He walked the dock where the regulation baskets sat in towers of ten. "Missing tags on some of these. Every pot has to have a number registered to the fishing license. You call in the inspector yet? He'll tag these."

"Tomorrow," Jill said. "Two o'clock."

"Because you're a new skipper, he'll scrutinize every trap and inspect equipment. The freezer, especially. He'll take swabs of the tank and if it isn't free of bacteria, he won't let us start the season."

Ray nodded. "I cleaned the hold. Let me give it another go, just to be sure."

"You can carry 300 pots. Why are you short twenty?"

Jill put her hands on her waist. "This is all Al had in storage. Maybe 280 is what he preferred to carry. Something about weight and distribution? Truth is, we've spent a couple thousand dollars for the inspection and fees for the season. No money to buy more traps. Let's stick with these." She gave the stacks a jaundiced eye. "Doesn't look like 280 will fit on the boat."

Jim chuckled. "Balance is key. But they'll fit. *Jig's Up* will look like a porcupine once we get her loaded." He lifted a bucket, filled to the brim with hooked elastic cords of all colors. "We'll use bungees to attach the baskets to the boat and to each other. We have any more of these?"

"More inside if we need them," Jill said.

Another kick at a trap. "Bait? We've gotta bait these before we stack 'em."

Ray said, "Jill asked me to do the research and buy the right stuff."

Scowling, Jim ran a hand to his shaved head. "Don't tell me we'll use real meat."

"Nope. Bait cakes."

"Good. We dollop each with my secret ingredient and we're good to go. Got mesh bags for the cakes?"

Ray nodded.

"Line between traps. How much?"

"Twenty yards; ten fathoms. Good enough?"

"Yup." Jim stepped to the stern of *Jig's Up.* "Ray sits the baited pot on the midship table, I clip the line on it and let it slide out the back of the boat. When it drops off, I clip the line to the next trap Ray sets down, and so on." He jerked a thumb at Jill. "This happens while you're moving the boat ahead at a steady clip. You goose it too fast or take waves funny and we'll lose pots and dislocate arms."

With an eyebrow arched at the baskets, Jill said, "I understand. 50 traps to a line, spaced ten fathoms apart."

Jim squinted at the traps. "Just to be sure, let's bring some extra buoys so we can set a few more strings than normal."

"Okay," Ray said. "I'll bring a couple out of storage."

"All the pots are the right height, twenty-four inches. Did you check tunnel sizes?"

Jill said, "Fifteen inches in perimeter, allowing juvenile shrimp to escape. The mesh is stretchable 1.75 inches. Made sure of that, too." She paused. "We're catching males who are at least two years old and females no less than three years old, at the time of the year when females are not carrying eggs. We return smaller prawns and egg carriers back to the sea."

Jim let out a breath. "Along with other by-catch, both dead and alive. We get turtles, fish, and octopi in our baskets. Hope they are alive. When we sort the critters, we keep track. On the fish ticket we make out each day, we count everything. Coonstripes along with the Spots."

"Good thing there are three of us."

Jim's side-look spoke volumes. "I wish. You two will fumblefart the first week." He shook his head. "Settin' pots, picking 'em up, and sorting Spots into the right boxes are the skill areas. Big learning curve. Keepers go into the spit tank first where they regurgitate their stomach contents. After that we apply a chemical to twenty pounds of shrimp at a time, so they keep their color and don't stink. You have the 4-hexylresorcinol on board?"

Jill nodded. "For ambient temperature dipping. If we want to add chemicals to ice-water slurry, I have the sodium metabisulfite."

"I prefer the 4-hex. Next we arrange 'em into separate large, extra-large, and jumbo boxes. Flash freeze 'em to meet sashimi grade. The Japanese buy ninety percent of our catch and they are picky about size and color."

"You'd think they'd want live prawns, air-mailed like lobster," Ray said, bringing out the bait and bags.

Jim grabbed a bait cake, stuffed it into the mesh and popped open a basket. "Not possible." Jim squirted the cake with his smelly sauce, hooked the bait inside and locked the basket. "Prawns don't survive air transport." He hefted the prepped trap. "Which means we freeze 'em. A million pounds of frozen Spots, a forty million-dollar industry. If we catch our quota I won't complain."

Jill stuffed bait and handed off the baskets to Ray. "Are most prawn boats boxing their catch and freezing them on board?"

"Sixty percent are FAS—frozen at sea, like ours. Best for us and the shrimp." Jim hopped aboard *Jig's Up* and surveyed the deck. "Enough talk. Every boat's different so I need to figure out how to stack 280 baskets in this small space. It's gonna take some experimentation, so let's get at it. Leave the untagged traps on the dock; I'll load them after the inspector tags them."

Ray picked up a basket and thrust it at Jim, noticing Jill remained immobile. "You okay, Jigs?"

She stared at the baskets.

When Oceans Rage

"Feeling underhelmed again?" He said it quietly, so Jim didn't hear.

"It's like Lynda dosed me with LSD again and I'm hallucinating. What a strange world this is, piling 280 baskets six high on a boat that looks like it will founder with only half that number." She squeezed her nostrils shut. "And whatever Jim squirted on the bait stinks like the devil. Multiplied by 280? We'll die of asphyxiation before we set our first string."

"We'll get the hang of it, Jigs. Teamwork." He smiled. "Mouth-breathing might help."

After a few moments, Jill picked up a filled bait bag and handed it to Ray.

Ironic. The truth was he needed her to fail at this. To give up on prawning and the boat. Yet here he was, prodding her to buck up and partner with him.

The duplicity was going to kill him.

***

On any given day, the ocean was a rebellious teenager. Mercurial. Unpredictable. Add a fleet of prawn boats all racing out of the marina at first light, and any skipper would be challenged.

Twenty boats churned up wakes while a six-knot current brought every eight-knot vessel to dead slow. Dangerously close together, bouncing wildly in the chop they all produced, boat collisions seemed inevitable.

In the melee, fighting the wheel at the helm, Jill forgot to breathe until Ray put a hand on her shoulder.

Jim, standing at her left, read the knot meter and growled a curse. "This speed, they'll beat us by two hours." He held his index finger on the GPS screen's rendering of the south side of Malcolm Island. "Hug the coast and you'll pick up four knots, guaranteed."

She'd studied the currents for days, the Malcolm Island course chosen if this very problem arose, yet she'd forgotten her plan. She was determined to get out first and race to Al's secret spot before any other boat saw where she was going.

What a joke.

Their agreed-upon strategy was to cruise to Al's first treasure trove and begin laying down traps. Regulations mandated a seven a.m. basket drop, no earlier, followed by a single long soak. Baskets had to be brought to the surface by seven p.m. Only one pull per basket was allowed in the twelve-hour time frame.

A look at her watch told Jill she'd make it to the first location at eight o'clock.

Ray's touched her shoulder again. *Deep breath*.

Jim said, "Shit. I thought you said Billy was a friend. *Sea Star's* crowding us." He leaned out the pilothouse door and gave Billy the finger.

Turning the wheel to the left, cutting across *Sea Star's* stern wake, Jill headed for Malcolm Island and picked up three knots. Not four.

In due course they hit Queen Charlotte Strait where Jill cruised at seven knots, GPS homing in on Al's prime prawning ground. Four-foot waves were the worst of it.

Twenty minutes into their voyage, rival boats disappeared and Jill's stomach slowed its churn. Only a little. Setting traps was ahead.

Another two hours and they reached Al's two-starred location for the beginning of the season. Were the prawns still there?

Ray peered at the fish-finder read-out. "Should be pebbly on the bottom with coral because they like to feed off the algae. They forage up and down mounds on the bottom of the ocean."

"But they don't range far, which is why Al's chart should still be good. I read they migrate no more than a mile," Jill added. "Funny how we have all this expensive equipment to target a creature with two or three inches of edible meat."

With a huff, Jim said, "Spots go for eighty dollars a pound in a restaurant. They are gold to us."

"Interesting the prawning industry only took off after 1980," Ray said.

"And we've had some scary declines. Commercial shrimping takes careful management and Canada is still learning those ropes." Jim put his hand on the wheel. "This is it. Put her in idle and we go through the steps. One more time."

Ray put on his jacket. "I think we've got it, pal."

"I'm good, Jim. I agree with Ray. You've been a good teacher. But it's time for us to do it, not talk about it. We set the pots."

Jim gave a slow smile as he shrugged on his jacket. "Cocky rookies. I like it. 'Course we have something no other boat has, so maybe we have cause to be confident. We set the pots, go off to a nice anchorage and relax while the drone patrols above our soaking baskets."

"Not happening, Jim. We only trotted out that myth to get a leg up on the dock."

His eyes rounded and for the first time, confidence faded from his expression. "You're shitting me."

"We set traps the old-fashioned way, over so many miles it's impossible to watch over them all. My drone doesn't have enough range or battery power for that kind of surveillance. Ray? You ready?"

"I am. Let's do it."

Lips pursed, Jim clomped out after Ray.

The anger puzzled her. Fishermen were constantly bragging about mechanics they carried on their boats giving them the edge. Half of the time their facts were fake. Why would Jim be so pissed about her tall tale?

With a shrug, she adjusted the intercom so she could speak to Ray and Jim from the helm. "Let's fish!"

12

"A Pelton or a Turgo, that is the question." Jill paged through an issue of *Off the Grid*, a magazine written by and for homeowners who harness sun and water power. She caught Ray's puzzled expression. "These are turbine engines for Dennis and Camryn's hydro plant. Just so you know, I'm leaning toward the Pelton."

Ray sat next to her on the bench seat, studying the picture of her machine.

Though *Jig's Up* was safely tucked into its moorage at Port McNeill marina, a wave of anxiety moved through her. She put her hands behind her head, closed her eyes and leaned back against the cushion, glad they'd sent Jim to town for parts. Opening one eye at Ray, she said, "And I thought the weeks of preparation were backbreaking." She straightened her spine. "Every day is tough. A few more weeks of this? We'll surely die."

"But we'll die happy," Ray said. "Al's fishing holes are gold mines. We've been able to return early three out of five days so far. Hell, we've already offloaded our shrimp to the freezer truck before most of the other prawners tie up at the marina. It's getting everything ready for the next foray and leaving the marina at 0-dark-thirty that's killing us."

"We were looking for a cake walk with Jim rounding out our crew, but it's the hours, not the help. Lack of sleep, too. So why are we sitting here when we could be resting?"

"I'm strung out on a high. We'll have the boat debts paid off by the end of our second week of the season. From the middle of May, on, it's all gravy."

"I know." She held up her hand for a high-five. "When you think about it, a couple months of hard work with this kind of payoff is the way to live. Hell, in another twenty-some days, I'll have enough money to take exotic trips, help Dennis and Camryn build the hydro plant, plus upgrade every machine on *Jig's Up* at my leisure."

Ray was quiet.

"Or not." She blinked. "Because your court case marches on." When he opened his mouth to speak, she held up a hand. "I know you got a call from your attorney."

He remained quiet, honoring their agreement not to share details of the case.

"The Port Hardy Fisheries office shows no record of Bill Parrish paying for *Jig's Up's* fishing license, yet you're moving ahead with the suit."

Ray opened his hands in a gesture of helplessness.

"And I can't do a damn thing about Lynda Flynn, either."

"Told you she dosed you with psilocybin."

Jill raised an eyebrow. "So says the tox report. But because she fled to China, Lynda may never have to pay for her crime. Constable Burns says the offense isn't serious enough for the Feds to demand her extradition."

Ray put his hands on the table. "Let's stick to the positive, Jigs. You're a good boat captain, and you've earned respect from some of the fishermen."

"Don't sugar-coat reality, Ray. I'm done without Al's help." She slid out of the bench seat, her interest in hydro engines forgotten. "Can't be a skipper without a boat."

***

"Where's she heading with Mae C?" Ray asked Greg Hanley when Jill walked past the marina office. He moved to the window, watching her push the drone in a wheelbarrow, its bed softened with a blanket. When she got to her Mazda she laid the machine and a large black bag in the bottom of the trunk and stashed the wheelbarrow in front of her parking place.

"Coupla times a week, mostly around suppertime when you're working at The Tides, she flies it over an empty field. For about an hour." He looked at his watch. "She's heading out early today."

"She calls Mae C her best friend."

"I can see why. I've watched her fly it. Beth usually shows up to watch. And others. People know her routine and they're interested in the drone."

"No kidding?" Ray tracked Jill's car as it moved out of the parking lot. "A lot going on when I'm stuck behind the bar."

Greg emitted a growl. "Go."

"What?"

"You have time before your shift at the bar. Watch her work with Mae C. Off McNeill Road. It's the best show in town."

Ray had his jacket on before Greg finished his sentence.

Though he wasn't far behind her, by the time Ray parked his Jeep in front of her Mazda, she'd already set Mae C on the ground and flipped up her little computer screen perpendicular to the handheld toggle board. A woman's voice came from the machine, simple sentences softened by a southern accent. Two sets of teenagers, two girls with Beth, and another group of three boys, sat on a bank to the right of the parked cars, and a couple men around Ray's age leaned against an old Toyota truck, one in a white Molson hat; the other in a black Modelo cap.

Jill raised her eyes to Ray, briefly, then refocused on Mae C. "Ready, girl?"

"Prepared for launch." Six blades whirred and the drone lifted off the ground delicately, seeming to bow to the audience before rising twenty feet into the air.

One teenage boy called out. "How many miles will she fly?"

Jill inclined her head toward the two men. Molson shouted, "Five miles."

"Speed?" another boy asked.

"Fifty miles per hour," Beth said.

"Battery power?"

Molson: "Two units. Fifty-two minutes total."

"Payload?"

Modelo asked, "Jill?"

"New tinkering. Up from three pounds to five. Going to try that now." Mae C whirled toward her and sat on the ground so Jill could hook on a five-pound fish weight.

The teenage boys wandered over to the two men. "Cameras?" one asked.

Molson pondered. "Two-axis gimbal stabilized FPV's?"

Jill winked at the guy. "Up you go, Mae C. New burden. Can you handle it?"

When Oceans Rage

A confident voice from the computer: "Ready to launch."

For the next thirty minutes, all eyes were on Mae C as Jill toggled her through one maneuver after another, the drone rising straight up into the sky, turning in circles, taking corners, moving at different speeds. Salt air mingled with the smell of newly shorn grass on a windless day, and the props of the machine sounded like a flock of birds taking off, wings working furiously. Set against powder blue skies, Mae C's black silhouette crawled around the air, Samuel's version of an upside-down tarantula on the move. Mae C flew as if tethered to Jill's handheld machine by invisible webbing, her slim figure anchoring the delicate-looking drone. Now none of the observers spoke, but Jill talked quietly to herself and to Mae C, laughing out loud when Mae C managed a tricky turn, but swearing under her breath when she erred at guiding the drone.

"Come on home, Mae," Jill said, and the drone landed at her feet obediently.

"Recharge battery," Mae C insisted, several times.

"That heavy load sapped your energy, didn't it? We're done for the day."

When she closed the screen, Ray approached. "Put her in the trunk for you?"

She nodded. "Thanks."

"That was so chill," Beth said, edging next to Ray.

"What's the new tweak?" the guy in the Modelo hat asked.

"Upgrade her obstacle sensing system." She pointed to a small hill at the edge of the field. "I'll work her around that mound."

"Next week? Usual time?"

"We'll be here, souped up." Jill smiled at Beth. "I'll text you. Hi to your grandmum. See her soon."

Gently, Ray lowered Mae C into the trunk and placed Jill's bag to the side of the drone. All the while, he searched for words to describe what he'd witnessed, to compliment her. But guilt robbed him of a sincere sentence. His very presence was a threat to her. He could never be the support he wanted to be for Jill, because Eileen needed him more.

***

"Tell me again the prawns you're catching?" Jill's mother asked. "Your dad says they must be Spot prawns."

Jill put the phone on speaker as she cleaned the glass dome covering the compass indicator. Using a pointed wood stick she routed out dirt from her instrument displays. "He's right. We're going for Spots, the shrimp with white dots on their tails. They're the biggest and most desired by our Japanese buyers. Spots fresh frozen, nestled in boxes, eight big ones across and three layers deep. They're gorgeous."

"How many do you catch at a time?" Rose asked again, as if she couldn't get her mind around the numbers.

Jill said, "Let's see. 280 traps. Up to ten pounds of keepers per trap. A good pull is 1800 pounds of shrimp."

Rose clicked her tongue. "Ray and Jim are doing the heavy work."

"Mechanized pulleys lift the traps. I help the guys box the shrimp and put them in the freezer."

"Be careful of your back, honey."

"Mom..."

Rose sighed. "I can't believe Al was a prawner all those years. It sounds so hard and so lonely."

"I think he favored solitude until he met Adrienne and Beth. They need him, Mom, and that makes me feel guilty."

"How are you responsible, Jillian?"

"Think about it. A long as he stays in jail, I get to keep the boat." She sighed. "And it's stressful to have a father who admits to shooting someone. Like you said, it weighs like a reflection on me. He forbade me to investigate the crime, but I'm ready to defy him for the sake of Adrienne and Beth. And myself."

Rose was quiet for so long Jill figured the connection was broken.

"Mom?"

"I'm here."

Jill waited, realizing her mother was crying when she heard the *swish* of a cloth Rose must be using to dry her tears. *It's painful, but we have to talk about this.*

Rose's voice was pensive. "I loved Al to distraction the five years we were together. We were soul mates, honey. On his good days we were so deeply connected, it takes my breath away even now, thinking about it. But the good days got fewer and fewer. He tried not to be around you and me when he was down."

Jill pulled in a breath. "Did he think he was a danger to us?"

Rose was silent for the longest time. Finally, she said, in a firmer tone, "He'd get upset with himself when he felt low and pessimistic. I always thought that was why he stayed away. Toward the end, I think he worried about controlling his mood swings. But no, he would never hurt us. I'm sure."

Jill exhaled, relieved. "He speaks of you with such warmth, Mom. And he looks at me with these proud eyes that tell me I'm perfect." Her eyes filled with tears and she choked out her next words. "Why do I believe what his eyes say to me when he hasn't lived with us for almost thirty years? For the life of me, I don't understand why his approval is so important. It's not logical."

"Al showed you how much he loved you for four years, my dear. That's emotion a child never forgets."

Jill let the tears roll down her cheeks, realizing how much she'd missed as a child. Her stepdad's smiling face popped into her mind and she smiled. "Mike was a good choice, Mom. He's been a great dad for me, loving me wholeheartedly from the start. Dependable, smart, and funny."

Her mother's voice was sunny. "I can pick 'em, can't I?

"Damn straight. And damn silly of me to dwell on a relationship I can't recapture."

"I wonder if I've helped you with your dilemma."

Jill swiped the tears off her cheek and straightened. "Actually, you have. You reminded me Al loved me the first four years of my life. Needing his approval now is irrational on my part; his request to respect his wishes is unreasonable, as well."

"You're planning to disobey him."

Jill chewed on her lip. "I'll think on it. Tell you more next call. Extra big hug to Mike, okay? You know why."

"I do, sweetie. Talk to you next week."

Jill set down the phone, sadness sweeping over her. If she defied Al, even for selfless reasons, would he ever forgive her?

When Oceans Rage

***

"Last line in!" Ray said to Jigs over the intercom before he reached back to rub his aching shoulders. The boat picked up speed as Jigs pulled away from the last marker buoy he'd dumped in Tribune Channel. "Breakfast is served," he muttered to the shrimp.

Rain 'plock-plocked' on the shoulders and hood of his yellow slicker and water sluiced off his visor whenever he dipped his head. "Crappy weather, but the prawns don't care." He smiled at their luck. Rain or shine, shrimp mobbed their baskets.

The boat slowed to an idle, a signal Ray could cover the pulley and get out of the rain. Jim had already gone in, but Ray was too wired to escape the deluge and waited for his adrenaline to ebb after setting traps. Worse, he kept replaying the scene when a basket slipped out of Jim's grasp and hit Jig's leg. She'd grunted in pain when the trap hit her, and he'd asked to look at her wound, but she'd waved him off.

If he went in, he'd want to ask how she was doing and stand close to her when she answered. Touch a curl, breathe in her honey-almond scent, draw warmth from her body.

Nope. Smarter for him to stay out in the rain.

"Ray!"

He whirled around to see Jigs standing at the cabin door. "Yeah?"

"Are you a masochist? Jim came in twenty minutes ago and hit the sack."

"Nah. Just working out some things in my head." He checked if he'd covered the pulley engine with tarp, nodding when he saw the job was done. "I'm comin' in."

He hung his dripping slicker in the head, made instant coffee, and stepped beside her at the helm.

They were quiet for a long while, sipping and watching *Jig's Up* drift, a silence made more comfortable because Jim slept below.

"Let's head over to Waka Bay to visit with Camryn and Dennis for a couple hours," Jill suggested. "We're fishing so close to them today."

Ray homed in on her smile. "Sure. Good idea." He felt off-center and immensely humbled by so many recent events and feelings he couldn't express. "I could use a dose of their razor-like focus on life."

"We have some time to kill while our traps fill." She checked their coordinates on the computer and consulted the weather radar. "It'll soon stop raining. When we get to Waka, why don't we hike to the foot of the waterfall? I need to make some measurements for the hydro plant piping."

Ray sat in the co-captain's chair, smiling at the excitement in her voice as she put the boat in forward gear, pointed to Waka Bay. "Oh, so this is not a social visit. It's an engine junkie interlude, eh?"

She cocked an eyebrow, but her mouth twitched. "I beg your pardon. First and foremost, I'm trying to build friendships. Working on the hydro plant is a means to an end."

"Oh, really?"

Jigs wrinkled her nose. "Of course. The family gets cheap and unlimited power to their home so visiting boats can hook up to power and pay for it. Their profits will soar."

"*After* they pay for the Pelton, the pipes, and the power shack, you mean?"

"Right. Initial expenses are big, but the rewards, enormous."

Her eagerness turned him on, but he quelled the feeling. "Tell me how the system works, Jigs."

"You really interested?"

He nodded. "I want to know."

She pulled in a breath. Her grin and the rise and fall of her breasts had him entranced.

With a dreamy look on her face she began to talk, glancing at the seas to check for debris in between sentences. "It's pretty simple, really. Water rushes through pipes from the falls, turning a turbine which rotates the shaft of a generator. Magnets spin inside a cylinder of tightly wound wire, creating a magnetic field transmitting electrical current. I'm going to have to install a regulator since the falls delivers water at different pressures. I'm thinking…" She stopped, both eyebrows up.

Ray smiled indulgently. "You're the only woman I know who gets excited by machine-talk."

She opened her mouth, but instead of saying something, she put a hand to her cheek. Turning her back on him, she checked the seas, muttering something.

"What did you say?"

Not turning, she said, "That was a set-up, Ray. You knew what would happen if you asked me about the hydro plant."

Ray bowed his head, remembering why he was better off riding on the stern. *Everything she says and does turns me on. I'm hopeless.* He took a breath. "I'm not making fun of you, Jigs. We wouldn't be here today crowing over our success if you weren't knowledgeable about our engine." He tried to figure out what would mollify

167

her. Finally, he cleared his throat and said, "I guess I'm jealous. My work has never thrilled me the way machines do you."

"Hmpf," she said, but seemed willing to accept his compliment.

He went on. "When Graham McDonald checked over our Deere engine, the two of you yakked like long lost friends, sharing a vocabulary and a passion I couldn't understand. I was jealous."

She stared at him. "You're good with people in a way I'll never be. We each have our own grooves."

"Where'd you go to school, Jigs. I've heard rumors at the dock, but I'd like to know the truth."

"Does it matter?"

"I want to know."

"MIT."

"That fits with the gossip. I say: Wow."

"I was thinking the other day, until *Jig's Up,* those days at MIT were the most exciting of my life. People wired like me, working on such amazing projects, with the focus on technology, not people." She smiled at the memory. Then she frowned. "Baldur was a disappointment. The higher I rose in rank, the more I had to manage humans, who are, in so many ways, unmanageable."

Ray found himself desperate to track her expressions, so he jumped off his chair to stand by her side, peering first at the water, then glancing at her face. A waft of honey-almond shampoo came his way, drawing his attention to her hair. *Hell!*

"What?" she asked

"How is *Jig's Up* like MIT?" He paused. "Since your team on *Jig's Up* is nothing like your MIT partners."

"The boating world is dependent on machines and electronics. *Jig's Up* presents me with unlimited technological possibilities. To you, it's one hassle after the other, I suppose."

He grinned. "The captain-slash-chief mechanic can be troublesome, I'll give you that. Moody and demanding."

She socked him in the arm and frowned.

"What?"

"I wish the MIT thing wasn't on the gossip chain."

"Why?"

"I'm having enough trouble fitting in."

She licked her bottom lip, a gesture Ray had come to recognize as contemplative. A gesture that muddled *his* ability to think. Leaning his shoulder on hers, he took her chin in his hand, turned her face his way, and kissed her. Quickly but soundly. And long enough to feel her enjoying the kiss. Briefly. Afterward, as speculative chocolate brown eyes focused on his, he cleared his throat.

"I'll, uh, check around outside and get ready for docking."

"But we won't be tying up for another fifteen minutes."

"I need some air." *Cold, preferably.* He pulled his slicker out of the head and put it on. Her unexpected look of confusion halted him at the door, and he took pity on her. If she was feeling even the slightest bit as disoriented as he was... "Doesn't look like we'll get up to the waterfall today, though, in this weather." His heart clenched when her shoulders dropped in disappointment. All he wanted to do was wrap her in his arms and tell her everything would be okay.

"We'll come next week, Jigs. Today, we focus on socializing, eh?"

Her confusion rapidly coalesced into mock horror. "Me? You want *me* to practice small talk? Not a chance. They're about to get an earful about my Pelton and all the glories of water-powered electricity."

Ray pushed open the door, shaking his head at the prospect of watching her explain mechanics while he urged his libido to stand down.

13

"My new life is a study in darkness," Jill grumbled, picking her way through the moonless blackness of the marina car park.

Ray took her elbow. "Few streetlights in little Port McNeill. But the void at sea on a cloudy night is even more overwhelming."

"A void to avoid."

"Ha. You brought your special flashlight. Use it."

"Maybe on the way back when I'm on my own. You have good instincts in the dark, plus we're almost at the restaurant." Sprays of light from the windows of The Tides beckoned, promising relief from darkness as well as hunger.

As they crossed the parking lot, they spotted Donna emerging from the restaurant balancing takeout bags.

Jill pulled her elbow away from Ray and smiled at Donna, who paused next to a car.

"Hey, Ray. Jill." Donna nodded politely, placed the bags on her car hood, and unlocked the door.

Jill said, "I'll leave you two here. Thanks for being my guide dog, Ray."

Ray opened his mouth as if to say something, but nothing came out.

As she entered the restaurant, Jill suppressed a need to look back at the couple, even though she saw them clearly in her mind's eye. Ray, tall, rangy, and dark-haired, paired with petite Donna and her beautiful long blond hair and fine complexion. A handsome pair.

Once she stepped into the empty vestibule of the restaurant, Jill put her finger to her lips, remembering Ray's kiss and how much they'd both enjoyed the moment.

For two people well-practiced in keeping their distance from people they cared about, the next days were about to get very complicated.

***

The lump in her throat was as big as a sea scallop when she saw the raw hope in their eyes.

Adrienne and Beth sat on each side of her in a booth, their desserts consumed, when Jill made her announcement. She held the whale pendant in her hand. "Al left this charm in *Jig's Up.* It represents the prosperity of a clan, our family, but it also ensures our safe journey home. I'm wearing it for luck and Al approves." A throat-clear. "I don't believe our clan can be healthy with Al in prison for the next five years." She circled the form of the whale with her thumb. "I'm going to go against Al's wishes and devote extra hours to find the person who killed Bill Parrish. Starting tonight."

Beth ducked her head a moment, looking uncomfortable with Jill's announcement. Was that guilt in her expression?

"I thought you be pleased about my decision, Beth."

The girl glanced at her grandmother before she addressed Jill. "I am, for sure. I'll do boat chores every day after school to help free up your time."

"I appreciate the offer, Beth, but—"

The girl sat up taller in her chair, narrowed her eyes, and surveyed the diners. With a quiet voice she said, "The true killer could be in this room."

"Let's not get carried away, honey," Adrienne said gently. "Don't forget, I could be the one who shot Bill Parrish." She touched Jill's arm. "Now that we know where Al is, we can write to him. Support him."

"But that won't get him out of prison, Grandmum. Jill's going to have to get tough with Al. Make him remember details and help us with the detective work." Beth pursed her lips. "We all need to focus on those few key hours before Parrish was shot.

"I'm so fuzzy about that night. Maybe I need to be hypnotized to jostle my memory." Adrienne looked across at her granddaughter. "You, too."

Jill said, "Parrish hit you, Adrienne. A blow to the head can erase memories."

"But what if my subconscious has a recollection. Shouldn't the constable use his resources to dig information out of me?"

"When Al confessed, the Mounties never took statements from you two or any other witnesses. In the next days, it would be helpful for both of you to write down exactly what you do remember. I'm going to ask Pete to do the same." Jill chewed on her lower lip. "The men in the bar, as well. I need to build a clear picture of that evening."

Adrienne wagged her head. "Bunch of drunks. Maybe you and I could double-team them. But we've got to catch them sober, one by one."

"I read somewhere that most murderers know their victims." Beth said, sounding excited about her role as a sleuth. "Al suspected Grandmum did it, or I did it. Grandmum's right. You have to start with us."

Jill sipped ice water, then nodded. "Correct. I must remain objective." But could she? Al had spent such happy times with Adrienne and Beth. Adrienne was vivacious and generous. Beth, at thirteen, brimmed with brightness and naiveté. How could Jill regard the people Al loved as suspects?

"Bring Al back to us. Please." Adrienne stood and hooked her purse strap over her shoulder. "Beth, you've got an hour of homework to do before bedtime. We better get going."

After their thankyous and goodbyes, Jill waited for the bill, stymied by the dodginess of a murder investigation. *Think about this like a machine you have to fix, components all laid out on the table. Where would you start?*

Beth's contribution slammed back into her mind. *Bill Parrish was probably killed by someone he knew.* Al would never forgive Jill if she pinned Bill Parrish's death on Adrienne or Beth. He was in prison to protect them.

Her heart heavy, she signed the credit card receipt, tucked her purse under her arm, and marched to the bar to talk to Pete, the bartender. Pulling a written statement out of such a taciturn guy might be a challenge.

At the entrance of the saloon, she waited for her eyes to adjust to the dark room. The man behind the bar had his back to her, but he looked too tall to be Pete. Another guy who might have known Bill Parrish? She slipped onto a barstool.

He turned.

"Ray."

He dipped his head. "Jigs."

"This is how you play bartender."

"It is."

"Pete off tonight?"

"Yes."

So no opportunity to quiz Pete about the night of the murder. "I need to talk to Milly, as well. Another day, I guess." Jill observed Ray's posture, back straight and chin jutting, as if daring her to comment on his apron or question his knowledge of mixed drinks. "You like the job?"

"I need the money." A sheepish grin. "Keeps me out of trouble, too."

"With who?"

"You."

She wasn't about to go there. Not tonight, or any night. She absolutely, positively did not want to feed the small sense of joy she felt upon learning Donna was not his reason for disappearing each evening after they'd unloaded their catch. "So what does it take to get a drink around here?"

He asked, "What's your pleasure, ma'am?"

"A tot of Baileys, no ice."

"Baileys it is."

She took a sip. Made a face.

"What? Has my Baileys gone bad?"

A deep breath. "The drink is fine. I'm girding. Homing in. Wired."

"For what?"

"I had dinner with Adrienne and Beth. Made a decision. I could lose Al, his boat, Adrienne, Beth. Even you."

His expression fell, but she didn't have time to analyze why.

"Lynda Flynn's dose of psilocybin wired up my relationship side, and I don't mind fostering that aspect of my personality. But for a while there, I forgot what MIT and Baldur liked about my brain."

Ray smiled. "And me."

A nod. "Al asked me not to analyze, critique, examine, dissect."

"Yet..."

"Yet, inquiry is in my DNA. Deep down, he knows what I have to do. Even if he killed Bill Parrish. Or Adrienne did. Or you." She gripped her glass. "I have to take apart this messed-up machine to understand it."

The sudden sadness in his eyes wrenched her heart. "I can't help you with this, Jigs."

"I know." She stood, handed over her credit card, and picked up her Baileys. "Kindly send a round of drinks to that table of fishermen over there." Jill consulted her watch. "I'll cross my fingers that they're still fairly sober at this hour."

She glanced behind the bar. "And hand me that tablet, please. Some pens, too. My goal is to get a written statement from each guy. If the booze helps loosen their words, so much the better."

He handed over the paper and pens. "I'll send the waitress to get their orders. Be careful, Jigs. Good luck."

As she approached the men, she wondered if a thief sat among them, a man gunning for her shrimp or her boat gear. Or maybe Bill Parrish's murderer was at the table, soon to be upset she was investigating the crime. Like Al said, ocean rages were predictable, but a sea of people presented unexpected dangers.

Once at the table, she dragged over a chair and gestured for Billy and Ken to make room for her. They were surprised enough at her appearance to open a space.

"Ken. Billy. Gentlemen. My name is Jillian Morrell, the new owner of Al's prawner, *Jig's Up.*" She noticed they weren't surprised. "I hear the men at this table are regulars at The Tides with intimate knowledge of what goes on in Port McNeill." She waited for their expressions to soften. Some even smiled proudly. "I want your help in finding out who killed Bill Parrish."

Ken said, "You're assuming Al didn't kill him?"

"Forget assumptions. I want the truth. And I don't like the way rumors are flying about Parrish's death because the Mounties never investigated the crime. I'll bet you're all ticked no one asked you, officially, what happened the night Bill Parrish died. The fact you didn't get to say your piece is wrong in so many ways."

She waited while the men absorbed her words.

"I'm buying a round for this table." Again, she waited a beat, the men nodding, grunting, or verbalizing their thanks.

"In exchange you get a chance to reveal what you know. I'm asking for written statements from each of you about the night Bill's life ended. Any little details you can offer from the time Parrish sat down with you to the minute he left. That's all. Simple. Quick."

Jill waited a couple seconds. "Now, I could sit here and ask questions of the whole group, but the problem is I might miss certain observations only one or two of you made that night." She glanced at the bar where Ray was amassing eight drinks while she ripped pages off the tablet. "I care about what each one of you remembers, separately." The waitress came to the table, her tray heavy with glasses. "One drink. One statement. Deal, gentlemen?"

As the waitress distributed drinks, Jill stood and circled the table. "Questions?"

"Care about spelling? I'm a for-shit speller."

"Nope. Details are what I'm looking for, not good grammar."

Almost in unison, each man slugged down a generous portion of his drink and began writing. One guy squinted at his blank sheet and gestured for her to come over. "I wasn't here that night ma'am. Do you want the drink back?"

She laughed. "No way. How about writing down anything you can tell me about Bill Parrish? I need all the information I can get."

Fifteen minutes later, she'd collected statements, thanked the men, and explained her next steps. "Anything you remember you didn't have a chance to write down, find me on *Jig's Up.* I'm out of your hair, now. Have a great night. And thank you."

She folded the papers, tucked them inside her jacket, and walked to the bar. "I'm going to the boat, Ray. See you later."

"If I had a relief I'd walk you."

"I'm fine with my newfangled flashlight."

He nodded, his eyes unreadable against the backlit bar. "Hood up. It's raining."

Halfway through the dark parking lot she flipped the switch on her flashlight, feeling smug about remembering to bring the thing. She'd spent a bundle for the technology, a sweet little machine that had three purposes. One button sounded a screeching warning louder than a car alarm. A second button, armed with a safety catch, set off a stunner, delivering ninety-five million volts of power to an attacker. Third, she got to shine two-hundred lumens of light ahead of her. She punched the flash. "Well, I'll be damned!" Stopped short, she realized the light glinting off sheets of rain made it even harder to see than before. A gray wall of raindrops appeared impenetrable. She trained the light on her shoes. "At least I can see where to put my feet."

She picked her way forward the next few minutes before she stopped and looked up, disoriented, the hood of her raincoat limiting her view. *Not right.*

Slowly, holding one hand in front of her and the flashlight to her shoes, she looked ahead and behind. *Can't go back, girl.* She took a step forward, holding out a hand, and scratched her fingers on the stucco of a building. "Damn!" Then she smiled. *I know this place. Once I'm past it, I'm home free.*

Keeping the building to her left, she walked on, the fear seeping out of her. She was thinking ahead to her work on the Internet when she heard a "Whoosh!" and sensed movement on her right.

"What the—?" was all she got out before something came down on her head and darkness enfolded her.

***

Ray eased his weight aboard *Jig's Up,* trying to avoid rocking the boat and waking Jigs. Once inside, Ray pushed the door closed as quietly as he could. He breathed in the smell of her and the first flush of arousal hit him. *Like clockwork, eh?* Was it possible for horniness to be comforting? "Not unless you know you can act on it," he muttered. "Eventually."

He scrounged around in the galley for something to eat, determined not to turn on the light and bother Jigs. Irritated he couldn't find the tin of peanuts in the dark cupboard, he reached over to grab the self-defense flashlight Jill kept in a saddle by the door. The container was empty.

He felt the skin on his neck prickle and peered into the dark corridor leading to Jigs' cabin. He scrambled down the stairs and pushed open her door to find an empty bed. "Jigs?" he yelled. A quick glance into the head. No one. Bunks empty, too. He grabbed an extra flashlight from a kitchen drawer and sprinted up the gangway to the restaurant before he remembered to take a breath. "Jigs!" he yelled. "Jigs!" *Hell. It's been two hours since she left The Tides. Where did she go?*

He traced his way back to the restaurant, stabbing the light in every possible corner, calling out her name. Rain fell hard, making it difficult for him to see. If he couldn't find his way in this stuff, how could she?

He returned to the darkened restaurant, still yelling her name into the rain. "Where'd she go?" And then he remembered the direction she'd walked the other day on their trek back to the boat. "But she had a flashlight. She couldn't possibly—"

He sprinted through the parking lot into the inky black, still yelling her name.

When he found her crumpled up against a building, still as stone, his brain refused to process the scene. "Oh, my God." He kneeled to get a better look at her. "Jigs, honey. Wake up for me. Please." He propped up her chin and trained the flashlight on her face.

Blood. Her hair was matted with it. Blood, some darkened and some bright red, striped her face and soaked her jacket collar. The eaves of the building hadn't protected her enough from the rain, so from waist down she was sopping wet. And shivering. He gathered her body close and held her, willing his own blood and energy to seep into hers, all the while trying to figure what to do next. He could carry her to the protected area of the restaurant entry and call an ambulance. But if he moved her, lifted her, he might hurt her more.

"Ray?"

He jumped, startled at her voice.

"Ray?"

In the darkness, he couldn't distinguish her eyes from the blood blotching her cheeks. He shined the light on her face and saw her eyes were open. When she held up her hand to ward off the brightness, he jerked the light away.

His voice came out husky. "How ya doin', Jigs?"

She pulled her butt against the building. "Someone hit me on the head."

"Someone *did* this to you?"

At her nod, he moved closer and looked around, wondering if danger still lurked. Was someone watching them? Gripping the flashlight as a weapon with one hand, he used his other hand to push hair out of her face. "How bad is it? Can you tell?"

Her fingers explored her face and gingerly probed around her skull, stopping on the left side. "Big bump here. Source of the blood, I think. Head wounds bleed heavily, you know. I'll bet I look scary."

Words clogged in his throat. "Any other injuries?" he managed.

She shifted her body. "I think my left arm."

"We'll get you to the hospital. Can you walk with me to the marina parking lot? We'll go to emergency and have you checked out, eh?"

She was attempting to rise when he stopped her. "You let me get up first and help you. No superwoman stuff, eh?"

Her smile cracked his heart. "You use a lot of 'eh's' when you're excited."

"You making fun of me?" he said, gently helping her to rise.

"Hell, yes," she grunted, trying out her legs.

"Right arm around here, sweetheart. No walking on your own, eh? Lean on me."

As she complied, he surveyed the darkness of the parking lot.

Who in Port McNeill would hurt Jill Morrell? What had she done to raise someone's ire to this level?

And what could he do about it?

***

"One day, that's it!" she grumbled. "We go out tomorrow, no quibbling, Ray."

From her chair beside the pot belly, she leveled her sternest look at him, but he chuckled in response.

"What's so funny?"

Ray raised his hands. "You're the picture of the walking wounded with a bandage across your forehead and your arm trussed up. "You can captain, but Jim and I will have to do all the heavy lifting."

She hoisted her right arm. "This one works fine and the doc said my left shoulder is merely bruised. We can manage, Ray. I would have gone out today except you tricked me."

He smiled. "The deal was a day at the hospital for observation or a day at the dock." He shrugged. "You picked this."

She hunched over her tea. "Two lousy options."

"You might be right about getting out of here. For the first time, I don't feel comfortable at the marina. A lot safer out on the hook, eh?"

"You think one of the prawners did this?"

"Constable Burns raised the question when he found out we were having such good luck fishing.

Since the person who attacked you didn't take your money or credit cards, he wondered if someone held a grudge against you, me, or both of us." Ray put his hands on the table and bowed his head, shaking it back and forth. "He even asked about Donna."

Jill sat up in surprise. "He wondered if *Donna* might have attacked me?"

Ray raised his eyes to her. "He said he had to ask."

"And your answer?"

He looked out at the marina. "I told him I couldn't imagine it. I mean, she might be mad at me, but why take it out on you? I think I know her well enough to say she's not a violent woman."

Grudges? Violence? Jill's stomach felt hollow and her head buzzed. She tried to clear her brain of thoughts of Donna as well as the pain pulsing in her head and shoulder.

He touched her arm. "Lynda Flynn came up. He questioned me, too, since I'm suing you for the boat."

She raised a brow. "But you found me." Jill put her hand to her forehead, willing the jackhammer-pounding to cease. *I never had friends but now I have enemies. This is progress?* "In the end, the constable wasn't much help, was he?"

Ray started counting on his fingers. "Burns doesn't like how the negatives are piling up. The pseudo diver who tried to break into our boat. Lynda dosing your wine. Someone attacking you in the parking lot. You'd taken statements from my stepfather's drinking mates just before someone decked you. Could be a vindictive guy amongst them, someone who didn't like being pressured to write a statement."

She gasped. "I tucked the pages in my jacket, Ray."

"They're still there," he reassured her. "Burns heard our tall tale about our drone protecting the boat and our traps," he added. "Thought we might have made a mistake talking up Mae C's abilities."

"I suppose he reminded you of the rules about drone use."

"Of course. He also advised no more solitary evening walks for you and a cell phone always at hand. Watch for suspicious characters and put an alarm on the boat. Show him the statements from the bar, too. Meanwhile, they 'continue their investigation'." He got up as she stifled a groan. "You're ready to go to bed."

"I'm fine," she snapped.

Ray raised an eyebrow. "How long have we worked together, Jigs? Day and night?"

She looked up at him. "Almost two months."

He nodded. "You're dead on your feet. Very cranky with the pain, too."

Jill started to protest but couldn't find the energy. *He's right. I need one day of rest.* "I researched proper security systems."

"Of course you did."

"Ordered it. Fast-shipped." She yawned. "To be delivered today. Wake me when it arrives and I'll install it." She rose, wincing at the pain in her elbow.

He went to the bottom of the stairs, reached for her good arm and helped her step down.

In her cabin, she closed the door and sat on the bed. Sadness washed over her when she thought of her attacker. *Why would someone knock me down? Who is my enemy?*

When Oceans Rage

Glancing at her drone, stilled on the teak wall of her cabin, Jill asked: "Who wants to steal you, Mae C?

Why are we both targets?

14

Awkward.

Jill stood inside the entrance of Donna's gift shop, wondering why she'd returned. She wasn't the kind of person to chat up people, much less Ray's girlfriend. Ex-girlfriend. Whatever she was. All Jill knew was there was unfinished business between them.

Could Donna be the person who attacked me? Because of Ray?

Shifting a bag of groceries to her hip, she surveyed the store, thinking about what to buy, a rationale for a revisit.

Donna finished ringing up a customer and came toward her. "What's up, Jill?"

"Hey, Donna. I'm in the market for...uh...some rubber-bottomed mugs. For the boat. For coffee. Tea. Whatever."

Donna moved to the far corner of the store. "Right over here."

After examining an array of cups built to stay put on flat surfaces in rough seas, Jill handed over a wide-bottom version, white with bright blue anchors decorating the surfaces. "Four of these, please."

When Oceans Rage

As Donna wrapped the cups behind the register, she said, "I heard about the mugging. A startling piece of news for this little town. How're you feeling?"

"Healing. Pissed." She touched the place on her head, where her hair hid the cut. "After three days, still no leads on the culprit." Jill purposely used her injured arm to reach into her purse for her credit card. Damn appendage still hurt when she extended it.

Donna studied Jill as if trying to understand her. "At least you, Jim, and Ray are having a good season."

"Knock on wood." Jill fumbled her credit card and it flipped to the ground. She placed her grocery bag on the floor and retrieved the card. "Ray prawns during the day, tends bar at The Tides five nights a week, and patrols the marina at night. He's still working three jobs."

Donna ran Jill's card through the reader. "To help his sister."

Jill took back her card and blinked at Donna. "I guess that's why I'm here. Ray and I agreed not to talk about the suit, but he's not offering much information about his sister's health, either, probably because her condition and her needs are central to the case. I get the idea he's really worried about her."

"She's worse, I'm afraid. Stays in her room most of the day and won't eat much. Ray's presence unsettles Eileen, but he checks in with her attendant daily." She paused, her focus on the card reader. "I'm impressed he's sticking by her even when Eileen doesn't want him around. That's new for Ray."

Jill stuffed the mugs in her grocery bag, lifted it to her right hip and grabbed her purse. Thinking. Puzzled. As a prawning partner, Ray was more than committed. A tireless worker. Dependable. Upbeat. At least he was now. Would she wake up one morning to find Ray had left Port McNeill? Her stomach hollowed out at the thought. She had begun to trust him. Like him. Depend upon him. Was Donna warning her that she shouldn't?

She refocused on Ray's needs. "He must be embarrassed and confused by Eileen's rejection."

Donna narrowed her eyes. "He's working side by side with you while he does everything he can to take your trawler. Add to that someone in town wants you out of here." She glanced at Jill's injured arm. "Maybe you need more help than Ray does."

***

"You take mildew duty and I'll focus on rust. Deal?" Jill waited for Beth's nod. "I'll mix a bleach solution for scrubbing every inch of the rain slickers, life preservers, and shower curtains. You can lay them all out on the dock and operate on them like an assembly line. I'll search and destroy the rust on this pulley system."

Beth put her hand on her hip. "Then?"

Jill grinned. "I'll order a giant pizza." She looked around, pretending furtiveness, then leaned near Beth's ear. "Ray's away tonight. We get a whole pizza for ourselves."

"Good," Beth said, a twinkle in her eye. "He eats so fast I can't keep up."

While Beth laid the slickers on the dock and Jill applied a wire brush to the pulley chain, Jill thought about Beth's original offer to help spiff up the boat, giving Jill time to exonerate Al. So far Jill had failed miserably at her end of the bargain. Beth seemed to enjoy working with her, but Jill owed the girl more. Adrienne, too.

"How's your grandmother?"

Beth shrugged. "Kinda depressed. I hear her crying at night sometimes. She told me she's gotta work more hours to start building my college fund. Makes me feel guilty."

"What's changed, Beth?"

"I'm not sure. When Al was around, she never worried about money." She looked around, as if to see if anyone was listening. "I think we need to do something to help her."

"Like what?"

Beth pushed her hands through her hair and her bottom lip quivered.

Jill set down her wire brush and hopped off the boat. "What's wrong?"

The teenager lowered herself to the dock and sat cross-legged, her head down.

"Beth?"

Beth raised her eyes to look at Jill, tears coursing down her cheeks. "Al said I wasn't supposed to talk about that night. I figured he was right because it would make things worse for my grandmother."

"You haven't told me everything."

"I haven't. But Grandmum gets sadder every day, so Al's plan sucks." The girl swallowed and brushed away her tears. "That night the man got shot in our house, I *did* wake up. When Grandmum was yelling at the guy, I snuck into the living room and saw the guy hit her. I was too scared to help her myself and I was gonna run for help." She shuddered and more tears came. "But he saw me, grabbed me and threw me into a chair."

Jill knelt and touched the girl's wrist. "Did he hurt you?"

She sobbed, "I thought he would. I was so scared. He yelled at me. Weird stuff like 'whore,' 'tease.' I didn't understand all he said, but it was like he thought he knew me. Believed I was bad."

"Then what?" Jill asked, fear for the girl so strong she could hardly speak.

"I should have stayed to help Grandmum, but I was too scared. We heard some banging and he turned away from me to look out the window. I ran to my room, locked the door, put on sweats and a jacket, climbed out of my window, and took off for the woods." She closed her eyes. "I heard the gunshot, but I was so scared, I couldn't move until I heard Al calling me. I ran to him, crying and tried to tell him what happened, but he wouldn't let me. He told me he shot the guy. Told me to tell the police I slept through the whole thing, to lie to protect Grandmum."

Jill reached over to wipe away Beth's tears, remembering Al's words. *Jillian, you will not look into this murder.* Her father must have assumed Beth killed Bill Parrish.

"You said you heard a shot. Do you know what happened to the gun?"

"I never saw a gun. I heard it, but I never saw it." She grabbed Jill's arm. "I lied to the police when I said I was sleeping the whole time. Is that what put him in jail?"

What do I say? What would Al say?

Jill moved closer to Beth and gave her a side hug. "Al came up with the best way to protect you and Adrienne. You followed his instructions. Instead of worrying about this, he'd tell you to do your best to catch up in school, take good care of your grandmother, eat right, get enough rest, and exercise. To be happy."

Beth's mouth twitched with a smile. "Almost sounds like him. He'd bring up science and English. Ask what I was learning and what I didn't understand."

Relieved to see a break in Beth's tears, Jill said, "When I visited him in prison, he talked about you and Adrienne. He loves you both. He wants all of us to focus on good things, on being happy."

You would honor me most as a daughter, to let me decide how to live these next years. It's too dangerous for you to play investigator, Jillian. I want you to stop.

But if Al's plan were perfect, why were Adrienne, Beth, and Jill miserable? He'd left behind two sets of women in his lifetime. Maybe it was time for said women to speak up.

With a reassuring squeeze to Beth's shoulders, Jill got to her feet and said, "I don't think Al realized how guilty and sad you'd feel. Let me be the one to persuade him to come up with a better approach. In the meantime, you and your grandmother stop worrying, okay?"

Beth's smile was weak, but she rose, grabbed the scrub brush and got back to her job.

15

"Someone cut the hose."

Jill eyed the open seas before she re-examined the hydraulic pipe snaking to the power block, now refusing to lift baskets of shrimp to the surface. Jim and Ray edged in to see the damage.

Rubbing her fingers together, showing her crew the fluid oozing from the rubber hose, Jill said, "Look. It's been sliced halfway through, in a place we couldn't easily see when we inspected our equipment. Damn it."

Jim's expression clouded. "Can't raise our traps without the pulley."

Ray said, "Not if we're hauling traps full of prawns."

With a vigorous shake of her head, Jill said, "Thank God we bought parts in Campbell River. I've got piping along with a union gizmo in case we have to sever and rejoin the line." She tested the slack in the hose. "A union should do." Moving to the lazarette, a watertight trunk holding supplies, and opening it, she calculated how long it would take her to fix the problem. Ten minutes?

She gasped at the disarray in her tool and parts bin.

Ray reached her side and swore. "I saw you put new parts in there, Jill. Now half of them are missing!"

With his arms crossed, Jim said, "Duct tape won't work, not on a pressure hose. We're screwed. All our traps down and we can't bring 'em up. We're gonna have to return to Port McNeill." He punched his diver's watch. "By the time we get to town the parts store will be closed."

Jill waved a hand. "Greg could buy the union for us and hold it at the marina." She peered out at the empty sea. "But if we leave our pots here, someone could steal them."

"It's never possible to watch all our traps since we lay them down over several miles." Jim picked up his binoculars and surveyed the area. "No other boats are around. We should be fine."

Ray scoffed. "Whoever cut our hose is after our pots, accept the fact. They figure we'll have to go back to Port McNeill for a part. They'll watch us leave and steal our shrimp."

"Time to get Mae C up and running, right, Captain?" Jim asked.

Jill frowned. "Mae C?"

"You and Ray said you'd use your drone to keep our catch safe. So let's use her."

Ray knelt at the lazarette, staring at the spare contents of the box. "Where the hell did our stuff go?"

"Stolen," Jill said. "Sabotage. The hose was cut by the same person who grabbed the parts we would use to fix the problem. Someone with knowledge of hydraulic hoses."

Ray stood, his hands on his hips, squinting northward. "Whoever cut it is aware our traps are down, right here. We have a transponder on *Jig's Up,* and our automatic information system is turned on so robbers can track us."

"What if we turned off the AIS so the poachers think we're still here?" Jim said while he rummaged in the lazarette.

Jill counted off hours with her fingers. "As soon as we shut down our AIS, they'll get suspicious. We have a six-hour trip back to Port McNeill. Current could slow us and extend the return trip to eight hours. Sixteen hours away from our catch. Lots of time for poachers to check whether or not *Jig's Up* put down anchor here."

"They'll lift our pots unless we use our wild card," Jim said, fingering his mustache. "Or were you really blowing smoke up everyone's asses about your drone?"

"*Do* you have a plan for using Mae C?" Ray asked Jill.

"Now's the time to prove we mean business," Jim insisted.

Jill grabbed a bucket and set it under the busted hydraulic hose. She took a knife out of her pocket, opened it and quickly sliced the line in two, letting fluid drip into the bucket. As she cleaned off the oily knife with a rag, she glanced at the empty horizon. "Mae C isn't all we've bragged her up to be."

"How's that?" Jim asked.

"First, Mae C can't fly longer than fifty-two minutes. Her battery recharge takes an hour. Sixteen hours of surveillance? No way."

"Shit."

A look at her watch made Jill sigh. "It's getting dark. I'd have to use Mae C's lights."

"She's got lights?" Jim rubbed his hands. "Cool. How much area can she light up?"

"If she's lit, hovering over the pot-snatchers, she might scare 'em off." Ray scanned the seas. "Mae C has cameras. She'd film them in the act of pulling up any trap that belongs to *Jig's Up*. They'd lose their license and go to jail."

A nod from Jim. "I say we use every trick Mae C has to catch the turkeys. You know they're hiding out someplace, waiting for us to cruise home. They'll jump in and grab our traps as soon as they're sure we're cruising back to Port McNeill. That's when we light up the drone, get her cameras going, and buzz 'em." He grinned. "I'll bet you've got her rigged to shoot bullets, too. At least give 'em warning shots so they don't steal our pots."

Jill was quiet, a complete contrast to the excitement coming from Jim.

After a moment of silence, Ray touched her shoulder and looked into her eyes. "You're in charge, Jigs. Use Mae C the way you think would help us the most."

Jill made eye contact with Jim, then Ray. "We haven't touched on the biggest problem of all."

"What's that?" the men asked in unison.

"Using her at night. Putting her lights on. Filming people and places without their permission. Letting her fly out of our sight." Jill took off her hat and shook out her hair. "All are illegal under Canadian law. We'd go to jail and not a frame of what we film could be used in court. Plus we'd lose our catch. And the chance to fish. Ever again."

Both men blinked.

"What's more, I have dual citizenship and Jim is working for us on a work permit." She took a long look at Ray. "You're the only 'real' Canadian on *Jig's Up.*"

"And Mae C belongs to you," Ray said, rubbing his forehead. "Probably time to call the RCMP."

Jim made a sound of disgust. "They aren't triple A, for God's sake. We're not in trouble. Not technically. We're safely anchored with an engine that works and no crime has been committed. Yet."

"But this is sabotage," Ray said. "The Mounties would be interested."

"Jim's right. It's a stretch to think they'd drop everything for a split hydraulic hose." Jill plunked her hat back on her head and straightened the visor.

"Zero cell service out here," Ray checked his watch. "We could relay a message to the Mounties through another boat using VHF. Let's check the computer for other vessels in the area with AIS transponders on." He growled. "With our luck we'll hail the very boat waiting to steal our prawns. I say we stay here and let the Mounties decide about investigating the crime."

"Fine. You try to reach the RCMP with VHF," Jill said. "I installed taller antennas, so you might get through."

Ray headed for the pilothouse with Jim trailing behind. Jill returned to the sliced hose, thinking about alternative ways to repair the damage. Hoses under pressure were tricky to fix, but easy to ruin. Someone probably cut the line late at night when *Jig's Up* was docked at the marina. Since the pulley sat out in the open on the boat's stern, in a matter of seconds, someone could hop on, slice the hose, grab parts out of the lazarette, and jet off into the darkness.

Was it another prawner? Someone trying to end her season? More likely it was a thief who expected her to leave her traps unattended.

When Oceans Rage

A list of people who might have cut the hose formed in her mind. Greg, Daryl, Ken, Billy, Chuck, Jim, and Ray. Ray? Did she trust Ray? Was his situation with Eileen influencing her? Making her feel sorry for him? Worse, did Ray vandalize the pulley to frighten her, discourage her from keeping Al's boat?

What was the difference? No matter who the villain was, his efforts were successful, because fear was scrambling her thinking. She'd been drugged, attacked, almost burgled, and now someone had deliberately disabled a machine on *Jig's Up.* The present problem was fixable and not a safety issue, but the next act of sabotage could be calamitous.

***

No one was coming.

Ray lay wide-awake at one in the morning. He and Jill had remained on the boat in a bight near Waddington Bay, sending Jim off in the dinghy for the hydraulic hose junction. The seas were calm enough for Jim to reach Port McNeill safely in the tiny boat, but he'd have to wait until morning light to return to *Jig's Up*. If the weather kicked up, he'd have to rent a bigger runabout.

Meanwhile, their trawler sat on anchor within sight of one string of traps with no ability to raise them to the surface. If thieves came to steal baskets belonging to *Jig's Up*, Jill and Ray couldn't stop them. Sure, she'd set alarms on the buoys so they'd squeal if someone raised them out of the water, but Jill and Ray had no recourse if the robbers ignored the noise and ripped off their shrimp traps.

The RCMP was busy with a drug bust in Vancouver. Meet you in Port McNeill, they said. In the next day or two.

How had events turned to shit so fast?

The *Jig's Up* crew had been catching their quota of shrimp for two weeks and Ray thought the other fishermen were beginning to treat them with respect. Genuine? Who knew? Someone had tried to break into the boat. Jigs was attacked. A vandal had damaged vital equipment and stolen the parts to fix it.

No. Sleep was not coming easily this night.

Jigs' response to the sabotage was to fix things. She'd struggled to rig a temporary hose-fix for hours after Jim left, but without luck. "I can't wait to get my hands on those rat bastards. I put cameras inside the boat because I was worried about someone taking Mae C. Installed an alarm system, too. But now I've got to set up trip lights and surveillance cameras on the *outside* of the boat. This is crazy."

They'd spent the rest of the evening at separate chores, coming together for a late sandwich and a beer, calling it an early night. "Let's get some sleep so we're ready for the grunt work when Jim returns," Jigs had said.

On his back, eyes open, Ray's brain whirled like a carousel.

Crrrunch!

He sat up, listening.

Crrunch! He felt the bottom of the boat vibrate as if it scraped against something.

"Damn, we're dragging anchor."

He jumped out of bed, pulled on boxer shorts, and scrambled to the bow through the pilothouse door. Disoriented in the dark, he caught sight of a ghostly movement at the anchor windlass. "Jigs?"

"Umm?"

"We dragging?" He peered across the water, trying to see land.

When Oceans Rage

"Since the anchor alarm didn't go off I think it's the chain scraping rocks on the bottom." Her words, disembodied, drifted toward him. "I can't see well enough to figure out if we've moved."

Inching closer to her, he gradually adjusted to the darkness. He tried to judge their distance from the shore in juxtaposition to the landmarks he recalled when they anchored, looking in all directions. Once he calculated their distance from the shore, he released the breath he was holding and said, "You're right. We're hearing the chain rattle on the rocks and telegraphing the sound through the boat hull. We haven't moved off our pivot point."

Still juiced by adrenaline, he ran his fingers through his hair before he set his eyes on Jigs. A tight tank top over some yoga shorts brought his body to full attention.

A sliver of moon emerged from behind the clouds and must have made his interest clear to Jigs. She moved away from the anchor and took a seat on the bench below the pilothouse window. "Looks like we have another dragging problem, eh?"

He smiled, but remained standing, his back to her. "I'd say so. Not something I haven't dealt with before."

She was silent for a long moment. "I wonder if part of the attraction is the forbidden aspect?"

"Wanting what we can't have?" He turned and sat next to her on the bench, his thigh against hers. The warm night, ebbing adrenaline, the scent of her subtle honey-almond shampoo and sleep-smell, had him putting his arm around her.

She sighed and leaned her head against his shoulder.

"How you doing, Jigs?"

"The truth? My behavior remains a puzzle to me. My headaches are gone, but now I have heartache over Al, Adrienne, Beth, my mother." She shook her head. "Funniest thing. Since I started calling my mother every week, and meet up with Beth and Adrienne regularly, I've never felt better." She paused. "And then there's you."

Ray didn't pretend innocence. He knew what she was talking about. "Dennis predicted casualties if we act on the chemistry between us."

"Imagine what Al would think. I didn't even have the nerve to tell him I was living with the man who is suing us. If I...if we... Oh, God."

He removed his arm from her shoulders and took her hand, entwining his fingers with hers. "I'm destined to make life difficult for you."

"And if I follow my instinct to share all my thoughts with you, I might reveal too much and hurt Al's chances to get his boat back."

"Damn."

Cheek on his shoulder, she asked, "How can this feel so good but be wrong?"

"I'm making every effort..." He let go of her hand. "Not to hurt you...uh...more than I have to." Pushing his fingers through his hair, he said, "Shit. I sound like a sadist."

Eyes on his, she leaned back and said, "We've worked together for almost two months, day and night. I'd have thrown you overboard by now if I thought you were a physical danger to me, despite Daryl's warning."

"Thank you for that." To avoid losing himself in her eyes, he stared up at the starry sky, feeling mostly regret and sadness. Was he destined to fail the people he cared about? His father, his mother, Donna, and Eileen. Jill would be one more name added to the list when the season ended.

Her smile rueful, she said, "I need to go. Get some rest."

Ray wouldn't sleep another wink, feeling the way he did. "I think I'll stay up a bit."

When she rose from the bench, he caught her wrist. He squeezed her hand, hoping by the gesture she understood his words were sincere. "No matter what happens next, Jill, please believe my intentions are good."

Her eyes narrowed at his forewarning and she left him without another word.

***

"Mayday, Mayday! Mayday!"

Jill leaped out of her bed before she'd opened her eyes, throwing her sweatshirt over her tank top and pulling on long pants. She scrambled up the stairs to the pilothouse, followed closely by Ray, already buttoning up his slicker.

Receiver in hand, Jill punched the on button and said, "*Jig's Up, Jig's Up.* Responding to a mayday. Over?"

"Tender taking on water in Thompson Sound off Tribune Channel. Need help!" The man's voice was shaky, loud, and high-pitched. "Need help, now!"

"This is the Comox Coast Guard Radio responding to a mayday on channel sixteen. Time is 0500 hours, 26 May. Tender, state your name, how many on board and what is your location?"

"We're taking on water! My eight-year-old son is with me. I'm Frank Smallet. On tender, *Little Trip*."

"Copy that *Little Trip*. State your position."

"I don't have equipment on my dinghy to give exact latitude and longitude. I'm in the opening of Thompson Sound, Tribune Channel."

"This is Comox Coast Guard Radio. Stand by for mayday alert." A wake-the-dead squawk pulsed three times before a firm voice said, "This is Comox Coast Guard Radio. Mayday alert. Tender, *Little Trip* taking on water in Thompson Sound, Tribune Channel. Vessels in the area please respond."

Jill turned to Ray. "A boat in Thompson Sound at five in the morning with a kid in it? Where's the mother ship anchored?" Her brain replayed Smallet's words. "The man's voice sounded muffled, unnatural. What's up with that?"

"Beats me."

"I studied that area because the mouth of Thompson Sound is a favorite fishing spot on Al's map. It's steep-to around there with no place to safely get an anchorage. If *Little Trip* is out there fishing, where did it come from?"

With his finger on the chart marking the location from which *Little Trip* had sounded the mayday, Ray traced potential paths for the tender. "No radar on *Little Trip* and no signal coming from an AIS transponder in the area. Doesn't make sense to me. You're right—Where is the mother ship?"

"If we had our own dinghy this would be a no-brainer. You could get to Thompson in fifteen minutes." She looked at her watch. "Jim won't return for a few hours. Too late to help."

"Odds are stacked up against us in a way that feels fishy."

"After losing our hydraulics, I'm skeptical, too. Someone wants our prawns and our traps. If we go after this man and his son, we leave part of our catch unsecured. This stinks of premeditation. Manipulation."

Nodding, Ray said, "The guy *sounds* scared, and he says he has a kid with him. Unless some boat is closer to *Little Trip* than we are, we're obligated by law to rescue them. Damn it, it's all we can do. No one has answered except for us." Ray paced the length of the pilothouse. "Shit, shit, *shit!*"

His vehemence startled Jill. "What?"

Before Ray could answer, the Coast Guard came online, "This is Comox Coast Guard Radio. Vessel, *Jig's Up,* come back to us on channel six-niner. Copy?"

Ray flipped the dial. "*Jig's Up* on channel six-niner. Go ahead."

"*Jig's Up,* describe your vessel, occupants, and location."

Jill took the handheld. "We are a prawner, length five-one feet, anchored in Waddington Bay. Two adults aboard." Jill cleared her throat. "A vandal cut the hydraulic hose to our pulley system. We sent our fast tender to Port McNeil; a crew member will pick up a part to repair the hose. So we don't have a small vessel to rescue *Little Trip.* Traveling at 7.5 knots, our trawler is more than an hour away from the tender in distress."

"Copy that, *Jig's Up.*"

Ray touched Jill's arm and reached for the handheld. "May I?"

Puzzled, Jill gave him the VHF.

"Comox, this is *Jig's Up.* Shift to secure channel, please. Suggesting two-two alpha."

"Comox Coast Guard Radio switching to two-two alpha."

Ray flipped the dial and the Coast Guard answered. Ray said, "This is Constable Ray Stewart, formerly employed by the Fishery and RCMP Tactical Team of Nova Scotia. Since no vessels are answering and we are an hour away from the boat in distress, we'd like permission to fly our drone for a reconnoiter."

"What the hell?" Jill said, hands on her hips.

"This is Comox Coast Guard Radio. Your superior, Constable Stewart?"

Ray said, "Doug Stendal of the Fishery Department in Nova Scotia. Quicker, check with Constable Burns, RCMP Port McNeill. He's aware of my RCMP career."

"We're checking, Constable Stewart. Weather conditions in Tribune Channel?"

"You won't get a chopper in here. Super-low cloud layer."

Jill tapped Ray on the arm. "We'll send Mae C. She'll e-mail pictures to the Coast Guard in real time so get their address."

"She will?"

Waving her hand at him, Jill said. "Tell them. I'm going to get her ready." She donned her slicker and with Mae C in hand, Jill stepped out to the stern, muttering, "Damn men and their secrets."

Ray followed her out the pilothouse door, briefing the Coast Guard, saying he would monitor channel sixteen in case Frank Smallet on *Little Trip* called back. He then came to her side with the VHF and relayed the Coast Guard's e-mail address to Jill. "She okay in this weather?"

With a nod, Jill booted up the computer, and typed in the Coast Guard email address. "She's ready, but I'm less than calm, having learned I have a cop as a partner."

He let out a breath. "I had to come clean, Jill, otherwise the drone couldn't legally fly, or worse, we'd lose our catch."

Palm up to stop his excuses, she focused on the remote. "We'll talk later. For now, let Mae C do her magic."

Without another word, Mae C's six tiny propellers whirled and she buzzed away.

"Can she see obstructions?"

"Yup. I've upgraded her obstacle sensing system. She'll travel mid-channel most of the way."

"But it's so dark and foggy. Wet, too."

"Mae C uses infrared tech. She's dust and water resistant."

"Using both her cameras?"

"Yup. Redundant capability. Two going all the time, both two-axis, gimbal stabilized. If there's a boat in the water at the mouth of Thompson Sound, she'll show us the same time she sends pics to the Coast Guard."

Ray's smile gleamed. "Samuel wants one. So do I."

"Seems like Mae C interests a lot of people," Jill mused.

"She'll come back? Could someone grab her or overpower your remote?"

"Absolutely not. She's my homing pigeon, mechanized. Better. No eagle's going to pluck my big girl out of the sky."

"How long will it take her to get to Thompson?"

Jill smiled as she scrutinized the TV screen. "At fifty miles per hour, she'll be rounding the curve to Thompson in two minutes."

With his cheek next to hers, Ray studied the pictures, streaming through Mae C's camera.

"Light 'em up Mae C." Jill punched in a setting and the photos brightened as if the sun had come out. "Wait a minute. She's making the turn. Watch. Watch." Jill studied the scene. "Damn! Nobody. Not a soul in Thompson."

"Could the current move the tender?"

"Mae C is on it. I'm taking her all the way to the end of Thompson and down to the tip of Viscount Island."

Minutes passed. Jill said, "She sees debris, but no boat. Her infrared registers no human bodies. Tell the Coast Guard I'm bringing her back. I want to listen to your conversation, so stay by me." Jill pulled her hood over her head and protected the remote next to her chest.

"Comox Coast Guard Radio, this is *Jig's Up.* Channel two-two alpha. You see what we see?" The line was quiet for so long Ray was about to restate his question when a man said, "Copy that, *Jig's Up.* We will go to Channel sixteen and rescind the mayday. You saved us time and money, and worry, Constable Stewart. Canadian Coast Guard thanks you. We'll investigate this criminal activity from our end." He paused. "And I want the drone, sir."

Ray laughed. "Copy that, Comox. Report to come. *Jig's Up* out.*"

Searching the sky, Jill spotted Mae C and heard her buzzing home at the same time. "Good, girl," she said as Mae C gently lowered to the stern deck, said, "Mission completed, Jill," and shut herself down.

Ray handed her a cloth and without a word, she wiped down the machine. After she'd stowed Mae C in the master cabin, she quietly took a seat at the table. Irritated. How many more times would Ray Stewart blindside her?

He cleared his throat. "We should talk this thing through before Jim gets here. I prefer he doesn't know I work for the Mounties."

Jill raised an eyebrow. "I assume Greg's in the dark."

"Correct. Locally, except for Burns, no one knows I'm doing some informal surveillance for the local RCMP."

"Eileen and Donna aren't aware?"

"Correct."

"You've blown your cover. Why?"

"We were cornered, Jigs. I had no choice."

"Yes, we did. We could have pulled up anchor and spent an hour checking out the mayday. Found nothing, returned here, and only killed two hours."

"In that time we could have lost our catch. Lost money."

"That's a prawner talking, not law enforcement."

Brow furrowed, Ray said, "As I said, I'm trying to help you all I can."

"Bullshit. I don't buy it. Eileen is first, and I understand why. But your undercover work is second, not my needs. You've been trying to get me to use Mae C against the poachers from the moment you learned about her. What? Would that put a feather in your cap? Earn a promotion or an edge into getting a job with the local cops?"

Ray blinked. Said nothing.

"For all I know you manipulated this whole scenario. Did you have one of your government people call in the mayday so I'd strut Mae C's stuff?"

"Absolutely not. The mayday was real. Or should I say, it was a genuine fake. The Coast Guard had nothing to do with the mayday."

"Then who did? Surely a bunch of prawners aren't responsible for something so slick." She shook her head. "What the hell is going on around here? And why do I feel manipulated at every turn?"

16

"I'm in trouble, Al," Jill said over the prison phone. "I know you asked me to keep out of your business, but I have to talk to you again."

When she met him in the fake living room two days later she expected him to be irritated, so she was ready to face him down, strong and insistent. His smile was a surprise.

"Jillian." He stood with hands in the pockets of his faded blue overalls. "You were smart and stubborn at four. I should have known you'd be back."

She relaxed a little, warmed by the compliment. "Aren't all four-year-olds?"

He chuckled as they seated themselves in chairs they pulled close together, keeping their conversation private from another woman visiting an inmate. "I admit to limited experience, but I'd say you were off the charts." He sat back and rubbed his eyes. "When I bought an erector set for you on your fourth birthday, Rose was upset. You hadn't developed hand-eye coordination, you had stubby, chubby, clumsy fingers and you couldn't read the directions. Still, you were determined to build the crane in the picture. You wouldn't let me help and proceeded to stay up all night to work on it.

She remembered. "I fell asleep before I finished."

He smiled. "Wouldn't eat breakfast until you had the last piece in the next day."

"Pretty self-sufficient, huh?" *Maybe he thought I was fine on my own.*

"I wish I could say the same for myself." He pursed his lips, looking disgusted. "It took me twenty years to get up the nerve to consult a specialist about my depression. In the meantime, I'd found some therapy in prawning. Once I had a prescription that worked, I began to feel halfway human." He hitched a shoulder. "By then, Rose had married Mike and you had a complete family again. I didn't want to mess up your new life, so I stayed away. I felt guilty and embarrassed."

Jill's heart clutched. "I should have come looking for you."

"No!" he said his eyes drilling into hers. "You were a child. It was up to me to contact you. I'm not proud of my decision to stay away." He narrowed his eyes. "Clearly you're the braver of the two of us."

She raised an eyebrow.

"You're here."

"I am." Impulsively, she reached out to take his hand, squeeze it and let it go. "You know, the money you sent me for MIT was key to my staying there, Al. I'm grateful. I'm not sure I ever made that clear to you. In fact, I know I didn't."

He smiled. "No need."

Her own eyes stared back at her. "But you were wrong to leave, permanently. You were even more wrong to go to jail and forbid me to help you get out."

He straightened in his seat, and she sensed a protest coming, but plowed on. "I've tried to focus on prawning. God knows I'm green at it and I have a ton to learn. But this case of yours is on my mind all the time. I can't stand having you in jail if you don't deserve it." She stood. "And Beth needs you now Al, not in five years. She does boat chores on weekends, mostly to free me up so I can to get you out of prison. She's such a good kid, with a grandmother who is struggling to raise her, alone. Both of them need you."

He said nothing.

"I believe you're in here because you think Beth killed Bill Parrish."

His face crumpled.

"She told me what happened that night, and she thinks you went to jail because *she* did something wrong."

"Damn it!"

"It's what kids do, Al. We blame ourselves. It's irrational, but it's what our undeveloped brains come up with. We think if we'd been better kids, our moms or dads would have stayed with us."

"Jillian—" Al stood.

"She's already lost a father and she's got a mother who isn't capable of caring for her. Don't let her lose you, too."

Tears glistened in his eyes.

"Okay, now that that's out in the open, my engineer's brain wants the floor. I don't do well with emotions. So let's cut the drama and fix this."

He gaped at the change in her tone.

She laughed out loud. "Yes, this is the real Jillian. At least it was before I had a mind-altering experience."

Al's forehead puckered.

"A story for another time. Anyway, *usually* I fix machines."

Pulling notebook paper out of her purse, she said, "Let's go over this information." Jill smoothed out the paper. "First, you. I've talked to every prawner, Greg Hanley, the guys at the bar, and Pete, the bartender. To a man, they call you a loner, a quiet, nice guy. The prawners say you're a good shrimper. They get a little squinty-eyed at that, thinking you and I share some kind of voodoo master-shrimper gene. Superstitious lot."

Al nodded, offering a quick smile.

"I've quizzed the neighbors around Adrienne and Beth's house. Several heard the gunshot but they can't agree on a time. One says 1:30 a.m. and another, 2:00 a.m. Beth is fuzzy on the exact time, too. Adrienne's no help because she was unconscious. In the police report, you gave 1:45 a.m. as an 'approximate' time."

Al didn't respond.

Jill rolled her eyes. "You aren't going to help me, are you?" She looked at her notes. "Adrienne says she might have shot Parrish. I don't think Beth could have, frankly; she sounds too scared about the whole incident to have pulled the trigger, much less kill him with one shot. But how do we know? By confessing, you made sure Adrienne and Beth were treated as witnesses." She eyeballed him. "They didn't find gun residue on any of you, yet you convinced them you killed Parrish. Makes me wonder how smart the cops are."

She ran her finger down the page. "The bullet that killed him entered his chest at close range. Why would Parrish let you get so close to him?"

"All these interviews, Jigs, stirring up emotions. It's going to hurt Adrienne and Beth."

"That ship has sailed. I'm here because Adrienne and Beth are already in pain. Adrienne has taken on more work hours to build a college fund, and Beth is an emotional wreck, her self-esteem shot."

"I can get extra money to Adrienne. I—"

"And me," she snapped. "How do you think it feels to meet people in Port McNeill for the first time, introducing myself as the daughter of an admitted killer?"

"That's why I told you to leave the thing alone."

She shook her head. "Three against one, Al. We don't like your decision." Jill consulted her watch. "I've got to get back. We didn't fish today because of a bent prop and problems with the freezer unit, but both should be fixed by now and tomorrow we can get back to prawning and sleuthing."

He made a noise in the back of his throat. "And when you find out I *did* kill Bill Parrish?"

"At least we'll know the truth!" She folded the paper, stuffed it in her purse and stood. "You're on notice I'm disobeying your orders. I *will* investigate this murder, so you might want to help me. If not, at least I've warned you."

Taking a fortifying breath, she said, "We're catching prawns because your charts are golden, Al. Ray, Jim, and I make a damn good team." She paused. "Which someone doesn't like."

He rose from his chair, chuckling. "I can imagine—"

"No, you can't. Some creep cut our hydraulic hose to the block and stole the parts we'd bought to fix such a problem. But we protected our catch and repaired the damage."

Al stared, stunned.

When Oceans Rage

Jill reined in her frustration, deciding not to tell him about the drugging, the mugging, or the fake mayday. One shocker at a time: "Full disclosure, Al. Ray Stewart, my partner, is the man suing you for half of *Jig's Up*."

Al stared at her. "Stewart? How is he—?"

"He's Parrish's stepson. He hired the attorney fighting you for the trawler on behalf of his younger sister, Eileen, who is not doing well, health-wise. She insists Parrish told her he paid half a million for the 'W' fishing license."

"But he didn't. I kept up payments on the license, not Bill."

"Eileen says different."

"Ray? Ray is Bill's stepson? And you work with him on the boat?"

She lifted her chin. "He has as keen an interest in keeping the boat in saleable condition as I do."

"Does he know anything about prawning?"

"Not a thing. Just like me. But we're working our asses off to save your livelihood. We have a veteran shrimper on board, a guy we hired out of Seattle. Bottom line is, we've caught more prawns than any other rig. And we have two weeks left, all profit. I'm hoping Ray makes enough money prawning to help his sister and drop the suit. I looked up 'fraudulent conveyance,' Al. I think they could get you on that."

"They would if it were true, but it's not." Al shook his head. "I'll talk to my attorney. You finish up the season. Don't worry about the suit."

"Adrienne and Beth send their love. I told them I was coming and they both wrote letters." She plucked them from her purse and slapped them in his hand. "Be mad at me, and not them for writing."

213

Al stared at the letters in wonder. "I appreciate this," he murmured. "Tell them thanks and I miss them."

Jill nodded, satisfied. "See you, Al. I'm going to keep in touch whether you like it or not."

"I guessed as much. Would you be careful? This thing with Ray and his family sounds dangerous. And don't underestimate jealousies in the marina."

Jill nodded and swallowed, glad she hadn't told him about the other suspicious incidents, or that Ray had ties to the RCMP. Al had enough to worry about.

"I have to go now."

As she was walking to her car, a new thought struck her. Was working with a cop making her less—or more vulnerable to danger?

17

I can't cook in a child-sized kitchen.

Jill owned up to her current disability in Port McNeill's one coffee shop while sipping a chai latte, and added to Ray's grocery list, food she was happy to buy, but thrilled she didn't have to prepare. Putting together any kind of meal in *Jig's Up's* tiny galley baffled her. With two square feet of counter space, two burners and a doll's house oven, Jill created chaos, not dinners. Somehow Ray knew how to put together a tasty meal with minimum fuss.

The switchover had happened after her third meal disaster, when she'd concocted a spinach salad, stuffed pork chops, and roasted potatoes. She'd run out of pans, time, and patience, while Ray sat at the table, drinking wine and splicing an eye into the end of some line. He'd stopped what he was doing and looked at his watch.

"I know. I know. It's eight o'clock and we won't be eating for another half an hour. Live with it." She glanced at the dirty dishes filling the sink and cursed.

"You wash and I'll wipe," he said, getting up. "I hate doing dishes, but I like to cook. Interested in a job change, Captain?"

Life was better with Ray cooking. She shopped and cleaned-up; he was permanent chef.

She finished her provisions list and drank the last of her latte, preparing to rise when a woman walked in, stopped at the coffee shop doorway, and stared at her, hard.

Jill sat back in her chair, took a deep breath and said, "Hello, Eileen." The resemblance to Ray was unmistakable.

The woman frowned and walked a couple steps closer. "I look that much like him?"

"You do." She had Ray's dark brown hair and dusty blue eyes. Tall, too. But she was an unhealthy version of Ray, anorexic-thin, with a pale complexion and dark shadows under her eyes. Jill gestured to the chair. "Want to join me?"

"You're finished."

"I'm in no hurry."

Eileen pursed her lips and plopped into the seat across from Jill. "I heard about you from Donna." She looked out the window and said, dreamily. "Al's long-lost daughter." Her eyes hardened. "Our fathers disappoint us, don't they? At least yours left you with assets. Mine left me with debt."

When Jill shifted in her chair the woman flapped her hand. "Never take offense when a crazy person says something outrageous. Expect trashings from a nut case."

"Excuse me?"

Eileen smiled for the first time. She glanced out the window again. "This whole town wonders about me. How do I heal from a nervous breakdown when everyone assumes I'm cracked forever?"

Jill kept quiet.

"You don't have pity written all over your face. I'm surprised."

"You seem angry with me. I'd like to know why."

"You're messing up things. I need money from the sale of your father's boat."

Jill stared at her. "But our season has been phenomenal."

Eileen laughed. "Did Ray tell you the shrimp money will be enough to get me the help I need?"

"Isn't it?"

"Profits from the season settle my father's past-due mortgage payments with nothing left over for my new shrink."

"I'm not following."

"Your father murdered mine. You owe us *Jig's Up* for restitution." She picked absently at lint on her pants.

"But Ray gave me the idea the suit wouldn't make it to court for a year."

She rolled her eyes. "Ray wouldn't stick around that long. He runs when things get messy. He has no staying power. Ask Donna."

"You need more than profit from the catch?" A detail Ray had kept from her.

"Do I hear an echo in here? We have a court date in two weeks. Your father will have to testify."

Jill's heart fell to her stomach.

Eileen smiled. "Ray didn't tell you? See how lucky I am? Loonies don't have to beat around the bush." She settled her long brown hair behind her ears in a slow-motion gesture that raised goosebumps on Jill's arms.

Maybe she's making all this up.

"I'm sick, but I'll find sanity once I can afford a decent therapist." She raised her hands to her shoulders and squeezed herself so hard Jill could see her fingers turn white with the pressure. "Our local shrink is an idiot. I need someone who can take this weight off my shoulders." Her face suddenly sagged with fatigue. "It weighs a ton," she whispered. "I can't manage much longer." She wagged her body side to side, loose-limbed, like a ragdoll. Suddenly her head popped up, erect, alert. "But when I sell your boat, my head clears, and Ray can go back home, relieved to be rid of me and my problems."

Home? Where was Ray's home? Jill didn't know what to say.

Eileen growled and Jill drew back, ready to defend herself. Instead, Eileen began crying silently, tears dropping unfettered to her lap.

Jill glanced at other patrons in the coffee shop, all with faces turned away.

Eileen wiped her tears with the backs of her hands the way a child would. "You might think I enjoy doling out pain. To you, to Ray, to Donna." She rolled her head, acting like it was also too heavy to carry. "I'd give anything to end the suffering. Anything."

Jill decided to take Eileen's advice and ignore what she could of the woman's disturbing rantings. Gently, she said, "Why don't I walk you over to Donna's store?"

Eileen nodded and stood, dabbing the last of her tears with a napkin. She straightened her back and seemed to work up a smile for the people who were now staring at her. Quietly, leaning in so only Jill could hear, she said, "That got me a good month's free pass for saying and doing what I want to in this town." She started for the door and threw back to Jill, "At the end of that month, I leave Port McNeill." She stopped and turned so quickly Jill almost bumped into her. "You go, or I go. Could I speak more plainly?"

Jill stared into Eileen's eyes, startled by the agony she saw there. "I get it, Eileen. I get it."

Once again, Eileen made her achingly slow-motion move to tuck her hair tidily behind her ears before she turned away and stepped out of the coffee shop, leading the way to Donna's store.

Jill followed, feeling a new burden loaded onto *her* shoulders.

18

"Ray! Where are you, you lying coward?"

He froze on the aft deck, paintbrush in mid-stroke, gray paint dripping into the pail, and prepared himself for Jill's wrath. Guilty as charged.

He felt oddly relieved.

Jig's Up dipped with the weight of Jill hopping on board.

After wiping the paint off the brush and placing it in the thinner, he met her at the pilothouse door and opened it for her.

She remained on the deck, red-faced, scowling, hands on her hips. Explodable.

He wiped his hands on a rag and said, "I'll pack my things."

"Damn right, you will."

He entered the pilothouse.

"You would have done anything to get *Jig's Up,* wouldn't you?"

He turned slowly. "Throw you overboard. No."

"I mean manipulation."

He held up his hand. "I didn't..."

"Oh, yes you did."

"I like you, Jigs. I genuinely respect you."

She growled. "Pretending again. Conveniently omitting a whole swatch of your cop life in Nova Scotia. No, you played aw-shucks laid-off mill worker pluggin' away at helping his baby sister."

"We agreed we wouldn't talk about the suit. We'd work hard at fishing. Take care of the boat. That's what we did."

"You gave me the impression your sister's health was your only big expense. Surprise! Your stepfather is behind on a couple mortgage payments. You made me think the profits from the season would be enough to help Eileen. Surprise number two: She needs more money than you've earned prawning *and* bartending. Surprise number three: You have a court date in two weeks. Not next year. In two weeks." She scrubbed at her forehead and yanked off her hat. Her energy sapped, she said, more softly, "I don't have enough time to prove Al is innocent."

"My stepfather had debts, yes, but I never hid the fact Eileen needs extensive treatment. Look, I'm willing to admit Bill Parrish was a grade-A asshole with shit for brains, but that doesn't mean your father didn't shoot him and illegally shift his assets to you."

She bowed her head, her shoulders hunched. "You worked me, Ray. Made me think I had plenty of time to get Al out of jail. Pretended a good prawn season would be enough to help your sister."

He reached out to her, but she stepped back as if he were poison.

"Go. I'm sitting here until you leave."

"I never told you I dropped the suit."

"We agreed to focus on fishing because we thought the suit would take months to get to court."

"I didn't realize how hard she's been hounding our attorney." He ran a hand through his hair and sighed. "She's running out of time, Jigs."

"But did you give me an update? A sign? A red flag? I had to find out in a coffee shop with twenty people listening that you can't wait to pull the rug from under me."

"I was surprised her lawyer worked so fast."

"Ha! *You* were surprised?"

"You won't let me finish out the season with you?"

"What the hell do you think?"

"You and Jim can't do the job alone."

"I'd rather work with Ted Bundy than have you as a third."

"A crew of two isn't enough, especially since you've been targeted. You're in danger, Jigs. I could get deputized and help your through the legalities."

"It's still my boat, buddy. I do what I please with it."

"We signed a contract," he began. He made a sound in the back of his throat. "I'll take my salary up to today and call it good."

"Fine. I'll drop your check at the Marina office."

"My sister is my priority."

She shook her head.

Ray kept going. "You're a great boater and prawner. How could I have predicted that? I wasn't pretending to enjoy working with you. You're skilled, smart, and hard-working."

Jill shot him a disgusted look. "More softening? You're certainly good at that. Pack. Get out. Take care of your sister." Her anger deflated into sadness. "There's one truth I'll give you. I met your sister; she is definitely ill."

"You talked to Eileen?"

"Who the hell do you think—?

Ray moved toward Jigs. "Donna. I thought you'd squeezed Donna for information."

"No. Eileen showed up at the coffee shop."

"She got away from Sasha?"

"After she unloaded on me, I took her over to Donna's. I'm sure she's home by now."

Ray exhaled in relief.

Jigs plopped into the helm chair, clearly dismissing him.

Ray went to his cabin and packed his clothes, his emotions roiling. Eileen was out of control so helping her had to be his priority.

But the boat. She and Jim couldn't handle *Jig's Up* by themselves. And Jigs. She wasn't safe. Who attacked her? Who cut the hydraulic hose? Who faked the mayday?

Duffle bag over his shoulder, he left the boat, casting a last look at Jig's stiff-backed, silent form—a woman alone at the helm.

19

Jill packed her last batch of shrimp for the day, working in silence, too fatigued to carry on a conversation. Daryl transferred filled boxes to the freezer while Jim stuffed bait into traps on the dock.

"Last week of fishing and we're hitting our quota every day. We should celebrate." Daryl raised a box in salute.

She straightened. "Good haul, this."

Daryl threw a smug smile her way. "Better than with Ray, huh?"

Jill ignored him, hoping he'd shut up.

"Best season ever for me. My crew takes my boat out to catch fish and I get to rub shoulders with you for extra cash."

She barely nodded.

"Jigs!"

She jumped at the nickname, thinking Ray was calling to her.

Greg Hanley hurried her way. He beckoned, so she stepped off the boat and met him on the dock, out of Daryl's hearing.

"I have a friend who works in the emergency room at the hospital. She just called me." Greg hooked his thumbs in his belt loops, his solemn eyes on hers. "Ray's sister attempted suicide. Her attendant found Eileen in the bathtub, bleeding from her wrists. She's lost a lot of blood, but the doc says she'll make it."

Jill closed her eyes and took a deep breath. "Is he with her?"

"Yup. She's stabilized and under suicide watch."

Jill glanced at *Jig's Up,* stuffed to the gills with frozen prawns. Hard to enjoy a successful haul while Eileen suffered so much.

A pink starfish clinging to a rock, left dry by a dropping tide, reminded her of Ray's position. Her heart ached for what he must be going through. "Devastating."

"Think they'll postpone the court date next week?" Greg asked.

With a vigorous shake of her head, Jill said, "Eileen's health has to be a priority for Ray, but any delay would certainly help Al's attorney prepare."

"And allow you to finish the season," Greg said.

A dull pain pulsed in the surprisingly slow-to-heal cut on her left calf and a feeling of malaise washed over her. "I'm making more money at prawning since I hired Daryl, yet I'm enjoying it less."

"Daryl's good at what he does, but his bragging can put one's teeth on edge."

"I'll get through the season. Pay my bills, pay off Jim and Daryl. Then I think I'm done."

"But you're good at this, Jill. You're a natural." Greg gestured to the other prawn boats. "Even they say so."

"Oh, sure."

"Okay, not all of 'em. But since you took Daryl on to finish the season, he's spread the word. You've got some fans on this dock."

"Did he collect the pool, yet?"

"He hasn't asked Ken for the money."

"He's lying if he says he won."

"The guys on the dock figured that out. They're giving him shit about it." He touched her arm. "Seriously. Daryl has a mean streak; he can be vindictive, too, and right now you are not his favorite person." Greg glanced at Daryl as the prawner transferred boxes to the freezer. "Go see Ray, will you? I think he could use a friend." He touched her arm. "So could you."

Al's wise words crawled like a banner through her mind: She had less to fear from the sea than from humans. Had she made a mistake hiring Ray just as Al had erred in partnering with Bill Parrish?

"Seeing me won't make him feel better, Greg. You go. Check on him. Make sure he's okay."

As Greg walked away, Jill's thoughts turned to Eileen, remembering her erratic behavior in the coffee shop, a desperate cry for help. When Jill had escorted Eileen to Donna's store, she'd witnessed a transformation in Eileen's behavior. The woman had smiled sweetly in Donna's presence and thanked Jill with a firm handshake. That glimpse of normality was all the evidence Jill needed to spark her next move. She'd go to Donna and get her help in making this right.

***

Ray banged on his head to bring his muzzy mind back to full attention. Donna dozed in the corner of the hospital room while his sister slept fitfully, her rent wrists hidden beneath the sheets. She had dark hair like his, longer, though, and spread out in a fan around her face.

When Oceans Rage

Ten years younger than he. Too thin. Fragile. So vulnerable.

Only noon? His second-hand dragged around the clock, the smell of alcohol and bleach clogging his senses. On the third day of suicide watch, all he thought about was how he'd screwed up with Eileen. His mother. Jill.

He worried about his sister's reaction to him as soon as the drugs cleared out of her brain. For the last few days, she'd been calm in his presence, giving him hope she might be recovering. But the hospital was releasing his sister in less than three hours with a stern warning: "If you can't care for her at home, the Provincial Sanitarium in Vancouver is your next best choice. She needs intense therapy and 24/7 monitoring."

Ray and Donna's research showed a better alternative: White Sands Rehabilitation Center in Victoria. The facility had an opening for her, but at $20,000 a month, he couldn't pay for it. Second best? Keep Eileen at home and increase her time with the local psychiatrist. Donna and a neighbor would fill in when Sasha needed breaks. The doctors had adjusted Eileen's medication so she'd be more even-keeled than before. Still they'd warned him she could try suicide again, even on drugs.

"Why, Eileen? Why don't you want to live?" he asked her. He stood up to stretch when he heard a knock on the door. A man in an orderly's uniform entered, pushing a wheelchair. "Eileen Parrish's room?"

"It is," Ray answered. "Aren't you early?"

Eileen opened her eyes and stirred, frowning at the commotion.

"I'm from White Sands. Mr. Stewart? Joe Natches. We have our transport here to take Ms.

Parrish to White Sands. She's been checked in and her doctor released her to us. You're the last person who needs to sign."

"What?" Ray glanced first at Donna then Eileen. "I didn't check her into White Sands. I mean, I wanted to. I did inquire if there was a spot for her, but..."

The orderly looked puzzled. "She's in, sir. Two months paid in full, the fee sent in your name." He showed the form to Ray. The man zeroed in on Donna. "You want to help her dress, ma'am, while Mr. Stewart and I do the paperwork outside?"

Donna rose from her chair. "It's what she needs, Ray."

Ray lifted a hand to stop Donna and took the form from the orderly. He scrutinized the paperwork until he saw 'Jillian Morrell' typed in next to Ray's name. She was listed as 'intermediary.' He turned to Donna. "She sold the boat."

Donna nodded. "Jill made me tell her about White Sands and explained she fronted the money the civil suit would have handed over eventually. She wants you to think of it as an early judgment."

Gesturing for the attendant to wait outside, Ray watched Natches exit the room, his thoughts swirling. To Donna, he said, "I can't let her do it. Jill needs *Jig's Up.*"

"And you don't? You didn't lawyer up to get the boat for yourself. You need the money for Eileen. Jill's a healthy, bright, educated woman. She'll find a way to get another boat if she wants one."

"It doesn't feel right anymore. I should have dropped the civil suit." He rubbed his eyes, frustrated with the turmoil in his mind. He checked to see that Eileen had fallen back asleep and kept his voice low. "My stepfather was a monster, Donna. I'm beginning to think Al had more than one good reason to stop Bill Parrish that night. And Jigs?" He rotated his neck to relieve the tension. "She's an innocent bystander. She doesn't deserve to pay for the sins of Eileen's father, or hers."

Folding the document and stuffing it into his pocket, Ray said, "I can't accept this sacrifice."

"Listen, Jill bought some time for you. Use it. Let Eileen go to White Sands so you can concentrate on finding a job you're actually trained for." Donna reached out and gave his arm a squeeze. "I never thought you'd stick it out like you have with your sister." She gestured toward Eileen and the chair from which Ray had kept watch. "You've proven yourself through this ordeal." She paused. "And I have been far from helpful. Maybe even hurtful."

"What do you mean, hurtful?"

"Remember the night I wouldn't let you into the house because someone was visiting?"

"Yeah. So? You're entitled to a private life."

"It was Jim Livingston."

"What the hell? You're seeing Jim? The whole time we were shrimping you and Jim were together?"

"We'd gone out a couple of times before he took the job on Jig's up, ticked when Jill wouldn't give him room and board." Her complexion pinked. "Everything was booked in town because of the prawn season, so I let him rent the room at the back of the store. He was interesting. Kind. Attentive. With an obvious antipathy toward Jill." Donna looked at the floor before she made eye contact with Ray. "She wasn't my favorite person at the time, either."

"Kind? Interesting? You're not describing the man Jill and I know."

Donna closed her eyes for a long moment before opening them again. "As we've been sitting here with Eileen, I've made myself think back on every conversation with Jim. Since I know people in town and every bit of gossip is traded in my store, he used me. To learn about Jill. Not you. Jill."

"He set you up?"

Donna's expression turned sour. "Why didn't I question why Jim was interested in me? In my business. My friends. My ex-boyfriend?"

Ray sat down and put his head in his hands, trying to think. Jim's focus on Jill worried him. The guy was playing Donna in order to get information about Jill?

"What did you tell him?"

"That you were intent on taking the boat away from Jill to pay for Eileen's special treatment." She jerked off the elastic ring from her ponytail, the pink of her complexion darkening. "He seemed supportive of your effort to get back what you rightfully owned. I was on your side. And Eileen's. But now, when I think about it, I made Jill the enemy because Jim pushed me there."

One look at Donna's expression and Ray lost the energy to criticize her. Jim was the culprit and Donna was the victim here. Jim had an agenda. What was it?

He walked to Eileen's side and looked down on her pencil-thin body lost in the big hospital bed. So pale. So frail. Turning to Donna, he said, "Fine. I'll follow Eileen to White Sands, talk to her doctors, and figure out what my role in her recovery will be. Could take days." He paused, questions whirling in his head. "Will you go see

Jill, thank her, and tell her I'm with Eileen? Check to see how she's doing, especially after hiring that egomaniac, Daryl. I've had nightmares about her fishing with him." He pushed his fingers through his hair. "And warn her about Jim, will you? Come clean with what he got out of you. Help her figure out his motive, please."

Ray was quiet for a moment. "We've grabbed a ray of light for Eileen, but I'm afraid we've just pushed Jill into a very dark place."

20

"I hate boats," Donna said as Jill opened the starboard door to *Jig's Up.* "Just too wobbly."

Jill gestured for Donna to enter the pilothouse

"My store has a nautical theme, but I don't like boats." Donna slid into the galley bench.

Jill put a dinner plate in the cupboard and wiped her hands on a kitchen towel. "We're tied securely to the dock. No worries about rough seas. Have a seat. Tea?"

"No, thanks. I'm not really here for a social visit. Ray asked me to come."

"Oh? He took Eileen to White Sands this afternoon, right?"

"Yes. He asked me to tell you he'd pay you back and to thank you."

Jill hitched a shoulder, as she broke apart inside. "It had to be done."

"We watched over Eileen in the hospital for three days, praying she wouldn't hurt herself again. White Sands is her best hope."

"I agree."

"Ray has a repayment plan."

"Oh?"

"He won't let you sell the boat. His words."

"But—"

"This is hard enough already. Let me finish with the direct quotes, okay?"

Jill clamped her mouth shut and nodded.

"He's gone to White Sands with Eileen to formally check her in. Then, when they tell him it's time, he'll leave, using his freed-up days to get the money and the boat back for you. He quoted, 'we should not suffer for the sins of our fathers'."

Jill frowned. "After paying for Parrish's funeral, doctor bills, mortgage payments, and Sasha's salary, does Eileen have any money left?"

"I asked the same question. Ray might try to sell the house to pay you off and keep Eileen at White Sands. I have no idea how long she'll need to stay there. Four months? Six?"

"So he'll stay in Eileen's house, not on *Jig's Up.* He knows I hired Daryl to finish out the season." She eyed the second cabin. "Thank God he's sleeping on his own boat."

"Ray wasn't happy about Daryl joining you," Donna offered. "He says he doesn't trust him."

Jill shot her a look. "Slim pickings for Ray's replacement. I had to talk Daryl into finishing out the season with me. Tell Ray I'm interviewing for a new position in Seattle the first of next month. If he understands I'm moving on, he might give up on selling Eileen's home. She needs a place to live after she leaves White Sands."

Donna sat quietly, seemingly lost in thought.

Jill said, "It's best this way for Eileen, Ray, and you."

Donna gave a slow nod. "Eileen, yes. Ray and me? I'm not so sure."

"Once Eileen is well again, Ray can return full time to his career in law enforcement. Seems simple to me, if he can find an opening." Jill focused on a seagull on the dock. "I'm sure he'd like a second chance with you, Donna."

Donna leaned back on the bench and sighed. "I wouldn't mind." She cleared her throat. "We'll see." She pushed strands of hair behind her ears, revealing eyes glistening with tears. "When I tell him Daryl's on your crew and you've got job interviews set up, I can predict the expression on his face. I watched him carefully when he found out you sold the boat to help Eileen. Anger, anguish, desperation. Unguarded. I'll see it again. Deep, palpable emotions." She took a breath. "I never saw such remorse in his eyes or heard it in his voice when it was about me, even when I told him I wouldn't see him anymore. He was disappointed, sure, but the despair was missing."

Jill couldn't think of a thing to say. Desperation? Despair? Over *her*?

Donna pulled in a breath. "Those same emotions ran across your face just now."

She dropped her head, suddenly too tired to hold it up. "Thanks for all you've done to help Eileen. And Ray."

"The third thing Ray wanted me to tell you..."

"Right."

"Where's Jim?" Donna asked, scanning the immediate area.

"I don't know, he's not on the boat. What about him?"

"A warning from me...and Ray." Donna pursed her lips, her face flushing. "Jim Livingston played me."

"I don't understand."

Donna rubbed her eyes. "Everyone knows he's renting the room in the store, but they're unaware of our romantic relationship." She cleared her throat. "I got drawn in."

"Why is that a problem? You have a right to—"

Donna put up a hand. "He used me to gather information about you."

"What?"

"He stopped coming to my house the day before Eileen attempted suicide. Wouldn't return my calls and I haven't seen him for four days while Ray and I sat with Eileen. I had time to think about my conversations with Jim. He wanted to hear about the way things worked in Port McNeill, but his favorite topic was you."

Jill frowned. "That's odd."

"I agree."

"Ray knows?"

"He does now. I apologized to Ray, and now to you. Ray believes Jim and Daryl are both sketchy. He urged me to help you find a reason for Jim's subterfuge." Donna shivered. "Jim used me and I'm not proud of it."

Jill pushed her fingers through her hair. "Damn humans. I swear, all I want is to take *Jig's Up* and my drone out to sea and never tie up to a dock again."

Slipping off the bench, Donna stood. "Ray's worried about you, Jill, but Eileen has to be his focus."

Nodding numbly as she watched Donna climb off the boat, Jill's heart cracked in two. She'd thought helping Eileen, Ray, and maybe even Donna, would finally bring order to her world, but she was sure she'd never been more disorganized in her life.

***

Why did success feel like failure?

Jill sat at the table late at night with a mug of tea in her hand, staring at the calendar. Only three days in the last seven weeks were circled in red. *Jig's Up* had come home with bulging traps nineteen out of twenty-two days. Daryl called it a record.

Daryl. *Can I stand a few more days with the man?* She'd never dreamed living with Daryl would the hardest part of her scheme.

The easy part was talking Jack Canter into buying *Jig's Up*, the boat *and* a license, a rare commodity in B.C. When Jack understood she planned to finish out the season and cut him in on part of the profits, he'd pulled together the $40,000 Jill had asked for up front, and wired it to her as soon as they'd agreed on a price and signed a promissory note. Jack was working out the financing with his bank while Jill made money for Jack as his employee.

After she'd made the proposal to Jack, he said, "Much as I've always wanted to own *Jig's Up,* are you sure this is what you want to do, Jillian? And Al? Will he be upset you sold the boat?"

"He was shocked I was thinking about *keeping* it. He said the money from the boat was to free me up so I could design my future. And that's what I'm doing."

"You're sure Al would lose the suit?"

"More to the point, Al promised the trawler is mine, to do with what I wish. Actually, selling to you may help him in court."

"How's that?"

"This way, the boat no longer belongs to a family member. The courts won't accuse me of 'holding' *Jig's Up* for him until he gets out of jail. It's no longer a family asset, and I can prove the money I received from the sale went to a needy person, not to my bank account."

"Your word is good with me." He paused. "You still have your partner, Ray?"

"He's not with me anymore. I hired another guy to finish out the week."

"Sure he can handle the job?"

"I guarantee it. This crew will bring a fine finish to the season."

She'd been right about one thing. Daryl knew how to prawn. He was experienced, strong, and quick, a perfect teammate with Jim. They cut a good hour off their time at sea each day, returning with full traps far ahead of the rest of the fleet. The problem? With some long evenings stretching before them, it was Daryl's idea Jill would spend them with him. After off-loading the shrimp, Jill would ease *Jig's Up* into her moorage at Port McNeill. Soon as she turned off the diesel engine, Jim would disappear, without so much as an 'Adios.' Three seconds after Jim's departure, Daryl would begin spouting 'plans' for the evening.

On the third night, Daryl started down a darker road. Freshly showered, he stood at the bottom of the cabin steps looking up at Jill, wearing a towel and a grin. "Wanna go get a hamburger or stay in?"

Jill was sitting with her wounded leg propped on the bench, resting it, wishing it would stop aching. They'd put in a full day, and not for anything would she show weakness to her new crew, so she wore jeans to cover the injury, even if the day was hot enough for shorts. When Daryl began speaking, she quickly lowered her leg to the floor and said, "You do what you want to." With a screwdriver, she pointed to the guts of a switch laid out on the table. "I'm going to fix this and decide about dinner later."

Daryl climbed the stairs and crossed the room to stand close to her, his toweled body inches from her arm, an offensive earthy cologne nearly making her gag. Catching the smoldering look in his eyes, she slid over a bit so he couldn't touch her. "What?" Jill said, letting irritation color her tone.

"For the last few days, you've been dancing away from me like I'm contagious." He put one foot on the edge of the bench, so his towel parted.

She focused on his eyes and set the toggle switch aside. "I wanted a partner who could fish, Daryl. I needed the best and I was lucky to hire you."

"Really? You came prancing over to my boat, crooked your finger like act one of a seduction, and convinced me to finish up the season with you. Why wouldn't I expect more in payback than shrimp?"

"Not my fault you got that impression," she said, her fingers loose around the screwdriver. "If you were seduced by anything, it was the prospect of doubling your income."

"The hell I was." He put a knee on the bench, leaned in next to her and sneered. "Women don't play me."

Her grip on the screwdriver tightened. "You confused persuasion with a come-on, Daryl. Not my problem. I promised to double your money by partnering with me. Threaten me, and I will throw you off this boat, leaving you short $15,000," she said evenly, her eyes locked on his. "Is that what you want?"

He stared at her long and hard, cinched the towel around his waist and resumed standing next to the table.

"A few more days with the ice queen for fifteen grand?" He pulled a nasty grin and dropped his hand to his crotch. "I guess I can handle it."

She worked hard to keep her face empty of emotion. "And from now on, shower and nap on your own boat when we're tied at the dock, please."

Once he had dressed, tromped up the stairs, and turned to exit by the starboard door, she let out the breath she was holding, discomforted by prickles on her neck and her arms. The boat swayed when Daryl hopped off the boat, and she heard him stomping up the gangway. So childish. So different from Ray.

She remembered Ray's gentleness, his kindnesses. Lying in bed with her while she shook off a drugging. Holding her tightly after she was attacked in Port McNeill.

She put her head in her hands and groaned.

I miss Ray.

***

Go home, Ray.

He sat in the marina parking lot with the car running, the simple task of opening the car door beyond his capability at the moment.

He was desperate to see Jill, yet he wanted to avoid her at all costs.

After overseeing Eileen's intake at White Sands and hours of one-on-one discussion with Eileen's new psychiatrist, Ray was exhausted. As much as he wanted to go home and sleep, the long drive from Victoria had ended at the marina.

He needed to get out of the car. Talk to her. Thank her for Eileen's two-month stay in White Sands. Stop Jigs from selling the boat.

Most of all, see if Jigs was okay. A week had passed since he'd seen her and the season was winding down. Had her leg wound healed? Was Daryl giving her trouble? Were they catching shrimp?

He hoped Daryl wasn't around. Or Jim.

I can't think straight until I talk to her.

He stood on the dock watching as she washed windows on the port side of the boat, fiercely concentrating. She wore a loose tee shirt over long pants, but he could see the bulge of a bandage around her calf. Did that mean the injury from the trap banging her leg was still a problem?

When she turned to look down on him, his heart stopped.

"Hey, Ray."

"Jigs. How are you?"

"Good. You? Eileen?" She turned the squeegee in her hand and wiped it off with a rag.

"She's settled in, thanks to you."

"Do you like the place? Will they help her?"

Ray nodded. "Unbelievable. So professional. It's taken me two days to get everything done...debrief with doctors and tell our life story." He leaned against a piling and squinted up at her. "That part was hard."

Jill sat on the bow bench, peering at him through the railings.

He closed his eyes, as the memory of Jigs sitting close to him on that very bench on a warm moonlit night punched into his heart.

"Ray?"

"Sorry. Long drive from Victoria. I'm on my way to the house. Thought I'd stop by and thank you." He straightened. "And tell you to stop the whole process of selling the boat. Now."

She rose and put a hand on her hip, the squeegee and rag still hanging from her little finger. "It's done, Ray. Get used to the idea."

He raked his hands through his hair. "You can't sell her."

"You always said I was playing at this." She waved her hand to include the boat and the marina. "You're right. I'm going back to a tech job where I belong. Al would have lost the civil suit, anyway. I read up on fraudulent conveyance and studied some precedent-setting cases. Figured I'd save you, Al, and me a whole lot of time and lawyer's fees. Jack is prepared to send the rest of the boat money to you." She pulled the brim of her hat down so he couldn't see her eyes at the same time Daryl emerged from the pilothouse door and sauntered to Jill's side.

Daryl nodded. "Ray."

"Daryl."

The man put his arm around Jill's shoulder and pulled a grin. "Wish you'd told me what a great partner Jill was. Now I understand what attracts the shrimp *and* the men to this boat."

Jill jabbed him with her elbow and scooted away. "Only a few days left in the season. Glad to see it end."

"I'll be on my way, then," Ray said, needing to leave before he did something stupid. "Greg's hired me back on as security here at the marina, so you'll see me around."

She nodded.

He started to turn away, then swiveled back. "Jigs, about the boat?"

"Let it go, Ray. Take the money. Let's move on. Good luck to you, Eileen, and Donna."

Ray wanted to ask about her leg and find out if Daryl was more than a nuisance. But both questions were too personal, and Jill had made it clear the conversation was over. "Thanks. You, too." He walked slowly up the dock, willing himself not to look back. But before he turned to go up the gangway, he stole an over-the-shoulder glance.

Jill sat on the bench, her head in her hands, and Daryl was nowhere to be seen.

21

She'd wakened with a headache and it worried her, reminding her of the brain-pain she'd suffered all through her years with Baldur. Her mother had labeled them symptoms of depression, because Al had suffered from headaches, too. Migraines, Jill had been told by her doctors. A lifelong burden.

Yet, for weeks, on the boat, she'd been pain-free.

Why had the throbbing returned? Maybe a little vacation from dock life was in order.

Once she'd offloaded the shrimp with Jim and Daryl, Jim pulled her aside. "Why don't we take *Jig's Up* to Waka Bay for an overnight?"

She put a cool hand to her pulsing forehead. "That's a good idea. I have to take measurements and go over the hydro plant drawings with the Hudsons. Most important, I'm bidding on a machine on E-Bay. I'll need to find out if the Hudsons can afford it."

"And you'll send Mae C up to reconnoiter?" Jim paused, watching Jill wipe a napkin across her sweaty forehead. "Unless you don't feel well enough to go."

When Oceans Rage

Her excitement about the project took over, and as was her habit, she pushed through the headache. "Ah, it's just a migraine. I'll take a couple pain pills and be fine. Jill put her hands on her hips and reviewed the trip to Waka. "Maybe I will put Mae C up in the air today and map the mountain like I promised Samuel.

Daryl left the boat without a word. "Good riddance," she muttered, pleased to see his overnight bag in hand. "Won't have to see his scowling face until morning."

"I say we head out now," Jim said, rubbing his hands together.

His eagerness surprised her. "Really? I was thinking of taking a nap first. Try to get rid of this headache."

He shrugged. "We better go now, while it's light. Might even be bright enough when we get there to send up the drone."

Jill hesitated, remembering Ray and Donna's warning about Jim. The man was self-righteous, for sure, confident and controlling, too, but she'd never seen a malicious side to him. Plus, she needed him for this trip to Waka Bay. Sometimes her headaches made it hard for her to see, especially on a foggy evening.

Her energy spiked at the thought of a restful night at the Waka dock. "I'm ready. Let's go."

Jim ran a hand over his shaved head and smoothed his mustache. Was he nervous? Maybe Jim was aware of Donna criticizing him. In all the weeks she'd worked with Jim Livingston, she'd learned very little about the man. Ray and Daryl were dominating personalities, each in their own way. Jim's quietude, in contrast, made him easy to ignore. And he worked hard for a know-it-all type, so he was a good asset to the team.

Jim rubbed his hands together again. "Tell you what. Just to prove you can single-hand *Jig's Up*, remove lines as if you're alone, and handle all helm duty. Just pretend I'm not here. Of course, I'll step in if you need me."

"Fine." Jill clicked on the weather report. "Some wind out in Queen Charlotte Strait. Could get eight footers before we make the turn to calmer waters. Still game?"

"Piece of cake. I've got a call to make, so I'll step out on the aft deck. Start her up and prep the lines."

Jill loosened the lines, noting Jim's tight expression as he spoke on the phone, but the roar of the engine covered his words. Once he'd stuffed the phone in his pocket, she opened the pilothouse door and yelled out to him. "Ready?"

"Roger."

Jill eased *Jig's Up* from her moorage. In reverse, she had to goose the engine because the wind was determined to hold her on the dock. Once she'd cruised free of the harbor, Jim entered the pilothouse, his expression grim as he pointed to the weather report.

Her headache came back, full force, pounding in time with the pulsing in her leg. In the back of her fuzzed-up mind, the notion that Jim had persuaded her to go to Waka Bay, feathered so lightly through her subconscious, she couldn't grasp the warning.

***

The waves hit *Jig's Up* broadside as soon as she reached the point Queen Charlotte Strait met Johnstone Strait, the ocean raging south from the former, north from the latter.

The havoc of wind against current.

"Shit." Jim yelled over the sound of waves crashing on the pilothouse windows. "We're going to have to cruise north so we can take these seas at forty-five degrees."

"Agreed," Jill said cranking on the wheel, her adrenaline spiking. "We head for the east part of Malcolm Island and make a 'u' turn when we can."

Jim pitched to the left and grabbed an overhead handhold to keep from falling. Jill came off her chair, taking a standing position in front of the wheel for more stable maneuvering.

When a wall of green water came at them, Jim helped Jill wrench the wheel to the right. Still, the wave slapped them down with such ferocity the hull pounded on the sea. The boat groaned and creaked, rocking so hard that Al's stash of bungee cords fell out of their cubby-hole and Jill's tea mug crashed to the floor, broke, and splashed liquid everywhere. Jill wondered about the damage done by the murderous wave to her equipment on the stern, but had no time to look behind her because the next wave hit like a battering ram. How many more shots could *Jig's Up* take? One look at Jim's calm features answered her question. "We're on a roller coaster," she said, trying to erase the panic from her voice. "Can't use autopilot in this stuff so I'll be worn out at the wheel by the time we get to Waka. Should we turn around and return to Port McNeill?"

"Look at the radar. Weather's deteriorating behind us. Can't go back."

He was right. But radar showed better weather up Tribune. "You told me seas like these were common out on the Pacific. Are we in trouble?" Nausea had her swallowing hard, her headache and leg wound pulsing in time with the throbbing engine.

No response from Jim.

"Brother," Jill winced as she fought with the wheel to keep the rudder on course. "I've got a lot to learn." She reached over, unhooked the flashlight from its cradle and tucked it in her pocket. "I might have to go down in the holy place. Let's hope seawater doesn't leech into the bilge."

Jim squinted to the north. What he saw must have pleased him, because a tight smile came next. "Get ready for the 'u' turn, Jill. After the next wave, we'll take a hard right and resume smooth sailing."

Once again, *Jig's Up* bucked and bounced as she cut through a ten-footer and pushed east, then northeast, and finally, south.

The quietude was astonishing, the three-foot waves feeling gentle after chaotic seas. The pain in her leg banged away, but she was so relieved she pivoted to congratulate Jim.

Her eyes met the barrel of his gun.

"Jim?" she said, her heart taking up a frantic fibrillation. "What's this?"

"You're done, Jill Morrell. Your season is over. In fact, your life as sea captain is finished." He reached to click on the autopilot, preset to guide them to Waka Bay, more than an hour away.

"What's going on? Why are you holding a gun on me?"

"Keys," he said, wiggling his fingers. "Give 'em to me, now."

"What keys?"

"Mae C's. For all those sophisticated locks you put on your fucking drone. God, I'm sick of looking for all your keys and codes."

"You want Mae C?"

"I don't want your stupid drone, but Lynda Flynn does."

"Lynda? You and Lynda are...?"

"Temporary cohorts. If she hadn't paid me good money, I would have given up this asinine job months ago. What you and Ray have put me through. Shit, on a normal shrimping job, I could get four times the money Lynda promised me."

"You want Mae C?"

"Didn't you hear me? The woman wants your fucking drone. For some reason she thinks the technology you've installed on Mae C is stuff she can use in her work with the Chinese."

A shock of pain ran through her leg, and Jill inadvertently stumbled toward Jim, who stiff-armed her away. "Stay back and get me the keys and the codes. Now."

"But Jim—" She grasped the whale charm, closed her eyes for a moment to stop her swaying, and pulled in air. "If I give you Mae C, I'm a dead woman."

"Smart gal. No techie tricks will save you from a gunshot to the head."

"They'll find my body. Connect you to the crime."

"The ocean critters will get to you first. Fact is, I don't think anyone knows for sure I went out with you today because I made you do all the line work and witnesses only saw you at the helm when you cruised out of the marina. I stayed out of sight the whole time. Even if they did reckon I was aboard, I'm taking the dinghy and your drone someplace no one can find us. I'll get my money from Lynda and leave the country."

Jill's mind was swimming. "You cut the hydraulic hose."

"Yup."

"You called in the mayday."

"Affirmative."

"You mugged me in the parking lot."

He frowned. "Nope."

"Okay, then. You were the fake diver."

"You see why I deserve four times what Lynda's payin' me."

"But—"

"*Jesus,* Lady. I'm tired of holding the gun. Fuck. I'm *really* tired of you and Ray and stupid Daryl. Goodbye."

At the same time the gun 'clicked' and no shot followed, Jill stepped toward Jim's outstretched arm, cracked down on his forearm in a double hit from her own forearms, then pulled his gun arm against her hip, hauling him toward her while bringing up her right knee. He screamed as she connected, dropping the gun before he fell to the floor, grabbing his crotch.

Whipping out her flashlight, Jill released the safety and tasered him. With a low groan, he stilled. She grabbed a fistful of bungee cords and set to work, wrapping and hooking cords on his wrists and ankles, and then attaching an extra-long one from the ankle bungees to his wrists. She slid her trussed-up turkey to the head of the stairs and pushed him below.

Jill approached the helm breathing hard, adrenaline waning, set to call the Coast Guard, when a white hot dagger of pain from her left leg snaked into her brain.

The VHF in hand, she collapsed to the floor.

***

Ray was waiting for the blender to mash ice into margarita slush when Daryl entered the bar with a woman, his arm slung around her shoulders. He squinted into the darkness of the dimly lit bar as the couple ambled to a corner table where the woman removed her baseball cap to reveal short blond hair. Not Jigs. Some of the tension left his shoulders as he turned to pour four drinks.

When Oceans Rage

"Hey, barkeep. How about a double bourbon on ice for me and a Molson for my little lady?"

Damn. "Coming right up."

Daryl leaned on the bar, his eyes already glazed by too much booze. "I figured it out, Ray."

"What's that?"

"Why you never nailed Jill. And why you couldn't claim the pool."

Ray wanted to slug him. "Here's your bourbon."

Daryl grinned. "Bitch is frigid." He leaned over like a confidante. "You coulda told me. Warned me, at least."

Ray's hand trembled as he set the beer next to the bourbon, took Daryl's money and gave him change. "*Jig's Up* in port tonight? I didn't see it earlier."

"She went to Waka Bay. Fucking *hydro* plant."

A new worry shot through Ray's veins. "Jim went with her?"

"Hell if I know. Or care." He drew up to his full height, drinks in hand. "Woman doesn't need a man. You or me. She's got some kinda bug, but she insisted on going anyway. Only thing she's good at screwing is herself." He laughed like a maniac, shaking his drinks until they spilled. "Shit!" He stopped laughing and steadied himself. "He carries, you know."

"Who?" Ray asked sharply.

"Jim. Keeps a gun in his bag."

"He showed it to you?"

"Hell, no. I searched his backpack and saw it." Daryl scoffed. "Gotta know who I'm crewin' with."

Ray struggled to keep his voice calm and his fists to his side. "You said Jill's not feeling well?"

Daryl took a swallow of his bourbon. "PMS, I figure. Kinda dizzy and pissy." He shrugged as if all women acted this peculiar way. "See ya, buddy," he said and walked back to his date.

Ray picked up the phone, called Greg Hanley at the marina and asked him to make a VHF check with Camryn and Dennis to see if Jill had shown up in Waka Bay. He held the phone and listened as Greg made contact. Dennis answered. "She's not here. She said she was on her way. Should have arrived an hour ago. The wind whipped up in the strait, so we figured she'd be a little late. But not this overdue."

Ray dropped the phone and ripped off his apron, beckoning to the waitress. "Call Pete," he said, as he grabbed his coat. "I've got a feeling I won't be back tonight. If I haven't returned in fifteen minutes, tell him to come in. And tell him I'm sorry. It's an emergency."

He ran, covering the distance from the restaurant to the marina office in less than ten minutes. Cursing at the boat's vacant spot, he rushed into the marina office and with a nod from Greg, picked up the VHF.

"*Jig's Up, Jig's Up, Jig's Up,* this is Ray Stewart. Answer me, Jigs.*"*

On his third try, Jigs' voice came back weakly, "Ray? This is *Jig's Up.* Over."

"Switch from channel one-six to six-eight."

Silence.

On six-eight, Ray tried again. "*Jig's Up?* Hey, Jigs. It's Ray. Where are you, baby? Camryn and Dennis are worried."

"Ray? I'm not feeling so good. I...I can't stand up."

He heard the vulnerability in her voice and sucked in his breath. "Jigs, I'm coming to get you. Where are you?"

"Hanging on to the wheel." She was quiet for a moment. "Location? I don't know. I can't stop shivering."

She sounded ready to cry. He tried not to think of her draped over the helm in order to stay upright.

"It's raining, Ray. So cold. You come, okay?"

"Can you send Mae C to me so I can check her coordinates and find you?"

She didn't answer.

"Send her to me and we'll make you warm again, baby. She's already programmed to land at the marina, Jigs. Start her up, open the door and let her fly away. I'll catch her. I promise."

"I don't know, Ray. Jim. He's down there. He's..."

Ray gripped the handheld, fear crowding out all sense of reason. "Jim's there? He went with you to Waka?"

Silence.

"Jigs, where is Jim?"

A little giggle, then, "Asleep. With Mae C. He likes her. Wants her."

Greg shook his head and whispered, "She's delirious."

"Jigs. This is Ray. Send me Mae C, honey. Right now."

Silence.

"Jigs. Touch your necklace, babe. Get some energy and send Mae C to me. The whale will bring you home, remember?"

Minutes later, still silence.

Ray called the Coast Guard to report the mayday, borrowed Greg's extra handheld VHF, and snagged a coil of line from the office. He put on waterproof overalls and a jacket, stepped into rain boots, snugged goggles over his eyes, and pulled his hood tight around his face. "Keys for your tender?" He caught them in mid-air and hollered into the VHF as he ran down the gangway. "I'm waiting for Mae C, Jigs. Send her to me. Stay in idle unless you drift to land. Stay away from the land, Jigs. Do you hear me?"

He heard her breathe, so she must have pushed the answer button down. "Stay away from land. Stay away from land." She said it like a child repeating what a teacher told her to say. "Mae C and the whale will take me home."

In the tender, Ray and Greg buzzed over to the finger where *Jig's Up* docked, searching the gray skies for Mae C. Ray had told the Coast Guard where he thought *Jig's Up* might be, but if no one was steering *Jig's Up,* the boat could have drifted off course. The Coast Guard promised to send up a helicopter, but the chopper was a half hour away and visibility was poor. More than anything, Ray wanted to strike out in Greg's boat to look for *Jig's Up,* but such a move was foolhardy without some idea of the trawler's location.

So, with Greg, he looked to the sky for a drone.

And looked.

And looked until his neck ached.

The sound came first. A mosquito's buzz. The whirr of baby helicopters. Like a flurry of incessant insects. His heart soared as Mae C slowly descended to the dock, a graceful yet deliberate maneuver, one Ray had seen her undertake several times over the last two months. She shut herself off and sat expectantly, as if waiting for her next order.

Greg said, "Will you send her back?"

"Too chancy if Jill isn't alert to receive her. If the boat has drifted, Mae C might land on the sea. Truth is, Jill may not have programmed a return. Still I can read the lift-off coordinates on Mae C's instrument." Ray recited the longitude and latitude to Greg. "You take the drone to the marina office, call the Coast Guard with the coordinates, and I'll go get Jill."

"Let me come with you," Greg said.

"No." he said, clipping on a safety vest and stepping into the runabout. "I need you here to coordinate the search with the Coast Guard. You're our lifeline, Greg. Stay on the VHF. I'll take the handheld with me."

Greg picked up Mae C and headed back to the office.

Once free of the marina's protected waters, Ray's tender bucked two-foot chop, careening up one side of each wave and pounding to the bottom. With no canopy to shield him, he was blinded by pelting rain. Gritting his teeth, he settled in for a boat ride not meant to be comfortable at full-out speeds in rough waters.

He calculated current and wind conditions. Looking at the telltale water line on shore, he figured they were close to the end of a flood tide. Good. More water over the rocks and less current to fool with. He opened up the thirty-horsepower motor as far as it could go and bounced crazily toward Broughton Island, the apex of the longitude and latitude on Mae C's display.

He lurched through nasty chop for thirty minutes to reach the eastern point of Malcom and another hour to reach Jig's coordinates, the GPS calmly planning his route while the tender and Ray's heart raced full throttle.

Every five minutes, he'd yell into the VHF: "Jigs, talk to me. Stay away from land, baby. Idle out in open sea where it's safe."

Static from the handheld and crashing seas were the only sounds he heard in response while he pushed past Nickless Islet on his way to Raleigh Passage.

He buzzed around the southern tip of Broughton Island to Notice Point holding his breath. If Mae C's location numbers were right, *Jig's Up* should be sitting next to Bermingham Island.

And there she was, rocking crazily side to side in the deep furrow of a wave. When he saw how close she was to the island his heart sank. *She'll hit rock any minute.* "Reverse, Jigs. Reverse!" Ray yelled into the VHF. But he saw no one at the helm. He pushed the call button again. "Jigs, come out and take my line, now. Jill, do you hear me? Over."

No answer.

He yelled into the VHF. "Jigs, come out and throw me a line."

No answer. *Did she fall overboard? Pass out?*

He pulled up close and sat in idle behind *Jig's Up's* swim step as the current edged his little rig and the big boat toward Bermingham's rocky shore. In minutes, *Jig's Up* would be aground.

Ray goosed the tender engine to the narrow platform, where chop soaked the surface. Slick. Tricky footing.

Bang! The tender crashed into the swim step and knocked Ray out of his seat.

Try again.

Rev the engine, nose in until the starboard side of the tender was even with the platform, grab the tender line and jump.

He rose from the helm chair, line in his left hand, ready to grab the platform's edge with his right.

Bam! The tender crawled up the platform and bounced back off it, almost dumping Ray into the water.

He made another circle around *Jig's Up*, vowing to time the rise and fall more carefully. How the hell was he supposed to grab ahold of a rocking fifty-thousand pound boat? He had to be crazy.

One. More. Time.

Gun the engine, edge up, left hand holding tender line, leap, and grasp with the right hand.

He sidled closer, counting the feet he had between his boat and *Jig's Up*. Ten, eight, four, two! He grabbed the slippery swim step. Nothing to hang on to! He let go of the wheel and used both hands to search. His index finger located a large eyebolt welded under the swim step. He held onto the eyebolt, his arm nearly popping out of its socket with each jerk of the boat. Grasping the edge of the swim step with his left hand, he pushed the end of the tender's line into the eyebolt with his right hand, pulled the rope all the way through and tied down the tender.

Now to jump from one pitching boat to the other. He pulled the side of his boat to the swim step, stood up carefully, and hopped, his feet slipping so wildly on the swim step he almost missed grabbing the boat's rail-cap.

Got it! He held on tightly, sucking in air. Now what? No door into the stern. Only a couple of holes, hawseholes, for bringing through lines. He'd use them as footholds. Hoisting his right foot up to one hawsehole, he pushed off enough to get his left foot over the ridgecap. Straddled there on the bucking boat, he looked at the looming landmass of Bermingham Island.

I've got to get us out of here, fast.

He scrambled up to the pilothouse door and entered. Jigs lay on the floor next to the helm, her eyes closed and her body shaking, both hands at her chest, enfolding the whale charm.

Buzzing from the depth sounder alarm warned of shallow water. Remembering Jack Canter's story of how *Jig's Up* had saved his life, Ray eased the boat into reverse, monitoring the tender's movement to the side of the trawler. As soon as he was sure they wouldn't back into the little boat, he raised the rpms. He prayed they weren't close enough to land for the prop to hit rocks as they reversed. He tracked the depths aloud: "Come on, baby. Six feet. Please. Five feet? Oh, No!" He waited to hear the crunch of propeller on rock. "Give me more, give me more. Eight feet? Thank you. Ten feet! Yay! Jigs, we're out of trouble!"

He breathed a sigh of relief once he had the boat back into safe waters. He shifted into idle and leaned over to tend to Jigs, laying a hand on her forehead. "You're burning up."

A gun lay on the floor next to the helm, Jill's flashlight next to it. *What the hell?* Belowdecks Jim was oddly festive-looking with colorful bungee cords winding around his arms and ankles, but the man wasn't happy judging from his non-stop cussing. Jigs took him down. She'd won.

Ray grabbed the VHF from the console poised to call the Coast Guard when their inflatable pulled up on his port side. Good for Greg. Mae C's coordinates worked. He put a pillow under Jig's head, wiped her sweat-drenched face with a dishtowel and strode out to help the Coast Guard tie their boat next to *Jig's Up*.

Two of the orange-clad men jumped aboard, following Ray to the pilothouse. While a Coast Guard medic tended to Jigs, Ray gave out the important information requested by the other, including what Ray had surmised about Jim Livingston's condition. "The gun belongs to Jim

Livingston. I know for a fact the stunner is Jill Morrell's. Since she tied him up, we should consider him dangerous." All the while, Ray watched the medic work, his heart torn in two by the agony on Jig's face.

"What's your assessment? Did he hit her? Is she bleeding internally?"

"With a raging fever like this, I'd say she has an infection."

"On her calf. She's got a bandage there." He pointed to Jig's left leg."

"I'll check it out and let the doctor know where you think the infection is. We have to rush her to the hospital in Port McNeill. Let's lower her to our vessel." With astonishing speed and efficiency, they tugged warm clothing onto Jill, along with a life preserver, and in minutes had her lying in the bottom of the inflatable, prepped for a fast ride to the hospital. They asked Ray if he could bring *Jig's Up* in by himself. Ray nodded. "I'll come to the hospital after I dock the boat. You take good care of my girl, you hear?"

"Yes, sir. It's what we do. Good job getting on the trawler, sir." He glanced at the swim step where the tender bobbed crazily over the waves, and raised an eyebrow at Ray. "I can see it was a challenge."

"It was," he said, feeling woozy as the adrenaline seeped out of his body.

"You okay, sir? Can you bring in the man she tied up?"

Ray nodded. "He's not going anywhere. Have the RCMP ready to arrest him when I dock in Port McNeill. You go. Make sure a doctor tends to her right away."

"I will, sir. You be careful going back."

He went out with the officer, waited for the man to scramble overboard, then released their line. They jetted away at an incredible speed, hydroplaning over the tops of two-foot waves. Three orange-clad men in their orange boat carrying his precious Jigs to safety.

***

Ray was so focused on getting to Jigs that when he jogged through the front entrance of the Port McNeill hospital hours later he wasn't prepared for the sharp pain of déjà vu to hit him. Only days ago he'd felt the same desperation coming to see Eileen in the hospital, lying wounded by her own hand. He took a quick breath, striving for calm, invoking the pleasant surroundings of White Sands where Eileen was healing under the watchful eyes of competent doctors. Jigs would get well, too. He'd make sure.

Outside her door, he breathed deeply and squared his shoulders. She'd be sitting up, all piss and vinegar, mad at Jim. Buoyed by the thought, he pushed open the door, smiling.

He felt the blood drain out of his face when he saw her looking frail in a sea of white. Deadly still. His heart clenched as he lowered himself slowly into a chair and reached for her hand. When he felt warmth there, he groaned in relief. Her fingers closed around his and she opened her eyes.

"Hey, baby. Feeling better?"

"Some. You?"

"You brought a little excitement to my day. Good thing because I was bored."

"Boat okay?"

"Not a scratch. Let's talk about you. What's the verdict?"

"Infection. Left leg. Trap...banged me." The effort of speaking seemed to exhaust her. "Right leg...feels bad, too. Kneed Jim. Both...still there?"

"Oh, yeah." He sensed it wasn't a good enough answer for her in her fevered state. "Here. You tell me what you feel." He rubbed her right leg from foot to thigh.

She gave him a weak smile. "Right leg? Mine?"

"Intact."

He did the same for each limb, careful with the left calf, where a bandage covered her wound.

"All there, trust me. You want me to stay awhile and make sure your legs and arms stay put?"

Jigs opened her eyes, managing a sheepish grin. "Please?"

He pulled up a chair, held on to her hand and watched while she slept.

Around midnight her fever broke, helped by the antibiotics. The doctors advised another night in the hospital to make sure the leg's swelling subsided. She wouldn't be walking for another three days or so after that, they explained.

"I'll come by in the morning." He patted her hand.

Jigs grabbed his fingers and pulled her head up off the pillow, eyes wide. "The Pelton on E-bay. I lost it."

He smiled. "Oh, no, you didn't. You told me all about the problem while you were burning up with fever last night."

"I did?"

"Yeah. When you're delirious, you don't talk about people, you babble about machines."

"And so?"

He laughed. "Not to worry. I talked to Camryn and Dennis before I put in a bid. I'll check on our progress when I get home tonight, eh?"

Her smile of thanks shifted to a grimace. "Ray, what about—?"

"I'll finish the shrimping season with Daryl. The government extended the season a couple days, so we want to hang in there. Why don't you stay at my house until you're on your feet again."

She nodded and sighed, clearly relieved.

She seems so fragile, mortal. Not the Jigs I know.

He leaned down and feathered a soft kiss across her blessedly cool forehead.

"G'night, Jigs," He said gently. "I've got things under control. Sleep, now."

22

"Cellulitis," the doctor said. "You'll get over the infection because we found the right antibiotic, but we won't know for some time if your kidneys have been damaged."

"Really? Both of them?"

He held up his fingers to show her a quarter of an inch. "Very close to failure. They got you here just in time."

"You're kidding. You mean if Ray hadn't come looking for me..."

"Consider yourself very lucky." He drew a frown. "But not unless you stay off your feet for three days after I check you out of here."

Her expression was crestfallen. "But I'm a prawner."

"And that's what got you into this situation. The shrimp will be there next season." He turned to go out the door, hesitated, then glanced back. "Jillian, you need to recover on dry land where you can run a wheelchair. No standing or walking, no stairs, no climbing. Ergo, no boat."

She closed her eyes. "You and Ray, couple of mother hens." She wished him gone, but when she peeked out of one eye, there he was, still standing at the door, a picture of sternness. "I repeat. No boat. And stay in town so we can check your kidney function regularly."

As she settled back in bed, feeling bored and restless, her leg throbbed. She knew she could ask for a pain pill, but for now, the ache coupled nicely with her irritation at needing to depend on others.

Ray sent a message through her nurse he was out prawning. She wondered if Daryl was his partner. If he was, one of them would throw the other overboard before the day was out. She chuckled at the thought. So she wouldn't see Ray until late afternoon. Her mother would be flying into the room soon, and she'd want to take Jill back to La Conner to recover. When Jill explained she'd have to stay put for three or four days, her mom would want to remain with Jill until she could travel.

"I need a plan to get all three mother hens out of my hair."

By the time Rose bustled through the door at noon, Jill had developed a strategy for staying in town, but not with Ray. Since the pain pill she'd finally asked for had dulled the pounding in her leg, she was beginning to feel human again.

When Rose arrived and hugged her fiercely, Jill teared up, enjoying the comfort of her mother's arms around her way too much. It had to be the drugs, starting way back with the damn mushrooms. Since then, she'd become so uncharacteristically sentimental.

When she'd gained control over her emotions, Jill held her mother at arm's length, taking in her pretty, carefully made-up face framed by highlighted brown hair, shoulder-length. Silk white blouse and tailored black pants set off with black pumps. Jewelry dangled from ears, neck, and arms. And she smelled faintly of Chanel. A put-together mother with a slap-dash daughter. How had that happened?

Her mother smoothed Jill's hair, a cue to tell the truth, unvarnished.

"A shrimp basket hit me in the leg. It broke the skin. Must have left some bacteria in the cut. I should have cleaned it out right away, but I waited until we returned to dock to treat it. Too late. The bugs must have burrowed. I fainted so my boat drifted."

Rose shivered as she touched Jill's forehead. "Your fever's gone so the antibiotics are working. Good. But why were you alone on *Jig's Up*?"

"I wasn't. Alone. Jim, the crew member I hired, was aboard, but he was set on shooting me and stealing my drone."

"Shoot you?"

"I stunned him with my taser and tied him up. So technically I was alone when I fainted."

"Someone tried to shoot you? Jill—"

"I should add I kneed him in the crotch. I was angry, Mom. He was going to steal Mae C."

"I'm glad your self-defense classes kicked in, honey, but how you fought him when you were sick is mindboggling."

"It's called muscle memory, Mom."

"But you fainted on a boat in the middle of nowhere. How did you get here?"

"I sent Mae C to the marina with my coordinates and Ray came to find me on a small motorboat. The Coast Guard actually brought me to the hospital on a fast inflatable."

"God. Trawlers, motorboats, inflatables. I don't understand half of what you're saying. But I do understand you're in danger here."

"Not anymore, Mom. The bad guy is in custody."

"We'll see about that. But I'd definitely like to thank this Ray. Personally. I'll express my appreciation to the Coast Guard by letter."

Jill grabbed at the chance to redirect the conversation. "You'll see Ray later, before you start your trip back to La Conner."

Her mother looked startled. "I'm not leaving you here alone. You're going home with me."

Jill explained the doctor's orders not to travel, knowing Rose held a physician's opinion as sacred.

"Then we'll stay together in a hotel."

Jill took her mother's hand. "I won't be alone, Mom. I'll be staying with Ray."

Rose blinked. "What? You will? Is he your boyfriend now?

"No, Mom. He's a good friend and a partner with me on *Jig's Up*."

Forehead wrinkled in puzzlement, Rose said, "Your other partner tried to kill you. How do I know Ray's one of the good guys?" She swallowed noisily as she sorted through Jill's wild adventure. Finally she stood straighter, looking relieved. "I've never met one of your boyfriends. This will be a treat."

"He's not a boyfriend, Mom. He's taking my place on the prawner until I get well, and he's offered to let me recuperate at his house. In a wheelchair. No walking or climbing stairs." Jill scooted up in bed to make her next point. "You'll meet him around four. Shortly after that, I want you to be on your way home while it's still light. You need to catch the eight o'clock ferry out of Sidney."

Rose consulted her watch. "That gives us only a few hours to visit. But if your young man is taking care of you..." She shook her head. "I should get back to the store. Mike's handling inventory all by himself."

"Exactly," Jill said. "Ray's a good guy."

Rose raised an eyebrow. "But how can he take care of you when he's shrimping?"

Jill reached for her water and took a sip to stall her answer, then cleared her throat. "Today I arranged for Sasha Morgan, an attendant from the hospital, to look in on me during the morning and early afternoon. Since the catches are dwindling, and Ray docks around four, he'll be home all evening and all night." She squeezed her mother's hand. "I'll be fine. You know how I hate people fussing over me."

"Starting at ten-years old. Remember when you had tonsillitis? After the operation, you refused to stay in the hospital."

"And I was so disappointed when it hurt to eat ice cream."

Rose looked out the window, smiling at the memory. She still looked happy when she turned to Jill and said, "How serious are you and Ray?"

Jill face heated up, which irritated her. She went for her water glass again to cover the discomfort. "We've prawned together for more than two months, Mom. Like I told you before, he's a great partner. I like him, but we live in different worlds." She patted her mother's arm. "You'll be happy to know I'm selling the boat and heading back to the life of an engineer." She forced herself to smile, even as a wave of grief hollowed out her stomach. "This was fun while it lasted, but I'm no prawner."

Her mother's expression crumpled to disappointment. "Call me selfish, but as much as I protested your taking Al's boat instead of selling it, I *liked* hearing your stories about fishing." She shook her head. "You never used to call and tell me about your work at Baldur."

"I'll keep calling, Mom. Along with phoning you once a week, I'm trying to make friends. Ray is one of my 'friend' projects." She smoothed the blanket. "Al taught me I don't want to wait until I'm sixty to develop close ties with people."

Rose nodded approvingly. "Good thinking, dear."

"I'll stay in Port McNeill for a few days to get healthy and finish up a project-design in Waka Bay, off Tribune Channel." She yawned, stretching her hands over her head. "I'm creating a hydro-electric plant for a small marina, harnessing the power of a waterfall. I'll be taking a few trips up here from Seattle to work on it, too."

Rose chuckled. "Now there's the girl I know." She refilled Jill's glass. "I think you need a little sleep, honey. You want to be fresh and pretty when your fella comes."

Jill rolled her eyes, but the conversation *had* exhausted her. Her fella, indeed. "We're *friends,* Mom."

Rose didn't seem to be listening. She hummed while she pulled Jill's blankets up around her shoulders and tucked her in. "I'll find your doctor. You get some sleep."

***

Ray pushed open the hospital room door slowly, juggling a vase of flowers, a book, and a sweatshirt he'd found next to Jill's bed on the boat. She'd likely be sleeping. Just as well. He'd nap in the chair. Two heads turned to him, both smiling. The broader smile came from the lady sitting next to Jigs' bed.

"Hey, Ray," Jigs said, holding up her hand in a weak wave.

When Oceans Rage

The woman stood to shake his hand. "I'm Rose, Jill's mother."

"Glad to meet you. I'm Ray Stewart. First mate." He focused on Jigs and let out the breath he was holding. She had some color in her face, looking tanned in contrast to the creamy thing she was wearing. He glanced at the sweatshirt in his hand. "Looks like you've already got something warm to wear over the hospital gown."

Jigs cocked an eyebrow at Rose. "My mother works fast. She bought this bed jacket, those flowers, and some make-up while I napped. My mother will take the posies. They're pretty. Thanks."

He gave the flowers to Rose and tucked the book and sweatshirt into a drawer. "I don't want to interrupt." He touched her forehead, the coolness flooding him with relief. "Fever's gone for good, eh?" He turned to Jigs' mother. "Looks like you've worked some mother-magic."

Rose waved away the idea as she took the flowers. "Jill wanted to look presentable for your visit."

Ray squinted at Jigs, who rolled her eyes.

"Mom, Ray knows me better than that." She pointed to a chair. "Pull it up and tell me about the day. Boat performance? Shrimp haul? Did you throw Daryl overboard?"

Ray laughed while he brought the chair over. He smiled at Rose conspiratorially. "Jigs is back."

Rose arranged Ray's flowers with the ones already in a vase. She took a chair on the other side of the bed. "You call her Jigs?"

Ray shrugged. "She needed lightening up, to make fun of her obsession with thing-a-ma-jigs. Still, I understand Al came up with the nickname first."

Rose nodded in agreement. "Suits her."

Jigs groaned.

Ray ran his hands through his hair, cleared his throat, and started a review of the day. What he had to say about prawning was routine, but Jigs listened raptly, begging for more detail. Rose sat quietly, wonder in her expression.

"Did you do a reading on the pressure gauge when you got in? I'm thinking I better change the filters soon," Jigs said, squirming like she wanted to get up and attend to the task immediately.

Ray put his hand on hers. "Normal range. I checked." He smiled when she settled back. "Let's get *your* pressure gauge back to normal, eh?" The memory of seeing Jigs lying on the floor of the pilothouse leaped into his mind and he felt nauseous.

She gave him a puzzled look. "What's wrong?"

He shook his head, grinning. "Not a thing. I live for conversations about fuel filters."

Pulling her hand away, she said, "No making fun of me in my weakened condition."

Ray turned to Jigs' mother. "Sorry, Rose. I'm still getting used to Jigs' romance with engines."

Rose waved her hand. "Didn't get that from me or her stepdad. Al's the culprit. Something about the way their brains are wired." She smiled at her daughter indulgently.

Jigs shifted in bed, giving them stern looks. She asked, "Daryl's not staying on the boat with you?"

He shook his head. "Thank God, no. If he did, I'd have killed the bastard by now."

She smiled at the idea. "You'd have my blessing."

"Really?

"He's a good prawner, Ray, but he has no other virtues."

When Oceans Rage

"Ethically challenged. Like Jim Livingston."

"Constable Burns stopped by to quiz me about Jim this morning. He's concerned because Jim confessed to me when I was fevered, weak, and delusional. Burns tracked phone calls between Lynda and Jim; he can't prove Lynda paid him to steal Mae C from me, but money did go from Lynda's account to Jim's. His attempt to—" she glanced at her mother "—to harm me may have been his own decision. Good thing is, Jim's in jail and can't come after me or Mae C."

Rose had listened wide-eyed, but instead of asking for more detail, she addressed Ray. "Jillian's telling me to go home, Ray, because you'll take care of her at your house. While you're shrimping, some lady named Sasha will look in on her. Is that true?"

Ray turned to Jigs, who was nodding as if this were old news. He covered his astonishment with a quick smile, taking back Jigs' hand for effect. "Absolutely. A good plan, don't you think? My sister's out of town so Jill can rest up in Eileen's room, whose bedroom is on the main floor of the house."

Rose frowned. "Are you sure? I can stay."

"You're welcome to bunk at my house as well, Rose. But Sasha, who was the attendant for my sister, is very capable. She'll look in on Jigs while I'm working." Ray was careful not to list all the jobs he held. Clearly Jigs was intent on persuading her mother to return to La Conner and Ray's hours prawning, bartending, and walking the dock, added to too many.

Jigs gave a thumbs up. "You need to help Mike in the store, Mom. All I'll do is sleep and Sasha will get me what I need when I'm awake. Ray returns from fishing around four in the afternoon. Three days of that, the season's over, and I'll be

269

ready to pack up my stuff and drive to La Conner." Jigs paused and swallowed. "I'll stay with you and dad while I prep for my interviews."

Rose directed a questioning look to Ray.

How should he respond? Jigs had given up her boat for Eileen's well-being, so he had to play along. "Our girl's talents are wasted on shrimp, eh?"

Rose pursed her lips. "If you say so." She stood and smoothed the blanket covering Jill. "You get a bit of sleep while Ray and I go to the cafeteria for a snack. After your nap, I'll come back and visit some more before I take off." She looked at Ray. "And leave her in your capable hands."

When Rose bustled out the door, Ray squeezed Jill's hand and searched her face. "Is this what you want?"

She nodded. "It's best for everyone. Mom'll pump you, but don't tell her about the boat going to Eileen. She knows I've sold the boat and thinks the money's for me."

He saw such sadness in her eyes his heart constricted. He sat on the side of the bed, bent down and kissed her forehead. Softly, into her ear he said, "But you don't even know Eileen."

She went still for a moment, then moved her head so she could see his face. "I don't need that boat, Ray. Now go tell your life story to my mom. Rose is waiting." She grinned unabashedly. "Get ready for an interrogation. She might have said she's ready to leave me with you, but Rose could change her mind by the end of the hour." Jill waved a hand in dismissal. "Go. Make a good impression. I need to nap."

Ray hunched his shoulders, turned, and left like he was heading for the gallows. He heard Jigs chuckle as he went out the door.

When Oceans Rage

***

Imprisoned in Ray's house with her leg propped up helped Jill identify with Al's bogus incarceration and focus on finding Bill Parrish's killer. She was sure Al was innocent, but how could she prove it, especially when she couldn't walk or leave the house?

She scrutinized her calf wound, which was healing more slowly than the doctor wanted to see. "On day four, you can walk a little." He prescribed two hours of leg exercises from sitting and lying positions. "Otherwise, keep your leg elevated," he warned. So, with her leg resting on an ottoman, she resumed her investigation.

On day one of her couch-stay, she drilled down on the weapon. Where the hell was it?

She phoned Beth and asked her to message her friends and the fellows who'd gathered to watch Jill fly Mae C. Next she enlisted the help of Dennis and Camryn Hudson, begging them to visit her in Ray's living room later that afternoon. An emergency, she'd called it. Bless their hearts, they came right away, leaving Samuel with a friend.

"I need a coordinated search of the woods behind Beth's house. I've made a matrix of the area and Beth has ten friends ready to help you look for the gun. I'm hoping you'll organize the search and offer every volunteer a twenty-five-dollar gift card at The Tides restaurant. Here's the money for the thirteen cards." Jill handed over $325.

Dennis said, "The cops never scoured the forest for the gun?"

"Al's confession stopped the normal procedure. And here's the dicey part, the reason why I'd like you two to observe Beth as she scouts the area. She says she ran into the woods

271

when Bill Parrish showed up at her grandmother's house. My read on Al is he thinks Beth could have shot Parrish and ditched the gun behind the house. If she hid it, will she help us find it?"

"How do we play this?" Dennis asked.

"I've told her finding the gun is key to getting Al out of jail. That's what motivates her. I'm not second-guessing her motives, plus I have Adrienne's approval to enlist Beth's help. The weapon is key."

"Why the woods?" Dennis asked.

"We've looked everywhere else. While I was in the hospital, I asked Adrienne to gather some friends to search her house, the area around her house, her garage and her cars. They found nothing."

Camryn said, "Well, we know Al didn't kill Bill Parrish, so the least we can do is buy the gift cards and lead the walkabout. What else?"

"Indulge me for a moment. I want to talk about the electric plant. We're still in a bidding war on E-Bay. Let's discuss how we pay for the parts and start drafting a schedule for the build."

Dennis laughed. "Al would support this sidebar." And he went on to tease out some of the elements he had in mind for constructing the power plant and paying for it.

Satisfied with her machine fix, she excused Dennis and Camryn to run the search while Jill waited. Wondering. Messaging Camryn on the hour.

After six hours of thirteen people canvassing, no weapon.

Day two: gun residue day.

Jill sampled the internet's knowledge on the intricacies of tracing gun powder on clothing, burying herself in arcane cases where residue was challenged. Armed with enough information to ask questions, she called up Constable Burns for the Canadian spin on residue.

"We use handheld residue detectors," Burns said. "Checked Al, the grandmother, the granddaughter for it. Nothing. 'Course they could have changed their clothing and hidden the stuff that was tainted. When Al Morrell confessed to the crime, we searched the premises for the gun, for residue, for bullets. Only one bullet was found—the slug in Parrish's body—and it matched those used in the type of pistol Adrienne described as her halibut shooter."

"Pictures?"

"Of course. Of the whole crime scene."

"Anything helpful there?"

"Nothing. You should know Al called an attorney before we arrived. He said nothing except for 'I did it.' The girl and the grandmother were no help. Two neighbors contend they heard a shot, but they disagree on the time."

"I had thirteen people look for the gun yesterday. Six hours and all we found was a blow-up doll. Deflated. Like I feel right now. Thanks for your information, Constable. I'll sample case precedents tomorrow."

"Why would you do that?"

"Strong-arming Al comes next. I need to learn how to get a guy out of jail when he's confessed to a crime he did not commit."

Burns was silent for a few moments. "He wouldn't let me help him, Ms. Morrell. Maybe as his daughter, having given up the boat he gifted you, you have the freedom to challenge his reasons for going to jail. But I'd be careful if I were you. Someone in this town doesn't want you to succeed. Watch your back."

Once she'd set down her phone, Jill considered Burns' warning. If the murderer was still in town and discovered Jill was beginning a robust investigation, would he try to stop her? Maybe he was the one who'd attacked her in the parking lot and his next move would be to finish her off

***

On day three of her investigation, Jill studied Canadian law. False confessions, restitution, and fraudulent conveyance sent her to myriads of cases, more than she could read and absorb than there were hours in the day. The only positive note to her analysis was Al had probably read the same documents. Yet another thing they had in common.

Yesterday Ray had quit fishing by one. What time today? She wished she had Ray's help, not his silence about the suit. If only they could work together instead of separately.

She surveyed Ray's comfortable living room, the cribbage board and playing cards ready for tonight's game, an hour out of the day when they could openly compete. As much as she liked the game, her face to face tussles with Ray over cribbage had lulled her into liking him more. His playful side helped her to forget her dead-end investigation and an ever-growing dread Al would hate her for scrutinizing Adrienne and Beth's part in Parrish's death.

She never should have come to his house.

What choice did she have? Her lies to her mother about staying with Ray had succeeded in convincing Rose to go back to La Conner, but Jill's actual plan to check into a bed and breakfast had fizzled because Ray anticipated her moves. From her hospital bed, she'd called the town's two B&Bs. "We're full up, Ms. Morrell," the first one said. The second one tipped her. "Yes, miss, we got word you'd be calling. So sorry to tell you we have no vacancy."

When Ray visited her the next day at the hospital, he looked smug as she glowered at him. "I never intended to stay in your house, Ray."

"I know. The act in front of you mother was pretty transparent, love. I made the calls in the hospital cafeteria while you were napping. By the time Rose left for La Conner, my place was the only inn in town." He patted himself on the back.

"Manipulator!"

"Look who's talking."

She heard the key in the door and glanced at the clock. *Not even noon. The shrimping season is over.*

Ray grinned at her and put away his jacket. "Didn't have much time to miss me, eh?"

"No prawns?"

He kissed her forehead, lingering there this time. "We're done. Season's over. Thirty days of good hauls behind us. Daryl cleared his stuff out of the boat."

She sighed. "I figured. We'll pay him off and be done with him." A pause. "Did you thank him?"

"For being an asshole?"

"No. For emptying the bullets out of Jim Livingston's gun."

"It kills me to compliment him for anything because he's such an egocentric fool. But, yes, I did. His selfish act saved your life. And we'll forever be grateful to him."

"I'll bet he preened. Chances are the whole town knows by now." She wagged her head, hoping to avoid contact with Daryl in the future. "Since we're on the topic of turkeys. I called Constable Burns for an update on Jim Livingston and Lynda Flynn. The FBI's involved because of the international scope of their criminal activity. Lynda Flynn was being paid by China. The FBI has evidence she stole ideas from Baldur and sent them to Beijing. She was also tasked to recruit drone experts for the Chinese firm, calculating I was a good candidate because I left Baldur in a huff. At the very least, she wanted Mae C, thinking I'd given my drone super-powers."

"You did, Jigs. Mae C saved your life."

"She's well-rigged, I'll give you that, but the Chinese wouldn't learn anything new from her. Plumping up her virtues around the marina to protect our catch was a bad idea from the start."

"So when Flynn figured you couldn't be recruited, she hired Livingston to steal Mae C from you."

"Livingston turned on Flynn as soon as the FBI threatened him with industrial sabotage. He admitted to the burglaries and to holding a gun on me to save himself. To jail he goes; the Feds are trying to extradite Flynn."

"Good," said Ray.

"Baldur is two engineers short right now. Wonder how they'll beat China without drone experts?"

Ray nodded and straightened, looking distracted. He paced a bit before he sat on the edge of the coffee table. "I got a call from Eileen's doctor today." He rubbed his eyes. "He wouldn't tell me over the phone what's going on. Said I needed to drive to White Sands to talk to him and Eileen. I didn't like the tone, eh? And I don't like leaving you alone."

Jill flipped a hand. "Go. I'm fine. Camryn and Dennis are in town and Sasha's at my beck and call."

His eyes drilled into hers and he shook his head. "But I can only keep you here if I stand guard." He swallowed and looked down. "Otherwise, you and Mae C will fly."

"Look at my leg, will you? Does it appear I can walk, much less fly?"

"You can drive," he said softly.

She nodded, still scrutinizing her leg. "You're right, Ray. I'll be gone when you return from White Sands. In fact, I want to catch the afternoon ferry out of Sidney, so I'm leaving here at the crack of dawn tomorrow. Not that the hospitality hasn't been superior." She gestured with her hand to include the whole house. "Great place to recuperate. Good cook, you are. Rousing cribbage games and fine conversation." She paused. "I liked working with you on *Jig's Up* even more. Best fun I've ever had, with good memories to take back with me to Washington." She met his eyes. "I won't forget."

He nodded slowly, his gaze not leaving hers. "I plan to work full time with the RCMP. After some coursework. After more training. You?"

"Back to the world of technology." She tried to smile. "I'll be pickier about the position this time. Something more hands-on-things and hands-off-humans."

"May not work. Prawning, spiked by a dose of mushrooms, transformed you into a people person." He paused. "Listen, I'm almost finished cleaning *Jig's Up,* in and out, and I'll send anything of yours to La Conner." He looked at his watch, shaking his head. "I'd better go. I said I'd meet with the White Sands guy tonight." He chewed on his lip. "The only reason I'm glad you're leaving tomorrow morning is I still worry about your safety in this town. Whoever pushed you that night is still around. I don't want—"

Jill wouldn't let him finish. "Burns warned me, too. I'll ask Sasha to stay over."

He let out a breath and smiled. "Perfect. She's a black belt, you know."

"I didn't, but I do now. Be sure to call and tell me about Eileen."

He put on his leather jacket, reminding her of the moment she'd met him on *Jig's Up.* Today, the thought that Ray was moving out of her life made her physically ill. But she wouldn't show him how she felt.

"Jigs?"

"Hm?"

"Look at me."

He came back to her bedside. She smelled leather and a hint of spicy aftershave. Clean. Two-showers-a-day clean. *I smell good.*

He sure did. Then and now.

"Are you okay?"

She forced a smile. "Of course. Mae C and I will stay with my parents for a time. I'll mend, research Al's case, and prep for interviews."

He reached out and touched her hair. "We've been together for months, Jigs. I'm having a hard time saying goodbye."

"You've had a crash course in loyalty, Ray. Saving my life put you over the top. Medal winner."

"You rescued Eileen. And sacrificed so much." He tucked a stray curl behind her ear. "I hate to see you go."

And if you don't nix this line of conversation, I'm going to fall apart. "This is triage, Ray. Eileen needs you. The court case looms, and I'm off to restart my career." Purposefully she smoothed down her shirt and placed her feet on the floor, preparing to get up with her weight on the healthy leg. "Time for you to jet, wonder boy. Why don't I help you make a sandwich for the long drive?"

He offered a hand to steady her as she rose. His kindness, along with his concerned expression, brought a lump to her throat.

He's the best friend I've ever had. How can I let him go?

***

Jill walked into Donna's store that afternoon with frayed nerves and a bum leg. One last thing she needed to do for Ray.

"Donna." Jill saw the store was empty.

"Jill. Or should I say 'Jigs'?" she said with a bite in her tone and shoulders straight.

"Jill."

Donna glanced at Jill's leg. "Mending?"

"Uh-huh. Doc says I can leave town tomorrow."

Donna relaxed a bit and her mouth twitched with a smile. "Really? You're giving up on prawning?"

Jill shrugged. "It was fun while it lasted." She cleared her throat. "Has Ray been by?"

Donna's face clouded. "No, but he called me a couple of times to keep me up on Eileen." She straightened and made direct eye contact with Jill. "You did a good thing by paying for Eileen's rehab."

With a nod to acknowledge Donna's compliment, Jill said, "I thought you should know he left for White Sands at noon. The doctor asked to speak to him in person about Eileen. Sounded pretty important."

"Poor dear. I hope this means they're getting somewhere with her."

"Me, too." Jill pulled in a breath. *Be tough. Say it!* "If I caused a rift between you and Ray, I'm sorry. I'm leaving tomorrow and I won't be coming back."

Donna stiffened again. "What? Is this a handover?"

When her leg began to throb, Jill limped to Donna's desk and leaned against it, easing the pressure on her calf. "I think you and Ray had unfinished business when I entered the picture. Consider giving him another chance. For sure, he'll need your support."

Donna's eyebrows shot up. "You mean take your place in his bed? Are you kidding?"

Jill drilled Donna with a stern look. "I never slept with Ray."

Donna put her hand over her eyes. "Yeah, right."

"He's my friend," Jill protested, her voice a thread of sound. "But I won't ever contact him again to complicate your relationship with him. He needs someone to help him through this thing with Eileen. Maybe if you were there in the house when he got back..."

"I see what you mean." Donna rubbed her forehead, clearly considering the idea. "Let me think about it. He doesn't ask for help easily. Maybe instead of being offended by having to wait for an invitation, I should be more assertive. Like you."

Jill struggled to smile naturally and strip sarcasm from her words. "That's me, all right. Going after what I want." *Leave before she sees you tear up.* "Gotta go. I'm packed and out of here early in the morning." She hobbled to the door. "Take good care of yourself, Eileen, and Ray."

"I will and...good luck," Donna offered.

"Good pluck," Jill muttered as tears blinded her painful walk back to her car.

23

"I can't see her, Doctor Munson?" Ray asked, his heart pounding with worry. Something must be terribly wrong with Eileen.

The psychologist, about Ray's age with rusty-red hair and a pale complexion, stood behind his desk and reached out to shake Ray's hand. "I'm afraid not. Not yet, at least. Grab a cup of coffee over there and have a seat on the sofa. We're casual here. No lab coats or suits. Polo shirts and jeans take some of the formality out of the place."

Ray sank into the office couch and Munson lowered himself into an armchair.

"Coffee okay? Need a zap in the micro?"

Ray took a sip out of the mug. "No, this is fine."

"Sorry you had to make the long drive, but I wanted to talk to you tonight so we could plot out a strategy for tomorrow. Time is of the essence."

"Is she that ill, Doctor?"

"Oddly enough, she's better. She's been carrying a heavy burden she refused to acknowledge. We've helped her lift it off her shoulders and look at it. A monumental step for Eileen."

"Something big, eh?"

Munson looked out the window and smiled ruefully. "About as big as they come. To tell you the truth, we may uncover more in the next months Eileen works with us, but my colleagues and I agree we have to act on some of the information now."

Ray nodded, leaning forward. "Go ahead."

Munson consulted the first page of the folder he held open in his lap. "Eileen is the quiet one of the two of you, I understand. It seems when your stepfather drank, he was abusive to your mother and to your sister. Were you aware of that?"

"I knew he drank, of course. Sometimes he yelled at my mother. If my sister or I came in late, he'd start arguments with us. We learned to avoid him when he was drinking." Ray stopped, his gut clenching when he realized he might have missed something. "Verbal abuse only. Right?"

"No. When she reached puberty, her father slipped into her bedroom late at night."

Ray could barely breathe. "The bastard raped her?"

"No. For about two years, when she was most vulnerable, he berated her for her sexuality, haranguing her about the dirtiness of intercourse. He demonized boys who might want to have sex with her, demonstrating how they'd try to seduce her. On more than one occasion, he frightened her by masturbating in front of her, to prove how nasty the act was. It was brainwashing, motivated by self-hatred as well as misogyny, we presume. He probably convinced himself he was protecting Eileen from predation, but we think his underlying effort was to make sure Eileen hated herself and her sexual urges as much as he hated himself and his own."

"And my mother? Why didn't Eileen tell my mother?"

"He made her feel so embarrassed about the topic and her so-called weakness of character that she couldn't make herself talk about it with your mother. We asked her if he threatened her not to tell her mother, but she can't remember."

"So he scared the sexuality right out of her? Why didn't he do the same to me? Wouldn't it make more sense for him to transfer his self-hatred to another male?"

Munson shook his head. "Seems logical, doesn't it? But history bears us out. It's a 'shoot the messenger' kind of thing. Women bring sexual feelings to men, so why not hate women since it's too hard to admit you hate yourself? Why not try to keep women from sending out signals, then we men won't get turned on by them? Completely irrational." He massaged his neck.

"Jesus." Ray stood, walked to the window, and looked out into the darkness. He mourned Eileen's lost youth most of all, but his guilt over not being able to help her, to shield her, wrenched his heart. When he could speak he asked, "I still can't believe I didn't know he was a pervert. Why didn't I pick up on what he was doing? She was *his daughter*!"

"You were ten years older, Ray," Munson offered in a soothing voice that nevertheless grated on Ray's nerves. *I should have known, should have been there, should have put two and two together.*

"You were probably very involved in your own life, so different from a girl's," Munson added.

"Adept at avoiding the sick bastard, anyway," Ray muttered. He swore again, then took a deep breath to calm himself, and wished Jigs were here. "Why did he stop harassing her after two years?"

"Eileen had a hard time figuring that one out. We think it was a combination of things. Your mother got sick and Eileen became brave enough to lock her bedroom door at night."

Ray pushed his fingers through his hair and stared out the window. "I installed a lock on her door during a holiday trip home. She said it was so no one would read her diary."

Munson smiled. "She trusted you."

"A little too late, eh?" Ray rubbed his eyes and sighed. "Why in hell did she return to live with the son of a bitch after her divorce?"

Munson took off his glasses and twirled them with his fingers. "We're helping her dissect the reasons for moving in with him. From the pragmatic view, taking the store manager position was her only avenue for making money. And moving from Campbell River to Port McNeill was a wise decision. Her ex-husband and his buddies, a toxic bunch of men, remained in Campbell River."

The psychiatrist was quiet for awhile. "Denial can be a powerful thing. Eileen had nursed your mother and succeeded in school, including college. When her marriage failed...was she thinking clearly about her relationship with Bill Parrish? We'll never know. For all intents and purposes, Eileen and her father appeared to have mended fences. Do you agree?"

Ray nodded. "After Eileen's divorce, her friend, Donna, moved her store from Campbell River to Port McNeill. To my sister, it made sense she'd move north to manage the giftshop and save money to buy her own place by staying with Bill. They developed some sort of truce, I guess." Then he remembered. "But he'd get drunk and create havoc in the local bar. Why would she pick him up from The Tides every midnight?"

Munson looked down at his notes. "They rarely saw each other during the day and her evenings were her own because he hung out at the bar. Still, she knew he couldn't drive home drunk with two DUI's already on his record, so she made the deal with Pete. He'd remind her to pick up Parrish around midnight. By that time, he was wasted, went to bed right away, and slept until noon. Since Eileen worked at Donna's store during the day, the only time they interacted was the two-mile car ride at midnight, from the bar to his house."

Ray lowered himself onto the couch. "This routine went on for months while I was still working in Campbell River. Eileen was happy, more content than I've ever seen her."

Flipping to another page of his notes, Munson cleared his throat. "Your theory was the trauma around your stepfather's murder made Eileen sick."

"Right."

"Well, you were close." Munson took a breath and pursed his lips.

Ray tensed. Jesus, what could be worse? "What is it?"

Munson cleared his throat again. "Eileen killed her father."

"What?" Ray held onto the arm of the couch, feeling like the earth had opened a hole beneath him. "That's impossible."

"We were as surprised at her admission as you are. That's why we called you down here to talk to us."

Ray kept shaking his head, lost in a nightmare. "Al Morrell killed my stepfather. He confessed. Eileen's still deluded, Doctor. She didn't do it. I'm sure of it." Worse yet, why hadn't he, a law enforcement officer, considered the possibility?

Munson turned to a new section of his notebook. "Let me read a transcript of what Eileen has to say about that night. You can help us judge the veracity of her story. Are you ready?"

"About as ready as I am for a brain transplant, but go ahead."

Munson said, "In her own words, then."

Eileen: That night I fell asleep watching TV and Pete didn't call to have me pick up my father. By the time I got to the bar, it was one o'clock, a good hour later than when I normally brought him home. My father was gone.

Dr. Munson: In his own car? When you picked him up usually, would he leave his car in the bar parking lot?

Eileen: Right. Pete would never let him drive home drunk. It was our arrangement. But some other guy was tending the bar that night.

Dr. Munson: So you went looking for your father in your car?

Eileen: Uh-huh. I checked a couple of places before I decided he might have gone to Adrienne's. My father had had a thing for Adrienne for years, and when she started seeing Al, my father dogged her about it to the point Al ended their partnership on *Jig's Up.* Anytime my dad drank too much he turned mean. Sure enough, his car was parked out front of Adrienne's house.

Dr. Munson: You went in?

Eileen: (crying) I went in. I went in. I went in. God. I wish I hadn't.

Dr. Munson: Take your time, Eileen. Tell us what happened, step by step."

When Oceans Rage

Eileen: (crying) I looked in the living room window. Adrienne lay on the floor, not moving, her head bloody and a gun lying next to her body. My dad was standing over the little girl, Beth. She was cowering in a chair. The look on her face was pure terror. She could have been me. She *was* me. I didn't stop to think. I banged on the window, yelling at my father. He turned around with this hateful expression I remembered all too well. Beth scrambled out of the chair and ran toward the back of the house, but I knew he'd find her and scream at her some more, repeating the awful things he used to yell at me. I knew better than anyone once he found a target, he wouldn't let up. So I ran into the open garage, through the kitchen, and into the living room. And faced him. Finally. To stop him from ruining another girl's life. He'd already destroyed me and any chance I had for a decent marriage. I couldn't let him do it to Beth.

(Takes a shaky breath) I picked up the gun and shot him. (She frowns at this, then smiles) Beth has nothing to worry about anymore. She's safe now.

Dr. Munson: Did Beth see you pick up the gun?

Eileen: No, she ran away before I shot him.

Dr. Munson: Did Adrienne wake up before you left the house?

Eileen: No, but I heard her moan and saw her moving. She was safe, too.

Dr. Munson: So you left?

Eileen: I got in my car and went home. I was finished.

Dr. Munson: And the gun? Where is the gun?

Eileen: I hid it in my house.

Dr. Munson: Your house?

Eileen: (nods)

Dr. Munson: Where?

Eileen: Next to my diary, in my closet. It's safe, too. (wipes her eyes) That's why I never wanted Ray in the house or near me. He's a cop. He'd make me tell him I killed my father, and he'd never forgive me. (sniffles) I've missed Ray. I'd like to see him now. Could I?

Dr. Munson: Very soon.

Munson looked up from the transcript, his eyebrows raised. "Is it possible?"

Ray held his head in his hands, filling in the end of the story. So Al drove up after Eileen left. He saw Adrienne lying beside Bill Parrish's dead body, assumed Adrienne had killed him, or Beth did. At the very least, when he couldn't find her in the house, he suspected Beth ran off with the gun. Maybe threw it somewhere in the woods. To him, it didn't matter which of the two killed Parrish, his goal was to keep both of them out of public scrutiny.

Lifting his head, Ray said, "It's possible. If the gun is where she says it is, Eileen...my little sister...is guilty of murder, not Al Morrell."

"Eileen also admitted to lying about Bill Parrish having paid for any of the fishing license."

"What?"

"She needed expensive treatment and she knew you would believe her. She did what she could to save herself."

Oh, God, Jigs. The boat. What have I done? He groaned and looked up at Munson. "I was flat-assed wrong about *everything*...and everyone."

"How could you have known?"

This time Munson's soothing voice sent Ray over the edge, and he exploded. "Al Morrell has spent months in jail because of *me*! His daughter gave up their boat to pay for *my* sister's medical needs. Why did I assume the worst about everyone except for my sister?"

"Because you love her." Munson's calm voice came back at him. "I repeat. There is no way you could have known. Nor could you have prevented these crimes. Eileen snapped that night, blanking out the horror of patricide. Now she's facing her guilt instead of letting it consume her. She will heal from this trauma. You'll do the same."

Ray shook his head, unable to believe Munson's words. "Damn."

The doctor closed his notebook. "We'll call the Port McNeill constable tomorrow morning to pick up the gun. If it's there, they start the paperwork to get an innocent man out of jail."

Thoroughly shaken, Ray stood to leave. "Jigs. God. Jigs." He turned to Munson. "She leaves early tomorrow so I'll make sure the the constables confiscate the weapon after she heads to La Conner. I can spare her that, at least." He scratched his head hard, feeling stupid for being so blind and stubborn. "Once the RCMPs find the gun, I'll visit Al to apologize and work with my lawyer to get him out of prison immediately." He shook his head. "And then there's the boat money. And Jack Canter thinking he owns *Jig's Up*. And Al, freed from prison, but boatless. Oh, God. I've destroyed a man's livelihood."

Munson stood. "Come back here in the morning so we can make the call to the constable together. I'll work on a written statement to email after the phone call. Get some sleep, if you can. We have a lot of work to do tomorrow."

Ray said nothing.

"Things will work out, Ray. Eileen is mending and we're going to get an innocent man out of jail. I can't help with the money or the boat, but I'm sure you'll do the right thing."

He turned and stumbled out of Munson's office, thinking Munson had more faith in Ray's ethics than Ray had. His right hand twitched, yearning to lift his cell out of his jeans pocket to check flights to Nova Scotia. Instead, Ray buried his phone hand in the right front pocket, and worked his mind around the fact his sister killed her father.

24

A few days later, Ray showed up at the prison during visiting hours, arranging the event through his own attorney and Al's, after briefing them about Eileen's patricide.

Meeting Al for the first time was stressful enough, but having to tell Jill's father he'd spent months in jail when neither Adrienne nor Beth were guilty, set his heart pounding. Worse yet, was seeing so many of Jigs' traits in her father. When he shook hands with Al, Ray stared into Jigs' brown eyes and the same features but a darker complexion than hers, reminding him he'd betrayed the trust of father *and* daughter.

When Al learned who Ray was, he asked, "Is something wrong with Jillian?"

"No. She's fine. She's with Rose in La Conner, recovering from an infection in her leg. Jill doesn't even know I'm here." Ray told the story of her aborted cruise to see her friends in Waka Bay. About Livingston's attempt to kill her and steal Mae C. How Ray and Mae C helped save Jill and *Jig's Up*. He lauded Jigs' bravery in taking down a killer even though she was too sick to know what she was doing. Her sense of right and wrong ran deep.

"First she's attacked in a parking lot, then a member of her crew tries to shoot her. Why are they after my daughter? And why would you let her take the boat out when she was sick?"

Ray shook his head. "We weren't working together at the time. I had to stay in Port McNeill to take care of my sister, so Jigs, uh, Jill, picked another partner to finish out the season. She decided to sell the boat to pay for my sister's care."

"She sold the boat?"

Ray nodded. "To Jack Canter. I couldn't stop her from doing it, but I tried. God, she's stubborn!"

Al raised an eyebrow.

"Okay, she's determined. Without my knowledge, she sold *Jig's Up* and paid for my sister's two month's stay at an expensive rehab center."

Al narrowed his eyes the way Jigs always did. Ray smiled at the memory. "Could we sit, Al? I've got a lot to say and my adrenaline's shot."

After they seated themselves, Ray took a fortifying breath before he narrated Eileen's revelations. Al listened intently, pumping out questions as Ray's story unfolded.

Ray added details to the crime based on a conversation he'd had with Constable Burns. "We think you showed up immediately after Eileen left. You assessed the situation, figuring you'd take the fall for Beth or Adrienne. It didn't matter which one pulled the trigger."

"I couldn't imagine a third person did it."

"None of us could." *Well, except Jigs.*

Guilt stabbed Ray anew. "Burns found the gun exactly where Eileen said it was. Bullets match the one that killed Parrish." Ray was quiet for a moment, thinking about how happy Jigs would be to learn Al would soon be free. "Your lawyer and Burns are doing the paperwork to get you out of here. I thought I'd leave it to you to contact Jigs, Adrienne, and Beth about the good news."

Al blinked, clearly overwhelmed. "Jigs?"

"I call her that."

"What will Jillian do when she learns your sister killed Bill Parrish?"

"She was sure you didn't kill my stepfather. From the beginning. I'm the wrongheaded one."

Al growled. "You call yourself her friend?"

"Actually, no. I sued her for the boat, based on the lies my sister told. Your daughter deserves friends who are loyal."

"You think she still wants *Jig's Up*?"

"I think she enjoys the life and had success as a prawner. She earned respect among some fishermen and wants to help the Hudsons build their power plant, a project you started. But she might be ready to return to engineering. I know she has interviews set up."

"Well, I'm done fishing. Prison and Jillian's experiences have convinced me I need to devote more time to family." Al winced. "Pretty bad when it takes a man sixty years to wise up."

Ray nodded. "So you'll call Jillian?"

"And you'll walk out on her?"

"I'm the last person she needs in her life. I'm sure of it."

Al looked hard at Ray. "I figured I was doing the best for her and Rose when I left them, in the same way I was sure Beth and Adrienne were better off on their own." He shrugged. "I decided for them what was best. It's not fair, Ray. I wasn't right, and neither are you. Jillian has a say."

"I'm all wrong for her. Look what I've done to screw up her life."

Jill's father drilled him with a glare. "That's for her to decide. I'm not calling her. It's your place to explain your sister killed Bill Parrish." He paused for a moment. "And you say she lied about the fishing license?"

"Eileen admitted it to her psychiatrist. It was a desperate move to cover the cost of high-end therapy." He drew in a deep breath. "I'm so sorry for all the trouble my family has caused yours, and I'll do everything I can to get you out of here as fast as I can."

"I can wait. My daughter comes first. Go to her."

The thought of unveiling his mistakes to Jigs and asking for forgiveness terrified Ray.

I can't forgive myself.

How can she *forgive me?*

Al rose. "If you know her well enough, you'll figure out how to convince her. Take some time to plan. You can be sure I won't be out of here for weeks." He put his hands on his hips and locked eyes with Ray. "Be snappy with a strategy, you hear? I won't call Adrienne with the news until you tell me you have a plan."

With that, he eyed the door. "You providing limo service when they spring me?"

Ray jerked up, surprised by the request. "Absolutely."

"Good. Now get outta here, young man, and solve your problems."

25

Jill wandered through the aisles of her parents' gift shop guided by sunlight. Where the sun's rays revealed dust on the shelves, she cleaned. The hot afternoon in La Connor was the kind of day when customers ducked into shops to cool off rather than buy. Still, she had few browsers. Her last customer left an hour ago, empty-handed. Jill wondered how her parents managed the boredom. Donna, too, at her store in Port McNeill. Surrounded by gifts they hoped customers would buy, their livelihood dependent on the whims of shoppers. Jill shuddered at the thought.

She focused on a picture of fishing boats, artfully arranged and brightly colored, chuckling at the idea of working vessels as pretty as those in the picture. Not in her experience.

Had Ray finished beautifying *Jig's Up* before handing off the trawler to Jack Canter? Jill wished she could have seen the boat one more time before Jack took possession. She'd left Port McNeill without giving *Jig's Up* a proper farewell, the idea of saying goodbye too painful.

The door chime rang and Jill waved to a pair of women, offered her assistance, then left them alone to browse.

Her parents were off on an extended buying trip to Seattle. Some kind of convention thing, they said. Her Mom had planned to go alone, but Jill had offered to handle the gift shop so both could attend. "You guys need a vacation together. Take more than one night. Take three. I don't have any interviews lined up until next week. Go!"

She'd expected them to protest, but they'd jumped on her offer and started planning their trip like it was a second honeymoon. Which meant her task of rigging Mae C with a metal detector would have to wait. Beth and her friends had searched the woods behind Adrienne's house for hours and hadn't found the murder weapon. Maybe Mae C could find the gun if she were outfitted with special sensors.

Also on hold because of her parent's trip, was Jill's plan to make face-to-face visits with each of Adrienne's neighbors. She needed to quiz them on the exact time they heard the gunshot. Next she'd drill down on how long Adrienne was unconscious, the duration of time Beth hid in the woods, the exact time when Al came on the scene and the police arrived. Jill's notes had fifteen to twenty minutes unaccounted for. Maybe Constable Burns could help. Even better would be to consult Al about the timeline. As if that could happen. Damn stubborn man!

Jill drew her feather duster over an otter figurine, its fur askew. *Ray. What are you up to now?* She'd heard from him twice, brief phone calls. The first one telling her the doctors were happy with Eileen's progress and he'd give her more details soon. Later that day, he'd called to ask for the combination to Al's lockbox. He said he needed the title of the boat for Jack Canter. "She looks good, Jigs." Then he'd asked her about her interviews. "Where, when, and how are you getting ready for them?"

She'd spoken positively about three appointments she'd set up with engineering firms, keeping her dread about the interviews to herself and not telling Ray about her dead-end attempts to find his stepfather's killer. Why not focus on the positive?

Nor had she mentioned her daily Mae C workout at a soccer field and two or three times-a-day wanderings down to the marina, only a few blocks from the store and less than a mile from her parents' home. Her goals were to exercise her now-healed leg and be around boats, breathing in the brine of fish and saltwater. In the past, she'd been offended by the smell. Now, she craved it.

Jill checked the time as the two customers left, empty-handed. Three hours until closing. The doorbell rang again. Thank God. Anything was better than dusting. She turned, smiling, ready to welcome yet another stranger.

"Ray!"

"Hey, Jigs."

She gripped the feather duster harder, fighting the urge to wrap him in a hug. His grin, unkempt hair, and oh, God, the soapy-spicy smell of him. *I've missed him.* Dizzy with her desire to embrace him, she leaned against a cupboard while memories tumbled into her mind: He'd lain with her all night as she climbed out of a drugging, he'd held her close after her attack, and he'd saved her from crashing *Jig's Up* and dying from sepsis.

He's as loyal as a man can be under the circumstances.

A new thought barreled into her consciousness. *I gave up the boat for him. Not for Eileen. For Ray.*

"I like this clerky look with the feather duster in hand. Quite domestic for the Jigs I know."

"I'm filling in for my parents." Sweat formed over her lips. Why was he here? "They've gone to a buying convention in Seattle."

"Warm day." He swiped at his forehead, and his expression changed to serious. "We've got some things to talk about, Jillian."

Her heart leapt to her throat. About Eileen? Donna? Why would he drive all the way to La Conner from B.C.? She glanced out the window in front of the store. Where was his car?

He followed her view of the empty street. "Any chance you could close early?"

Blood turning to syrup, she took a slow-motion turn to meet his eyes. "Sure. If you're in a hurry to get back, I can take a break. Let me get my keys."

When she locked the store's front door behind them, he grabbed her hand. "Let's go find some shade out by the water. It'll be cooler there."

"Uh, okay." She looked at their joined hands. Maybe this wasn't about Donna.

"Something wrong, Jigs?"

"Not that I'm unhappy to see you...but I'm wondering why you're here. Why a phone call wouldn't do."

"You deserve more than a phone call, eh? I did talk to Rose, just to make sure you were still in La Conner. She told me about the conference, that she'd be gone but you'd be here."

"I see. Why not tell *me* you were coming?"

When Oceans Rage

"Rose thought my surprise visit might add a little zest to your life. Your mother said clerking was, for you, one of the rings of hell."

Jill laughed. "Funny, and accurate. But I can't imagine you two colluding on anything."

Even so, she decided to go with the moment, strolling with him to a shaded bench near the marina.

He glanced at the docks and when she sat, he stood over her, waiting. Hesitating.

She patted the seat next to her. "If it's bad news, please don't hover."

He lowered himself to the bench a foot away from her and combed his fingers through his hair, still not speaking.

"Spit it out, Ray. I can handle it." He was making her nervous, now.

He took her hand. "I don't know how to tell you this, Jigs. My recent pledge to stick by my sister was meant to be a positive move, but the blowback has been massive."

So this *was* about Eileen? Jill waited for more.

He cleared his throat. "I was on my way to see my sister at White Sands when you and I last talked specifically about Eileen's problems. Their doctors had something important to tell me. A breakthrough, they called it."

"Sounds upbeat, but your tone says otherwise."

"Good catch. I'm still reeling from the news, myself, so bear with me, okay?" He swallowed and squeezed her hand. "Eileen killed my stepfather."

Jill's heart leapt to her throat for a second time. "What? How could...?"

"She shot him with Adrienne's gun. In that short time after Bill hit Adrienne and before Al showed up, Eileen shot him close range and left with the gun. The Constable found the weapon in Eileen's closet, where she admitted she hid it."

"But that means..."

"Eileen may plead self-defense."

"Do you mean because she was defending Adrienne?"

"No. Eileen was saving Beth."

"Beth?" Jill moved closer to Ray, her hand anchored on his knee. "Oh, no. Was Parrish hurting Beth?"

"Eileen...witnessed her father harassing Beth. She recognized his aberrant behavior, some of the same fearmongering he'd used on her when she was a kid." Ray looked to the sky. "I was ten years older, and living in Nova Scotia when all this was happening. I had no idea the bastard harangued her regularly about boys and sex. Called her names, demonstrated sex acts. Awful stuff."

"And he went after Beth? That's why Eileen killed him?"

Ray nodded. "Eileen was horrified by what she'd done but she was also desperate for help. She kept me away from the house because she was afraid I'd find the gun and send her to prison.

"How old was Eileen when her father abused her?"

"Thirteen. Beth's age. It went on for two years."

"Oh, my. How sad."

"The night of the murder, Eileen banged on the living room window to distract Bill so Beth could run away. Beth never saw Eileen enter the house through the garage."

He finished the story, then looked down for a long moment. When he raised his eyes to her, they were filled with a deep sadness. "Eileen also lied about the Bill owning part of the fishing license."

Having met Eileen in the coffee shop, Jill could believe that. "Doesn't really surprise me," she said gently.

But Ray would have none of her forgiveness. "I've been blind to the truth, assuming Al deserved to be in prison when he was innocent. And you. Watching over you so you didn't steal or damage a boat I was sure was Eileen's. To help a sister I considered a victim." He growled. "*She* hit you over the head that night in Port McNeill, harboring some wild idea I needed help getting rid of you."

"What?" Jill shivered at the memory of the night she was attacked.

Ray squeezed her hand. "You were right, I didn't know my stepfather at all and I didn't have a clue about my sister's secrets. I am so sorry, Jigs. For all the pain I've caused you and your family."

She sat back, taking in the breadth of Ray and Eileen's suffering. The police had been contacted, an attorney was working on Eileen's case, and experts in White Sands were leading Eileen through an intricate healing process. Her big brother would stand by her every step of the way. She couldn't have asked for a more loyal supporter.

As for her own family? Rose and Mike were stolid cheerleaders. Jill's thoughts jumped to the joys of her shrimping days. A vision of Al walking out of the prison into the arms of Adrienne and Beth made her happy, too. "You're accepting responsibility for all of our troubles when the only thing you did was stand by your sister. Misguided, but noble."

Ray shook his head.

"Eileen isn't a reprobate, Ray. Your sister is ill, mentally fragile, made even more so by her father and her ex-husband's abuses. Lynda Flynn and Jim Livingston are the true villains here, people we had little power over because they are so evil. They tried to *kill* me when Lynda couldn't recruit me, intent on stealing Mae C. None of that was your doing."

He looked out at the marina, as if considering her point.

"Bright side? The woman gave me a nice brain tweak. Not one I would have chosen on my own, but…"

He smiled. "It rounds out your personality?"

"Other positives…Eileen's on the mend. She'll get her mind sorted, too."

He nodded, slowly. "I hope."

"Al's free, right? Determined to devote all of his time to Adrienne and Beth."

"He'll be out soon. And yes, he's retiring."

"So what did we lose, Ray? Maybe all this had to happen to pull Eileen out of the dark and help my dad sort out his priorities."

He shook his head, clearly unable to accept her positive spin. "Be enraged. I'd feel better."

She laughed. "I *do* feel better." She reached out to grab his chin and make him look at her. "We're getting Al out of jail."

"At a snail's pace. The red tape to spring him will take another week. I used some money I'd set aside for the civil suit and arranged for Adrienne and Beth to stay in a hotel near the prison this coming weekend.

She nodded, feeling a blur of sentimental tears come to her eyes. Sometimes she didn't recognize this new Jillian at all. She fought for control, determined to ask the question she dreaded most. "And Donna?"

"Donna's fine. She's been amazing with Eileen. In fact, she's at White Sands right now, spending time with her."

"I'm glad to hear it. Good."

Ray frowned. "That part is, anyway. The oddest thing happened. She was waiting for me in my house when I got back from visiting Eileen. Surprised the hell out of me."

Jill felt her heart constrict.

"You promised her you wouldn't contact me." Ray's dusty blue eyes locked onto hers and she stopped breathing. "Why?"

She couldn't speak.

Ray frowned. "Breathe, Jigs. Breathe."

She waved her hand at him, annoyed, while she took in air slowly, soundlessly.

"You put us in an awkward spot. I had all this stuff to do with Al and Eileen and you threw Donna at me, too."

"I figured...you needed her support."

He studied a fishing boat maneuvering up the channel, then nodded slowly. "I know it's a failing of mine, not asking for help from others."

"Hey, I can match and raise the size of that flaw any day."

Ray smiled. "You've changed since I've known you, Jigs. Look how you went to bat for Adrienne and Beth. And Al. He refused your help, forbade it, even, and you waded into investigating the murder anyway. Then, the ultimate sacrifice. You gave *Jig's Up* to Eileen, a woman who not only called you out, but attacked you and lied to all of us."

Quietly, Jill said, "I hardly recognize myself these days."

A laugh from Ray, then he got serious again and took both of her hands in his this time. "Trouble was, when you put Donna in my house a

303

day after you left, it made me realize it was you and not her I needed."

Jill swallowed.

"I lived with you for two months, Jigs. You said it yourself. We've built a loyalty to one another."

All she could do was nod once.

"Anyway, I helped Donna pack and brought her back to her place. It was painful for both of us. Embarrassing for her, especially."

"I'm so sorry. It was—"

He raised an eyebrow. "The push I needed, Jigs. Don't be sorry." He stood and extended a hand. "I've got one more thing to do before I leave you to your clerking."

What? He's going to leave? She felt the blood drain from her face and wobbled as she stood. Ray grabbed her at the waist to steady her and she leaned into him to catch her breath. *I can't do this. Not again.* The last time he said goodbye broke her heart.

***

Ray led her to the marina, thankful Jill wasn't questioning why. A few more steps and he'd be home free. At the top of the gangway, he pointed to the prawner, shining in the sun.

Jigs gasped. *"Jig's Up?* She's here? Jack let you bring her here?"

He nodded, smiling. "Jack's a generous guy. He figured you deserved one last look at her before he took her to Campbell River." He tucked her arm around his elbow and led her down the gangway.

"What a gesture. Hey, maybe Al can partner up with Jack and eventually buy back *Jig's Up* with his earnings."

Ray shook his head. "I think Al's done with fishing, honey, but you can ask him yourself."

When Oceans Rage

They stepped onto the main dock. Ray said, "*Jig's Up* handled the trip from Port McNeill to here without a hitch. Only problem I had was with the damn diesel pump for the stove. I took it out, but I haven't had a chance to see what's wrong with it."

"Really?" She frowned in disbelief. "I thought I fixed it for good."

He watched her ruminate over the problem. *God, she's fun to watch when she chews on machine problems.* He cleared his throat. "Don't worry about it. Jack said he'd work on it later."

They approached the prawner, Jigs squeezing his arm. "She looks so good, Ray. You repainted the name, I see."

"Yeah. It was faded. Needed clarity."

"You're assuming Jack wants to keep the name?"

He ignored her question while he unlocked the door, stepping aside to let her in first. He watched her take in the pilothouse, stopping her survey briefly on her new chairs. He smiled when she looked longest and last at the control panel at the helm, reaching over to caress the instruments while touching the whale charm at her neck. Then, as he predicted she would, Jigs looked around for something she couldn't find.

"What?" he asked, pretending he didn't know.

"Where is the fuel pump?"

"I put it in the master cabin, to get it out of the way."

She was down the steps and opening the door of the cabin before he finished his sentence.

He followed, hearing her gasp when she saw the room. He'd bought and laid out a bright blue comforter with blue, white and green striped shams. "Egyptian cotton, 800- count sheets under there, Jigs."

She touched the comforter and smiled before she focused on the curved wall where Mae C used to hang. "Her hooks and locks are still here. We should take those out."

"This room doesn't feel right without Mae C." He chuckled. "She caused us some problems, but she saved our catch and she helped me find you when you were in trouble." A pause. "Remember the day you explained to little Samuel how Mae C operates?"

Jill nodded, her thoughts zipping to the hydro plant, the Pelton engine, the—"

Ray touched her arm. "Uh, Jigs. Stay with me, baby." When she'd refocused on him, he continued. "I think I fell in love with you that day. Using simple terms a six year-old—and I—could understand, you explained to Samuel how your pet drone worked. Dennis, Camryn and I saw how much love and respect you have for Mae C and all things mechanical. I made up this crazy story in my head, right there on the dock of Waka Bay marina, that if I could somehow become the second object of your devotion, I would die happy."

Jigs' laughter bubbled over, giving him hope.

"I always say humans can learn from machines." Raising her index finger for a moment of quiet, she gave a love pat to the space Mae C used to occupy, and looked at two items he'd attached to the wall, smiling at the silly one he'd framed of the two of them with Camryn and Dennis at Waka Bay. Samuel had taken the lopsided snapshot.

He held his breath when she turned her attention to the framed document hanging next to it.

"What's this?" She leaned over to read the small print. She looked back at him, her forehead furrowed. "It says I'm the owner of *Jig's Up.* How could that be, Ray?"

"Because it's true." He swallowed. "Al bought it back from Jack for you. He's agreed to let me repay the $40,000 in installments. We've settled on an interest rate and I had my lawyer draw up the papers." He pointed to the date on the title. "The boat never actually changed hands."

He watched a smile play on her lips as she touched the frame. She turned to him, her expression grateful but concerned. "How will you manage your sister's care?"

"I'm selling the house. Too many painful memories in it for Eileen, the doctors advise. And I'll take a fulltime job with the RCMP. No worries. We'll be fine." He opened a drawer, pulled out an envelope and handed it to her.

"What's this?"

"Open it."

She sat on the bed and stared at the stack of twenty-dollar bills inside. "Is this what I think it is?"

"Yup. The pool. You won."

She frowned. "They think *you* won."

"I told them you won the pool because you ended up getting screwed by not one, but two hires. I shamed 'em into giving it up."

She thumbed through the bills and smiled. "I can imagine how reluctant Ken Bailey was to part with his wad of dough. Thanks, Ray. But what will I do with a prawn boat when I'm employed in Seattle?"

Ray shrugged. "It's your decision, babe. Like it was your decision six months ago. You deserve the chance to make up your own mind, especially after what you suffered at my hands."

She looked up at him, puzzled. "You said I was playing at prawning."

"I was wrong. I've never seen anyone take to a boat and prawning like you did. I'd partner with you any time."

"You would?"

"In a New York minute." He waited a beat, looking into her eyes, then stood and cleared his throat. "I'll be heading out now, Jigs. I'll walk you back to the store, eh?"

He held out a hand and she stood as well. "You taking the ferry out of Anacortes?"

He nodded, distracted by her curly hair, the angles of her cheekbones, the lure of her lips. The bed behind her. He yearned to tumble her into it and kiss her in so many places.

"Are you in a hurry?"

The question surprised him. After days of jumping through hoops and strategizing how to get Al out of jail, working with Al and Jack Canter to get *Jig's Up* back in Jill's hands, and bringing it down to La Connor, he couldn't think of a time when he wasn't in a hurry. *I can finally relax.* "No."

"If you really want to go, I'll drive you to the ferry—"

"No, no. I'm—"

"But I think we've got a little celebrating to do, don't you?" She affected a distinctly un-Jill-like pout, one that seared into his heart. "You wouldn't leave me to celebrate all by myself?"

He reached out to wind a flyaway curl around his index finger, remembering Al's words. *She has a say.* Ray felt the air whoosh out of him. "I...I figured you'd had enough of me."

"I see. Well, that's for me to decide, eh?" Gesturing with her hand, she said, "This is my boat, right? I'm the captain and what I say goes. You, sir, have anticipated my moves from the start. Think back to all the arrangements you've made, based on what you know about me." She eyed him critically. "Like creating no vacancies in the B&Bs." She took his face in her hands. "Helping get Al out of jail, making sure Adrienne and Beth could be close by to support him. Checking with my mother on my whereabouts. Working out the boat finances with Al and Jack. And bringing *Jig's Up* to La Conner. You knew all those moves would make me happy."

He shrugged. "Elementary."

"But you haven't got a plan for what comes next, do you?" She opened her eyes wide, clearly surprised by her own observation. "For the first time, you, Ray Stewart, haven't figured out the future." She squeezed his cheeks, insistent. "This loyalty thing. This 'not running away' habit is new to you. Am I right?"

He felt the hair rise on his arms. Jigs must have sensed his reaction because she took her hands from his face to rub his arms, soothing and arousing him all at the same time. He stumbled with the words. "I...I was busy with—"

She cocked an eyebrow.

He muttered, "I was afraid to look ahead."

Calmly, she waited for more.

It all came out in a rush. "I hurt you, Jigs. I used poor judgment. I'm capable of screwing up again. You deserve more."

She frowned, flattening the last of his goosebumps before stepping back. "You aren't the only one who's been transformed and humbled. I'd convinced myself I'd given up the boat for Eileen."

"You are a generous—"

Jill touched his hand to stop him. "No. I gave it up for you."

"Me?"

"You."

"But Jill, I don't deserve—"

More pressure on his hand "You think my life is better off without you? All the scenarios you could come up with had me turning you away. Letting you go?"

He forced a smile. "Kinda."

She grew very still.

"What?"

"You forgot one thing. I'm the captain, here."

Hope sparked in his heart. "Indeed you are."

"And as such, I request your presence at this celebration. It's not every day a woman has a boat returned to her."

A slow grin bubbled up. "Aye, Aye, Captain."

Wordlessly, she tugged him down onto the bed with her.

"Seems we were here once before," was all he could think to say.

She nodded, watching his eyes.

"And you want to know something?"

"Of course."

"Ever since that night, when I watched you sleep, I've wanted to get back to this cabin." Tentatively, he lay his hand on her stomach. "With you."

She closed her eyes and sighed.

"Jigs?"

"Hmm?"

"Remind me why we didn't come back here sooner."

She raised an eyebrow. "Donna. I thought you and Donna still had a chance."

He slipped his fingers under her T-shirt.

Another soft exhale.

He had to know. "Was there...anything else that stopped us then?"

"You lied to me. Chill factor there." She reached for him as she said it, but he intercepted her hand, bringing her hand to his mouth, kissing each finger.

"I have learned how to stick around, Jigs, even if things get tough."

"Yes, you have." Her free hand went to the whale charm while he resumed caressing the strip of skin above her waistband. "And I've gained some wisdom about relationships with people."

He cleared his throat, suddenly so terrified he could barely get his next words out.

"If we go down this road, Jillian, separation is not an option."

She hesitated, then smiled. "I know." One eyebrow lifted. "I think I knew that about you the day we met. It scared me at first and I fought it for quite a while, but you rescued me anyway." Her smile grew stronger. "I wouldn't fight that kind of determination."

"Jigs?"

She smoothed wrinkles of concern from his brow. "No worries, Ray. I'm yours." She scooted over in the bed to give him room. "One hundred percent yours."

***

The evening sun woke her, a porthole spotlight blinding her when she opened her eyes. Jill turned away from the light to see Ray sleeping soundly beside her.

She snuggled up to him, kissed his neck and breathed in his warm scent, an alluring combination of sex, sleep, and soap.

Yes, indeed, you do smell good.

Ray opened one eye and smiled. "Again?"

"And again," she whispered. She'd had a moment of panic when she'd realized what Ray meant the night before. *Separation is not an option.* Could she be constant? She really had no experience with solid emotional attachments beyond her parents, but Ray, Al, Adrienne, Beth, Camryn, Dennis, and Samuel were essential parts of her new life. Now and forever. She understood the basis of an enduring relationship for the first time. Not possession, not ownership, but a fearless commitment to supporting one another, in good times and in bad. She squinted at him, trying to absorb the overwhelming concept.

"We're going to get better and better at this, aren't we?"

He nodded confidently, then burst into a grin. "Over the next seventy years, give or take."

Now *that* scared her. But he stroked her hip, somehow already aware his caresses calmed her. *And I know what he needs, too.* She relaxed a little, enough to let in an errant thought. "Which reminds me. Where *is* the machine I'm supposed to repair? The damn fuel pump." She propped herself up on an elbow and looked around the room, scowling when the broken parts weren't visible. Ray laughed and pulled her attention to his mischievous smile.

He pointed to his chest and hers. "We're it, Jigs. Fix us."

She nodded solemnly as he traced the contours of the whale charm resting above her breast. Prosperity for her clan. Wisdom. Safety. Home. She'd need them all. Human issues created turmoil more ominous than raging seas, and much trickier to tame.

But people were damned interesting, *sometimes* as intriguing as machines.

The End

DEDICATION

To all our boater friends who explored the San Juan Islands, the Gulf Islands, Desolation Sound and the Inside Passage with us

ACKNOWLEDGEMENTS

My husband, Steve, and I co-captained boats starting in 1980, even if we had never owned nor operated large vessels before that year. Our first purchase, *Ro-ven*, a 34 foot Tollycraft sedan with twin gas engines, took us around Lake Washington, Puget Sound, the San Juan Islands, the Gulf Islands, and Desolation Sound. More 'extreme' adventures began in 1999 when we bought *Intrepid,* a Kady-Krogen trawler, 42 feet, 40,000 pounds, and powered by a single diesel Lehman. When we gained enough experience, we cruised up and down the Inside Passage from Washington State, two times making it all the way to Alaska and back. The scenery, the weather, the friendships, all transformative, unforgettable adventures.

I wrote about the isolated reaches north of Vancouver Island, B.C. in my first novel, *Last Resort. Lie Catchers* is my paean to the amazing town of Petersburg, Alaska. *When Mountains Fall,* the first of my Woman at the Helm Mystery Series reveled in the people and places around the Broughton Islands, with a focus on a tiny struggling marina in Waka Bay. This novel, *When Oceans Rage,* a prequel to When Mountains Fall, drills in on commercial fishing and the town of Port McNeill, B.C. Truth is, the settings are so grand and the people living in the Broughtons are so special, that capturing their essence is not easy. I encourage you to witness the rustic beauty yourself, cruising the fjords, stopping at marinas, fishing for cod, prawns, and crab. Sublime experiences!

Since my passion is writing page-turning mysteries, I took great freedom in changing certain names and places, and I ramped up local conflicts to darken my plot. Still, I hope I captured the loveliness of the area and honored the hardy, friendly folks who live and work in the Archipelago. For some reason I've always been fascinated by men and women who make their living by fishing. Prawning in particular. Twenty years ago I met a man named Fred in the Broughtons. I buzzed up to his prawn boat in my dinghy and asked him about his vessel and his career. He even gave me his phone number so I could give him a follow-up call. Since it took me another ten years to write *When Oceans Rage,* and I needed a more recent update on the business, I contacted prawners Yvonne and Albert Maximchuck. They graciously answered my questions with the kind of brilliant detail that made my characters sound authentic. I am in awe of locals who forge a livelihood out of fishing. Their knowledge of boat mechanics, the nature of weather and ocean conditions, and how and where to catch prawns...amazing skills! As much as I tried to learn from experts, I remain a pleasure cruiser and recreational fisherwoman. Any errors I made in capturing the life of a prawner, are mine.

When Oceans Rage

Many generous people helped me with this story. My faithful book group, Barbara Wyckoff, Marti Valley, and Sue Ratty-Seeman critiqued my polished draft before my talented friend and editor, Laura Kelly, helped me make the story shine. The patience and insight of Laura Kelly defy superlatives. She has guided me through eleven novels since 2011; I can't imagine what my creative process would look like without her. I also thank my Beta reader, Barbara Cutshaw, for giving my story a close reading in the spit-polish stage.

To my sweet husband, Steve, my biggest cheerleader, and to all of you who inspire me to publish my stories, a heartfelt thank you.

PRAISE for Rolynn Anderson's Ten Novels
Find information on all her books here:
https://www.rolynnanderson.com

CEZANNE'S GHOST: "Anderson knows how to keep you turning the pages. Besides creating a compelling mystery, she peppered it with her well-researched historical facts to add value. Aline and her handsome guide were a perfect match for each other, as each was challenged to play their roles. You'll need to be on your toes to figure this one out." *-Amazon Reviewer*

BAD LIES: "Thoroughly delightful read from start to finish! It has it all-humor, suspense, even a little romance. A must read for fiction lovers!" *- Amazon Reviewer*

FEAR LAND: "…well written, exciting, and will keep you on the edge of your chair from page one through its final chapter"… "an incredibly well-written and well-researched suspense novel that slowly reels you in"…"a well written story that shows great attention to detail and will have suspense lovers glued to each page." *-Amazon Reviewers and InD'Tale Magazine*

FAINT: "an intricate, suspenseful story"…"with characters, setting and story so believable, the reader feels like a part of the story." *-Amazon Reviewers*

"Don't miss **SWOON** by Rolynn Anderson! If you like an interesting cast of characters, a heavy dose of mystery, and a lot of fabulous surprises, you'll be happily turning pages late into the night."

When Oceans Rage

FADEOUT: "Rolynn Anderson develops her characters and relationships beautifully, deftly painting Jan's interactions with Roman, her dad, Bella, Frank, even the terrier Elwood, to delightful perfection, making this a great read and a 5 star rating!" *-InD'Tale Magazine*

"FADEOUT has humor, healing and plenty of heat to satisfy. It also has a strong suspense element to keep you turning the pages. I highly recommend it." *-Amazon Reviewer*

LIE CATCHERS: "I adored the setting and the quirkiness of the characters in the small Alaska town. That kind of authenticity comes from an author who knows her setting, who understands its people, and can then convey that knowledge richly. Her mystery/suspense, is carefully woven with the right amount of history to engage the reader, and enough mystery to keep the reader guessing. This was my first novel by Rolynn Anderson, and I would definitely read this author again." *-Amazon Reviewer*

"LAST RESORT is an interesting read that will keep your nose firmly planted in its pages. Make sure you leave enough free time to enjoy this one from cover to cover!" *-Long and Short Reviews*

FIRE IS NICE: "Forced to work together to investigate an attack on a park ranger in addition to ongoing thefts of national treasures, law enforcement rangers Sable Chisholm and Carter Glass come to an uneasy truce. But can this truce grow into something more than a partnership?

You must read this fast-paced, well-researched, suspense story to find out. I give it 5 Pig Snorts, 5 Donkey Brays, and 5 Stars!" -*Amazon Reviewer*

WHEN MOUNTAINS FALL: "When Mountains Fall is the perfect blend of romance, mystery and emotion. Camryn is a great heroine, and her love for her son comes through in every interaction. The story is intense and heartbreaking and the setting comes alive. I'm not a boat person but the author did a great job conveying the information in a way I could understand and relate to. I was at the edge of my seat, wondering how this story was going to play out and I was not disappointed, other than by the fact that the book was over. Highly recommended!" -Amazon Reviewer

I hope you enjoyed WHEN OCEANS RAGE. Please consider writing a review of my book on Amazon, Goodreads, and/or Book Bub. Your rating and your few words about the story gives this author a vital connection with her readers!

Now I offer you an opportunity to 'keep cruising!' Here's the first chapter of **WHEN MOUNTAINS FALL**, another Woman at the Helm story, which also takes place in the Broughton Archipelago.

To whet your appetite, I give you a teaser for **WHEN MOUNTAINS FALL**
https://www.amazon.com/dp/B07XXFB1LC
Running a marina in isolated Waka Bay, British Columbia was her husband's dream, not hers. But now he's dead and a prime suspect in a murder.

Shattered by grief, **Camryn Hudson** must return to the bay to exonerate her husband, protect her seven-year-old son, and save a failing business.

Loner **Finn Weber's** mission seems equally impossible. He left a top job in Seattle to work in tiny Port McNeill. Fulfilling a bargain with his ailing mother, he must sail to Waka Bay every weekend. He never imagined the danger of cruising into Camryn's heart while withholding a family secret.

A killer roams the land and vultures demand possession of the marina. Can Camryn solve a crime *and* survive in Waka Bay?

When Mountains Fall
By Rolynn Anderson

1

The ocean regurgitated Oda Osland in a record eight months.

A wonder because he'd sunk six hundred feet to the floor of Tribune Channel, British Columbia, cocooned in a zipped bag weighed down by a fifty-pound anchor.

Chilly saltwater slowed Osland's spoilage. Better yet for Oda, big crustaceans smelled the decomposing body, yet minimal oxygen at those depths kept them at bay. Undeterred by conditions deep in the ocean were sea lice, piglet squid, snake pipefish, sea angels, and football octopi, all enticed by the hemp rope tied to the anchor.

While the critters snacked on the line, the container rubbed against rocks, friction creating pinholes in the plastic. Soon, the tiny roaches of the sea squeezed into the bag to feast on the body. Eventually, filled with decomposing gases and free of its weight, the yellow balloon made its lazy way to the surface.

Osland's bag popped to the surface, surprising a seagull so much it squawked and flapped awkwardly into flight. In size, Oda's zipped container measured less than six feet by four, but the color didn't mesh with the channel's normal debris. Amongst dark brown branches, logs, and water-soaked lumber littering the channel, a neon-colored bag would be noticed. Boaters would stop at its sight. Investigate.

The color yellow meant WARNING to North Americans. CAUTION. DANGER. But the bag also presented itself as something to forage.

Lucas Mitchum, a solitary prawner, who had pulled his pots out of a bight in Tribune Channel and was putting his way home to Finger Bay, saw the yellow blob from a distance. His brain registered a weather buoy, with dollar signs attached to it. The Canadian government would buy back such a machine for hundreds of dollars. Since his catch for the day was paltry, his sighting of the bobbing treasure brightened the day.

But his hopes dwindled as he pulled his boat beside the floater. The smell hit him, a fetid odor so strong it made him jerk away. "Fucking luck, eh?" he said to his black lab, who barked at the thing. Lucas stared at a deflated balloon, its zippered closure mocking him like a smile. Was the bag useful even if it stunk like the die-off of a thousand fish?

He grabbed a boat hook and stabbed at the bag to stop it from drifting. Quickly he reversed the engine to keep his vessel in place. Next, he worked the hook through a grommet at the far end of the bag. "Argh," he yelled when he tried to lift the bag. "Need a tool," he muttered, then secured the bag, opened his lazarette, and pulled out an elk hoist. Once he'd attached the pulley to a stanchion, he tied the business end around the yellow bag and heaved the heavy thing aboard.

Lucas was patient, waiting for seawater to dribble out, his arm shaking with the effort to keep traces tight. Finally when the water reduced to a steady drip, he said, "Let's get the sucker on deck, eh?"

He was surprised at the weight of the thing as he lowered it to the transom. His dog stopped wagging and growled, so Lucas hesitated, his thumb and index finger poised over the metal tab.

Unzipping slowly, punctuated by the raucous barking of his dog, Lucas uncovered a man.

Dead. A jagged wound at the side of his skill.

His face a pincushion for hundreds of sea lice.

***

Camryn Hudson stationed herself in the kitchen for the intricate dance around pre-dinner cocktails. She rolled her neck and straightened her back against the massive kitchen island, warding off the tension that built inside her every afternoon. Eight months—two hundred forty days of tensing up.

Five o'clock marked the hour Morrie Hudson returned home from his Vancouver, B.C. law office. Her father-in-law had a way of making his four thousand square foot house feel like a one-room cabin.

A booming voice.

A propensity for directing every family member's life.

A proclivity toward money, status, and the status quo.

A predilection…

Camryn's ten-cent 'p' words got a workout with Morrie. Suffice to say, Camryn's father-in-law was the opposite of his son, Dennis. Her former husband, Dennis.

Holly Hudson scurried into the kitchen wearing a fitted red jacket and matching A-line skirt, breathless. Camryn's mother-in-law was a small, squarish woman with a chubby, childlike face and short wispy brown hair. "No time to change. Morrie's coming home early. Sounded harried. Wouldn't tell me why."

"I'll make an appetizer. Why don't you put on something more comfortable while I put the drinks together?"

Holly wore a tight smile, still wound up from her job in West Vancouver as a systems analyst. She shook her head and went for the ice.

Five days a week Camryn had the big house to herself until five-o'clock. Evenings and weekends with Dennis's tightly wound parents were murder. She took heart that tomorrow, Saturday, she and Samuel would spend the day at the zoo.

Holly slashed a lime in two. "Where's the little guy?"

"In his bedroom."

Holly's face fell. "Sleeps too much, don't you think?"

"I'm hoping he'll rally for our trip to the zoo." Camryn held up a bottle of gin. "He sleeps his grief away. A good G&T helps me."

"Your job search must be exhausting," Holly said as she quartered the lime.

"I lived off the grid with Dennis and Samuel for eight years. My resume has gaps as wide as the Grand Canyon. I don't know how to make the empty years look productive."

"Why not let Morrie find you something?"

"I might. I haven't given up on returning to the marina, either. It's low on my list, but it's there. In the meantime, I'm looking for a job and an apartment near a good school."

"Even though we've begged you and Samuel to stay with us."

The front door shut with a bang. "Where are my little women?"

Holly rolled her eyes. "Kitchen."

Morrie entered, his woodsy cologne striding into the kitchen with him. He embraced Holly and kissed her on the cheek. Camryn hid her grimace when he enfolded her in a hug. The smell of him would remain with her for the rest of the day.

While he straightened his expensive suit jacket over his ample belly, his eyes swept over their preparations. "Good work, girls. I'm dying for a bourbon."

Holly handed him his drink and said, "Where's the drama, Morrie?"

Morrie took a swallow of his drink and glanced upward. "Samuel in his room?"

Camryn tensed. "Yes."

"Best if he doesn't hear."

Holly gulped. "Tell us."

He took another sip, his baldhead and ample nose shining in the afternoon light. "The Royal Canadian Mounted Police from Campbell River visited me today."

"Something about Dennis's death?" Camryn asked.

"That was my thinking. But no. They wanted to talk about an incident in the Broughton Islands." He quirked an eyebrow at Camryn. Accusing.

"Spill it, Morrie," Holly said, lowering herself to a barstool.

"They found a dead man floating near your marina. In Waka Bay."

Camryn set her drink down. "Who was it?"

Morrie pulled a business card from his wallet. "Inspector Wallace."

"No, I mean, who died? Whose body was found?"

"A Norwegian named Osland."

Camryn squeezed her forehead, thinking. "A fish farmer. He wanted to raise Atlantic salmon in a pen close to our marina. I never met him."

"Evidently Dennis did. In a Port McNeill bar. Where they fought. Physically got into it."

Nodding, Camryn said, "Oda Osland was drunk. Dennis told me about it. The man wouldn't listen to reason...to *all* the reasons why his particular plan to farm fish would be a disaster." She drank from her glass, dread building. "Dennis died eight months ago, so how could he have anything to do with Osland's death?"

Morrie glanced at Holly before his attention settled on Camryn, a strange mixture of sorrow and righteousness in his expression. "The police say Osland was killed by a blunt weapon and dumped into the ocean, probably weighted down with something heavy. The body popped up after months underwater. Forensics shows he could have died before Dennis's accident."

"They're accusing Dennis of killing someone?" Holly plunked down her drink. "He was a pacifist. He *hated* violence."

"Exactly what I told the inspector," Morrie said. "Supposedly Osland was drunk and acting crazy. He picked a fight with Dennis. Witnesses at the bar say so."

Camryn closed her eyes, overwhelmed by Morrie's news. She felt her father-in-law's hand on her arm and opened her eyes. "They actually think Dennis is responsible?"

Morrie was quiet for a moment. "They do."

"There's more."

He hesitated. "They consider you a possible accessory to the crime."

"I wasn't at the bar, Morrie. I was home with Samuel."

"But you signed the protest letter and you're the one who knows what time Dennis returned from the bar to the marina. If Osland was killed that night, the Mounties think you have the power to fake an alibi."

"Dennis signed my name." She waved a hand. "Any handwriting analysis will prove it. Accessory? Come on, that's nuts. A distraction. Our focus has to be on who murdered Oda Osland."

His mouth set in a grim line, Morrie said, "I agree."

"Dennis is a hero to Samuel. "I can't...we can't..."

Morrie squeezed her arm. "Dennis isn't alive to fight this, so I'll have to do it for him."

Camryn thought about the money and power Morrie could use. He'd employ the best lawyers and apply massive amounts of money to knock Dennis off the suspect list. Would he fight as hard to have her exonerated? She wasn't sure.

And then she remembered how life in the British Columbia islands resisted big-city forces. Morrie's methods and influence would be useless in the rugged, sparsely populated Broughton Archipelago. Investigating a murder on the B.C. coast? Like trying to hold water in your palm.

"The Norwegian government is involved. Pressure is also coming from Osland's family and his insurance company." Morrie swallowed some bourbon and put the icy glass to his forehead.

Holly groaned. "The Mounties are eager to close the case."

"And since Dennis is dead and can't defend himself," —Morrie took a swallow of bourbon— "it's easy to pin the murder on our son."

***

Camryn Hudson palmed her seven-year-old's forehead, feeling for a fever even though she knew her son wasn't sick.

"Having fun, Samuel?" Camryn prodded, smoothing the boy's silky rust-blond hair.

"Sure," he whispered in front of Vancouver's seal exhibition, where three of the shiny water-slicked animals played with a ball in their pool.

When a seal slapped water on Samuel, bringing a smile to his face, she felt a ray of hope. Yet in a flash, his passive expression returned. With shoulders hunched, he stared at the ground instead of the seals. She took his hand and led him to the otter exhibit, where her son's favorite sea creatures splashed about in a rollicking game of tag.

Camryn thought about how much she liked watching animals cavort from a safe distance.

In a zoo, they looked cuter, more like pets.

Benign.

Not like the nasty otters in Waka Bay that shit on the marina dock and grumbled all night long while she tried to sleep. Her husband and Samuel had named one frequent interloper Otto. Camryn called him pestiferous. Pernicious. She had a plethora of 'p' words to describe the messy creatures.

Camryn was sure antics of the round-faced, whiskered animals, irresistible to any child, would delight Samuel. Instead, he kicked at a rock, his small hands grasping the top rail of the barricade as if he needed help standing. When she stooped for a better look, his crumpled face had Camryn staring in surprise. He was crying soundlessly, tears racing down his cheeks.

"Oh, sweetie. Come here."

He fell into her arms, almost knocking her over. She settled on her knees, bracing herself as he drew shallow breaths between sobs, his chest hitching against hers. In moments, the shoulder of her tee shirt was wet with his tears. She rubbed his back. "I've got you, honey. Let it out. It's okay to cry."

She stood up with difficulty, her hefty son velcroed to her body.

"Let's sit awhile and figure this out. Deal?"

His head moved in what she took as a nod, so she hauled him to a bench and settled him on her lap.

"You don't have to talk, Samuel. Take all the time you need."

She'd transferred him to her dry shoulder when they sat down, alarmed when air hit the giant patch of tear-soaked shirt. Since Samuel rarely cried, Camryn realized she didn't know what to do if he kept crying. Should she order him to stop? He could make himself sick if he carried on much longer.

When he struggled to breathe through his stuffed nose, she reached into her purse for a tissue. "Here. Blow your nose."

He hiccupped and grabbed the tissue, pulling his arm from behind her back so he could use both hands to clean himself. She looked the other way, knowing he didn't want to be watched. In his typical effort to play the tough guy, he might not tell her why he cried.

When he handed back the tissue, she glanced at Samuel's eyes, her own filling with tears at the sight of his red, swollen face. Camryn blinked rapidly, forcing herself to stay in control.

He took a deep, raspy breath and relaxed against her chest. It killed her to wait him out, but while Samuel calmed himself she got busy watching people.

The five minutes she stayed quiet felt like fifty. She expected him to crawl off her lap, say, "I'm ready to go," and lead off to the next exhibit. Instead, he pulled away from her body and looked straight at her with puffy, heart-breaking pink eyes and a quivering bottom lip.

"What is it, Samuel?" she asked.

He pulled in an uneven breath. "We gotta go to Waka Bay, Mom. Back to our marina."

When her heart picked up an extra beat, she put a hand on her chest to stop the fibrillation. "I thought you were getting used to living in the city with Grandda and Grandmum. Soon as I get a job, I promise I'll find a place of our own."

He shook his head slowly with his palm on his forehead, his father's gesture, signaling impatience. "But see..." He pointed over to the otter cage and looked into Camryn's eyes to emphasize his point. When she raised her eyebrows, he said, "Otto's there and our friends, Bryan, Katie, Jigs, Ray, Milly, Greg, Bobby, and Jessica. All the boaters, the 'ventures. And Dad."

He must have expected her to shake her head, because he sighed and looked away, in the enervated way he'd approached every day of the last eight months. Another round of their familiar debate was coming. His distraught expression told her so.

This time, she kept quiet, working on the big 'p,' perspective, an attribute she yearned to call her own. *How does Samuel process his father's death?*

Her son seemed to be watching the otters for inspiration. Finally, in a heaving exhale, he reached into his pocket and cradled an object in his palm.

She stared at a small crude carving her son had carried for some time, among a fistful of coins and little toys. She reached for it, fingering its hardness and smooth edges. "It's a cool raven, honey."

He took it from her and closed his fingers on it to mark its preciousness.

"Did Grandda give it to you?"

He shook his head. "I got it back at the marina, at Waka Bay."

The weight of distress seemed to push down on his shoulders as he traced the surface with his thumb.

"Tell me more, Samuel."

"This is a present. A secret. I also have different kinds of rocks. Someone put them behind the tool shack next to my fish net."

Hair rose on her arms. "At the marina?"

He gave one nod.

Wiping a tear from his cheek, she said, "I'm sure it was Dad's idea of a surprise. Kind of a mystery game."

"Dad didn't put them there."

Instead of arguing with him, Camryn asked gently, "You never showed me the presents. How come?"

"'Cause you might stop him."

"Him?"

"It's gotta be a him."

"Because of the kinds of gifts these are, you mean?"

"Yeah."

She held his face in her hands. "Honey, these are artifacts of native tribes once living in our bay. Someone found them on shore or in the woods, and since I know it wasn't me, Dad must have brought you the presents. We're the only people who live in Waka Bay." Camryn smiled at the thought of Dennis hiding the treasures for their son.

Samuel's face sagged like he was ready to cry again. Shaking his head as if he couldn't believe what he was about to say, he whispered, "The last present came a day after Dad died."

ABOUT THE AUTHOR

Rolynn Anderson loves makeovers! She crafted curriculum to spark student learning as a high school English teacher and opened a cutting edge high school as a principal. From scratch, she learned how to co-captain a trawler with her husband, cruising the Inside Passage for twenty-five summers. Rebooting her golf game and renovating her California home's interior and landscape are her most recent projects. In her role as author, she delights in creating imperfect characters faced with extraordinary, transforming challenges. Her hope: You'll devour her makeover suspense/mysteries in the wee hours of the morning, because her stories, settings, and characters, capture your imagination *and* your heart.

Find her website/blog at
http://www.rolynnanderson.com

NOVELS BY
ROLYNN ANDERSON

Suspense/Mysteries:
Last Resort
Lie Catchers
Fear Land
Bad Lies
Cézanne's Ghost
Fire Is Nice-Sable Chisholm Mystery
"Links to Evil"-Sable Chisholm Mystery

The Boutique Funeral Planner Suspense
Series:
Fadeout
Swoon
Faint

Woman at the Helm Mysteries
When Mountains Fall
When Oceans Rage
When Winds Howl